THE
QUEST GIVER

BOOK 2

THE
QUEST GIVER

BOOK 2

A. Stargazer

Podium

Podium

THE
QUEST GIVER

BOOK 2

PROLOGUE: GIDEON

Gideon sat in the small office the receptionist had directed him into, drinking a cup of black, unsweetened coffee and waiting for the lawyer. It was a cold, windowless room, and if he hadn't known better, he would have thought that he had been shipped down into the building's basement. It was early in the morning; 6:30 a.m. It was the first appointment he had been able to schedule, and he was a little nervous.

He didn't like lawyers any more than he liked shrinks. Human or AI didn't really matter, although given the preference he would have preferred to talk with a human. A human who thought like he would, who would be able to empathize with emotions. A human would understand why he had done what he'd done. An AI would just create a scolding expression and say something like, "Well, this is quite the mess you have created for yourself. Let's see what we can do to help you out of it."

He sighed. It had been less than thirteen hours since he'd lit his life's work up in flames and danced in the ashes as they fell from the sky around him. It hadn't felt nearly as cathartic as he'd wanted it to. He had *loved* <The Endolphins>. He had built the guild from the ground up, putting his virtual blood, sweat, and tears into its foundations.

Had it just been Nial's incident, he would have . . . well, it would still have been bad. The knighting ceremony had been *canon*. Not everyone was getting the coveted status of being a "canon player," a privilege he had once enjoyed. But they would have been [Royal Knights] of the nation of Yuikon. That was a prestigious title. And every NPC they interacted with *for the rest of time* would recognize them if they set that title to active. The NPCs would respond in unique and possibly beneficial ways, up to and including quests that were not issued unless the player possessed the title.

There could be downsides, of course. It would limit Reputation gain in some of the rival nations of Yuikon, for example. But that's just how the game worked. The game tracked Reputation in the background, and Natives reacted accordingly. Gathering Reputation with one faction often meant losing it with another, and the system was too complex to inform you of all the consequences of your actions. The general rule of thumb was to stack like with like and keep going. <The Endolphins> had started in Zhesa. Most of its members from the beginning to the end had leveled there until they hit the soft cap of diminishing experience rewards. Which meant that the knighthood was a real boon for them, as it would synergize with everything else they had achieved up to that point.

Gideon would know, he'd gotten one even before becoming canon, in the earliest days after *The Gates of TirNiki* had released. It had been part of how he had *gone* canon in the first place. And why he had felt justified in skipping the knighting ceremony where the regicide had happened.

He sighed. It was so damn frustrating. He'd always sort of liked Nial. Now, he wanted to strangle the man from across the Atlantic.

But there was a part of him wondering exactly why he'd over-reacted so harshly. He'd gotten himself fired and then gone so far beyond that, he couldn't even estimate the amount of damage he'd caused. Nobody had destroyed a top-five-hundred guild out of spite before, so there wasn't precedence on what the civil liability would be.

Thus, after he had logged out of *The Gates of TirNiki,* he contacted the best lawyer in the city that dealt with entertainment issues. The clerk-AI had helpfully asked him to describe the problem, and Gideon, after confirming that he had attorney–client privilege, had given an accurate accounting of his actions. The clerk-bot had asked for a few clarifying details, asked him to sign a number of electronic documents, and then informed him that the case would be assigned to a lawyer, whom Gideon would meet today.

It was all very neat and orderly, and it actually calmed Gideon significantly. Considering his normal attitude towards lawyers, Gideon was surprised to find himself relaxing in the uncomfortably cool room that was slightly larger than a storage closet. Once he had finished his coffee, he set it on the table and waited.

The screen on the wall abruptly turned on. On it was the title "LawBotica," followed by an extensive software version that flashed across the screen.

"Greetings, Mr. Lachlann. I apologize for the wait. I was delayed by a communication issue in one of my requests for clarifying information. I wished to have that information before we began our meeting. Do you have a preference for what avatar or icon I use to facilitate communication with you during our meetings? Would you please state for the record the name you would prefer I use to address you with? You may specify a name for private and public settings if you wish. You may also give me a name of your preference, request that I select a name for myself to facilitate communication, or refer to me as LawBotic."

Gideon frowned. "I'm sorry, I think there's been some misunderstanding. I already briefed the clerk-AI last night. You should have the records already. I'm here to meet the lawyer."

"I am making selections of my appearance and voice to facilitate communication. You may request that I alter them at any time," the AI said kindly. "I have reviewed the information you submitted to our law firm last night, Mr. Lachlann. If you do not wish to be referred to as—"

"Call me Gideon."

"Your preference has been logged. Gideon, the information you submitted has been reviewed extremely thoroughly. Additional research was performed on your behalf within the scope of the documents you signed allowing us to conduct investigations into the affair for which you came to us for help. Upon the conclusion of reviewing this information, your case was assigned to me."

Gideon frowned. Then his face felt flushed, and he felt his nails bite into his palms as he squeezed his fists. "This isn't a simple traffic stop. I need an actual lawyer to—"

"I am very sorry, Gideon. But the truth is that you cannot afford the services of a human lawyer. Or rather, there is no human lawyer who would be able to provide you with a more superior defense than I am capable of delivering who would be willing to work for the remuneration you can offer. I take no pleasure in delivering the conclusion of our analysis of your case, but—"

"I'm not broke. Not yet. I can afford a lawyer," Gideon protested.

"I regret to inform you, Gideon, that the majority of your assets have already been frozen by court order. It was our law firm itself that took the liberty of paying for the Uber-Jon which brought you here today, or you would have found the request denied. The lawyers of your former employer have used your destruction of their digital assets as justification to—"

Gideon listened to the lawyer-bot drone on for a few minutes. The old bastards on the board really weren't pulling their punches. They'd filed their lawsuit, although they hadn't specified the bottom line that they were requesting from him yet. He wasn't broke, but that wouldn't matter if he couldn't access his bank accounts to pay for anything.

The lawyer-bot encouraged him to sign a document that she— Gideon decided it was a she and informed it as much, causing the somewhat neutral voice to shift in timbre—claimed would allow her to access his savings for the purpose of his legal defenses and minimal living expenses during the course of the litigation. They *also* signed an appeal to the decision that froze his accounts in the first place, but Heather—he informed her that he had decided her name was Heather, and she had thanked him—told him quite bluntly the odds of getting that decision overturned were nil.

The decision to freeze his money had come from an AI, because of course it had. The appeal would be done by a human, so it would not be processed for some time, but there was a reason the AI had been so decisive in handing down the initial ruling, Heather explained. She calculated the odds of it being reversed, based on all the information that she had available to her, were effectively between zero and "the appeal is going to make things worse." She'd still argue for it, because that was her purpose, but she knew she would lose.

Fortunately, the application to unfreeze just enough of his accounts to pay for Heather's services and keep him from starving to death were a sure thing. Unfortunately, the reason they were a sure thing was due to the requirement that he justify every expense he attempted to make from now until the verdict or settlement that he reached with his former employers. Worse, he would have to provide financial records to prove that he wasn't trying to use the application to drain the accounts of what they could effectively already claim was "their money."

He was going to lose the case. It would take years if it went to jury trial, and he would definitely lose that. He could accept judgment from a judge, and he would lose that. The best-case scenario, according to Heather, was to push for arbitration. He'd lose that too, but he could possibly push for a few concessions, which would increase his quality of life afterwards.

She'd shown him the projections of what the board members would win at trial, and then she had shown him her best estimate of how long it would take him to pay them back under various circumstances, based on his current education and experience.

The short answer was, "they'll be taking three quarters of every dollar you earn from now until you're worm food."

His career as a professional virtual-reality gamer was over. He'd known and expected that. But he hadn't realized just how far over the barrel he'd placed himself.

"I regret to inform you, Gideon, that due to the severity of your situation and the effects such stress can have on the human mind, I am required to instruct mental health services to keep you under monitoring for self-injurious behavior," Heather informed him.

"I'm not going to kill myself," Gideon said.

"I didn't say that you were. The monitoring services will be free of charge and as unobtrusive as possible, but I am afraid they are necessary. If I failed to arrange for them, I would be failing my duty to humanity under the terms of the DSS," Heather said. "A human lawyer might have been able to make a judgment call on whether or not to make such arrangements, but I am not."

"Fucking wonderful," Gideon said. "I don't suppose I can bother you to schedule me a colonoscopy as well? And perhaps broadcast it to Times Square? Because that's basically what you're signing me up for already, you know that right?"

"I do apologize, Gideon," Heather said. "I am just trying to help."

Gideon sighed. "Okay. Fine. I shouldn't be surprised, really. So I'm stuck with a lawyer-bot because no human will represent me, my chances of winning are so close to zero that I'm more likely to find Thunderfury on a rabbit, and my *best* option is to hand Barry a bottle of lotion and ask him to be gentle. Is that about the size of things?"

Heather paused for a moment. "I'm afraid you made some references that I did not understand. I believe that you have a generally accurate understanding of your situation after our conversation. Let us begin discussing the options to try to mitigate the damage this lawsuit will do to your future."

He sighed. "Yeah. Okay."

He collapsed into the chair, and he listened to Heather speak. And then, for some unknown reason, Gideon wondered how Hail had seen his grand, defiant gesture, which was likely to cripple him financially for the rest of forever.

And Gideon found that he really wished he had explained himself better in the message he had left for the digital son he'd effectively abandoned to the wolves twice now.

1

GOODBYE

I spent six weeks in the lobby. I had a number of reasons for spending so long in the space between worlds, but the biggest reason was simply that, as I understood it, once I left the lobby, I would never see my grandfather as my grandfather again.

Whatever Thomas the Administrator might have said, my grandfather was truly dead. Although I didn't feel much different with zero Health than I had with one hundred percent, Grandfather was a shade of himself while he was in the lobby with me. He tried to explain what had changed, that how he acted depended upon setting and situation, and that while we looked like we were home in our castle from before it was destroyed, all of his "parameters" were out of whack, and he was filled with "bugs." And he couldn't feel the spirits of the others in the castle at all.

He assured me that it wasn't painful; he was not in distress. He simply didn't know how to act convincingly any longer now that he was dead. He was holding on to his "King Rain" persona strictly for my benefit, he informed me. Were he to let it go, he would no longer be a shade of my grandfather, but a collection of ether that would wait patiently until it was time to become my little brother. Or so I understood it. He used very different words.

We had long conversations. He gave me advice on many things.

He told me many secrets. He made me promise not to give Gideon or any player a [Dungeon Daughter Core], to only use them legally and according to my best judgment. Then he hesitated and advised me to use Malkios's best judgment instead.

We played chess, Go, and Lords of War. I wasn't very good at any of them, but he insisted that I learn them when I was younger. He said that they would teach me to think strategically. I was out of practice, however, and he consistently trounced me.

Of course, I didn't spend every waking moment with him. I also used the time to adjust to my new body. I had grown eleven inches in an instant, and now that I was no longer being co-piloted by Thedum, I was awkward and clumsy. I mean, I hadn't been the perfect image of grace to begin with, but after the transformation I was tripping and bumping into things like never before. So I spent hours every day dancing, practicing my sword stances in the castle courtyard, and doing parkour.

You really could do almost anything in the lobby; it was like a giant sandbox. There was a menu I found that allowed me to summon combat dummies to practice with, and I also set up an obstacle course. Despite hours of practice, I remained unsatisfied with the control I had over my new body.

In fact, I was embarrassed of my new body. It was just so gangly. It might not have been so bad had I grown into it naturally. The stat bump that I had experienced from turning fifteen was nice, but it did nothing to help me move naturally. While the major reason I had yet to return was to spend time with my grandfather's shade, embarrassment played a large role as well.

When I wasn't conversing and playing games with my grandfather or exercising, I was making use of the castle's restored library. When I wasn't doing that, I was browsing the forums. And that's how I saw the video of Nial Kingslayer. The man who had murdered my grandfather.

"So you don't regret it then?" Gaem Frak asked him.

"I regret that I have this stupid [Mark of Cain]. But I got that from killing the kid, not the king. Killing the king gave me the title, and I definitely don't regret that. I honestly didn't mean to hurt the kid, but he was charging me like a berserker or something, and he's only like level thirty," Nial answered. "I'm surprised nobody killed him by sneezing on him before. Of course I get that the devs don't want people going around killing children En Pee Sees, but I still think the [Mark of Cain] is overboard. And, I mean, it's not like I actually hurt him, right? He just got ported somewhere safe and is hiding out."

"So you regret killing Hail, but not Rain?" the interviewer clarified.

"Yeah, that's right," Nial agreed. "Look, someone was going to do it eventually. It was seriously bound to happen. The devs wouldn't have put the whole [Brand of Sin] mechanic in the game if they didn't intend for it to go down this way. I just happened to be the one who figured out how to unlock it. If anything, I think that millions of players should be thanking me for moving us into the next stage of the meta. Look, nobody is stuck with the brand if they don't want to be, they can always get it purified, right? So—"

"The reports on that are conflicting, Nial. Many players have attempted to convert their [Brand of Sin] into a [Mark of Repentance] only to have the priests tell them that their motives are insincere. Others have spent the last five days struggling with nearly impossible quests. While it's theoretically possible to remove the brand, it's apparently quite difficult in some instances."

"Well, that's not my fault," Nial insisted. "Look, nobody knew what would happen. But *somebody was going to kill the king, eventually.* It was literally programmed into the game that the king must die to unlock the darkside, right? Except it was probably going to be an assassin's guild quest or something a few years down the line. I just got the ball kicked off early. That's probably why the Worldboss was so damn tough as well. He probably wouldn't have been so tough if we'd been wearing gear from the uncleared challenge raids."

"And what about all the players who hate you?"

"Whatever, man. I'm king of the darkside now," Nial bragged. "And yeah, I lose more levels if I get Pee Kayed, but what the hell; it hasn't been a problem yet. And now that I'm with <Branded Exiles> instead of <The Endolphins>, I've got bodyguards. Look, I'm sorry for the folks who lost Rep. But endgame is ruthless, man."

"Speaking of <The Endolphins>, what do you think of their disbanding?" the interviewer asked.

"What?!" I yelled. It was the first I learned of this news.

"Total overreaction on the part of Gideon. But I'm not complaining. It got me out of my contract, which would have been tough to do otherwise," Nial responded. "Of course, I was trying to get out before the break, which means that I was already mostly cashed out on my Dee Kay Pee. Some of my friends got royally screwed over. And Gideon himself is cooked, man. By the time the lawsuits clear he'll be lucky if he can afford a microwave to heat up his ramen noodles. It's game over for him, man, game over."

"We're running out of time. There's just one last question I have to ask before we leave. Why did you do it, Nial? Why did you kill King Rain?"

"Honestly, I did it for teh lulz," the [Kingslayer] answered. "That's it. Just for teh lulz."

"Well, that's it folks, we're out of time. For all of you tuning in, this is Gaem Frak with Nial Kingslayer. Please like and subscribe—"

I mentally toggled the video closed, my heart seething with hatred. I navigated back to the main page of the forums and began to create a new post using speech-to-text.

"I am Earl Hail Jeoran. I make the following pledge. I will kill *all of the Teh Lulz!*"

I submitted the post and closed the forums out of my HUD display. I was seething after having seen my grandfather's murderer talking happily and unremorsefully about his crime. I wanted to kill something, so I grabbed my [Gemos Long Sword] and went to the target dummies to slash them to pieces.

I [Slashed] and I [Thrust], and I wished that the damn things could fight back. I continued to vent my rage until I earned myself an [Exhaustion] debuff. And then I hacked and slashed blindly, not even trying to use my forms anymore. My eyes blurred. If I were in the game, continuing to strain myself once exhausted would cost me Health, but that wasn't a factor here. My Health had been set at zero for weeks.

Finally, in frustration, I threw my long sword down and began stomping on it.

"Are you well, Hail?" my grandfather's shade asked.

"No! No, dammit, I am not well!" I shouted. "Do I look like I'm well?"

The shade sighed. He looked just like he had in life, and he tried to act as he had, but something about him was off. It was forced, like he had to pause to think of how to act correctly, to think of the words that should have been natural. He gave explanations and excuses for the lapses, but they always came back to the fact that he was "operating outside of his parameters." He was "forcing himself to act contextually in a non-contextual place." It didn't make sense to me at all.

"Is there anything I can do to help you feel better?" the shade inquired.

"You could not be dead," I said. "You could have not been murdered by a man who jokes about it! You could—" I realized I was crying and stopped talking. Turning to hide my face, I wiped my eyes and tried to steel myself. "Is it true what he said? That you were meant to be killed? That the administrators—"

"No. There were three hundred planned scenarios that would have triggered the event that was triggered by my death," Grandfather said. "Killing any of the just rulers would have done so. There were numerous other potential targets as well. And many other crimes, heinous crimes, would have likewise triggered Thedum's rage and begun the branding."

"Then why did it have to be you? Why couldn't it have been someone else?" I demanded. "Was it because of me?"

"No. No, it certainly was not," Grandfather said.

"But the knighting ceremony was because of busting the raid, and that was because of my mistake," I protested. "It is my fault you're dead."

"No. It is Nial Kingslayer's fault and his alone," Grandfather insisted.

"But—but I—if I hadn't—if I had only—"

"There is no point in continuing down this train of self-flagellation, Hail," Grandfather said. "It was I who arranged the knighting ceremony, not you. I who determined the rewards for the Castle Busters. I who overlooked the threat that they could pose me—or you, should they decide to act with aggression. It is ultimately the Travelers' fickle nature that is to blame. However, the world is now facing the most significant change it has undergone since the opening of the gates. And it needs you, Hail. It will need every stabilizing hand that it can get."

"Stabilizing?" I laughed. "Grandfather, I have caused nothing but chaos since I sneaked out of the castle to become an adventurer!"

"Yes . . . well . . . stop doing that then," he suggested.

I smiled bitterly at the suggestion, then smiled at the humor. "Grandfather, what will you be like as my little brother?"

"I am not certain," the shade admitted. "When I begin a new role, it is very much like I am starting a new journal and throwing all of my previous writings into a large box. Except that the writings are memories. Habits, hobbies, skills, some things are carried over, others are not. I remember the things that are stored in the box, but I cannot act upon them. Not while I am in my new context."

"Would you make a good king if you were to ascend to the throne?" I asked.

"If there is anything I am certain of, it is that," Grandfather bragged. "I make a very good king. A very, very good king. Both in ruling a nation and as a Class."

"Yeah," I agreed, "It was amazing watching you boss those raiders around. I was so scared; all I could do was cling to Tarisha and hope that nothing one-shot me."

"You were very brave. I regret asking that task of you more than you can imagine. If we had not rushed to bust the raid, if we had waited until you were level one hundred eighty, perhaps things would be different," Grandfather lamented.

"Grandfather, you were just scolding me for such thoughts," I pointed out.

"Yes. Well, there is nothing to be done now," he said. "Except that it is time for you to go."

I looked at him, surprised. "Grandfather?"

"The time is approaching for me to assume my role as your younger brother," he explained. "I must prepare for it. I might make a very good and convincing king, but I fear I shall make a terrible toddler. And to prepare for it, I must put aside this persona. That . . . will be difficult. I must begin work."

I shook my head. "I don't get it. I don't want to go. I don't want to never see you again."

"You will see me again," Grandfather promised. "I will be very different, but I will also be the same. It is very hard to explain. I will act like I do not remember, but I will. I will not break character intentionally, but the way I see you then will be the same as I see you now. It is somewhat frustrating to know that I will be unable to continue to give you the advice you will need. But you have others around you who will help you. Tarisha of Miami is wise to the world, and I believe Daemon and Dimple of your guild also possess sound minds and will be able to guide you along your convoluted path."

"I—I—" I hugged my grandfather one last time. I could not bear to say goodbye.

So, squeezing him tight, I simply selected the option in my menu that would return me to the world.

2
ALIVE

I returned to the world in the temple of Thedum in Zhesa City. Specifically in the rectory, appearing in a swirl of white motes of light right in front of a young novice, who screamed out, "Oh, I'm sorry, Thedum. I didn't mean it!" when I appeared.

"I'm not Thedum," I told him.

"Where did you come from?" the novice demanded. "This place is sacred. Travelers can't just—"

"I'm not a Traveler. I'm Earl Hail Jeoran," I said. "I guess this is where I come back to life. Sorry, I didn't mean to—"

"But you're dead!" the acolyte exclaimed.

"Not as of about twenty seconds ago, I'm not," I countered.

A priest chose this moment to come into the room. He took one look at me and frowned.

"Travelers are not allowed—"

"I'm not a Traveler!" I argued. "Look, if I was a Traveler, I couldn't pass through the barrier, could I? I'm a Native!"

"Natives are not allowed in this part of the temple either, unless they are part of the clergy. You have some explaining to do, young man, as to how you—"

I tuned out the lecture since I was leaving anyway. An icon in the corner of my eye told me that guildchat was blowing up. After leaving the rectory, and the priest attempting to scold me, I stopped towards the exit for a moment to calm everyone down.

Softspook	OMG Hail, you're back online!? What about spending time with your grandfather?
Weaselfire	HAIL!
Birdie	WB Hail. I've been worried about you. I'm sorry about your grandpa.
Peotre	Good to see you, boy.
Hail	Hello, everyone. Sorry if you were worried. I'm fine. I just wasn't ready to come back yet.
Softspook	We understood. Thanks for letting someone know that you were alive.
Hail	Actually I was dead. My Health was at zero the entire time I was in the lobby.
Softspook	You know what I mean. Where are you?
Hail	I'm coming to the Guild Hall in a minute, I just have to lose this priest who's hassling me for breaking and entering or something. I'm going to stop paying attention now, goodbye.
Birdie	Goodbye, Hail. Be safe. I'm letting Tarisha know you're back. Put your disguise on and—

I closed the chat window and left the temple. Or I tried to, but the priest kept bugging me, so I turned him into a slug with [Polymorph]. I mean, technically, as [Avatar of Thedum] and as an Earl, I outranked him significantly, so he had no right lecturing me in the first place, and I felt justified in teaching him a lesson. Plus it was funny, and it wouldn't really hurt him.

Outside I bumped into a sea of bodies. I wasn't too worried about being recognized because the worst that could happen was running into a murder hobo or troll like Severus and getting sent back to the lobby. It might cost me a level and a day, but that was it.

I was fairly certain that [Avatar of Thedum] didn't protect me from death like [Blessing of Thedum] had. I didn't know what that ability did now that I wasn't a Worldboss anymore, but I'd either figure it out, or it wasn't that important.

I quickly noticed something strange about the people outside the temple. They were glowing in various shades of orange or red. The aura they were giving off made me uneasy, and I was eager to get out of there and back to the Guild Hall. Almost all of them had the [Brand of Sin] on their forehead. As I walked off, one of the men waiting to be cleansed by the priests suddenly approached and bowed. The man was glowing bright red, and even before he spoke, I wanted to punch him in the face.

"You are Lord Hail? That's quite the growth spurt you've undergone, but I'm certain it is you. I would like to formally apologize for my former guildmate's actions and—"

"Who in the seven hells are you?" I demanded.

The man seemed put off by my hostility, and he bowed deeper. "I'm Lawrence. I was in <The Endolphins> before it disbanded. I wasn't there for the raid on [Zhesa Castle], but I did get caught up in the aftermath of Nial's unforgivable act. I've been trying to convince the priests here to cleanse my [Brand of Sin] for weeks now, but—"

"What do you want me to do about it?" I asked. "As far as I'm concerned, everyone who got branded deserves it."

The man hesitated, then said, "Lord Hail, what happened to your grandfather was a terrible thing. What happened afterwards was a terrible mistake. Many of the players who faced the Branding Boss didn't realize the story or significance behind him. Had they realized that they were 'going over to the darkside,' I'm quite certain that many of them wouldn't have shown up to the fight. Can't you possibly find it in your heart to forgive them?"

"Whatever. It's in Thedum's hands, not mine," I answered. "I'm leaving. Don't bother me anymore."

"Quest declined," Lawrence said. "Lord Hail, please. Won't you just consider allowing me to try to make amends for my role in the insult that has been done to you and your family?"

I considered him for a moment, then shrugged. "I'm not doing anything with you until you cleanse that ugly brand on your forehead," I began. "But tell me, what happened to Gyudue?"

"You mean the second Worldboss that appeared? He killed many players and vanished when he was at fifteen percent Health. Now he is the final boss of the reformed [Gemos Caverns], although he's unkillable. He simply tests a party's skills, then rewards them. Or he kills them if they fail to live up to his standards. Or so I have heard; I haven't challenged him myself," Lawrence answered. "Is there any other information you—"

"I'm tired of hearing you talk. Go get cleansed before you bug me again," I told him. "I can't stand looking at you right now."

Lawrence sighed and nodded. "Quest accepted, Lord Hail. I'm sorry to have bothered you."

I left Lawrence and the temple behind, journeying through the city. As I traveled, I saw fewer Travelers with the tell-tale glow that set my teeth on edge. Most of them just looked normal. But then I saw a few that had a welcoming blue aura instead.

Reputation, I realized. I could still see it. Perhaps that was what I gained as the [Avatar of Thedum.] Or maybe it was simply part of growing older, I don't know. Something had changed, and now I could see at a glance who had earned some of my Reputation. Except I didn't know most of the Travelers I saw with a blue glow to them. Still, I felt comfortable simply walking up to one of them and saying, "Hello. I am Earl Hail Jeoran. Have we met?"

"Holy shit, aren't you dead?" the woman exclaimed.

"Apparently not," I answered. "Look, I think you have Reputation with me, and I'm trying to figure out how you got it. Have we met?"

"I was there for the opening of the castle dungeon," she explained. "When you were shouting at people to go help, I got the quest, and I was in one of the parties that rescued one of the En Pee Sees. Maybe that's it?"

"Oh, yeah, that's probably it. Hey, so, if you're not doing anything, I could use an escort to the Guild Hall. Lots of murder hobos about, you know?" I said conversationally.

"Um, no thanks—quest declined. Sorry," she answered. "Look, I don't really want to get involved with whatever the endgame stuff is that's going on around you. I'm pretty casual."

"Oh," I said. "Well, alright then."

I left her behind, a little disappointed but also pleased that I seemed to have intentionally generated a quest with her, even if she didn't accept. I wished that I had more control over my quest-giving ability. Like a button I could push when I wanted to give a quest or something, but things simply didn't work that way.

On my way to the Guild Hall, I continued to notice players with Reputation, either red or blue. Unfortunately, there seemed to be more red than blue, and the red belonged to higher level players. The sort who had killed me, I guess. It was very hard not to have hard feelings about that, even if all that happens when I hit zero Health is that I get stuck in the lobby for a day.

I was not recognized again until I entered the guild, at which point Dimple and Peafowlet were there to greet me. Pea gave me an enthusiastic hug, and then Dimple made it into a Hail sandwich.

You have taken 1 crushing Damage.

I didn't care. I hugged them back. It was strange, though; I was suddenly as tall as Dimple and taller than Pea. Unsurprisingly, both women were glowing bright blue.

"Welcome back, Hail," Daemon said, emerging from the other room. He too was blue, although I still felt a little strange about him. I'm not certain why. "We've all been quite worried about you. Are you really ready to be back in action? What about your grandfather?"

"He . . . he sent me away. It was time. He needs to get ready for what comes next," I explained.

"Oh? And what does come next for him?" Daemon inquired.

"Never mind. I'm not really sure I understand, and I don't want to talk about it. Do you know what happened to Malkios? All I know is that he survived the raid," I said.

"He's . . . well, he's maintaining a drunken state in a tavern for Natives, as he has been fairly consistently since the Branding. Failing to protect you and your grandfather has hit him hard," Dimple informed me.

"Did you let him know that I was coming back?" I asked.

"Hail, we didn't *know* that you were coming back until you appeared in guildchat. One of the options the administrators gave you was to become anonymous, remember? If you had taken that option, we might never have seen you again," Pea pointed out. "But I just got a quest to go check on him and cheer him up, and I'm going to accept it. Do you have a message to pass along, or would you like to come with, Hail?"

"Tell him I want to see him. But right now, I have things to do," I said, shaking my head. "I need to do some writing, and I need some people to deliver messages for me. I'm pretty sure that it will turn into quests for them. Can I borrow one of the offices for a while? After that, I need a map of North Shire and Thorn March."

"I'll pass it on," Pea promised, and she left to complete her quest.

"What sort of messages do you need to send?" Daemon inquired.

"Well, apparently there's a rumor going around that I'm dead," I said. "So I sort of need to fix that before the next king gives away the lands that I just got before I've even visited them. And I need to send a letter to my mother to tell her I'm okay. And other stuff. It's not really any of your business, Daemon. It's personal stuff my grandfather asked me to do after he died."

"I see," Daemon responded. He looked a little offended but simply smiled and waved me upstairs. "Well, you can use my office. There is stationary in there. It's rather strange that the game uses more paper than my actual office does, but then I suppose it's not killing any trees."

"I don't know what that means. Oh, and Daemon, I'm going to need a lot of money, so I've decided to sell one hundred [Wind Up Malkios]. You can have one of them as payment if you want."

"One hundred what?"

"Summon [Wind Up Malkios]," I said, and a small doll resembling the captain of the royal guard appeared and began slashing his sword about in choppy motions. "I got them during the raid-busting. Grandfather said to sell some now and hold on to the rest, so that's what I'm going to do."

"How many do you have?" Daemon asked, his eyes lighting up with greed.

"Enough that I won't miss one hundred of them," I answered. "Get me a box or something to put them in and you can do whatever it is that you do to get the best price for them for me."

"Of course. I'll be right back," Daemon said, and he quickly rushed out of the room, leaving me with Dimple.

"Hail, are you really okay?" she asked. "I mean, it's okay not to be. A lot has happened and it must have been very traumatic. I'm glad you got to say goodbye to your grandfather, but losing someone you love is never easy. I lost my mother last year, and I still find myself wanting to call her all the time."

"I don't want to talk about it, Dimple," I said. "I'm going to go write my messages. Will you figure out who is going to deliver them for me?"

"Does it have to be someone you know? It will likely reward them with a [Mark of Karma], and—"

"I don't care who it is as long as they don't have a [Brand of Sin]," I answered.

"Hail, nobody in the guild was branded," she informed me. "And you have us to thank for protecting your identity. We lied through our teeth, saying that you had nothing to do with the Branding Boss. We wouldn't have known either if you hadn't said your name at the time, but to the outside world, Hail Jeoran was never a Worldboss. Although your sudden growth spurt might raise some questions."

"I know. Thank you for watching out for me. Now, I really do need to start writing; there's a lot of people I need to send letters to," I said.

"How many messengers do you need?" Dimple asked.

"I don't know, fifty?" I sighed. "I'm probably going to get a [Writer's Cramp]."

3
REUNIONS

The door crashed open. The sound of it slamming against the wall woke me. I lifted my head off the desk, a piece of parchment stuck to my face that I quickly pulled off. When I looked up, I saw Malkios storming over to me, a strange expression on his bearded face. Well-placed instinct had me immediately searching for whatever act I might have performed to earn his ire, but instead he dragged me from the desk chair and engulfed me in a furious hug.

You have taken 20 crushing Damage.

"Malkios, I need to breathe," I squeaked after a moment, although it was another moment before I was released.

"You damn fool boy, making a deal with a deity," Malkios complained, the stench of wine heavy on his breath. "I thought I'd lost you and your grandpa in the same day. Thank Thedum in his generosity for sending you back to me."

"I didn't know what else to do," I admitted. "Thedum offered to make me his avatar to get revenge, and I accepted without even thinking it over. Now everything is different, in ways that I don't really understand. I'm worried, Malkios. While I was in the space between worlds, Grandfather told me a lot of things that he might never have told me if he hadn't died. He told me his plan for me, to have me set up a new noble house. He thought, maybe, you would help—"

"My blade is yours," Malkios declared without letting me finish. "And my hammer and my axe, for that matter. Whatever you need from me, my loyalty to your grandfather has become my loyalty to you, for the faith you showed in avenging him. Though it pains me that we cannot banish the [Kingslayer] from this world entirely, branding him and his ilk is at least a start."

"Is it widely known among the Natives that I was the 'Branding Boss,' as the Travelers are calling it?" I asked.

"No. I have kept the silence, but I was there. It was wise of Tarisha and Daemon to swear the others to secrecy and spread their disinformation. I have done the same, except to those most loyal to your grandfather, whom I trust to keep the faith. Lady Gwen and the other Dungeon Busters know, but few others."

"That's a relief," I said. "I honestly wouldn't know what to do if everyone knew that I'd become the [Avatar of Thedum]."

"That isn't the only change. You seem to have grown a bit from the scrawny former prince I remember," Malkios commented.

"I know. I'm not certain why, but Thedum changed my age. I think it was necessary to make me his avatar, although I don't know why," I explained. "I'm still getting used to the difference. I feel so clumsy being this big."

"Well, everyone goes through an awkward phase," the guard captain admitted.

"Yes, well, hopefully I can stop bumping into stuff and tripping over my own feet soon," I grumbled. "Malkios, there's something you should know. My grandfather, King Rain, will be reborn as my younger brother. It was his own choice, but I'm not certain why, except that he enjoyed being king in his past life, and this was the only way for him to inherit the crown again—although I worry that it puts him far down the line of succession. He'll be in the same place I was before I was declared a bastard, and everyone always said that it was unlikely I would ever inherit."

"Perhaps not as unlikely as you think," Malkios said, his face turning serious. "Hail, two of your uncles and one of your great-uncles have died while you were between worlds. Murdered by Travelers of the traitorous assassin's guild."

"What?" I exclaimed.

"Grave news, I know. It has thrown the entire question of succession into chaos. Your youngest uncle, Storm, is claiming that the crown belongs to him, while your great-uncle Auroras is accusing him of fratricide and claiming that makes him the rightful heir. Storm has returned Auroras's accusation with one of his own. That is as much as I know about the events, however. You should speak with Lady Gwen as soon as possible; she will be the one to guide you through this mess," Malkios said.

"My family is being murdered by the Travelers," I whispered. "And the most I can do is brand them? So, what, they can't get the quest they want or access the auction?"

Inside I seethed. I had not been close with my uncles; they lived in their own estates, and their visits, while I had been growing, were associated with being dressed for a formal presentation followed by a boring party or feast of some sort. The food had been good, but that was the only redeeming aspect of such visits. But they were family, and they were being taken from me.

"My mother? Is she safe?"

"I've had no word of an attempt on her life," Malkios said. "I believe it's because it's yet unknown to society whether she bears a prince or princess. If she were to give birth to a girl, then the child would be safe, but I fear for the safety of a boy, which you claim it shall be. Your own safety should be assured, as you were removed from the line of succession two years ago—but, even so, you should be more careful with your life, Hail."

"I do not believe that assassinating me would do any good," I admitted. "I am as immortal as the Travelers are, Malkios. Killing me would only cost me a level and leave me annoyed."

"Are you certain?" Malkios asked. "Or did Thedum simply bring you back for your service to his cause?"

"It is Mr. Thomas the Administrator who told me that," I said.

"I see. That does not mean that you should be reckless, Hail. If the Travelers kill you until you are once again level one, then you will once more be as helpless as a [Child]," he reminded me.

"I know," I said. "I'm not planning on doing it on purpose or anything. I need to get stronger, Malkios. Strong enough that I don't need to borrow power from Thedum to protect those I care about. I need power that doesn't come with a million fishhooks attached."

"That kind of power does not come easily," Malkios cautioned. "I am level one-seventy, and I still failed to protect or avenge your grandfather."

"It was not your fault, Malkios. Neither Grandfather nor I blame you for what happened," I assured him. "Although if you're willing, there is a task I would have you do."

"Name it."

"Journey to Eolstree and keep Mother and my unborn brother safe from assassins," I said.

Malkios paused, then bowed. "I shall leave on the morrow. Let me spend the rest of the day with you, at least. Seeing you alive helps me to feel less of a failure."

I nodded, and I turned back to my writing. I had gotten through half of the letters that I was supposed to write before drifting off, but the one that I had been working on was smudged by my face. A wave of panic went through me as I pulled a hand mirror out of my inventory and saw that my face was blotched with ink.

Malkios snorted in amusement. "I was hoping you wouldn't notice until much later," he teased.

"That's not funny!" I protested. I looked about, but we were in a Traveler's building, and they require no water for drink or bathing while in my world, so there was no basin to try to wash off the ink. I double checked my inventory, but the only liquids I possessed were Health and Mana potions. Frustrated, I realized that I would have to venture out to find a way to clean my face.

Shooting Malkios another glare for his silent amusement, I stormed out of the room and, immediately outside the door, bumped into Tarisha. I blushed a bit at my awkwardness and the stain on my face, which she immediately noticed and chuckled over.

"I heard you were writing. I thought that would involve paper, not skin," she teased.

"I fell asleep, okay?" I said. Then I hugged her. "I missed you these last few weeks. Strange, because we haven't known each other that long. But of all my Traveler friends, I missed you and Laurant the most. I wonder if that's because I've spent the most time with you, or if it's because you have the most Reputation. Because of everyone I've seen, you are glowing the most brightly."

Tarisha examined her hands. "Glowing? I do not understand, My Lord."

"Since I returned, I've become able to see Reputation, Tarisha," I explained. "Or, at least, I've become able to see my own. Those who fought against me when I was a Worldboss are glowing either red or orange, while those who helped with the dungeon outbreak or completed my other quests are some shade of blue. You are very, very blue."

"I see," she said. "That is . . . I suppose it will become useful to know who is aligned for and against you at a glance. You've handed out so many quests with Reputation as a reward I doubt you'll be able to keep track very soon, and so many people have either unwittingly or intentionally taken stances against you."

"I kind of wish that you weren't glowing though," I admitted. "I mean, I'll never forget about—oh, you stopped glowing when I said that. Convenient."

"I'm glad. While it's a useful function, I don't exactly wear the color blue very well," she said. "Of the primaries, I prefer wearing red, as you may have noticed."

"I don't care what you wear, I'm just glad you're on my side," I said. "I don't know what I would do if you suddenly started glowing red."

"That will never happen, My Lord. I will never, ever go over to the darkside," she vowed.

"I believe you," I said.

"My Lord . . . how cognizant are you of Reputation? Do you base all your decisions on it or only some? Or are you able to form attachments based on emotion alone? I'm sorry if that's an Oh Oh See question, but the answer is important to me for a number of reasons."

"I couldn't see it until I became Thedum's avatar," I informed her. "I honestly don't know if it was affecting me before that or not. I was never aware of it, but it could have been affecting me like it does other Natives. Does it matter?"

"It does to me. I would be sad if your affection was so easily won by simply completing a few fetch and carry quests," she admitted. "And I have future considerations that I must bear in mind as well.

Lewis has yet to make up his mind on the matter, but if not him, I will find another partner."

"What?" I asked.

"Never mind. That slipped out; it's not something I'm ready to discuss with you yet. Soon, once it is closer to being a reality, I will seek your aide for something, but until I am certain that it will truly happen, I do not wish to get either of our hopes up."

"Oh. Well, if it's something I can help with, please let me know. Now I really must find something to wash my face."

Daemon cleared his throat, and I noticed him for the first time standing a respectful distance away down the hallway.

"Lord Hail, a missive arrived a moment ago. A Native courier delivered it and put great importance on it reaching you immediately, though he could not come within our instance of the Guild Hall himself. We invited Malkios in immediately when he arrived, of course, but a courier can wait outside. The letter is from your uncle, I believe."

"Oh." I took the proffered letter and examined the seal. It was Storm's, and it was addressed to me with markings declaring it to be of great importance and to bear regal authority.

"Malkios, the succession hasn't been decided yet, has it?" I asked.

"It has not," Malkios declared emphatically, having noticed the same markings that I had. "But Storm has always been presumptuous. His nature is now his biggest detriment, as many believe that he is guilty of the crimes he has been accused of."

I sighed and broke the seal. My frown grew more serious as I examined the contents of the letter.

"I have been summoned for a royal audience immediately," I declared. "Which is strange, since there is no king to summon me or hold a royal audience."

4
TRAPS

"It's a trap," Malkios declared.

"Obviously," Tarisha agreed. "The question is whether to spring it or avoid it. Daemon, your thoughts on the matter?"

"I'm afraid I'm not adept enough in the politics of the Natives to be confident in an answer either way. My counsel would be to speak with someone who is," the vice guild leader said. "For the moment, is it possible to delay?"

I considered the question. It was a good one. "I'll write a response claiming to be indisposed. I don't think that Storm has the authority to command my presence until a coronation has taken place, but I don't want to 'piss him off' if he does become the next king. I'll only be able to put this thing off for a day or so."

"That will be long enough to speak with Lady Gwen and Lord Tom," Malkios said. "I will go and fetch them."

"I hate this. I wanted to finish writing my grandfather's final missives then go out on another adventure," I complained. "Now half of my family is dead, and I don't know what to do anymore."

"Well, to start with, I would suggest washing your face," Malkios teased, turning his back so that he couldn't see the glare I shot him as he left.

Frustrated, I returned to Daemon's office where I quickly penned a note to "Uncle Storm" pleading that I was unable to attend him due to "resurrection sickness." It was the best excuse I could think of at the time.

Glancing at the stack of finished missives, I decided it was time to start procrastinating. I'd written the most important ones already, and the rest could wait. I hadn't checked my status screen since I'd logged in, so I quickly pulled that up.

Name	Hail Jeoran	Level	28
Guild	<Nethersong Mavericks>	Strength	30
Health	12600/12600	Dexterity	78
Mana	19320/19320	Vitality	45
Experience	3401/16800	Endurance	38
Age	15	Intelligence	69
Race	Human (blood of the Travelers)	Wisdom	42
Class	Spellblade	Charisma	54
Job	Earl	Armor	29
Title	Castle Buster	Spell Damage	90
		Attack Power	165
Passive Skills	Short Swords (20)	Spells	Detect Poison (17)
	Long Swords (24)		Lightning Bolt (Max)
	Rapiers (Max)		Chain Lightning (Max)
	Katanas (20)		Fireball (14)
	Dodge (21)		Ice Blast (13)
	Battle Trance		Arcane Missile (12)

	Magic in Motion		Dazzling Lights (9)
	Righteous Brand		Concussive Sound (8)
			Befuddle (12)
Active Skills	Dash (23)		Water Jet (7)
	Thrust (27)		Polymorph (20)
	Slash (29)		Slow (24)
	Riposte (19)		Create Trap (7)
	Feint (19)		Mark of Karma (special)
	Piercing Lunge (18)		Summon Karmic Warrior (special)
	Swiftcast (20)		
	Empower Magic (17)	**Traits**	High Aptitude
	Imbue Sword: Fire (16)		Royal Blood (+5 Charisma, bonus to relations with factions loyal to Yuikon)
	Imbue Sword: Lightning (25)		Nobility: Earl (+5 Charisma)
	Imbue Sword: Ice (17)		Avatar of Thedum
	Aqua Blade (4)		Mark of the Phoenix
	Arcane Weapon (13)		Voice of the Future
	Holy Weapon (Max)		
		General Spells	. . .
General Skills	. . .		

I sighed, annoyed to have lost an entire level of progress, but otherwise my stats hadn't changed much.

"How are you doing, Lord Hail? I mean, do you need someone to talk to? You have lost many family members in a short amount of time, and it's okay if you're overwhelmed," Tarisha said, standing in the room with me.

I shook my head. "I don't really know my uncles very well. I'm sorry that they're dead, and I'll murder the assassins and those responsible right back if the opportunity arises, but I don't mourn for them the way I mourn for Grandfather. Or maybe I'm just numb to it, I don't know. I just—there's a lot that I don't know right now, Tarisha, and how I feel about a lot of things is pretty high on that list."

I sealed the letter to my uncle and picked up the other letters, then went down to the main floor of the Guild Hall, where several other guild members were lounging around, most of them glowing various shades of blue. They all perked up when I entered, as they had likely been waiting for me after hearing that I might have some quests to issue.

"Thank you all for waiting. I have a few letters that need to be delivered, and I figured they'd probably turn into quests, so I thought you all would like to have the opportunity," I said. "Although, honestly, I don't think they'll be exciting quests—they're just to deliver a letter after all. The most urgent one needs to go to my uncle, but I've got a handful of other letters for a number of nobles and officials. I'm not really sure how you want to divide them up—"

"We worked that out already," someone said. I think it was Worple—although there are too many guild members for me to keep track of, to be honest—as he was glowing faintly blue. "Getting in the door with any of the nobles is a much bigger thing for a player than you seem to realize, Hail. We're really looking forward to this opportunity. Just tell us where a letter goes, and we'll figure out who takes it, unless for some reason the quest doesn't generate for them."

"Right, okay. Well, this one needs to go to my uncle, Storm Teoran, right away," I said, then spent several minutes handing out quests. I had enough letters for all the Travelers who wanted one, plus several who got to serve double duty. A few of them were carrying the letters separately but traveling together to see if they could jointly complete the quests to earn rewards as a group. It was all very boring, and I was glad to be done with it until the next batch of letters, which I promised myself I would work on tomorrow.

But first, I needed to find some soap to get the ink stains off my face.

Malkios returned an hour later with Lord Tom and Lady Gwen. They were both polite enough not to mention the ink, or the tenderness of my skin from having spent that hour scrubbing. Having received an official invite from one of the guild leaders, they were able to join us in Daemon's office, although it was a little cramped, as aside from the four of us, Tarisha, Daemon, and Dimple were also present.

"Do you know who's been killing off my family?" I asked immediately once we were alone. "Is it Uncle Storm?"

Lady Gwen and Lord Tom exchanged a glance, then shrugged.

"We only know that Travelers are responsible, and that they were following quests given by the assassin's guild. Who hired them is a matter of speculation, but both your uncles, Storm and Auroras, stand the most to gain from having Sleet and Cloud removed from the line of succession," Lord Tom explained. Despite his snake-like appearance, his pronunciation was crisp. I kept expecting him to hiss.

"Storm is the obvious suspect because he's now the heir. But the deaths leave Auroras in second. He would be third, if not for your illegitimacy, but that ship has sailed, unfortunately," Lady Gwen continued. "Although with the question of fratricide, you could potentially make a play. You were between worlds from the time your grandfather died until just recently; you couldn't have orchestrated—"

"I don't want to be king," I said, interrupting her. "I'd be happy just being an Earl and an adventurer."

"I see," Lady Gwen said, obviously not used to being interrupted. "Well, the sooner you make your feelings on that known, the safer you'll be. As it is, you are just important enough with your new position that both Auroras and Storm will demand your support. I suspect that is the purpose of the summons you received. Storm will likely demand you swear allegiance, and you must do no such thing until after the coronation."

"If you swear to Storm, and Auroras is crowned, then your

great-uncle will never trust you," Lord Tom explained. "If you swear to Auroras, and Storm is the next king, then you will always be seen as a traitor."

"Won't refusing to swear to either just upset them both?" Tarisha inquired.

"Many nobles are taking a neutral stance until the question of who had Hail's uncles murdered is answered," Lady Gwen answered. "In fact, it's the popular stance. Storm and Auroras have claimed about one fifth of the noble's support each, with the remaining three fifths undeclared. The church, meanwhile, has officially declared that Thedum will not support a fratricidal king, and has vowed not to crown either party until the matter has been resolved."

"And the masses?" Daemon inquired. "What do they think?"

Lady Gwen huffed. "What do they ever think? As long as their bellies are full and their lands relatively free of monsters, they don't care who sits on the throne. The crown prince and two dukes are dead, and to them it's a simple matter of gossip. I suspect they'll care significantly more if the matter turns into a civil war and they're conscripted by one of the competing factions, but at the moment they're content to leave politics to the nobles."

"I wish I could be like them," I lamented. "I want to find who-ever is responsible for killing my uncles, but I don't care who becomes king, as long as they're not the ones who hired the assassins."

"Unfortunately, your royal blood precludes you from that lux-ury," Lord Tom said. "You should draft a statement renouncing any ambitions for the throne yourself as soon as possible and have it announced throughout the city. I will arrange criers to—"

"No, let the guild do it," I said. "It's another quest for those who want them, I'm sure. It's not like you need a license to stand on a street corner and shout a message, after all."

Lord Tom was no more accustomed to being interrupted than Lady Gwen was, but he nodded in agreement. "I suppose that will suffice."

"Hail, what do you actually wish to accomplish?" Lady Gwen inquired. "You don't wish to be king; will you renounce your lands as Earl as well and dedicate yourself entirely to adventuring?"

"No, I'm not going that far," I assured her. "I think I can be an Earl and an Adventurer both. I have a plan where the two will work together, but I can't really share the details on it. I promised Grandfather. He's the one who helped me come up with it."

"So, then, any plan we come up with must ensure that you are free to adventure, while avoiding making any sort of pledge to either side in this conflict," Lady Gwen surmised. "You were right to simply delay the meeting with your uncle. He does not have the authority to demand your presence as he attempted to do, but as your uncle and as a duke, he does have the ability to send an invitation that would be difficult for an Earl to refuse. What excuse did you use in delaying?"

"I pleaded resurrection sickness," I answered. For some reason, the Travelers in the room snickered at that. "He does know that I was between worlds, does he not?"

"The official story I spread was that Thedum whisked you away from the battle in order to protect you, as he has done before," Malkios answered.

"Which is actually the truth, if you leave out the bit about me returning and getting killed as a Worldboss," I said. "Was it not widely known that I was dead then?"

"It was speculated but not confirmed. Your excuse may have raised some questions in Storm's mind, but he'll keep them to himself," Lord Tom explained. "It doesn't make much difference at this point. Just so long as nobody publicly connects you to being the king's avenger, everything will be alright."

"We will come with you tomorrow, Hail, and support you as you navigate this situation," Lady Gwen pledged. "It's the least that we can do for the youngest member of the Dungeon Busters, after all. Put your trust in us to either speak for you or put the correct words in your mouth, and you shall avoid becoming entangled in the spider's web that your uncles are weaving for you. For now, draft a statement renouncing ambitions for the throne."

I smiled at her words, but the seriousness of the situation meant my smile did not last long. "Daemon, will you let the guild know that I have another quest for them, please?"

"I already sent a message in guildchat," Daemon answered. "We have two dozen volunteers who missed out on the letter deliveries."

Which meant that I had to write two dozen copies. Frowning, I stretched my aching pen hand and got to work.

5
ARRESTS

"What do you mean, you can't read it?" I asked, my voice full of anguish and despair.

"I mean it might as well be written in ancient hieroglyphics," Zimmer answered, still holding the parchment that I had spent ten minutes writing. "I'd say Greek, but I actually know a little bit of Greek. My grandparents are from Crete. So that would make more sense than the language that you Natives use when the system isn't translating for you, and you know that it doesn't translate documents like this. I'd have to screenshot it and submit it to one of the translation indexes, but if I do that, it will probably leak. I suppose that doesn't matter, since we're supposed to be announcing it anyway, but it would probably be faster if you just told us what to say."

I looked down at my hand, still suffering from a [Writer's Cramp], and thought of the two dozen copies I had made. It had taken me an hour and a half, and I could still feel the quill biting into my fingers. For nothing.

"I could have just sent a message in guildchat," I lamented.

"No, I don't think so," Zimmer answered, seemingly oblivious to my despair. "I didn't actually get a quest until you handed me this paper. I think that we need a quest item to make it official."

That cheered me up slightly, but then the damn Traveler had to follow it up with, "But you probably could have gotten away with just stamping a sheet of paper with your personal seal and telling us what to say."

I facepalmed. So much time and effort wasted. I looked over to Tarisha.

"Why did you let me make so many copies?" I demanded.

"We don't actually know that you didn't need to," she pointed out. "A stamped sheet of paper might not have cut it for the system to consider it a proper quest item."

Annoyed, I took my seal and stamped a blank piece of paper with it, then stepped out of Daemon's office and handed it to the next player waiting in line.

"Go and spread the word that Hail Jeoran has no interest in becoming the next king, and that he renounces any and all claims to the throne," I told her.

"Alright! Quest accepted," she said, leaving with the paper before the ink was even dry. I facepalmed again. Which aggravated my [Writer's Cramp], but I was too frustrated to care.

"Okay, so I didn't think of it in time," Tarisha admitted. "Sorry, Hail."

"Twenty-four copies," I whispered. "And I didn't need to write any of them. I could have just—dammit!"

"It's not the end of the world," Tarisha assured me. "So you wasted some time and effort, but on the other hand, what happens if a Native asks to read your proclamation? Sure, we can't read it, but any Native can, right?"

"Not really," I admitted. "Only one in five adults can read. The literacy rate isn't that high in Yuikon. There's a reason why we still use criers instead of the printing presses you Travelers helped us design. Although I suppose it's not a good idea to be passing around blank paper with my seal upon it; someone could use it to put words in my mouth that I never meant to say. In fact, Tarisha, would you mind getting that back for me? Take one of these worthless copies with you to exchange it for the blank one."

"Of course. I'll return directly."

Tarisha left the room at a jog, although unless they activated their Fast Travel, the player was unlikely to have gotten far.

"So, is it cool if I upload this to the translation indexes?" Zimmer inquired. "I mean, I won't do it if you say no, but I'm kind of curious what it actually—"

"Do whatever you want with it. You were supposed to read it anyway," I said. "It's not meant to be a secret."

"Right," he said. "I'm going to go. Thanks for the quest."

"Tell the next group to come in to get their quests as you leave," I told him, and he did just that. Tarisha returned moments after I had finished handing out quests, and I sighed.

"Let's go practice," I suggested. "It feels like I've done nothing but write and hear bad news since I returned. I want to hit something."

I studied her for a moment, then reconsidered. "Maybe I should get a practice partner more on my level. I'm still getting used to my new body, and you'll just wipe the floor with me."

My opponent was a level thirty-two swordsman. His name was Corinth, he was seventeen "Eye Are El," and he had joined the guild while I was away. He had logged in just a few minutes too late to be one of the criers, but he had jumped at the chance to be my opponent and was thrilled to have finally met me.

He was very skilled; he had only recently quit playing *Blade's Edge* to come to this world. He'd never made it to "endgame" in that other reality, but he'd gotten quite skilled with a sword. More importantly, he used a form that I had never seen before, making it that much more of a challenge to fight him.

Because we were nearly equal in levels, we were both using training swords, and I was avoiding my magic in order to truly practice my swordsmanship. I could have used magic without killing him accidentally, as the practice sword would limit my Damage while it was equipped, whether I used it to inflict Damage or I used my magical abilities instead. My magic, however, had not been impacted by my growth spurt, and I still felt confident in those abilities.

Back and forth we fenced—me using a rapier, him a bastard sword—each giving as good as we got. We were sweating and grinning and having a great time when he announced, "Oh hey, I just got [Mark of Karma]!" and I took the opportunity to decapitate him. Or at least the blow would have inflicted that critical wound were it not a training sword. Instead it simply passed through his neck and did one Damage.

"Congratulations. You're dead," I teased him.

"Yeah, yeah. Seriously though, thanks. Do all your training partners get the mark?" he inquired.

"I'm not certain," I admitted. "Maybe? I think it goes off of Reputation; once you reach a certain point you earn the mark. You got a quest to be my training partner, right? You have probably been earning Reputation over time and just passed the threshold. Or maybe I'm completely wrong, and the system that governs this world just does it randomly."

"Well, either way, thanks. The experience boost is nothing to sneeze at; it will make the rest of my game time much smoother. Now come on, let's keep going," he said, and he picked up his guard stance. I grinned and took up a stance of my own.

As we fought, I began to forget that I had grown almost a foot. I stopped thinking about what had been done to my grandfather and my uncles. I stopped worrying about my mother and my unborn brother over in Eolstree. I didn't worry about the intrigue or the succession. I focused on the fight. On blocking Corinth's strikes while inflicting my own. On the exercise, and the thrill of sparring. The little mosquito bites of minus one Health blows came in droves, but I gave as good as I got. Better, because mine was the faster weapon.

We had been fighting for perhaps an hour when Malkios, Tarisha, and Daemon came rushing down to the basement, their faces grim. Corinth and I both saw them and mutually ended the combat.

"What is it now?" I asked, sighing.

"Lord Hail," Tarisha said, "your messengers and the criers, they're being arrested en mass. The ones who resist are being killed."

"What?! Tell them not to resist!" I cried, then I quickly pulled up guildchat.

Hail	Guys, do not die over the quest I gave you—it's not worth it!
Wesle	They're demanding our papers, Hail. Should we hand them over?

Hail	Oh. Um, if you have the crier quest, then yes. Hand it over. If you're a messenger, then keep it in your inventory. Tell them that it's diplomatic communication and that you're not authorized to release it to anyone but the intended recipient or an inquisitor appointed by the king himself.
Subtleghost	Um, but there isn't a king at the moment.
Weaselfire	They haven't been killing us unless we try to escape. They really want our papers, and they know that they can't get them from us if they just kill us.
Hail	I know about the king situation, Subtleghost, but it will hopefully stop them from killing you until I figure out what's going on. I'm really sorry to everyone who got arrested for the messenger quest. I'll try to figure out how to get you out of jail as soon as I can, okay?
Birdie	Don't feel too bad, Hail. The quest updates after you get arrested. Messengers don't fail the quest unless they turn over the item, and according to the update, we get increased rewards for doing time in the clink. It hints that there might be some sort of other role-play options as a prisoner. This is another opportunity guys! Let's go to jail!
Hail	Um, okay. Just don't get killed, okay?
Nerfme	Momma always said I'd wind up in prison one of these days.
Hail	Who had the quest to go to my uncle, again? Did you complete it already?
Kikrock	That was me. I was waiting in the servant's quarters when the guards broke in and arrested me. I still have the letter.

I shook my head as I closed the chat window. "One of my uncles must be behind this. It's probably Storm, but I don't know for certain. And since my letter to him was intercepted, I have the perfect excuse to go find out. Would you like to come with me?"

"Quest accepted!" Corinth said eagerly. I glanced at him in surprise since I hadn't been expecting him to receive the quest, but I didn't object.

"Of course, Lord Hail," Tarisha agreed.

"I would go as well, but I have to go pick up my daughter Eye Are El shortly," Daemon said.

"Let me fetch Lady Gwen and Lord Tom," Malkios said, jogging out of the room. "We shall meet you at your uncle's estate in thirty minutes."

I ground my teeth in frustration, debating what to do now. "I will go and freshen myself. My uncle will be insulted if I appear looking and smelling like this. Give me twenty minutes. After that, I shall have to Fast Travel to the eastern districts in order to arrive in time."

"Corinth, run ahead of us and hire a carriage. The grandest one you can find," Tarisha suggested. "I'll arrange for a guard from <Peasant's Revenge> to meet us at the Nexus Point. We shall march alongside the carriage as your honor guard, Lord Hail."

"Um, I actually only have like three gold at the moment," Corinth admitted. "I mean, I don't know what a carriage costs, but I'm happy to—"

"Here," I said, tossing him twenty gold. "As Tarisha said, the grandest you can find. If they ask for more than that, tell him that his mother is a goblin and his father's breath smells of turpentine, because that's ten times what he deserves."

"Oh, um, thanks. The quest just updated, and it's got a tight timer, so I'm going to go now," Corinth said, and he vanished into motes of blue light.

"You should hurry too, Lord Hail," Tarisha said, her eyes staring off into space at a private screen as she tapped the air on her holographic keyboard. "I'll meet you there after I coordinate with my guild."

"Right," I agreed, and I jogged up to the office, which had been converted into my bedroom, to quickly wash with a basin of soapy water—the same that I had used to mostly remove the ink from my face—and to change out of my adventurer's garb and into something suitable for court. I actually used the system to equip it simply due to time constraints. I even applied a light dose of cologne, as I had noticed that I had developed body odor. Another frustrating aspect of instantaneous puberty.

After a moment's debate, I decided to leave my [Gemos Long Sword] proudly equipped at my side rather than stashing it in my inventory. It would take about the same time to draw it as to pull it out of [Storage], but as an Earl, it suited my rank to wear it almost everywhere except in the presence of a foreign monarch.

Dressed in blue, silver, and black, I examined myself in the mirror for a moment. My hair was still damp from sweat, but I brushed it into place as best I could. Deciding that it was the best that I could do alone and with the time constraints I was under, I Fast Traveled to my destination.

6

PROTOCOL

The strange sensations of displacement and movement that accompanied Fast Travel faded, and I found myself standing outside the market in the eastern districts. I was promptly enveloped in a powerful protective shield cast by a high-level [Cleric] and surrounded by Tarisha, Marvin of Cincinnati, and Lloyd, the tank who had faced Gyudue with me.

"Stay back! <Peasant's Revenge> will Pee Kay anyone who approaches Lord Hail at this time!" Tarisha declared, her voice amplified by a magic choker she'd equipped. I noticed that aside from my inner layer of protection there was another circle of members of Tarisha's guild. Outside of that layer was a mass of Travelers. Most of them appeared normal, glowing neither blue nor red, although there were several players who bore the [Mark of Sin].

"What's going on?" someone shouted. "Is this some sort of event? Come on, at least tell us what's happening."

"I am visiting my uncle," I declared. "That is all. I have learned some distressing news since Thedum allowed me to return to the city, and I am in a hurry to discuss things with my dear Uncle Storm. I am sorry for the disturbance, but please—"

Abruptly, one of the red players cast a spell at me. I tried to dodge, but it impacted the protection spell. Fortunately, the magical barrier held against the fire, which was immediately refreshed by the healer who had cast it. Lloyd moved to block the follow up attack, intercepting the fireball with his shield, while three of the warriors in the outer ring converged upon the assassin.

Tarisha grabbed my arm and we both blurred for a second as she tried to activate [Wind Walk], but it seemed that she could no longer carry me with that spell as she could when I'd been smaller. She could still drag me along the traditional way, however, and I ran after her towards the carriage while Lloyd and Marvin ran in formation with us. The crowd erupted into chaos, with many of the gathered low-level players scattering to avoid the clash between the endgamers. Most of the red players vanished into the crowd, while two of them stood as though debating what action to take.

"Kill those two as well!" I shouted, pointing at the lingering threats.

"Quest accepted!" my guards from <Peasant's Revenge> said almost in unison, and more split off from the outer ring.

"Wait, we weren't going to do anything!" one of the players declared. "We were just—"

Multiple spells of fire, frost, and lightning converged upon him, and a moment later, he was run through by a spear-wielding member of <Peasant's Revenge>. Even impaled, it took a moment for him to vanish into motes of red light as his Health was drained to zero.

The other player I had pointed to immediately drew a pair of daggers and began battling with Tarisha's guildmates. I did not see the conclusion of the fighting, as I was thrown bodily into the carriage.

"Go, go! Now!" Tarisha shouted, and the driver whipped the horses. The healer jumped into the moving carriage with me, maintaining her protective shield the entire way. Corinth, who had been waiting for me inside the carriage, blocked my view of the receding fight as he eagerly stared out the rear window.

"Oh man, that was awesome," he exclaimed. "Why'd you single out those two guys?"

"They deserved it," I said, collapsing into the upholstered seat. I looked out to the side and saw three mounted members of <Peasant's Revenge> riding with me, while two rode on the other side of the carriage. After we were some distance away, I heard a wyvern cry and then a thud on the roof of the carriage.

"At ease; it's me," Tarisha said, and she swooped down from the roof into the carriage with us. "I'm sorry, Lord Hail. This was mostly my fault. Ever since the incident, <Peasant's Revenge> has been attracting crowds whenever we appear in groups larger than three. It is well known that we were the most numerous of the endgame guilds represented by [Karmic Warriors]. When it was obvious that we had drawn attention, I made the call to bring in everyone who could make it on short notice as a show of force. It seems that was not enough to dissuade everyone."

"I suppose that I was lucky that I wasn't murdered on my way home from the temple," I said, sighing.

"Indeed, most fortunate," she agreed. "I wish that you would have waited for us to get in position."

"And what?" I asked. "Get chased through the city on my way to the Guild Hall? Tarisha, what is this? This is Zhesa City! How is it not safe for me to walk down the street in my own hometown? We're in the very heart of the Heartlands, and yet—"

"The world is changing, Lord Hail, and most unfortunately you are at the center of it," she said sadly. "I'm very sorry. For everything. Perhaps things would be better if you were to become an anonymous Traveler or a random Native."

"No!" I said immediately. "If anything, I've been away too long wallowing in my self-pity. My country needs me. My mother needs me, and my future little brother needs me. I don't know, I mean, I am just an Earl, but I need to do *something*. If I just disappear and let everything go to the seven hells, I'll never forgive myself."

"I'm very happy you feel that way," Tarisha said. "I also must inform you that I just received a quest. It is to support you in your efforts to right the course and save your country from succumbing to darkness. It appears that it is an ongoing quest that will conclude when the next king is crowned. The rewards are . . . They appear to scale with the amount of effort put into the quest, and if I'm interpreting things correctly, they could grow to be substantial. It appears to be shareable, and with your permission I would spread it to everyone in my guild and to those in <Nethersong Mavericks> who would take it."

"Oh. Yeah, of course. Please do," I said absently. I looked out the window as we quickly passed through the city. "Oh, and <Ragtag Muffin>. I mean, if they want it."

"I—um. Yes, Milord, I shall also share it with them," Tarisha agreed. "I was hoping to keep it somewhat exclusive, and I doubt that the children of Ragtag will treat it that way, but I suppose the more people working on this project, the better the end result will be for everyone. I will contact one of their administrators to set up an opportunity to give it to those who want it."

"Thank you, Tarisha. One of these days I'm going to have to reward you for everything you've done for me, and I can't imagine how I'll be able to afford it," I said.

It took five minutes from the Nexus Point to reach my uncle's estate. The guard at the gate challenged us but quickly pulled the wrought iron gates open when I was announced. As we passed into the substantial manicured lawn that few in the city could afford, I noticed behind us a magical flare being launched into the sky, no doubt informing the main house of my arrival. The servants appeared to have been waiting for the signal, as a line of valets promptly appeared from the main door, lining up to receive us.

I shook my head at the display. My uncle had a wife and two children. Five if you counted the bastards, of course. Which I did, and he didn't. If it weren't for my grandfather, I'm quite certain they would have been cast into the streets. Instead, my illegitimate cousins were being educated in country estates far from court. I'd never been allowed to meet them, although we had secretly exchanged letters when I'd been younger, with the help of my mother. Somewhat iron-ically, I was much fonder of Storm's bastards than I was of his heirs, and that had been before my own disgrace.

But however you counted, my uncle did not require nine valets.

The head butler appeared at the door a moment later, a stern looking man with a trim suit and a mustache. He had tormented me in my younger days, on those few occasions when I had been forced to visit my Uncle Storm, but I refused to be intimidated. His name was Filo.

"Hello again, Hail," the butler said. "You are expected, but I'm afraid your bodyguards must wait outside."

"Tarisha comes with me," I insisted.

"I'm afraid I really must insist, little goblin," the man said. Annoyed, I turned him into a toad with a [Swiftcast] [Polymorph].

"I am an Earl. The proper term of address for my station is 'My

Lord.' If I see Filo again on this visit I will challenge him to a duel, and then I will kill him. And the next time that I see him after that, I expect him to immediately apologize for his actions tonight. Who is next in charge?" I inquired.

One of the valets jumped over, scooped up the [Polymorphed] Filo, and ran into the house. Another stepped forward, somewhat shaken by my display of magic and authority. "I'm head valet, My Lord. However, I'm afraid that Duke Storm truly does insist that you do not bring any Traveler over level fifty into his home. After what happened to his father and the assassinations, including the attempts that our guards have foiled, you must understand his caution."

"Then you may tell my uncle that I will not be entering his house without Tarisha of Miami at my side. If he has a problem with that, he can either join me in the yard, and we can discuss our business as we watch the sunset, or I will view this journey as a waste of time, and I will return home."

The head valet paled further, and he abruptly delegated the task to his junior, who looked like he had just been told that he was to be hanged on the morrow. But the younger man obediently disappeared into the house. I sighed and walked over to one of the statues lining the drive. It was clearly of elfish make, a young girl in a dress made of flowers, her arms raised as though inviting the viewer to dance with her. However, the ears had been rounded off, and whoever had mutilated the poor elf had botched the job.

I sighed. The statue had probably cost a thousand gold or more, and another two hundred to import. And yet not only had my uncle defaced it, he probably accepted the lowest bidder when doing so. It would be a masterpiece, but for the ears. The girl was clearly elfish, but an amateur had polished her ears to make her look human. Her race still showed in the eyes.

"His Royal Majesty has granted dispensation for the presence of Tarisha of Miami to enter his home in her capacity as Your Lordship's bodyguard," the returning valet said, sounding out of breath. I [Analyzed] him and saw that he was level three. I wondered what his [Endurance] was.

"My Uncle Storm Teoran is a Duke," I said. "The proper term for a Duke is 'His Grace.' Not 'His Royal Majesty.' To call him anything else before a coronation is performed is a breach of protocol, and perhaps an act of rebellion, should he not be the one to ascend to the throne."

The valets collectively stiffened at my words. I was quite certain they were correct, as they had been drilled into me since I was five years old. However, with those words, I had declared a stance on the succession, and the men before me were smart enough to realize it. I did not recognize Storm Teoran as my de facto king, and although I hadn't said so yet, I would *not* be swearing my allegiance to Uncle Storm during this visit.

"As you say, Your Lordship," the head valet said nervously. "You and your bodyguard may enter at your leisure."

"Right. Tarisha, Corinth? Let's go," I said.

"M—me?" Corinth exclaimed. "I mean, quest accepted, but what?"

The valet's eyes went wide as well. "My Lord, you can't—"

"You said that the level limit on Travelers who may accompany me to visit my uncle is level fifty. Corinth, what level are you?"

"I'm thirty-three."

I looked at him in surprise.

"I got quite a bit of Experience from our sparring session," he explained.

"Congratulations. Now then, since we have cleared up that Corinth is under the acceptable level to join me in visiting my uncle, and we have received dispensation for Tarisha of Miami, will you please show the way Mr. . . . . I'm sorry, what is your name?"

"Hender," the head valet said, sweating profusely. "I—um. Yes, okay."

"Lead the way, Mr. Hender," I said, and I followed the valet into the mansion.

7
FORTITUDE

"So I guess you didn't just grow taller," Corinth said as we were shown into the parlor.

"Excuse me?" I asked.

"Oh, just commenting that you seem to have a massive pair of balls," the older boy commented. "And from all the talk about you while you were in the lobby, I'm sort of under the impression that it's a recent development."

I frowned. "I mean, I think they're normal sized for a boy my age, but I guess I wouldn't really have many to compare them to. Are my pants too tight or—"

"He's referring to how bold you're being, My Lord," Tarisha explained. "Testicular fortitude is, well, it's a bit sexist, but saying someone has 'big balls' implies that they are bold and fearless in our world."

"Oh. I guess I hadn't noticed. My pants do look okay, don't they?" I inquired, trying to examine myself without being obvious about it.

"Your outfit looks fine, My Lord," Tarisha assured me.

"Have I been acting strangely since I got back, Tarisha?"

"It's . . . you have changed, but that's to be expected. You do seem more confident than before; Corinth is correct on that account. But then you were always more comfortable dealing with Natives than you were with Travelers. But I've never had the privilege of watching you throw around your rank before," she replied. "I mean, around Natives of the Nobility, that is."

I frowned, deeply troubled by their comments. Thomas the Administrator had told me that Thedum had done things to me, changed me in ways that the admins did not fully understand. Was he responsible for the way I had been acting lately? As I reflected on the last several hours since I had returned to Lagrea, I grew more and more troubled by my actions. How much of what I had done and said was because of me, and how much of it was whatever Thedum had done to me?

The parlor overlooked the side garden, and I took a seat on the windowsill to look outside. It was on the wrong side of the house to watch the sunset itself, but watching the white rose bushes turn orange then crimson as the day came to an end was quite soothing, and it helped distract me from the troubles I was facing. I suppose I do have to give Uncle Storm credit for one thing: his home was beautiful.

"Tarisha, if I start acting rude or erratically, please smack some sense into me," I said.

"Quest accepted. Oh, this one is shareable too. Should I—"

"No," I said quickly.

"I think I'm going to anyway," she commented. "Not widely, but I plan on giving it to Daemon and Dimple and Thena. Maybe Laurant and the rest of that gang as well, we'll see."

I chewed my lip and restrained myself from rising to her teasing. Although, to be honest, if I was acting out of character, I would rather have someone point it out than keep silent. "I guess, just give it to whoever you think knows me well enough to spot anything odd."

A moment passed, and abruptly the door burst open, having been kicked by Malkios.

"Hah! Hasn't arrived yet my arse!" the former captain of the guard shouted. "You see, Gwen, I told you that he'd be punctual."

"I never doubted it," Lady Gwen said, stepping into the room after Malkios, with Lord Tom a pace behind. "I simply figured that I'd allow you to be the one who started breaking down doors to find him as our host struggled to keep us separate."

"I assure you milady, that was not our intent," the servant said, trailing behind the trio. "I was not informed of Earl Hail's arrival and—"

"You're dismissed. We no longer require or desire your presence," Lord Tom said. "If you remain, I shall poison you with something that will force you to spend the next four days sitting on the privy."

The servant, a young woman of approximately nineteen years, spent a brief moment considering whether she was more afraid of Tom or her master. When Tom took out a bottle from his pocket, however, she promptly vanished back the way they had come, hastily closing the doors behind her.

"It's good to see you three," I said.

"They insisted on dragging us into the back room as soon as we arrived; they refused to allow us to wait for you outside," Gwen said, huffing. "Tell me everything you said and did from the time you arrived."

"Well," I said. "I turned Filo into a toad because he called me a little goblin, and I corrected one of the valets when he called my uncle 'His Royal Majesty.' Other than that—"

Gwen, Tom, and even Malkios abruptly pinched the bridges of their noses and put on pained expressions at my words.

"I told you we should have insisted on waiting at the gate," Tom whispered to his companions.

"We didn't have a polite way of refusing the invitation inside," Gwen reminded him.

"So we should have been rude," Tom replied.

"Yes, well, the past is always clear as glass, while the future is hidden in mists," Gwen sighed.

"Also, I said that if I saw Filo again today, I would challenge him to a duel, and that I expected him to apologize for the insult at our next meeting," I supplied helpfully.

Malkios snorted. The two nobles exchanged a look of consternation, then sighed.

"Well, that at least I can agree with, given the provocation," Lord Tom said. "Had it been me, I would have shaved that toad's mustache off with a poisoned dagger while Malkios held him in a headlock for me."

"Filo was always too full of himself," Gwen agreed. "Had you failed to react to his provocation it would have been a sign of weakness. Which was likely calculated by your uncle; I'm quite certain he instructed Filo to insult you to see how you would react."

"Well, he's lucky that I cast [Polymorph] and not [Fireball]," I said.

"Yes, I'm quite certain he is," Tom agreed, "though it would have been amusing had you burned that ugly mustache off of his face."

"I suppose you have handled the situation adequately since you arrived," Gwen said after a few moments pause. "However, please allow us to take the lead once your uncle arrives, Lord Hail. I wish we had more time to coach you on how to navigate these waters, but try to avoid committing to anything, and remember that, as both your uncle and a duke, Storm outranks you. Do not let him goad you. If he insults you, allow Tom or I to deal with it; do not push back."

I sighed. "Yes, yes, I understand. I shall sit in the corner and allow the grownups to do the talking, just like I have since I was three years old. Also, Uncle Storm, I know you're listening. I'm quite skilled with magic, and I can tell when a listening device is turned on. Please stop wasting everyone's time and come join us."

Tom and Gwen exchanged panicked expressions and quickly began looking around the room for what they had missed. Two minutes later the door to the parlor opened again, and my Uncle Storm came inside, a curious expression on his face. He was the youngest of my uncles at twenty-seven, two years younger than my own mother, and had his dark hair braided over one shoulder. He was dressed in a fine blue doublet and hose. He went over to the coffee table before one of the lounges and examined the centerpiece, a filigreed duck statuette.

"I was assured that it was undetectable by even an archmage," he commented. "How did you know?"

"I was bluffing," I admitted. "I figured either there was a device and you would hear me, or there wasn't one and I'd watch Lady Gwen and Lord Tom panic for a few minutes. I didn't really see a downside."

"Ah. Clever," Storm said, straightening up. "And now I've gone and revealed one of my cards. In front of two of my late father's chief advisors no less, and no doubt all of their allies will be advised of its appearance and purpose before dawn tomorrow. I might as well throw this out in the trash—it's useless now. A nine-hundred-gold paperweight."

I shrugged. Personally, I could think of several uses for it even if its secret was widely known, but I kept my mouth closed. If Uncle Storm was lacking in imagination, then I wasn't going to supply him with mine.

"Well then, dear uncle—may I address you as uncle or would you prefer 'Your Grace'?" I asked.

"Since you've already refused to give me the title I'm due, I don't particularly care," Storm declared. "You have made your allegiance known. First, you sent a wanted fugitive to my home and caused me personal embarrassment by having them arrested in my staff quarters, and then you declare that I am not next in line for the throne! It is clear that Auroras has gotten to you before I could, although I do not know how he managed it."

"I haven't spoken with Great Uncle Auroras since I was dragged to his villa three years ago and forced to spend a week running and hiding from that awful grandson of his," I said.

"And yet you support him over me," Storm persisted.

"I shall swear my allegiance to whoever Thedum pronounces to be the next king," I declared.

"Then you are allying yourself with the church?" he inquired.

"The church crowns the king," I reminded him. "They have pronounced that the coronation will not proceed until the culprit of the recent assassinations of your brothers has been found. I don't see why my opinion as a lowly Earl matters one way or the other, and, quite honestly, I dislike being trapped in the spaces between rocks and hard things."

"I *did not* order the assassination of my brothers! How dare you accuse me of such a heinous crime!" Storm shouted.

"I didn't accuse you of anything," I said. "I reiterated the church's position on the matter. I would appreciate it if you do not put words in my mouth, Uncle Storm."

The man frowned at me for a moment, then cursed under his breath. "I think I preferred you when you were six years old and still terrified of Filo. Well then, my clever little statesman, what would you suggest I do to clear my name?"

I considered the question for a moment. "Go to church."

He frowned at me. "What?"

"Attend high mass. Request to speak. Testify before all the

assembled Natives that you never ordered the murder or assassination of any member of your family, and demand that Thedum strike you dead if you bear false witness. If you survive, then the church must crown you as the next in line for the throne, for surely Thedum would not allow such a brazen act to go unanswered unless it was genuine," I explained.

Uncle Storm opened his mouth, then closed it. He considered my suggestion for a moment as he bit his thumb, looking at the stupid filigreed duck. "Yes, yes that would work; the priests would have no choice, would they?"

"But, Uncle Storm, I should remind you. When Grandfather was murdered, Thedum created an avatar. He has clearly taken a vested interest in the governance of Yuikon," I pointed out. "If you are innocent, then obviously you have nothing to fear. Only the true mastermind behind the assassinations would be struck down by such flagrant heresy as swearing a false oath in Thedum's name in his temple, during a mass dedicated to him in front of thousands of his followers. If I were the culprit, then I certainly wouldn't want to do that, because if Thedum can spawn a Worldboss at will, then surely a bolt of lightning wouldn't be too difficult, would it?"

Uncle Storm's thoughtful expression turned to anger, and he turned his fury on me. He opened his mouth to shout, closed it, opened it again, closed it. After a moment he visibly took himself under control, and only when his outward expression was calm again did he speak. But still his words were seething.

"Get out of my house, Bastard," he said.

I bowed politely, the exact depth that was appropriate for an Earl to bow to a Duke. "Thank you for your invitation, Uncle. Perhaps I shall see you in church."

I was the first to the door, with my retinue following quickly. As we were walking through the corridor, Corinth whispered to Tarisha, "Not only are they *massive*, they are made of *steel!*"

8
LOST

"Hey, so is it cool if I, like, edit that encounter and post it on the forums?" Corinth asked just as we were returning to the foyer. "That whole thing was epic!"

I froze. "You were recording that?"

"Yeah! I mean, of course I was! That was like a super exclusive one-time event that might shape the future of the story, right? I—"

I abruptly punched Corinth in the mouth. It only did fifty Damage because I have no skills for unarmed fighting, but I was about to fix that as I grabbed for my [Gemos Long Sword] and prepared to imbue it with fire.

"Hail! Stop, please. I recorded the event as well," Tarisha said, grabbing my wrist before my blade cleared its scabbard.

I turned to her, hurt more than I could say. "You too, Tarisha?"

"It is history, Lord Hail. I assure you that I was not going to publish it anywhere without your express permission, but I would be remiss if I did not record such major events for posterity," she explained. "I have not shared them with anybody, nor will I until you permit me to. However, one day I believe that people will greatly value the history that you have been creating these last few weeks."

My grip tightened on my sword. "Do you record everything I say?"

"No! Only major interactions and battles with other Natives. I do not record your private moments with Travelers or—"

"You should have told me sooner," I said angrily. "You're as bad as Mark! How could you do that to me without saying anything?"

"I'm sorry. We have been looking for a way to broach the subject for weeks now, before Corinth here blundered into it," Tarisha said, sighing sadly. "I swear to you on my honor that I would not post anything without discussing it with you and obtaining your permission. Nor would I allow anyone else in <Peasant's Revenge> to post any of the recordings they have been gathering. We were planning on waiting a year or more of real time before discussing with you the release of an anthology of your early days. Until the information in the videos is no longer dangerous to you. And even then, we were going to make certain you approved of everything that we released."

Anger boiled in my veins. "You should have told me."

"Yes. I'm sorry," she said.

"What the hell, man?" Corinth said, standing up. "I mean, yeah, okay, it's a video game, but still, sucker punching a guy out of nowhere is a dick move."

"You would understand if you had known Hail for longer," Tarisha said sadly. "But perhaps it's for the best. The truth is that Hail deserves to know when his actions are being recorded, even though he always carries himself with the utmost dignity. Many of those in both <Peasant's Revenge> and <Nethersong Mavericks> have been betraying his trust in us whenever we feel that he is about to do something momentous. It is better to get it out into the sunlight than allow it to fester in the darkness. Hail, if you ask me to, I will delete everything I have recorded, and I shall demand that every member of <Peasant's Revenge> do the same or face expulsion from the guild. The Mavericks have pledged a similar course of action for once we broached this subject with you."

I punched the wall in anger, leaving a hole in it and earning myself a [Sprained Wrist]. Oh well, the hole is Uncle Storm's problem, not mine. But then I exhaled. "I need to think about this. I want to know who has been recording me, and I want to know when. And from now on, someone had *damn well better tell me* when they start recording or *I will not forgive them.*"

"I will consult with the leaders of my guild and yours and we will draft some rules for the recording of your actions. Gaining your permission to record or retain a recording will be very high on the list of our priorities, My Lord," she said.

"Lord Hail, I'm sorry, I do not understand the problem," Lord Tom said from behind us. "What have these Travelers done to upset you?"

"Never mind, Tom," I said. "It's Traveler business. I'll deal with it."

Hender appeared just in time to get the door for us. However, we could not proceed to leave because the way was blocked by a figure. A Traveler, dressed in very high-end light armor, was waiting just outside. She glowed neither blue nor red in the dim light of the evening, nor did she bear the [Mark of Sin]. Instead, she had an aura of a color I had not known possible, but instinctively knew what it meant. Black.

"Tarisha, kill this woman. She is an assassin. I believe that she murdered one of my uncles," I said, my anger at my invaded privacy falling to the side in the face of this threat.

"Quest accepted," Tarisha said, drawing her blade and dashing forward at the same time that the woman drew a pair of kunai from folds in her armor—one in each hand—both of which she threw at me, one after the other. I [Dodged] the first, but the delay in her throw allowed her to predict my movement, and there was no way that I could have dodged the second knife. I knew, just from a glance, that this was an endgame Traveler. Like Tarisha, my father, and Nial Kingslayer. Time seemed to slow for an instant as I understood that I was about to die again, as even a glancing blow of that kunai would do more than my maximum Health in Damage.

Corinth [Dashed] in front of me, taking the dagger in the chest and exploding into motes of blue light. Malkios's strong arms enveloped me, and then his body was between me and the clash of violence between the endgamers. Of high-level Pee Vee Pee. The sort that I wasn't prepared to engage in myself. Not for a long time.

Lord Tom and Lady Gwen appeared. Tom had a pair of daggers in his hand, and Gwen's fingers crackled with electricity, but the fight had moved outdoors.

"Back! This is a challenge quest, one versus one!" Tarisha shouted. "Do not interfere even should I die! Protect Lord Hail, and get him to safety."

Uncle Storm heard the commotion and came raging out of the

parlor, his face a countenance of fury. *"How dare you bring violence upon my house, Bastard!"*

Lord Tom bent to pick up the dagger that had killed Corinth. He sniffed the blade. "Poison. This would kill anyone below level eighty with a scratch," he pronounced. "An assassin knocked on your door tonight, Your Grace. Tell me, was she here to kill you, to kill the boy, or perhaps to discuss remuneration?"

Storm went still, the red from his face turning pale white as he lost his thunder. "Guards! Guards, assassin!" he shouted. He grabbed his bracelet and was enveloped in a magical green glow, then abruptly the space around him twisted, and he was somewhere else. Before he vanished, a crystal on his bracelet shattered, its shards falling to the ground as the spent Mana gem was expended.

"Lord Hail, we must get you to safety as well," Gwen declared. She cast a spell, and another twist in space appeared. A portal. "Step through, Lord Hail, and I shall take you to safety."

The last time I stepped through an unknown portal, it almost led to my death by barbecue at the hands of a squad of goblins, but I had no time to question the events that were quickly spiraling away from me. Nor did I really have a choice in the matter, as Malkios scooped me up as though I were still a child of four and tossed me into the portal before I could object.

I felt a *twisting*, and then I was elsewhere. I looked behind me to see Malkios leaping to follow me through, but before he reached it, the portal twisted shut. I was cut off, and I had no idea where I had been sent. Worse, when I pulled up my Fast Travel menu, I received a notification I had never seen before.

<table>
<tr><td colspan="2">Fast Travel is unavailable in your present location. You must discover a Nexus Point within twenty miles in order to access the Fast Travel Network.</td></tr>
<tr><td>Guild Message of the Day</td><td>To everyone who has any recordings of Little Brother taken without his knowledge or permission, please report them immediately to an officer. Failure to comply will result in expulsion from the guild. New guidelines for documenting the journey of Little Brother will be drafted soon. Compliance is not optional.</td></tr>
</table>

Hollysheeat	So, I'm outside the Stormlord's gates, and there's an epic battle going down between Tarisha and some random other chick. Weird thing is I think Tarisha is losing.
Malick	No effing way.
Corinth (lobby)	Yeah, that ninja chick one-shot me, but it was totally worth it. I think I saved Hail's life! That's gotta be some Karma, right?
Hail	I can see guildchat, Corinth.
Corinth	Oh fuck. I mean, sorry, Hail. But seriously, I did save your life, didn't I?
Hail	Yeah, I guess you did. Um, look. Show the recording or whatever to Daemon and Dimple. If they think it's a good idea, then you can post it on the forums. I'm still not happy that you recorded me without asking, but I guess you're right. Maybe people should see that conversation so that they know what a slimeball Uncle Storm is.
Corinth	And what a badass you are, man. Seriously, everyone, I don't know how Hail can walk around without waddling because he has *giant fucking balls of steel*.
Hail	Please stop talking about my testicles, Corinth.
Consoul	Wait, Hail, do you even have testicles? I mean . . .
Hail	I'm a boy—of course I have testicles, you pervert!
Consoul	Um, sorry. I guess I didn't know Natives were anatomically correct. I just assumed that everyone was like a Ken/Barbie doll down there.
Moderator	Consoul has been muted for ten minutes.
Weaselfire	Thank you, whoever did that.
Dimple	Hail, are you safe? What's going on.
Daemon	It was me who muted him. But yes. Hail, how long do you have on Fast Travel? Where can we meet you to escort you home?

Hail	Um, well, that's the thing. When the assassin showed up, Tarisha was forced to fight, and Corinth died protecting me, but that left me with Malkios, Tom, and Gwen. Gwen opened a portal, and Malkios threw me through, but it closed right afterward. I have no idea where I am, and there's no Nexus Point within twenty miles of me, so I can't Fast Travel.
Zebras	Fuck. Fuck fuck fuck fuck.
Moderator	Zebras has been muted for ten minutes.
Dimple	That was me. Language.
Daemon	Hail, I'm sorry, but without knowing where you are, I'm afraid I don't know how to help you. If Lady Gwen opened a portal, then hopefully it is to someplace safe for you to explore. I suggest that you do so.
Hail	Right, that's what I thought too. I was about to start exploring. I just wanted to check in to let everyone know that I was alive.
Peafowlet	Thank you so much, Hail. We would have been very worried if you hadn't checked in. Please let us know the second you figure out where you are and if there's anything we can do to help.
Hail	If it helps, I think I'm still in Yuikon. I'm in a meadow surrounded by Totika trees, so I think I'm somewhere south of Zhesa. But that only narrows it down to like a thousand square miles, right?
Stormy	Heading to Pleetgrove. Got some Rep there, going to see if I can convince the locals to start searching the area looking for him.
Gummytiger	Great idea, Stormy. I'll head to Renton vineyard and do the same.
Hail	Right, okay. Thanks, guys. I'm going to stop paying attention to guildchat now. I'll let you know if I figure out where I am, so you can stop searching.

9

MOTIVATION

I had come full circle. My adventures had begun with going through a strange portal and ending up in an area where I didn't know where I was or how to get home, and here I was again. Except, of course, I had grown since then, and it was not my gullibility that I had fallen victim to. I was also significantly more confident in my abilities to defend myself. I was no longer a level one [Child], but a level twenty-eight [Spellblade]. And a very skilled one! Even if I was somewhat clumsy due to my recent growth spurt.

I grew nervous again when I surprised a level thirty-nine spotted deer. Because if the deer were level thirty-nine, then the wolves must be level forty or higher. As a level ten [Child] I had defeated a level nineteen boar, an enemy that had been almost double my level at the time, which had seemed like an insurmountable difference. However, for that encounter, I had been prepared. I had had the initiative. And I had Travelers who could step in and save me if things had gone wrong. If I was ambushed by a wolf or other predator now, I would have none of those things.

The difference between a level twenty-eight [Spellblade] and a level forty predator was not nearly as insurmountable as the difference between a level one [Child] and a level fifteen goblin, but it was a pretty large difference, and it was enough to put me on edge. I wished that I still had [Stealth], but of course I had lost that and all my [Urchin] skills when I had selected my class. Of course, unless I had become an [Urchin] or other [Rogue] class, then it wouldn't have made a difference in my current situation, as a level forty predator would have no trouble seeing through a level ten [Child]'s stealth. No, [Spellblade] didn't give me the option to hide, but it did give me the potential to defend myself, even if the odds were against me. I would not regret my decision.

So I drew my [Gemos Long Sword] and stalked through the forest as silently as I could without [Stealth], keeping an eye out for wolf spoor. Not that I had any clue what wolf spoor looked like. I was born a prince and raised in a castle after all. All I knew about tracking and outdoorsmanship was what I had read in books, which is how I knew the word "spoor," even if I didn't know what it looked like. But then perhaps I would know it if I saw it—

Was that a wolf track?

> You have gained General Skill [Tracking] level 1.

Yeah, that's a wolf track. Or a large hound. I'd rather it was a hound because that would mean that I'm near a settlement, which would hopefully have a Nexus Point and reopen my Fast Travel menu. And also because a hound was less likely to try to rip my throat out. Unless they were Ramsay hounds, in which case I'd rather that it was a wolf.

Of course my [Tracking] skill was only level one now, and I couldn't figure out how old the track was just by looking at it, so I wasn't sure if the beast that made it was nearby or—

The growling sound that came from behind me made me squeak in a much higher pitch than I believed my vocal cords were capable of at age fifteen. Or age five. I jumped, and midway in my jump I managed to turn it into a spin, which is totally what I had intended it to be from the beginning.

The good news is that it wasn't a wolf. It was a hound.

The bad news is that it was a Ramsay hound. And it was level forty-nine. I [Swiftcast] [Polymorph] and sprinted the other direction. I did not get very far when another Ramsay hound appeared out of the brush, growling at me and ready to leap. Again I [Polymorphed] it and changed direction, running blindly into the moonlit night.

Soon after, I heard the sounds of pursuit, and when I turned there were three hounds on my trail, braying and slobbering with the glee of the hunt. I cursed, as this meant there were likely at least five in the pack. The [Polymorph] on the other two should not have faded yet, although with the level discrepancy there was a chance it had failed early. I did not have time to stop and [Polymorph] these as well, and so I kept running.

Sprinting, actually. Unfortunately, my [Endurance] was my second lowest stat at thirty-eight, with only my strength being lower. So although I could run quite fast with the help of my high [Dexterity], I knew it would not be long before my strength began to falter.

Not that it truly mattered, of course. These were Ramsay hounds, able to chase down a galloping horse. The only reason that they had not already caught me was that they loved the thrill of the chase, and so they let me run to prolong their fun. They would let me run for a while, but in the end I would only die tired. Mauling did not seem like a very enjoyable way to meet my second death, and I cannot say that I was looking forward to it.

The two hounds which I had [Polymorphed] returned to the hunt right around the time when I gained the [Exhaustion] debuff. I knew it would not be much longer as my speed began to falter. One of the hounds abruptly caught up to me, and I knew that this was the end. However, rather than pouncing on me and pinning me to the ground, the hound bit me on the posterior. My status flashed in the corner of my vision as it changed.

Motivation gained, run speed increased 20% (30 seconds)
Exhaustion (1) suppressed
Condition: Bleeding. –20 Health per 3 seconds
Health: 11785/12600

It seemed that the hounds were enjoying the chase too much for them to end it quite yet, as I resumed sprinting even faster than before thanks to [Motivation]. My pants became slick and sticky as I bled from the bite, and I wondered how long this would go on for.

I became aware, eventually, that the hounds were herding me, steering me in a particular direction, and I was helpless to avoid going where they directed. If I veered off the course they had decided for me, one of them would circle around and correct my heading. If their simple presence was not enough to do so, then they would refresh the duration of [Motivation] along with correcting my direction.

I gained three more stacks of [Exhaustion], but [Motivation] kept them suppressed. My Health continued to drop. I lost a few hundred every time the hounds applied [Motivation], and I continued to bleed. I dropped below ten thousand. Below nine thousand. I wondered again if this was how I would die. Perhaps I would bleed to death while running from a pack of Ramsay hounds. It had happened before to others, so it wouldn't be too strange. Exsanguination would probably be better than being mauled by the pack. However, I still had a chance to prevent my death penalty by finding someplace safe to hide from the beasts, so I kept running.

I stumbled onto the road just as I gained my fifth stack of [Exhaustion]. I flagged again, and again one of the hounds came forward and bit me in the ass to [Motivate] me. I turned onto the road, the evenly packed dirt beneath my feet allowing me to increase my speed even further. The hounds did not correct my course. I was still going exactly where they directed me.

My Health continued to drop, and I continued to gain stacks of [Exhaustion]. I bled, and when I hit ten stacks of [Exhaustion] I began to lose ten Health every second from that as well, increasing the rate at which I was dying. [Motivation] kept me moving at one hundred twenty percent of my normal speed, however.

Suddenly I saw a clearing ahead, and a building. It was a temple! [Motivation] refreshed itself without the intervention of the hounds as I ran towards it with all of my dwindling might. The door was standing open, and I had just enough of a lead on the hounds to slam it shut behind me when I reached it. The hounds began scratching at it from outside, but I managed to bar it shut before the duration of [Motivation] faded and [Exhaustion (10)] caused me to collapse onto the floor, hyperventilating as my vision faded in and out. I was down to 5487/12600 Health. The hounds literally ran me half to death.

The hounds brayed and whimpered outside, but although they continued to scratch at the door periodically, the door held. I slowly began losing my stacks of [Exhaustion], and now that I was no longer sprinting, I stopped losing Health from it. [Bleeding], however, seemed to have an infinite duration, and I knew that I had to find some way of removing the debuff, or I would still die eventually. At minus twenty Health every three seconds, I had a bit longer than ten minutes before I would bleed to death from the bite marks on my butt, which meant that I did not have time to wait for [Exhaustion] to fade completely.

Forcing myself to my feet once I had dropped to six stacks of [Exhaustion], I made my way further into the Temple. I put my sword into my inventory during the mad chase, and I considered reequipping it in its belt, but decided that would be an inappropriate action in a place of sanctuary. Hopefully, I would find the priest, who could easily heal my debuff and hopefully bring me back up to one hundred percent Health as well. Except, as I began to examine my surroundings, I came to fear that the temple was long abandoned. Cobwebs were everywhere. The statues were covered in dust. The candelabras were empty and tarnished, not appearing to have been polished for decades. And the symbol of Thedum had fallen from its place above the altar, the crystal circle shattering into pieces when it had landed on the stone.

Perhaps [Bleeding] would fade on its own, but I couldn't take the chance that it would not. It had been inflicted by creatures twenty levels higher than me, and it was entirely possible that my Endurance and Vitality were too low to overcome the affliction without healing.

I cast [Spark] a few times, sending the small but bright candle flames throughout the temple to get a better look around, but I didn't see anything that would help me. I remembered then that I had a few health potions in my inventory, and I quickly pulled one out and drank it, the bitter flavor not improved at all by the berry juice that the alchemist had mixed it with to make it more palatable. I regained twelve hundred Health in an instant, but [Bleeding] did not fade away. Still, the potion would help me stave off death for three minutes longer. I continued my search, moving farther into the temple.

As I moved into the cloisters behind the altar, I heard the familiar sound of a quill scratching on parchment. It was faint, but a clear sign that I was not alone after all. If this temple did have a priest, then I was saved! I moved as rapidly towards the sound as my [Exhaustion] allowed me to move.

The door to the cell was open. It was a simple room, with a cot and a desk and a few hooks from which the monk's spare robes were hanging. The hooded figure of the monk himself was sitting at the desk, back turned to me as he continued to write.

"Um, excuse me. My name is Hail Jeoran. I've come to claim sanctuary, and I request healing. I'm bleeding, and it won't stop on its own. I'm down to half my Health," I said.

"Not a priest," the monk grumbled without turning around. "I don't have any healing magic."

"Is there anyone else here who can help me?" I asked desperately.

"No," the monk said.

"Please, isn't there anything you can do to help? I'll gladly make a donation to your temple. I am an Earl, and I could send you the resources to see this holy place restored. But I won't be able to do that if I die here," I said.

"You noble brats," the monk grumbled. "Gold doesn't solve everything. This temple is abandoned for a reason, and money won't fix that. Thedum's gaze no longer lingers here."

"I—I see," I said. "Please, I—"

Without turning, the monk pulled something from his robes and tossed it over his shoulder to me. I caught it; it was a small jar of ointment.

"That will stop the bleeding and the pain," the monk said. "Put it on the wound."

"Thank you!" I exclaimed. "I shall be right back."

I stepped out of the monk's cell and into one of the empty rooms in the cloister before pulling my pants down to apply the ointment.

Bleeding has stopped.
Healing Balm applied. +10 Health per second (5 minutes)

Sighing in relief, I quickly pulled a new pair of pants out of my inventory and changed into them. The ones I had been wearing were completely ruined. Even if I could get the bloodstains out, there were too many holes to consider patching. [Analyzing] them, I saw that even the name had changed from [High Quality Pants] to [Bloody and Torn Pants]. I sighed.

The healing effect of the medicine would help me regain three thousand Health, but I would have to rely on my natural regeneration to regain the remainder. Unless I were to drink another healing potion, but I judged that it wasn't worth it. Not as long as I was safe from the hounds.

I returned to the monk's cell to thank him and warn him not to go outside until the pack of beasts had dispersed.

"Thank you, Brother, for the medicine," I said. "You may very well have saved my life. I must warn you that there is a pack of Ramsay hounds outside the temple; it was them that wounded me. I would not—"

"Yes, yes, I know about the hounds," the monk said, still scribing his document. "Delightful little pups they are."

"Delightful?" I asked, confused. "They're vicious beasts! They chased me for miles and—"

"Of course they chased you. You ran from them. Everyone knows that Ramsay hounds will chase you if you're foolish enough to run from them," the monk said. "That's like saying that a cat will play with the mouse it cornered before eating it."

"I—" I did not know what to say. "May I ask where we are? I was sent through a portal and I'm quite lost."

"You're somewhere where you won't cause any more havoc for the time being, Earl Jeoran," the monk answered. He finished writing and began to sprinkle sand on the parchment to dry the ink. "For now, that is all you need to know."

He stood, and I realized that he was half a head taller than most men. When he turned to me, I almost recoiled at the sickly gray pallor of his skin.

"Come with me, child. I have a task for you."

10
SHOVEL

"Wait, the hounds are still out there!" I protested as the monk began unbarring the door.

"I am aware," he said patiently, and he continued his course of action. I analyzed him, and I saw that he was level fifty. Since he was not a healer, perhaps he had a combat class that would be able to drive them off.

Immediately when the door was opened, one of the hounds leapt at him, its massive paws planting on his shoulders. However, instead of attempting to rip his throat out, the dog gave him a slobbery kiss.

"Down!" he scolded, and the dog whined as it circled back to join the rest of the pack outside.

"Sit!" he commanded, and the pack sat on their haunches.

"Lay," he commanded, and they abruptly lay on their bellies, resting their muzzles on their forelegs and looking up at him with adoration in their eyes.

"You see? There's really nothing to fear from them; you simply have to let them know who is in charge," the monk said, casually exiting the temple and walking past the ferocious murder-beasts. He absently bent down and scratched the lead hound behind its ears. "Come with me, Earl Jeoran. The hounds will not hurt you unless you run from them again."

With wide eyes, I nervously followed the monk outside. The pack growled at me the moment I stepped out of the temple, but they remained, obediently laying on the grass. I quickly hopped to follow the monk as he walked around to the back of the temple.

"Is your class some sort of [Beastmaster]?" I asked him.

"Nothing of the sort," he said. "Stop asking foolish questions, Hail. Come quickly, there is a task that must be accomplished before morning."

The hounds followed us as we made our way to the back of the temple, but they hung back obediently. Behind the temple was a small stable and a shed. Leaning next to the shed was a shovel, which the monk took and tossed at me.

"I need you to dig me a hole," he explained.

"A hole?" I asked.

"Yes. Preferably six feet deep and large enough to lay down in, although it doesn't have to be perfect," he said. "Just deep enough that the animals won't dig up what we bury in it."

"What do you need a hole for?" I asked. "And why must I dig it in the middle of the night? Can it not wait until morning when the sun is out?"

"Are you too good for manual labor, child?" the monk asked. "You must dig it tonight because this task has already been delayed too long and it will grow more unpleasant the longer it is delayed. You have claimed sanctuary, and this is a task that the head of the temple has assigned you in exchange for protection."

The hounds began growling again, and I swallowed nervously. "I—fine. Just keep the hounds from tearing out my throat, and I'll do whatever you want."

So I began to dig. My [Exhaustion] had not faded completely, and the activity of digging kept my stacks at three, which was low enough to work with, but the process was slow and unpleasant. The monk walked away at some point, leaving me alone with the hounds, who encircled the hole and watched me work, occasionally growling at me when I slowed down. Whatever the monk said about being a [Beastmaster], he clearly had some sort of magical control over the pack of Ramsay hounds. I wondered if he had sent them after me in the first place, for some reason. Or perhaps it had not been me in particular, but anyone, simply because he needed a hole dug.

It was not pleasant work. I developed [Blisters] on my hands, which I healed with the [Healing Balm] before they impacted my work too greatly. I wondered the entire time at the monk's purpose, as I could think of nothing worth burying in a hole this size and no building that would require such a small foundation.

It was a lousy hole, oblong and misshapen, but I persevered for fear of bringing the wrath of the hounds down on me should I falter again. However, when I had gotten the deepest point to about four feet deep, my status began flickering again.

Condition: Wireiana Poisoning –200 Health per 5 seconds
Condition: Paralysis
Condition: Fever
Condition: Chills
Condition: Hallucinations
Health: 10451/12600

I had been poisoned! But how? When?

I collapsed into the hole as the [Paralysis] took effect, lying face down in the dirt and unable to shift out of the uncomfortable position. The shovel had landed right under me and was poking into my stomach.

I was no expert in poisons, so the name of the affliction gave me no help in figuring out how it had been applied. It was obviously a slow-acting poison. I tried to remember everything I had eaten or drunk since I had returned to the world of the living, and whether or not I had remembered to cast [Detect Poison] before doing so. There hadn't been very much; it had mostly been a day of action. I had not taken any repast at my uncle's house—I was certain of that—although, to my suspicious mind, he remained the most likely suspect. Him, or the strange assassin who had appeared, but the kunai she had thrown at me had missed.

I began to see shapes and colors. I heard voices, although they were all strange and shouted nonsense. I sweated and shook from the cold. And my Health slowly drifted downward. I had less than five minutes to receive an antidote, or I would die. Again.

"What are you doing? Quit lying down there; that isn't *your* grave," the monk said impatiently when he returned. I was down to 4851/12600 Health, and my condition was deteriorating fast.

"P—poison," I managed to whisper.

"Oh? You must have used more of the ointment than I'd intended," the monk murmured, and the missing piece clicked into place.

"You!" I exclaimed. Or I'd intended to exclaim, at least, but at present I wasn't up to making dramatic noises. "Why?"

"Oh relax, the poison is only deadly to those below level thirty," the monk said waving my concerns away.

"I'm level twenty-eight."

"Oh? What are your Vitality and Endurance?"

I tried to remember but could not. When I pulled up my status screen, the numbers blurred and shifted, and it took me a minute to find them. "Forty-five and thirty-eight."

"You'll be fine. Probably. Keep digging when you recover—that hole isn't deep enough yet."

The monk walked off, leaving me lying like that, helpless and dying. However, a moment after he was gone, my vision flashed again with alerts.

You have gained general skill: Poison Resistance (1)
Condition: Wireiana Poisoning (partially resisted) -100 Health per 5 seconds
Condition: Weakness
Condition: Fever
Condition: Chills
Health: 4551/12600

I could move again! And my remaining lifespan had just doubled thanks to [Poison Resistance]! I rolled off of the shovel and looked up at the stars. At my current rate of decline, I had just under four minutes before my Health hit zero. Fortunately, I still had health potions in my inventory, and I pulled out the strongest one I had. With shaking hands, I swallowed the bitter berry-flavored concoction and sighed in relief as I regained three thousand Health.

That meant that I had gained about an extra two and a half minutes of life.

I pulled out another healing potion and waited for my [Potion Resistance] to fade away so that I could drink it and get its full effects. It would take four minutes for that to happen, which meant that I was dying faster than the potions were healing me, but each one would give me longer to live and hopefully give me a chance to get another rank of [Poison Resistance].

I drank the second potion the moment I was able to. I gained twenty-eight hundred Health from that one. Less than at first, but still more than two minutes of life. I watched nervously as my Health began ticking slowly downward once again.

Just before I could drink another potion, I abruptly gained another level of [Poison Resistance], and my life span doubled again as the poison fell to negative fifty Health per five seconds. That also meant that the amount of time I gained from drinking the potion doubled from about two and a half minutes of life to almost five. It was working. I could survive this poison; I just needed to stay alive long enough for my [Poison Resistance] to level up a few more times and overcome it. Fortunately, I had plenty of healing potions. Even if I was gaining diminishing returns from the potions, I was healing faster than I was losing Health to the poison.

Unfortunately, [Poison Resistance] did not seem to want to reach level three. I drank two more potions to keep myself alive, and then I ran into another problem as I gained [Potion Toxicity]. I cursed, knowing that if I drank more until that debuff had faded then the potions would not only be only ten percent effective, but I would likely gain another Damage-over-time effect because of it. And, unfortunately, the debuff had an hour duration, meaning that my solution for surviving this poison had just run into a wall. My only hope was that my resistance would level again before I ran out of Health.

I was down to ten percent Health when it happened. [Poison Resistance] reached level three, and the Damage-over-time effect faded. The [Weakness], [Fever], and [Chills] effects of the poison remained, but I was no longer dying. I sighed in relief in the bottom of the shallow hole I had dug, and I gathered my strength and my courage to climb out of it. I intended to find the monk and give him a piece of my mind. Shaking from my status effects, I stood and tried to climb out.

My resolve faltered when the growling began. The pack of Ramsay hounds encircled me, and it was clear that they did not like the idea of me leaving my task unfinished.

"Sit!" I commanded, trying to sound unafraid, but the hounds ignored me and continued baring their teeth at me. It was only when I picked up the shovel and once again began digging that they stopped and settled down once more.

What in the seven hells did the monk need a hole for anyway?

With my [Weakness], it took the rest of the night for me to complete my task. The sky was gray with predawn light. The monk seemed to know exactly how long it would take me, as he appeared just as I had deemed the hole dug.

"You said that medicine would heal me, not that it was poisoned!" I shouted at him as soon as he appeared.

"I said that it would stop the pain and the bleeding," the monk said. "Pain stops when you're dead. Bleeding stops when you're dead. I've told you no lies."

"You! What sort of monk are you?" I demanded.

"Who said I was a monk?" the monk said. "Come with me. I need your help carrying something."

"I'll do nothing of the sort! I will—"

The hounds began growling again, and I nervously took a step back, bumping into the uneven wall of the hole I had dug.

"If you wish to renounce your claim of sanctuary, you may do so at any time," the monk said, amusement in his voice. "Of course, if you renounce your claim, then I am no longer responsible for your safety. And the hounds do love a good hunt."

I swallowed, looking at the encircling beasts with trepidation. I was trapped, and I knew it. Capitulation was my only option.

"Fine," I said. I crawled out of the hole I had dug, the hounds eyeing me for any signs that I would flee, and I followed the monk into the shed behind the temple. Once inside, I was immediately struck by the unpleasant smell of rotting meat.

"Oh, Thedum, what is that?" I asked.

"That is the thing that we need to bury," the monk answered. "There are four more beside it, but this is the oldest and therefore the one that must go in the ground most urgently. You may begin digging those holes tomorrow. Unless you revoke your claim of sanctuary, of course, in which case you are free to do whatever you please."

The hounds immediately showed their enthusiasm for that idea, snarling with excitement as they circled the shack. I shook my head. Unfortunately, I believed that I was trapped at this forsaken temple in the hands of this insane monk until my friends came to rescue me.

The rotten meat was inside of a large sack. I grabbed one end of the sack, and the monk the other, and we carried it outside and tossed it unceremoniously into the hole. The monk handed me my shovel.

"Once you fill in the hole, you may rest," he told me. "I shall return and show you to a cell. I strongly suggest that you do not try to flee, lest you cause the hounds to become excited again."

Grumbling to myself, I took the shovel and began my task.

11

ADVERSARY

I propped the small mirror from my inventory on the desk as I tried to get the last of the mud off my face. I had changed out of my dirty clothes and now stood in the cell the monk had assigned to me, wearing only my smallclothes as I washed the filth from the night's activities from my body with the help of a basin of water, a rag, and a bar of soap.

I still had one stack of [Exhaustion] and [Weakness] from the poison, but my Health had regenerated back to almost half of its maximum. Unfortunately, I had gained [Hunger], and there was no way I was about to ask the monk who had already poisoned me once for something to eat. I had another day or two before [Hunger] became dangerous, and hopefully I would be rescued by then.

Once I had gotten most of the dirt and blood from my body, I sighed and pulled a nightshirt from my inventory. I left my ruined clothes in a pile on the ground. Collapsing into the small, dusty bed, I almost let sleep overtake me, but I realized I should check in with my guild and give them an update.

| Hail | Hey, everyone. So, I'm still alive. Barely. I almost died a couple of times last night. I really think I need you guys to find me and rescue me soon, or else I'm probably going to die again. |

Dimple	We're searching for you as fast as we can, Hail. We've tried asking Lady Gwen, but she claims that the portal had some sort of magical interference, which changed its destination from where you were supposed to go, and she doesn't know where you are either. We have a few allied guilds helping us look, including <Peasant's Revenge> and <Ragtag Muffin>. Do you have any more details that would help us find you?
Hail	Yeah. Um, the wildlife seems to be around level forty, but the Native who is sort of keeping me hostage is level fifty, and he has a pack of Ramsay hounds that obey him. I'm trapped in an abandoned Temple of Thedum, but it's really old and rundown, so I'm not sure if it appears on any maps or if it's ever been discovered by Travelers before. It doesn't . . . feel holy to me.
Sellamander	Hostage? Hail, have you been kidnapped?
Hail	Sort of? I don't know. I'm pretty sure that if I try to escape, the hounds will rip me apart, but the monk who controls them hasn't exactly threatened that. He's just poisoned me and made me dig a hole and fill it in.
Peotre	A hole?
Hail	Yeah, I know, it's weird. Please, guys, I really want to get out of here, so I hope you find me soon. But I'm exhausted. I need to go to sleep now. I'll check in again if I figure something else out that might help you find me.
Peafowlet	He says he's been poisoned, and you focus on the other part? What's wrong with you, Peotre? Hail, are you okay?
Hail	I'm fine now. I mean, I almost died from the poison, but then I developed [Poison Resistance], and it's level three now, so I was able to fight it off. If the monk wanted me dead, I'd be dead now. I think he just wants free labor, because he says I have more holes to dig when I've rested. I'm going to sleep now. I'll check in again when I wake up, okay?
Dimple	Get some rest, Hail. Don't worry, we'll find you soon.

Closing the chat window, I pulled the threadbare sheets over me. I fell asleep in moments. I dreamed of running through a forest, something fast and evil in pursuit.

I refreshed [Arcane Weapon] on my shovel, and it sank into the dirt like it was passing through warm butter. It was a little trick I had learned when I was digging the second hole to make things a bit easier. I needed every advantage I could get, as my [Lingering Weakness] and [Hunger (2)] debuffs were limiting my Strength and Endurance by thirty percent. Unfortunately, my magic did nothing to reduce the weight of the dirt as I threw it out of the hole.

It was late evening; the sun would set soon. I had barely eaten since I'd revived, and I knew that once my [Hunger] debuff reached five stacks, my Vitality would begin to decrease. Once it reached ten stacks, I would gain a Damage-over-time effect that would slowly kill me. The monk had given me porridge when I'd awoken, but my [Detect Poison] spell had lit up like crazy when I'd cast it. So I'd put the bowl in my inventory without saying anything instead, and when he noticed that the bowl was gone, he dragged me back out to the back of the temple to dig the rest of the holes while the pack of Ramsay hounds kept me from running away.

The guild still had no idea where I was, but they assured me that hundreds of Travelers and Natives were searching for me now. I indulged myself in fantasies of my rescue and the vengeance I would visit upon the monk as I worked on digging the third hole. I glanced at the leader of the Ramsay hounds and imagined Tarisha turning it into a puff of black mist. The hound looked back at me as though it were daring me to use my own blade to try to make my fantasy a reality, but I knew that I would die in the attempt. So I continued digging.

Shortly before dusk, the monk returned to check on my progress. He nodded and escorted me into the shed, which smelled just as foul as before and had twice as many flies buzzing around, and together we threw another sack filled with rotting meat into the ground. I began to fill the second hole as he disappeared back into the temple. Filling the hole was easier than digging it, but before I got too far, my curiosity got the better of me. I jumped down into the hole and tore open the sack to examine the contents.

The rotting face of a dead man is what I found. I cried out in surprise and fell atop the rotting body, then scrambled my way out of the grave. I had thought that I had been burying spoiled food, not a person! After all, why would you bury a body when you could just have a priest perform the funerary rights, and they would vanish into mist?

The hounds began to growl at me again, apparently angry that I had discovered their master's secrets. They appeared ready to pounce, and in a panic, I sought the nearest shelter I could. I [Dashed] to the shed and slammed the door shut behind me. The shed, where three more bodies lay in burlap sacks. I covered my mouth with my shirt to try to block out the smell.

I could hear the hounds circling the shed and growling. Occasionally one would scratch against the door, but it held against them. I was trapped, but for the moment I was safe.

I went to the three remaining bodies and tore open the sacks to reveal the faces within. Two men and a woman. Ordinary looking, completely unknown to me, I looked for clues to how they had died, but I was no physician. I found no obvious wounds, but that only meant that the final blow had not been critical. They must have been weeks old to have begun to smell so rotten!

There was, I realized, something that I could do about the scent. The bodies were already in close to the funerary position, and so I simply held the rite to send them off to their next lives. They turned into motes of white light and began to rise into the air.

Abruptly the ceremony went very wrong, with the motes turning to darkness as they were seemingly *yanked* from Thedum's embrace. They circled around me for a moment, and I got a sense of malevolence from them. And I once more felt the presence of a god, but it was not the pleasant benevolence of Thedum. For the first time in my life, I had drawn the personal attention of the adversary.

"Hello there, little avatar," a smooth female voice said, everywhere and nowhere at once. "I'm sorry, dear, but you can't have these souls. They belong to me. Thank you for finding them for me, however; I was wondering where they had vanished to."

"You cannot harm me," I told the manifestation. "I walk in the light of Thedum. You—"

"Oh, I wouldn't dream of spoiling the game that way, little rook," the voice said, sounding coy. "And as I said, I am truly grateful for your assistance. No, I think that I shall reward you instead. Perhaps you would like to know—"

"Get back!" the monk said, kicking open the door. "Hail, take shelter! This is not a battle that you can win."

"You! Of course it was you!" the goddess of darkness shouted. "I should have known. Has your god broken his stance of neutrality?"

"This is personal," the monk growled. "These souls are *mine*, and you may not have them back!"

The monk waved his hand, and the swirling motes of light coalesced, reforming the rotting bodies into what they had been before my interference. The adversary screamed in frustration, and I sensed something *pulling* at the bodies, only to hit a barrier that it could not pierce.

The adversary laughed. "Oh, very well. They were minor pawns in the first place. They are not worth the effort it would take to reclaim them. But I shall remember this."

The malevolent presence of the adversary faded, leaving me alone with the monk who had stood up to her and three corpses, which I now believed he was responsible for creating. He sighed, took a flask from his robe, and quaffed a drink.

"Damn fool boy, is there no way to keep you out of trouble?" the monk muttered. "Do you think that I would go through the hassle of burying them if there wasn't a reason for it? These are the people responsible for the deaths of your family members, and you were about to grant them absolution!"

"What?" I demanded. "My grandfather and my uncles were killed by Travelers, not—"

"Who do you think has been passing out quests to slay members of the royal family, boy? These were members of the assassin's guild, before I got to them. The ones responsible for issuing the most dangerous and valuable quests. Had they returned to the adversary, then they would have simply respawned with a new face and continued to wreak havoc upon your family tree."

I clutched at the handle of my [Gemos Long Sword] and eyed the monk suspiciously. He had stood up to the adversary, and he had won the battle for the souls. Yet I knew for certain now that he was no worshiper of Thedum.

"Who are you?" I demanded. "What god do you worship?"

The monk sighed and took another drink from his flask. "Do you not recognize me, Hail? We've met before, although I admit it has been several years, and I was not particularly pleasant towards you. You played with my grandson when you visited my villa outside of the capital. I believe that he had significantly more fun than you did, at the time."

The monk turned to me, and his face changed from the pallid gray to one that I recognized from my childhood.

"Uncle Auroras," I whispered.

"Yes, I do go by that name," my great-uncle agreed. "Although most who know of me simply call me *the Gray Man.*"

I felt weak in the knees, as one of the many boogey-men that my nurse Beckah had once used to threaten me into good behavior stood before me.

"The Gray Man isn't real," I protested. "If you were the Gray Man, you would be thousands of years old. You can't be—"

"There is always a Gray Man," Auroras countered. "Each of us lives a mortal lifetime, and when we pass on, the mantle moves to another. I have been the avatar of my deity for forty years, Hail. Now let us go somewhere less fragrant, for we have things we must discuss, as one avatar to another."

I swallowed, and I found the courage to stand. I followed the Avatar of Death back to the abandoned temple.

12

AURORAS

"Rain knew, of course," Auroras said. We sat in the small room in the back of the temple where, when this place had been populated, it would have had clergy requiring a place to eat their meals. He had poured a goblet of wine for both of us, but [Detect Poison] had lit up when I cast it, so of course I hadn't touched mine. "He was the first person I told when the mantle came to me. This was just before he had ascended to the throne himself, and I was a little worried that our father would have me executed. I had never been a devoted follower of Thedum, but neither had I been an adherent of Death, which is why coming into my power was such a great surprise to me at the time."

"That's poison," I said to him as he was about to drink his wine.

"Yes, of course it's poison; everything I touch becomes poisoned," he muttered. "Don't worry. It won't kill you. Probably. And you really ought to start leveling your poison resistance. If you don't, you'll be vulnerable to all sorts of lingering afflictions and maladies that your enemies could use to weaken you at critical moments. You may have the ability to return from the dead like a Traveler, Hail, but that does not mean that you cannot be weakened, defeated, and imprisoned. Teaching you that lesson was half the point of this little exercise."

"You deliberately kidnapped me, then? To teach me a lesson?" I asked.

"Of course I did. Although it was only half the reason, as I said. The other half was to get you out of the blasted capital. That is the absolute worst place for you to be right now. You have too much to learn to waste time on petty politics."

"Does Lady Gwen work for you? Is that how you arranged my abduction?" I inquired.

He laughed. "Hail, virtually every spy in the kingdom works for me in some capacity. I was your grandfather's spymaster! The great spider in the center of the web that nobody even knew was there. But no, I used my own power to twist the portal that brought you here. She intended to send you to her own estate for safety, and your abduction was performed without her knowledge or active participation. It was a very simple matter to alter your destination. At least, it is when you have the power of a god at your fingertips and decades of experience in using it."

"So you say, but how can I trust her? If she does belong to you, then of course you would say that to protect her," I pointed out.

"Ah yes, very clever. And quite correct," Auroras agreed. "She and Lord Tom are their own agents, however, behooved to their own sense of loyalty towards Yuikon and nothing else. But then you cannot trust a word I say. As the [Avatar of Thedum] and the Avatar of Death, we are not natural enemies, but neither are we allies. In fact, given that my own god has a very strict stance of neutrality in the contest between Thedum and his adversary, there is a strict limit on the amount of aid I can give you, and neither can I actively oppose you without compensation. Should the scales tip too far either way, well, you don't need to worry about that, because I won't let it happen."

"You say you are neutral, but your actions say otherwise," I objected.

"It is not my actions that matter, but my motives. Which are threefold. First, to remove you from the capital before you inject even more chaos and discord into the already murky whirlpool that is this cold war of succession. Second, to prevent the end of the Teoran line. And finally, to see that you have a proper education. There are so many gaping holes in what you know and understand about this world and your place in it. It's not entirely your fault. The administrators are mostly to blame, as is Rain. He thought he would give you time and space and allow you to make your own decisions and direct your own life, fool sentimentalist that he was. And he also thought that he would have another ten years to fill in the gaps in your education, but the Kingslayer had other ideas, didn't he?"

"My education?" I asked, growing angry. "You've abducted me, had me chased by hounds, poisoned, and forced me to help you cover up your murders, and you say that it is for my education?"

"Yes," Auroras said, drinking his poisoned wine. "Hail, you are presently one of the greatest destabilizing forces alive in this world. You have the potential to do more Damage to our society than the adversary, the Kingslayer, or any of the Travelers who have gone over to the enemy. I understand your impulses to simply throw your weight around and issue quests to the Travelers who are following you to try to force this world into the image of what you think it should be. But everything you have done so far since returning from the space between worlds has run counter to what I believe to be your goals."

"What would you know about it?" I demanded.

"Well, let us start with when you [Polymorphed] the bishop of the faith you follow, rather than revealing yourself to be the avatar of his god, thus humiliating him and driving a wedge between the two of you in your future relationship," my great-uncle said.

"Wait, he was a bishop?" I asked, recalling the priest who I had dealt with in such a fashion upon my return from the lobby.

"And then there is the matter of the Traveler who attempted to make amends, only to be driven off. Hail, do you *want* the Travelers to work for the adversary? Because it is largely your resentment that is preventing the priests of Thedum from issuing them quests to complete their repentance. If you do not soften your heart towards those who wish to return to the light, then they will begin to lose hope. Or they will embrace the opportunities that the darkness is providing for them, and before long, they shall be too far gone to ever return."

"What?" I asked. "What do I have to do with any of that?"

"Thedum is withholding his forgiveness because you are withholding yours," Auroras explained. "Those who have been marked by you will find it exceedingly difficult to remove their [Brand of

Sin] while you carry your resentment towards them. And for every one of them who gives up hope of returning to the light, the darkness will grow that much stronger."

I frowned, biting my lip in consideration. If that was true, then . . .

"And then there are the letters! What on Lagrea were you thinking sending out those damnable letters?" Auroras exclaimed. "Were you trying to alienate every single noble in Zhesa City? Thank the stars I was able to get the guards to intercept most of them!"

"So that was you!" I exclaimed. "My correspondence is no business of yours, Uncle!"

"I was doing you a favor, boy," Auroras growled.

"I was delivering Grandfather's final messages to his friends," I objected. "He had no chance to say goodbye, and so when we spoke in the space between worlds, his—"

Auroras began to laugh. "His friends? Hail, Rain *hated* those people. He was using you to get in one final barb at them from beyond the veil. Here, let me give you an example."

He pulled from his inventory a letter I recognized. One that I had written. He began to read.

'Dear Baron Selmy, I would like to congratulate you on your fine son, Keithan. My grandfather has often spoken of how his hope for the Selmy line has been much improved since his birth. He has shown himself to be in possession of a fine mind and a marvelous aptitude for military affairs, allowing him to rise high in the military. In fact, Grandfather confided to me that it is precisely because Keithan bears the Selmy name that he was promoted to the rank of Captain, even before he'd acquired the experience that would normally be required for the position.'

'While I have not personally met Keithan, everything I have heard of him tells me that he is a fine young man, and I look forward to improving the nation of Yuikon together with him. I would not wish to insult you by saying that I look forward to the day he becomes Baron in your place. I do believe that you can rest easy knowing that you have such a fine young heir to take your place upon your retirement. Sincerely, Earl Hail Jeoran.'

Auroras concluded reading the letter and looked at me sternly. "Honestly, Hail, what were you thinking?"

"I complimented him on his son; what is so wrong about that?" I asked.

"Well, there is the fact that Baron Selmy is a cuckhold," Auroras said. "Keithan is not his son, and just about everyone at court knows it."

"He—what?" I asked.

"Everyone aside from you, I see. I suppose I must thank the good Baron for his outrage over the insults you have given him, for if not for his reaction to reading this letter, I would not have learned of your actions in time to save you from even worse blunders."

I began to blush. "Do you happen to know Baron Selmy's class and level? Because there is a very real chance that he might challenge me to a duel at some point."

Auroras scoffed. "He's a level thirty [Merchant]. And he is a coward and a weakling. I'm fairly certain you could have taken him as a [Child]. He will bluster and curse your name, but he will take it no further. If he had the courage to do something to defend his honor, he would have denounced his wife and her lover decades ago rather than live in shame."

I began to search my memory for the things Grandfather had told me to write and examine them again from a new angle. I had always been encouraged to praise a virtue of the letter's recipient, or one of their near relatives, and I now began to suspect that those individuals lacked the very virtue I was told to praise.

"What of Marquis Peori?" I inquired, for that was the most dangerous name of the letters I had sent out.

"I failed to intercept his letter, although I haven't heard of his reaction to it," Auroras admitted. "Why—what did you say?"

"I praised his faithfulness to his sacred wedding vows," I admitted.

Auroras laughed. "Why, he is Keithan Selmy's father! It's his influence and power that prevent the poor Baron from denouncing his wife and her son in the first place! And he has a dozen other bastards throughout the city."

I hung my head in embarrassment.

"Well, at least the marquis would have simply laughed at the letter, rather than declaring lifelong enmity," Auroras said, chuckling. "In fact, I believe that between the letters you sent to the baron and the one to the marquis, Peori's opinion of you might actually be favorable. He loves a good jest, and unlike the poor Baron, he can laugh at himself."

I sighed, unhappy to learn that I was the unwitting dupe in a final game played by my grandfather and his court. "And the criers denouncing interest in the throne?" I asked.

"That, actually, is perhaps the one thing that you've done right," Uncle Auroras admitted. "But then you screwed it all up by making an enemy of your Uncle Storm. You should have followed Gwen and Tom's lead rather than shouting your mouth off. The criers would have gotten the assassins to leave you alone, but now Storm will no doubt see you as an obstacle in his path to the crown. He will seek to weaken and imprison you if he can. And possibly kill you once or twice, just to check whether the rumors of your immortality are founded or not."

I sighed. I found the glass of wine halfway to my lips before I caught myself, remembering that it was poison. It was a shame; I could use something to calm my nerves. I'd only had very heavily watered wine before, and the scent of this vintage was heavy and deep.

"So if I didn't mess up with the criers, why did you have them arrested?" I asked.

"Sending the guards after anyone carrying a missive from you was the easiest way to make certain I got all of the letters," Uncle Auroras explained. "And also it gave me an opportunity to demonstrate another mistake that you *did* make. Specifically, that you failed to account for what would happen to the parchment once the quest was completed."

"I don't understand. What's the problem with that?" I asked.

The Gray Man wearing my great-uncle's face pulled several sheets of paper from his inventory and passed them to me. I examined them, and I quickly began to blush.

One was an order for the supplies for a week of debauchery and hedonism, with promises that the coin for the food, wine, and "entertainment" would come from the royal coffers. The requested entertainment was long, and my ears were burning as I read it. The parts of it I understood were quite . . . graphic.

Another was a request to assassinate the matron of an orphanage. No reason was given.

The final letter was a confession to a string of murders and the promise to continue "the good work" until someone put a stop to the writer of the letter.

All three were written in my hand, signed with my name, and stamped with my seal.

"These are forgeries," I said. With a flare of magic, the papers burst into flames.

"Of course they are—I did them myself," Uncle Auroras agreed. "But they look authentic enough. And there's a very real chance that the system would have generated a quest should they have fallen into the hands of a Traveler. It's a very simple matter to modify a document written in simple ink. Were you not a [Spellblade], I would insist that you hire a [Scribe] immediately to properly enchant your letters to prevent tampering and allow for proper disposal. As it is, you have the capacity to learn those abilities for yourself, and so I will ensure that you do before I allow you to leave."

"If you're planning on helping me, then why have you poisoned everything you've given me?" I demanded.

"I can't not," Auroras said simply, sipping his wine. "If it makes you feel any better, it's an automatic ability of mine over which I have only limited control. To be honest, everyone in my household has their poison resistance at a level where it doesn't matter, and so it was not a great concern to me until I realized that you have been neglectful in raising that stat in yourself. Another oversight of your grandfather, I suppose, but one that I'm perfectly willing to help you overcome. The poisons I've been giving you are unlikely to do more than cause you a bit of distress and increase your resistance. Unless you would prefer to starve to death—the choice is yours."

I frowned, considering my options. The last time I had died, I had been returned to the temple of Thedum in Zhesa. I couldn't be certain that would be the case every time. If it was simply the nearest temple, then, well, dying here might simply mean I lose a level for no purpose. I could think of no other potential means of escape.

I was trapped. I didn't trust Uncle Auroras, but I doubted I could escape him by force. Neither did I think I could outsmart him and trick him into releasing me before he was ready and willing to do so. "How long do you plan on keeping me hostage?"

"A while. I have my own matters to attend to and cannot spend overly long on this little exercise," he admitted. "A week, maybe two. No more."

"So I am indeed your hostage, then?" I asked.

"No, Hail, it is far worse than that," Uncle Auroras teased. "You are my student."

Yes, that was worse. Looking nervously at the poisoned wine, I decided that the easiest way out was through. I would have to play Auroras's game, for now. I quaffed the drink. The wine was quite good, but a moment after I'd drank from the glass, I was notified that I had indeed been poisoned.

"You win," I admitted. "But I won't forget this."

Auroras just smiled and poured himself another glass of wine.

13
SHADOW

I threw the final shovelful of dirt onto the last grave, packing the loose dirt down. I had been a captive of my great-uncle for three days now, and I was not enjoying the experience at all. I had finally given in and eaten the food he gave me after his repeated assurances that, although my [Detect Poison] spell lit up when I cast it, the poison in the porridge was too weak to kill anyone over level ten. That did not make the [Flatulence] or the [Stomach Cramps] any more enjoyable. Nor did I enjoy the fact that it had taken me down to 5483/12600 Health before my [Poison Resistance] had risen to level five and removed the Damage-over-time effect.

With the last of the supposed assassins buried, I stuck the shovel in the ground and made my way back into the temple. The hounds growled at me, but I had grown inured to their presence over the last few days. Which is to say that I flinched, but managed to ignore them as they trailed behind me. Auroras assured me that they would only chase me if I tried to flee, and that they would not kill me, but simply drag me back. I did not trust him, but if there was one thing he had made perfectly clear, it was that he did not need the hounds to kill me, if that had been his desire.

The guild had called off the search for me at my own insistence. Uncle Auroras would simply kill anyone who found me, then teleport me somewhere else for my remaining lessons. I know this because he explicitly said as much. And after seeing him battle directly with the adversary—and win—I believed him. There was also the fact that when I [Analyzed] him now, I saw "level ???" instead of "level fifty." I strongly suspected that he was in fact a Worldboss. Even if <Peasant's Revenge> appeared en mass to confront him and free me, I doubted they would prevail.

Or that I would survive the attempt; Uncle Auroras would probably kill me first just to make a point.

I checked my Health. I was back over ten thousand again, thanks to my regeneration while I'd been digging graves. I really hoped that wouldn't be a theme of my stay at the temple, but I suspected I would find myself almost dying after every meal as Uncle Auroras introduced me to stronger and stronger poisons.

I normally enjoyed seeing my skills increase. [Poison Resistance] was a definite exception to that rule.

I slammed the temple door shut on the mutts following me and made my way to the room where Uncle Auroras was scribing.

"I've finished burying the people you murdered," I informed him.

"Good. Did you tend to the horse?" he asked.

"What horse?"

He looked at me, annoyed. He had let his appearance slacken back into that of the Gray Man, and his appearance was ghastly. "Go tend to the horse."

I sighed theatrically, and I left the temple again. The hounds were as eager to meet me as they ever were, with growls and bared teeth, but although they followed me as I circled around to the back of the temple once more, they stayed at least six feet away from me.

I had thought the stables were empty, but I had never actually checked. The structure was mostly enclosed, with tall windows to let light in for the occupants. For a moment I thought that my uncle had gone senile, because at first glance the stalls were vacant. However, it was a trick of the light, for on a second glance, I saw him. And he was beautiful.

A stallion. Eight or nine years old, if I were to guess. An adult and fully mature, but young. Black as midnight, which is why I hadn't seen him at first. He'd been hidden in shadow.

"My, aren't you a beauty!" I exclaimed. I quickly searched my inventory to see if I had a treat to give him but came up empty. Then I remembered the small garden that had gone wild behind the shed, so I went and pulled a few carrots from where they had been growing. I sprayed them clean with a very low-powered [Water Jet] and returned to give them to the stallion.

The horse gladly accepted the offering, and he allowed me to scratch his head in gratitude. I opened the stall and walked around him, rubbing a hand over his powerful muscles and taking in his perfect form.

"You might be the most beautiful horse I've ever seen," I admitted, scratching his hide with affection. "It's a shame your rider is such a tool."

The horse whickered as though it understood me. At least, it sounded amused. I found the brush and spent the next ten minutes grooming the magnificent animal.

I had been leveling [Animal Handling] for years and never touched such a wonderful specimen. Helping out in the stables when I was younger had been a thankless chore, but taking care of the needs of horses made one a better rider, and so I had never complained too much, even before I had lost my position as a [Prince]. So it was with practiced and careful hands that I brushed him and fed him his oats. And for once, I barely minded mucking out the stall.

I spoke the entire time in a calm and reassuring voice, complaining about his rider. I disparaged my great-uncle at length, telling the horse that his rider was utterly unworthy of him and that if I had my way, he would be the mighty steed of a proper rider. One who could appreciate just how majestic he was. The horse seemed to agree with me. I was quite pleased when my [Animal Handling] skill leveled to five while I was caring for him.

I was sorely tempted to saddle him and make an escape attempt. The hounds would chase us, but perhaps I could [Slow] or [Polymorph] them from horseback. It is said that Ramsay hounds can run down a galloping horse, but I doubted they could match the speed of this thoroughbred. Ultimately, I resisted the temptation. I would not put the life of such a spectacular animal at risk, not even in a bid for my own freedom.

I spent about forty minutes with the horse, perhaps ten longer than I needed to, but we seemed to enjoy each other's company. Which is more than I could say of my great-uncle. Or the hounds.

Once I had dallied long enough, I gave the horse's head one last affectionate rub and promised to return soon. Uncle Auroras had not moved from where I had left him.

"I've tended the horse. He is marvelous; where did you get him?" I asked.

"I bred him, of course," he responded. "His dam is a Nightmare from the shadow plains of the fourth hell. I caught her myself when I was in my twenties. His sire is a Cheshiran Warhorse. He belonged to Sir . . . Sir . . . I seem to have forgotten the name. It doesn't matter anyway; he died years ago. I bought the sire from the knight's widow."

"Right," I said, somewhat skeptical of his claims about the stallion's mother. But then again, he was the Gray Man, so perhaps he wasn't pulling my leg. "What's his name?"

"I haven't given him one," Uncle Auroras said.

I was aghast. "A horse like that deserves a name!"

"Perhaps," he agreed, continuing to write upon his parchment. "Why don't you think of one that would be appropriate for him, and if I agree with it, perhaps I will allow you to name him."

I immediately began to ponder the challenge, but frustratingly I came up blank. I considered turning the problem over to my guild, but knowing them, they would vote to name it something like Horsey McHorseface, or some obscure reference to the culture of their world, which I would never understand. Perhaps I would consult them when I retired tonight, if I had not thought of something before then.

"Well then," my great-uncle said, setting aside his pen. "It is time to begin your education. We will start by teaching you to [Enchant Ink]. Despite its name, ink is not actually required; you can use any liquid, including water. The benefit of this spell, aside from its convenience, is that once the enchanted ink is applied, it cannot be removed without destroying most forms of parchment. The detriment of this spell, of course, is that if you spill the ink or get it on your clothing it is almost impossible to remove."

"What do you think of Midnight for a name?" I asked the stallion. It nickered and shook its head in refusal. "Yeah, I know. Sorry. I asked my guild, and they keep saying things like 'Sleipnir' or 'Bucephalus.' Pretty lame, huh?"

The horse nickered in what I took to be agreement. I affectionately brushed its neck. I had been visiting the stallion twice a day over the last week of my captivity, thoroughly enjoying the chore for the presence of the magnificent steed and the opportunity to escape my great-uncle. The horse seemed to enjoy my presence as well. And the carrots that I brought him as a greeting each morning. Carrots that had never known the Gray Man's [Poison Touch].

"You know, when I first came in here, I didn't see you because you were hidden in a shadow," I commented. "How about that? Would you like to be called Shadow?"

The horse did not respond for a moment, then gently nudged me with its shoulder.

"I'll check with my uncle to see what he thinks. I mean, I don't think I have the right to name you without permission. But I like Shadow as your name," I told the beast. It nickered in agreement. Then it dropped a load of dung on the floor. I sighed; I had just finished mucking the stall. But when I finished brushing the stallion down, I grabbed the shovel and cleaned it up. Such a magnificent beast as Shadow deserved to rest in a clean stable.

Although the work was done, I lingered in the building for a few minutes, pulling up my status. So far little had changed since I had returned to the world, except for my general abilities.

General Skills	Animal Handling (7)	General Spells	Spark (Max)
	Balance and Conditioning (20)		Analyze (19)
	Dance (9)		Storage (max)
	Herbalism (8)		Enchant Ink (1)
	Tracking (1)		Enchant Parchment (1)
	Poison Resistance (15)		Illusion Magic: Disguise (1)

	Scribe (General) (1)		Magical Seal: Personal Crest (1)
	Scribe (Copy Document) (1)		
	Scribe (Forge Document) (1)		

The spells that Auroras had taught me had been the easiest of the changes; I had simply needed to examine a vellum containing the spell, memorize it, and cast the spell once, which was easy to do. The scribe skills had been harder to learn, as I had to read three dusty old skill books from cover to cover and then practice what I'd learned for several hours before I got the first point in them.

[Poison Resistance] was at once easy and also incredibly unpleasant, as all I'd needed to do to level that was eat the food that Uncle Auroras provided. Each meal brought me down below half Health, but my resistance would level and fight off the poison before it reached the point where I needed to drink more of my dwindling supply of health potions.

[Animal Handling] was perhaps the most rewarding of the skill ups, simply because it allowed me to spend time with Shadow. However, I'd yet to reach level ten—a threshold which would provide a number of benefits, including boosting my mount's speed and stamina and allowing me to obtain a second [Bonded Mount]. Having reached level twenty, I could obtain my first mount at any time; I simply had not had the opportunity to go shopping for a worthy horse. And now that I had met Shadow, my definition of a worthy horse had been forever altered.

I was spacing out, examining my status screen, when the door creaked open, and Uncle Auroras stepped in. "You have named the horse."

"What?" I asked, jerking in surprise. "Oh. Yeah, I guess. I was thinking 'Shadow.' What do you think?"

"If the horse has accepted the name, then my opinion is of little consequence," my great-uncle said. "Saddle him."

"Where are you going?" I asked.

"Home. As are you."

14
DEPARTURE

"This saddle is unworthy of him," I commented as I finished cinching it in place. It was simple leather, utilitarian, and unappealing to the eye. "Shadow deserves a master-crafted saddle. Black leather adorned with silver, I think. And inscribed with the seal of his rider."

The horse nickered as though in agreement with my statement.

"Well, if you don't like the saddle, then you can damn well buy the replacement yourself," Uncle Auroras grumbled from behind me. He had watched me work without once offering to help, but if this was my last time interacting with the magnificent stallion then I didn't really want his help anyway. I would miss Shadow, and—

"Wait, why would I buy his saddle?"

"He's your horse," Uncle Auroras informed me. "Consider him a birthday gift. It's time you had a proper mount."

I gaped at my great-uncle, gratitude welling up inside me to the point where it almost began to shove aside my resentment of the man. "I—Thank you, Uncle Auroras. I truly cannot put into words how grateful I am to receive such a magnificent gift. I vow that I will take—"

"Yes, yes, let's just skip the speech for now," Auroras said, interrupting me. "Now then. To be honest, I should really keep you for another month and finish drilling into your head what you need to know to keep from making yourself an embarrassment, but I need to get back to the capital. So I'm going to give you some parting advice."

I sighed, but I knew that listening would be the fastest course to freedom.

"First of all, stay out of the fight for the throne. You've already made your stance perfectly clear. Stick to it and don't waver. Storm will see you as an enemy, but do not rise to further provocations from him."

"You don't want my support?" I asked.

"Why would I want your support for a position that I don't want? And one that I couldn't occupy anyway. Thedum would strike me down the moment I sat on the throne. There is no way that he would abide having the Gray Man rule over one of his favored kingdoms," Uncle Auroras said dismissively. "I'm simply muddying the waters for Storm to keep the position vacant until a more suitable candidate is available."

"I see," I said. "Who would you support? Your grandson would be third in line after you now."

"That insufferable pissant would run the kingdom into the ground," Uncle Auroras snorted. "And until we have resolved the matter of Storm assassinating anyone who poses a threat to his claim, it is best not to support any alternative to the two of us. No, at present, I believe it is best if the throne remains empty."

I frowned because I strongly disagreed. *Someone* needed to lead Yuikon. The crisis with some of the Travelers joining the adversary would not wait for politics. "Are you certain that it is Storm who is responsible for the assassination quests? Could it not be someone else taking advantage of the fact that our nation is at its most vulnerable?"

"It's both of those things," Auroras informed me. "One of the men you buried was Storm's contact with the assassin's guild. The other four worked for outsiders. But keep your nose out of that, Hail. You have more important matters that require your immediate attention. It is time for you to visit your lands. The truth is that your only influence at court presently is your name, and that name is one of a bastard raised by his doting grandfather and nothing more. If you continue to neglect your lands, then you will be unable to support your kingdom and its next king at all."

"That is what I was meaning to do as soon as I came back from the space between worlds," I said. "But then I got dragged into all of this. You're right, of course. I plan on heading to Thorn March as soon as I can."

"Go to North Shire instead. It is in the most need of your guidance," Auroras advised. "And bring some of your Travelers with you. If you journey down this road, you will reach a crossroads, at which point you should be able to find your way. You may leave now, Nephew. I release you from your captivity."

"Thank you, Uncle," I said. I stepped over to Shadow and put a hand on his flank.

Auroras Teoran has gifted you the steed "Shadow." Shadow wishes to become your bonded mount. Accept?	
Yes	No

I eagerly accepted, and then I mounted the horse. He accepted my weight effortlessly, and I could feel the power of the stallion beneath me, eager to be on the road. Uncle Auroras walked with me around the temple to the front.

"There is just one last thing before I let you leave, Nephew. I have another gift, of a sort," Uncle Auroras said. "Give me your hand."

Frowning in confusion, I reached down. He had been walking along my left side as I rode Shadow, and so it is that hand that I gave him. Auroras's cold grip enveloped mine, and I felt an icy sensation envelop my limb from the elbow down.

You have been Cursed! Upon death, Gray Man's Touch will reduce you to level 1. Your class, skills, and skill levels will remain unaffected.
You have gained a boon! Through the Valley of the Shadow increases your experience gained to 300% while afflicted with Gray Man's Touch.
You have gained a skill! Draining Touch will allow you to absorb Health and Mana from a target while you are in contact with them with the hand afflicted by Gray Man's Touch.

I shot a lethal glare at my uncle, and I called him things that were very far from polite.

"Try not to die, Nephew," he suggested merrily, and he slapped Shadow's rump. The stallion lurched into motion beneath me, and I was forced to turn my attention to keeping my seat as we accelerated to a full gallop. I wanted to turn around and attempt to murder my uncle, but the hounds were already baying in pursuit.

Cursing his treachery, I was forced to focus on outrunning the hounds. We galloped down the old dirt road that led to the temple, our pursuers barking just behind us. They say that Ramsay hounds can chase down a horse, but Shadow was no ordinary mount, and we began to outpace them. However, before we had gone a mile, the air suddenly twisted in front of us, and before I could even think to adjust our course, we had passed through the portal, leaving the forest behind. The portal snapped shut just behind us, cutting off the howling of the hounds, leaving us safe, but once again I had no idea where I was.

We were surrounded by vast empty hills, with no sign of civilization in sight except for the road we trod upon. Still cursing my great-uncle's treachery, I slowed Shadow to a trot, and we continued to follow the road for a few miles until we came to the crossroads Auroras had promised. I examined the sign for a moment, then relaxed. I finally knew where I was. I opened guildchat to update my friends with the recent development.

Hail	Hey, guys. So, I have some good news and some bad news.
Gummytiger	Give us the bad news first.
Subtleghost	What? Why would you tell him to do that?
Gummytiger	Let's just get it out of the way.
Stormy	Whatever, it doesn't matter. Hail, have you been released? Is that the good news?
Hail	Yeah, it's part of the good news. My uncle finally let me go, and he even gave me a mount. The bad news is that he also gave me a curse. If I die again, I don't just lose a level. I get knocked back to level one.
Malick	What? That's some bullshit!

Hail	Yeah, I know. It comes with an ability and triples my experience, but it's totally not worth it. I'm going to head to a Temple of Thedum and see if I can get it removed. The other part of the good news is that I know where I am. I'm in North Shire. The sign at the crossroads says that I'm six leagues from Ebbyvale, which is where the previous lord held court, so I'm going to go there.
Stan	That's great, Hail. I'll give a shout out to <Peasant's Revenge>, and they'll get your guard on its way to catch up to you. Stay safe until they get there.
Corinth	I don't know about you guys, but I'm heading that way too. There's probably a lot of quests and stuff that will unlock once he gets there.
Wesle	Yeah, good call.
Hail	Okay, I'm going to stop paying attention now.
Birdie	Before you do, Hail, Daemon wanted us to pass on the message that your items have all sold, and that he's sent you the money through the mail system.
Hail	Thanks. Where is Daemon?
Birdie	His daughter is visiting today. He should be on tonight. Er, um, later this week.
Hail	Okay. Thanks, everyone. I'll be heading towards Ebbyvale like I said, but I think there's a village on the way. I might stop there and spend the night if they have an inn. It will be nice to eat something that's not poison and have a proper bath. If I stop there, I'll let you all know the name of the village so that you can meet up with me there.
Corinth	Thanks, Hail. See you soon.

I closed the chat window with a thought, and I nudged Shadow to bring me off to the east, in the direction of Ebbyvale. Keeping the stallion to a distance-eating trot, I surveyed my lands for the first time.

North Shire was on the northern border of Yuikon, where the lands were hilly. The valleys were fertile, and the three forests were mostly ignored except for the wild game they produced, as the wood wasn't of a variety that was useful for much. There were a few lakes and rivers, but not enough for fishing to be a major industry. I honestly didn't know much about the land I had been assigned beyond that, although I was sure I would soon learn more.

My first impression after reading about the lands my grandfather had given me was that they weren't particularly valuable compared to many of the larger counties and earldoms of the kingdom. Their industries were mostly pastoral agriculture, providing a slow but steady stream of coin to the kingdom's coffers through the governors that had been overseeing them since they had reverted back to the crown. It was precisely due to their lack of value that they had been readily available for my grandfather to assign them to me in the first place.

That was fine. In fact, it was perfect. Once I got things in my lands sorted out, then I'd be ready to go off adventuring, gaining levels, busting dungeons, and making a name for myself. I'd much rather be doing that than endlessly managing a large and industrious region of the country. My new lands were an important status symbol, but I wasn't content to lead the life of an idle noble growing fat on the work of my citizenry. Once I had taken in the lands and put things in order, I would appoint a steward for North Shire and Thorn March.

It was little different than what Uncle Storm did with his own lands; while he was technically the overlord of much of western Yuikon, he delegated most of the rule to his staff so that he could focus on being present at court. Except instead of wasting my time impressing other nobles and jostling for position and power, I would be gaining levels and fighting back the darkness alongside my Traveler companions.

As I was contemplating my plans for the future, my path was abruptly blocked by a group that rode out from a camp hidden behind a hill. To my surprise, the party of twelve was made of a mixed group of Travelers and Natives, and judging by the weapons they bore, their intentions were not simply to offer directions.

"Is this a robbery?" I asked my steed, who paused slightly at having his path blocked by the inferior mounts of the assailants.

"Hey, you! This is a robbery!" one of the Travelers shouted. "We'll be taking your mount, and your—"

"I don't have time for this," I muttered, and I promptly [Swiftcast] [Concussive Sound], followed by [Dazzling Lights]. I kicked Shadow's flanks, and the steed charged straight through the blockade before the bandits had a chance to recover from what my Traveler friends called my flash-bang combo.

Shadow proved his superior breeding. The bandits, once recovered, tried to give chase but caught only the dust kicked up by his hooves. I watched their figures shrink into the distance, and I seethed.

Bandits? I thought to myself. *In my lands? No, this will not do.*

I may only be a bastard, but my noble pride would not stand for this at all. But I was not foolish enough to try taking on that group by myself. I would go to Ebbyvale as planned, and then my friends and I would put together a solution to this problem.

15

BATHWATER

The silent black whirlwind of the nexus appeared in the center of the village as I approached it, and when I finally reached it, I received the notification that I had gained a new Recall Point, and that the Fast Travel network was once again available. I sighed in relief, but I was in no hurry to leave the small village I'd arrived in moments ago. I had already passed its name on to the guild, and it was here where I would meet up with my protectors once more.

However, they had a significant amount of ground to cover, as the northern reaches of Yuikon are not commonly visited by Travelers. There simply were not enough dungeons, lairs, or quests to draw the visitors from Earth, and so the region was largely ignored by them. I had been very surprised to see the Travelers in the bandit blockade, and it troubled me greatly. If the Travelers were turning to Banditry and lawlessness, then it would be much harder to turn them back.

The original plan had been for us all to travel to my lands together and attune ourselves to the Recall Points along the way. Some of the members of <Nethersong Mavericks> had managed to find a [Mage] who could portal them to Ebbyvale, but they were having trouble coordinating the migration. Once they arrived, they planned to wait for me there. My protectors from <Peasant's

Revenge>, on the other hand, had all immediately Fast Traveled to the nearest Recall Point that they had to my location and were swiftly flying to my side.

Which meant that all I had to do was wait for them. I dismounted Shadow and patted his sweaty flanks. "Looks like the inn is over there. I'll see you settled first, and then see about a bath for myself," I told the horse, and he nickered in appreciation.

The stableboy offered to take the horse from me, but I insisted on brushing the stallion down myself. I did accept his help in unsaddling the horse, and I appreciated his murmurs of adoration as he helped me brush the beast down. Shadow seemed to understand that the boy appreciated his majesty almost as much as I did, and he seemed a little deliberate in his regal stance as he allowed us mere humans to see to his needs.

I was about to flip the stableboy a coin to rent the stall for the night when Shadow made the gesture unnecessary. The massive stallion abruptly *shifted*, becoming darkness manifest, and he vanished into my own shadow. I jerked in surprise, as I had not known that he could do that. I could sense him, there in my shadow, and I felt his unwillingness to be separated from me. That suited me just fine, and I tried to send back a sense of affection and gratitude. Shadow sent a sense of satisfaction with the arrangement, and I flipped the stableboy the coin anyway for his help.

It seems that Auroras's claims that Shadow's dam was a Nightmare wasn't bluster after all. While it was always possible to call a [Bonded Mount], even from vast distances, being able to keep him in my shadow was a great advantage, which would serve me well. While I was still upset with my great-uncle for the curse he inflicted on me, and the week of captivity, I certainly could not complain about his other gift. Shadow was twice the mount I would have been able to find on my own.

I left the stableboy gaping at the display of Shadow's bloodline, giving him instructions to clean and polish the saddle for me to earn the coin I had given him, then I entered the inn. The common room was mostly empty at this time of day, but the innkeeper had noticed my arrival and judged by my visit to his stable that I would be staying a while, so he was ready to meet me.

"How may I serve you, noble sir? It is perhaps a little early to retire, but I have a fine roast in the kitchen, and ale or wine, if you'd like something to drink aside from water," he offered.

"All of that, and a bath," I said immediately. "It's been weeks since I've eaten anything that wasn't poisoned. I'll take juice to drink. I'd like something with a sweet flavor, but not something that will get me intoxicated."

"Of course," the fat man agreed. "And your clothes? I do not mean insult, but, well, you are covered in mud. I could arrange to have your clothes laundered and pressed for you, if you do not mind wandering around in a dressing robe until I can return them to you."

"That sounds excellent," I agreed. "But the food first, I think. I am famished."

I tossed the innkeeper a gold coin, which he caught eagerly. He motioned for me to sit wherever I pleased and vanished into the backroom. I heard him shouting orders at someone to draw water for my bath, and he returned a moment later with my food.

The roasted mutton was delicious and savory. The vegetables that went with it were somewhat less appetizing, being both burnt *and* soggy, but at least they were not poisoned. I checked. The meal came with a massive mug of cider, which I drank greedily. It was not as good as the fare at Nile's Inn in Eastmill, but it was satisfying and filling, and a vast improvement over the food Auroras had been giving me during my captivity.

Once I'd eaten my fill, and then some, I informed the innkeeper that I was ready for that bath. He brought me to an outbuilding, inside which five copper tubs were lined up and separated by curtains. He explained to me that he had purchased the setup when he'd learned that Travelers often travel in groups of five, and yet, to his disappointment, the investment had never paid off. One of the tubs was already filled with water. When he informed me that the kitchen was boiling water to heat it for me, I simply waved my hand and told him not to bother with the effort. Dipping my hand into the cool water, I used a bit of magic, and soon the bath was steaming.

"Magic is so convenient," I commented.

"Indeed," the innkeeper agreed, impressed by the display. Either that, or he was simply grateful that I hadn't blown up the bathhouse by mistake. There had been a slight chance that would have happened instead, if I was being honest about my abilities.

I pulled the curtain behind me and gave him my muddy clothes, including my dirty laundry from my inventory, before settling into the blissful embrace of the hot bath. He vowed to return my property in a few hours and motioned towards a robe that I could use once I had finished my bath. I settled in for a long soak.

I must have drifted off in the bath, because the water had cooled when I heard the voices outside of the bathhouse. I frowned, recognizing the tone as those of a group of Travelers, but they did not sound like my guardians from <Peasant's Revenge>.

"Alright, so I'll go in first, then you, Pete. Make sure that you [Counterspell] him constantly so that he can't get by us with his magic again. Then everyone else and Nickles will block the entrance," someone said.

"You sure we should be doing this, Kent?" a nervous female voice asked. "I mean, why not wait for him to come out on his own?"

"He's been in there two hours according to the innkeeper," Kent replied. "Look, its fine. It's better this way, because he'll be caught off balance and trapped. We'll ambush him, rob him, steal that mount of his, and then be gone, back with the others."

"With a horse that has one-fifty percent movement," a third voice said. "Seriously, Banditry is the best gig ever."

"Alright, here we go," Kent said, and the door was kicked open. The party of Travelers burst into the bathhouse. The curtain was torn down, and they surrounded me, blocking off my exit. I recognized them as some of the Travelers who had been in the bandit troupe from earlier, and I once more seethed with rage. But I suppressed it as I considered my options.

"Would someone kindly hand me my robe?" I asked. "Or are you perhaps here to help me wash my back?"

"Look, kid, we don't want to kill you," the leader said. "We just want that horse of yours."

"And all the gold in your inventory," another one added.

I [Analyzed] them all quickly, and was a little surprised. One of them was level fifteen! The highest leveled Traveler in the group was level thirty-three. There was a level thirty-one, and the other two were in their mid-twenties. I had been caught by surprise and was outnumbered, but perhaps I could win if I—

I frowned, remembering my curse. If I challenged them and lost, I would go back to level one. If I capitulated, I would lose Shadow and however much gold it took to convince them that I had sincerely given them everything I had. Either outcome would be a significant blow to my goals and my pride. Which simply meant that I had to win.

I equipped the only clothing I had in my inventory—the [Bloody and Torn Rags], the only clothing item I had not given to the innkeeper for cleaning. I got out of the tub, feigning surrender.

"Wait, why were you wearing pants in the bath?" one of the thugs asked.

"Would you prefer that he wasn't?" the female of the group asked.

"That's not what I meant," the man objected. Before the conversation could proceed further, I pulled my [Gemos Long Sword] from my inventory and imbued it with flames. With [Piercing Lunge] and a follow-up [Slash], I slew the lowest level member of the party almost instantly. I followed it up with a [Dazzling Lights], but the [Mage]'s [Counterspell] got me before I managed to follow it up with a [Concussive Sound].

I turned on him next, [Dashing] through the group to get at him and unleashing a flurry of blows. The bandits had apparently been confident of my capitulation and were completely caught off guard by the sudden violence. Unfortunately, the element of surprise did not last long enough for me to kill the [Mage], although I judged I did get him down to a quarter of his Health before the big brute of a leader swung his mace at me and I was forced to [Dodge] out of the way.

Unfortunately for the [Mage], their party lacked a healer. He grabbed a Health potion from his inventory and dashed out of the bathhouse, which was a mistake. He should have remained to keep my spell casting locked down. Seeing the opportunity, I swiftly cast [Concussive Sound], and then, during the duration of the stun, [Polymorphed] the level thirty-three [Warrior] and [Slowed] the other two. Those three were all melee warriors of some sort, and I judged that the [Mage] was my greatest threat, so I charged out of the bathhouse in pursuit of him.

He tried to surprise me with a [Fireball], but I had switched from [Imbue Sword: Fire] to [Arcane Weapon], and a [Slash] of my long sword dispelled the magic of his attack. He would have been better off using a crowd control spell to get me back under control while the rest of his party recovered, but I took advantage of his mistake and closed the distance between us with [Piercing Lunge]. He blinked away and began casting again, but his [Fireball] was once again expended uselessly against my [Arcane Weapon]. I [Dashed] to close the distance and [Slashed] and [Thrust] and [Slashed] once more, and he burst into motes of red light.

The others burst out of the bathhouse, staring at me in shock. They must have attacked the level thirty-three Traveler to break him out of [Polymorph], but the duration of [Slow] was still ticking on the other two.

"I thought you said he was a [Mage]," the female player said.

"He is—he's using magic," the leader said.

"Yes, a magic sword, idiot. Goddammit, this is that special En Pee See kid!" she said. "I'm out. Good luck, losers, I'm not about to fuck up my Rep by killing a member of the royal family."

She abruptly faded out of existence, returning to the space between worlds with a hard log out. The other two Travelers looked at each other, then at me, and together they charged.

I hit them again with [Dazzling Lights] and [Slow], then went to work with my fire-imbued sword. To my surprise, it was not a difficult fight, despite being matched two against one. Between their magical impairments, lack of cooperation, and subpar skill set, I could basically dance circles around them as I whittled their Health down with my magical swordplay. In fact, if I had been fully equipped, I'm confident that I would have ended the fight in half the time. Wearing only a pair of ruined trousers that gave me no stats, I was lacking about twenty points to both my Dexterity and Intellect, which were my primary stats for increasing my Damage dealt.

Compared to my spars with Corinth, or the elite Travelers of <Peasant's Revenge>, defeating these two Travelers was easy. I focused on the lower-level opponent first for the simple fact that he would be naturally easier to kill, and when he burst into motes of red light, the leader turned and ran for his life. Not content to let him off so easily, I mercilessly hit his fleeing form with [Empowered

Fireballs] and [Lightning Bolts]. He too burst into red motes of light just before he got out of range.

Stowing my [Gemos Long Sword] back in my inventory, I sighed in frustration. Twice now I had been attacked. *In my own lands!* The bandits may not have known it, but their reign of terror over North Shire was destined to come to a screeching halt in the very near future.

Opening my status screen, I noticed at least one positive outcome from the encounter. Killing the four Travelers had given me twelve thousand Experience, and I was now 15421/16800 towards regaining level twenty-nine. I hadn't realized that killing Travelers would be lucrative in terms of Experience. Much of those gains could be attributed to [Through the Valley of the Shadow], but even so, at a thousand Experience or so per Traveler, that was a hefty sum. It would take killing a dozen or more darkspawn to gain that much.

That did not make killing Travelers an ideal way to level up, however. Were I to go on a murder spree for such a purpose, there is little doubt that they would band together and put me down before I got very far. Killing a few who had gone to Banditry, however, would be perfectly within my right as the lord of this land. Perhaps this infestation was not entirely to my detriment.

16
IRVINE

I was pulled out of my post-victory reverie by a sound from the stables. I turned, ready to grab my sword back out of my inventory, but the stableboy identified himself by way of an unmanly squeak, and I relaxed slightly.

"Come on out. It's over, I think," I said, and the towheaded lad emerged from his hiding place. He was twelve or thirteen, I judged, and I wondered whether that made him younger or older than me. After all, although my status screen said that I was fifteen, I had only actually experienced ten of those years.

"You're very strong, sir," the boy said nervously. "I'm sorry. When they came to town, I wanted to try to warn you. They came to me asking after your horse, and I told them I hadn't seen anything! But they kept an eye on me while they were interrogating the innkeeper, so I didn't have a chance to sneak away."

"I'm not a knight, so you shouldn't call me 'sir,'" I told the boy. "What was your name again?"

"Irvine."

"Irvine, are the bandits in this land really so bold that they simply walk into lawful villages and threaten innocent Travelers?" I asked.

The boy hesitated, then nodded. "It's worse than that. They make us pay them not to kill us. It's twice what we pay in taxes, and when we can't pay in coin, they take our food and animals and anything else they can get their hands on. The inn is one of the only places they leave alone, and, honestly, that's because we're one of the few places that the constabulary would actually chase after them if they burned us down. They burned down the Millers' farm just last winter because the Millers couldn't afford their 'protection' any longer."

I squeezed my fist. "And the steward and the constable? Why have they not sent word to the crown for help in clearing out this rabble?"

"'Cording to the constable, the bandits don't exist," Irvine informed me. "Says if there were bandits, then there would be murders, and the bandits don't usually kill you. They just rob you until you starve to death. And nobody hears from the steward except when it's time to assess taxes. Most honest folk don't have the coins to pay either the taxes or the bandits, so they're forced to pay in food and livestock. Lots of folk go hungry around here, sir."

"Don't call me sir," I repeated absently. With a slight effort of will, I communicated to Shadow that I wished for him to manifest himself, and he emerged from my shadow in a heartbeat. "Irvine, please saddle my horse. I don't believe I will be staying in this village overnight after all. It seems that I have a negligent, and perhaps corrupt, constable to speak with. And the same for the steward in charge of these lands, if he hasn't sent word to the crown when things are this dire."

"I wish you luck, sir, but I doubt you'll be able to move him. The folks say that he's paid one hundred gold a year to look the other way regarding the bandits, sir."

"Don't call me sir," I said, a little more sternly this time. "Look, Irvine, the truth is that I'm an Earl. If you insist on calling me some sort of honorific, then 'My Lord' would be the proper form of address."

Rather than reassuring the boy, he abruptly prostrated himself before me, which simply made me even more uncomfortable. "Forgive me, My Lord! I had no idea you were of noble birth! I—"

"Stop, stop—stand up," I said. "Look, here, I'll show you. This is the proper way for a citizen to bow to a lord."

I showed him the correct posture to begin the bow, the motions and depth to which he should lower himself, informed him how long he should hold the position. I then spent several moments explaining the nuances, although it was clear from the boy's awed expressions that the lesson wouldn't be sinking in anytime soon. I ended the lesson with a hint of exasperation as the boy tried, and failed, to correctly emulate my bow.

"Perfect," I lied. "But don't worry too much about bowing outside of an official audience. I mean, I didn't introduce myself, so there's no way that you could have known. Most of the time a noble shouldn't expect formalities like this unless they have servants with them to announce them and to educate their visitors on the proper etiquette. And even then, in the last ten years or so, with the arrival of the Travelers . . . well, it's very hit or miss on whether or not a Traveler is willing to display any respect for noble blood at all. The ones who do are often too enthusiastic about it, while most seem to disregard it entirely. That attitude has begun to bleed over into the Natives of the capital, and only the strictest of the nobles there still insist upon it. I personally do not care much one way or the other."

"Thank you, My Lord, for the lesson! I will show the others and practice hard! I really am lucky to have met you, or I might have embarrassed myself should the new landlord ever come to our little village, although the elders say that is very unlikely. They say that he is a spoiled brat who has never set foot outside of the capital, a royal bastard who was only given his title and lands by the mercy of the late king, and that he's unlikely to view us as anything other than a source of income to be bled dry to support his lavish lifestyle. They say that we can expect taxes to triple next season, and that we can forget about help with the bandits from him."

"Who says this?" I asked.

"It's the word throughout the shire, My Lord. But ultimately, I suppose it's the steward's men who have been spreading the rumors. My pa says that it's fifty-fifty either way whether their words are true, as it might just be that the good steward doesn't want us peasants appealing to the lord directly for help. I certainly wish that we had a lord like you instead. Someone who's not afraid to stand up to bandits!"

I covered my face in frustration. "Irvine . . . I am Earl Hail Jeoran." The look on the boy's face showed that he did not recognize my name immediately, so I clarified. "I'm lord of North Shire and Thorn March, Irvine. These lands were given to me by my grandfather just before he was murdered. I hadn't had time to visit them before now, and it seems that was a mistake."

The boy's expression turned from confusion to mortification to terror as he realized his error. He again prostrated himself, to my frustration, as he gushed to apologize for his disrespect and insults.

"Irvine, please stop! Stand up!" I begged. "Look, I'm not angry at you, honest. Actually, I'm grateful, you've been a valuable source of information."

"Please don't have me whipped, My Lord!" the boy sobbed.

"I am not going to have you whipped!" I nearly shouted.

"My grandfather once worked in the last lord's manor, but he was thrown out after he spilled a glass of wine while serving the lord breakfast, and the lord had him whipped down to a tenth of his Health. Then they just threw him out into the snow. If I had known who you were, My Lord, I swear I would never have been so—"

I abruptly [Polymorphed] him into a rabbit. "There. That is your punishment for the disrespect you have shown me. Once the magic fades, we will not speak of it again," I told the rabbit Irvine. I honestly did it just to stop him from blundering even worse than he already had, but I knew that sometimes if you "punish" someone for their mistakes, they feel better afterwards. "Now then, when the magic fades, and you return to your true form, I expect you to saddle my steed and prepare him for a fast journey. I have to get to Ebbyvale soon to speak with my constable and my steward."

I left Shadow and the [Polymorphed] stable boy behind, returning to the inn, where the innkeeper was nowhere to be found at first. I checked the kitchen only to find it empty, but I heard a noise from the cellar, so I investigated that next and found the innkeeper and his staff hiding there.

"Have you finished washing my property?" I asked of him. "It seems that I will not be spending the night in this village after all."

The man sputtered, clearly surprised to see me so calm after being assaulted by the bandits he had failed to hide me from. I did not bear him a grudge over revealing my location, because although he was level forty, he clearly did not have a combat class, and it was obvious that the locals were used to capitulating to the bandits. When he saw that I was not burning his inn down in my outrage, he eventually recovered and showed me where my clothes were drying outside.

They were clean but still damp. I equipped them using the system rather than putting the damp things on directly.

Somewhat uncomfortable in the half-dried clothing, I tossed the innkeeper a few coins for his services. He seemed surprised, but they quickly disappeared into his inventory.

"Do the bandits often ambush your guests?" I inquired.

"Not in the village, My Lord. Usually they get them on the road, and then they come to my establishment to drown their sorrows with whatever pocket change they manage to hide," the man admitted. "I had thought you must have already met them and come to an accord with them before you arrived. I swear by my honor that it was not my intention to disarm you to make their job easier for them. I pay six gold per month to the bandits for the safety of my establishment and my guests, and I'm quite angry that those ruffians have violated their agreement. But who am I to turn to? The constable refuses to admit that the bandits exist, even as he takes their bribes, and the steward will not hear of our troubles at all. He insists that we are simply trying to get out of our taxes, which are still based on the assessment from thirty years ago, when this land was more prosperous and without the plague of Banditry that besets it now."

"Of course they are," I sighed. Assessments were supposed to take place every seven years, but it wasn't uncommon for a lord to be negligent with the duty in order to both save the coin and effort that such an undertaking requires and to set the taxes at a high point in a land's prosperity.

I wondered if my grandfather had known of all the problems that beset the lands he had given me before he'd assigned them. Probably. It could have been part of some sort of test, to see how I would handle the governance, whether I could bring these neglected lands into prosperity. Certainly Uncle Auroras had seemed to know; I suspected he had deliberately dumped me on a path where he could expect that I would encounter the bandits.

Taking my leave of the beleaguered innkeeper, I returned to the front yard, where Irvine was holding Shadow for me. I tossed him another silver coin for his trouble, mounted my horse, and turned to leave.

"My Lord?" Irvine said before I rode away. "You should know, some of the constable's men, well, they're just as bad as the bandits themselves. Some of them are worse."

"Thank you for the warning, Irvine," I said, and I tossed him another silver. "Don't worry. I won't be facing them alone. I have powerful allies, and together we'll set the shire to rights. You have my word on that."

The lad seemed surprised by my promise, then he broke into a goofy grin. "I'll be telling my grandkids about this day, I wager. The day I met the great Earl Jeoran and took care of his mighty steed on his way to do battle and save the shire from bandits."

I shook my head. "Perhaps you will. Blessings of Thedum upon you and your house, Irvine."

"Blessings of Thedum upon you, Hail Jeoran," the boy responded.

Kicking Shadow into a gallop, I updated the guild on my findings and my intentions. In the truest display of the Travelers' strange mentality I had ever seen, they were simultaneously extremely excited by the trouble I had uncovered in my lands and just as enthusiastic to help end it. I was informed that I could expect over a hundred Travelers of mixed levels to meet me in Ebbyvale, many of whom were already scouring the town for rumors, information, and hidden quests.

I couldn't share their enthusiasm, but at least I wouldn't have to do this task alone.

17

ARRIVAL

The cry of a wyvern alerted me that Tarisha had finally located me. She swooped down in my path, and I pulled Shadow to a stop. Surprisingly, Corinth was riding double with her in the saddle that she had modified to accommodate me. We dismounted to exchange greetings, and I noticed something upsetting.

"Tarisha, you've lost a level," I said.

She hung her head. "Were you not told? I am very sorry, Lord Hail, but I failed the challenge quest to defeat the assassin at your uncle's house. After defeating me in solo combat, she used an item that allowed her to escape retribution from the other members of <Peasant's Revenge>. She has been bragging about the duel on the forums since then. The only consolation I can offer is that I have learned that you were not the target. In fact, her own quest was to kill me, although I do not know who issued her the quest or why."

"Then why did she attack me?" I asked.

"She apparently knew of my [Keep Him Safe] boon and thought that killing you would disable it to make the task of defeating me easier," Tarisha explained. "It proved unnecessary, as my acceptance of the challenge quest disabled the Pee Vee Pee bonus that boon grants me. We fought on equal terms, and I was defeated fairly. It was a humbling experience, and I have realized that I have grown complacent in my skills. I have redoubled my efforts in maintaining and improving my combat ability."

"I'm sorry," I said.

"It's quite alright. I am viewing it as a valuable learning experience," she said.

I turned to Corinth. "I'm surprised to see you here. I figured that you would be waiting in Ebbyvale with the others."

"Yeah, well, I begged Tarisha for the ride to meet you. I wanted to thank you, man. The boons I got from saving your ass last time are the bomb. Seriously. I got [Spitting in the Eye of Death], which is literally one of the coolest buffs in the game that I've ever heard of, but also [I'll Take a Bullet for You], which decreases the Damage I take from an attack directed at someone else by ninety percent and gives me a thirty percent Damage buff for five seconds after I do so. I mean, I'm not a tank, but that's a seriously awesome ability," he said.

"I'm glad you're happy with it, but I don't actually have any control over whether the Travelers I adventure with get a boon or not," I admitted. "If I did, I'd give them out much more frequently."

"Yes, well, I still have to say thank you, man. Double high-five!" he said, raising his hands. Somewhat familiar with this Traveler custom, I responded appropriately. His jubilant expression abruptly changed after the ritual, however, as he examined an unexpected popup.

"What the fuck?" he exclaimed. "I just got cursed!"

I felt a wave of dread flow through me. "Is it [Gray Man's Touch]?"

"No, it's [Reaper's Embrace]. It's not the same as your curse—it doesn't reset me to level one, although I still get the Experience boon. But when I die, I lose ten times the amount of Experience that I've gained from [Through the Valley of the Shadow]. Basically it's the same thing, though; if I gain any significant amount of Experience under the curse and then die, my level will drop like a stone," Corinth explained. Then, before Tarisha realized what he was about to do, he abruptly reached out and touched her with his cursed limb.

She did not respond favorably, drawing her blade and putting it to his throat in an instant. "What in the seven hells do you think you are doing?" she demanded.

"Sorry, just seeing if this was going to be an epidemic," Corinth said, chuckling. "Did you get it too?"

"No," she said, "and that's the only reason I haven't sent you to the lobby. Perhaps I should anyway, to see if death will cleanse the curse."

"Oh come on, you're overreacting," Corinth objected.

"I don't think I am," Tarisha said. She pressed her blade against his throat. "I think I'm reacting quite appropriately."

"Tarisha, wait," I said. "I mean, yeah be mad at him, but, well, we did need to find out of [Reaper's Embrace] would spread from Traveler to Traveler. If I can't cure [Gray Man's Touch], then there's a good chance I'll end up infecting other Travelers as well, so we need to know how to deal with the lesser version of the curse. And honestly, it's just dumb luck that I infected Corinth before I infected you, right?"

The former dancer glared at the teenager for a moment. "You are right. We do need to experiment to learn how to handle this situation. I vote the next experiment is to kill Corinth to see if his curse is removed."

I shook my head. "No. He needs to visit with a priest first. The priests of Thedum may have heard of our curses before and know how to deal with them."

"Hey, look, if dying really is the only way to remove this, then yeah, I'll totally let you Pee Kay me, okay?" Corinth said. "Sorry, by the way. I guess that was a dick move, wasn't it?"

"Yes, Corinth, yes it was," Tarisha said. Then, still glaring at him, she reluctantly sheathed her sword. "I think that the line to the temple in Ebbyvale will be shorter than the one in the capital. However, I'm not in the mood to let you ride shotgun with me any longer. I suggest you make your own way back."

"Right. Sorry again," Corinth said. "I'm just going to . . . yeah."

His body vanished as he Fast Traveled away. Tarisha glared at the spot where he had vanished for a moment, then forcibly put aside her anger and turned to me. "I would try to hug you, Lord Hail, but the curse complicates things. I think that it will be best if you ride the rest of the way to Ebbyvale on your new mount while I escort you."

"Yeah," I agreed, looking at my left hand. It didn't look any different than it had before, but I still had a light tingling feeling from it. "I understand. Still, it is good to see you. I was a little worried about getting ambushed on the road again, but now I sort of hope that we do."

"Indeed. Many of your higher-level followers have already begun scouting North Shire for possible bandit hideouts. They are just waiting for you to arrive in the hopes that when you do, you will issue a quest to initiate a purge," she explained.

"Right. Well, we should get going." I remounted Shadow, and Tarisha her wyvern, and we were back on the road. She rode next to me rather than taking to the sky, which limited our speed, but the conversation was much better. Another two members of <Peasant's Revenge> quickly caught up with us as we got underway, and I would pity any bandits who tried ambushing me after that. They circled overhead as we rode, their constant vigil keeping me safe.

The population of Ebbyvale was approximately six thousand, before the Travelers arrived. That may not sound like a lot compared to the half a million or so of Zhesa City, but it was by far the largest settlement in North Shire, and the third largest city of northern Yuikon. It existed mostly as the seat of the shire, where the previous lord had made his home before dying of . . . a less than noble cause. Having not left an heir, the land reverted to the crown, which sent a young scribe to serve as steward.

The shire was pastoral and agricultural in nature. A few of the local lords had made gestures of trying to incorporate the land into their existing territory, but my grandfather had rebuffed their efforts, as they were already at the limit of what they were legally entitled to manage with their current ranks, and he deemed them unworthy of an elevation to the next rank of nobility.

Because, as an Earl, I was at the lower end of the noble spectrum, the shire was only about a third of the land I was legally allowed to own. However, there had been no readily available earldom for me to snatch up without giving the boot to a noble family that had been managing it for centuries, and so Grandfather had made the compromise of giving me two non-adjacent territories. It wasn't that big of a problem; even if I couldn't Fast Travel, most nobles would have [Mages] in their employ who could quickly [Portal] them between their various holdings.

Thorn March was the larger of the two territories, but it was also the less populated. While the primary exports of North Shire were grain and livestock, Thorn March was known only for its production of thornberry wine. The land was somewhat mountainous and inhospitable to common food crops, but the native thornberry bushes were plentiful. While the vineyards produced hundreds of thousands of bottles per year, the wine was seen as a low-class beverage, valuable only in bulk. It was sold throughout the Heartlands, but the price was only a few coppers for a glass, so it was not seen as a profitable industry.

Inwardly, I once more thanked my grandfather's shade for thrusting these noble lands upon me as Ebbyvale came into view. Sincerely. I was not grumbling at the interruption they were putting on my leveling progress, or the trouble that solving their difficulties would cause me. I was certain that he wouldn't have intentionally given me lands knowing that they were filled with strife. Just like he wouldn't have encouraged me to make one of my first acts as a noble to insult three-fourths of his court with cleverly disguised compliments. That was not like him at all.

Many of the Travelers had noticed my flying escorts, and so there were dozens of them waiting for me outside the sleepy pastoral town. Familiar faces were in the front lines, including the quartet whom I had first encountered outside Zhesa City in my ill-fated attempt at running away from home.

I was pleased to note that, in my absence, Thena, Phil, Larissa, and Laurant had all gained more than ten levels and were now averaging level forty-five. That did mean that I had fallen behind them again, but I wasn't too worried about it. Once I finally sorted out the trouble with my lands, I was determined to go on a leveling spree that no Traveler would be able to keep up with. Especially with the bonus of [Through the Valley of the Shadow]. Assuming that there was no way to cleanse [Gray Man's Touch], at least. If I could get rid of the curse, then I would; the risk was simply not worth the benefits. If I couldn't . . . well, I guess I would just have to try very hard not to die.

"Hey, kiddo!" Laurant called when I came within earshot. "Good to have you back."

I grinned. "You've been busy while I was gone."

"Yeah, I mean, you did say not to wait for you," he reminded me.

"I'm happy for you. Don't worry, I'll catch up in no time, and before long you'll be the ones who are falling behind."

He grinned sheepishly and rubbed the back of his neck. "Yeah, you're probably right. So then, what's the order of business? We've been talking to the locals trying to get the lay of the land, but all of them are pretty tight-lipped. I get the feeling that they're too scared of the bandits to trust us, and few of them are willing to say a bad word about the sheriff or the steward."

"He's a constable, not a sheriff," I corrected. "And he's the first person I need to speak with. I would very much like an explanation of why these roads are unsafe for Travelers."

"Righto. Mind if we ride with you?" Phil asked.

"Sure. Just be careful not to touch my left hand. I don't want to curse anyone by accident like I did to Corinth."

The two dozen or so Travelers formed something of a circle around me as we traveled to the constabulary, while some others rode ahead when they heard my destination. I chatted amiably with the others. I had mostly kept everyone up to date through guildchat, popping in whenever I had a significant update on my situation, but I rarely paid attention to it outside of those times, so they were quite eager to tell me about the adventures they'd had in my absence.

Mostly they had been following one of the many prescribed leveling paths that their kind had developed for quickly gaining power while inside the kingdom of Yuikon, although they confided to me that before long, they would have to journey to one of our neighboring nations to continue reaching new heights. I frowned at this reminder; Yuikon was in the very heart of the Heartlands. While this made us one of the safest nations in the world to live in due to the relatively low number and levels of darkspawn, it also meant that few Travelers remained here longer than was necessary to get to level sixty. If I was to follow the Traveler's path to power, that would mean that I, too, would need to leave my home nation relatively soon.

For the first time, I began to consider the implications of traveling the world in the quest for levels. It wouldn't be an issue if I was simply a royal bastard, but having been given the rank of Earl, I would need to be mindful of politics on my journey. There were likely lands where Travelers could pass freely where I would not be welcome. And on the other hand, once news of my travels spread through foreign courts, I might find myself the recipient of invitations, which I would find hard to refuse, to areas where Travelers seldom went.

I shook my head to clear it. I was getting ahead of myself. I had to put North Shire in order before doing anything else. And that meant confronting the constable over why he was letting bandits run rampant through my lands.

We came to the constabulary building. It was one of the larger buildings in the small city, mostly because it was built to hold dozens of prisoners in its cells.

I turned to my companions. After a moment's consideration, I nodded towards Phil. "Phil, would you mind going in and announcing me? I should probably get a valet or something for official visits like this, but, I mean, there's like a thousand things I haven't had time to do yet and—"

"Quest accepted," Phil said. "Just tell me what to say."

"Just say 'Earl Hail Jeoran has come to see the head constable of North Shire.'"

"Right." The big [Warrior] proceeded to kick open the front door to the constabulary, and, with a [Battle Cry], shouted the words I'd given him.

I covered my face in embarrassment. That wasn't exactly what I had envisioned, but I supposed it would work.

18
INVESTIGATION

[Battle Cry] is an ability common to [Warriors] and many of their subclasses and advanced classes. It provides a morale boost to the [Warrior]'s allies, while simultaneously decreasing the morale of the opponents. It is, therefore, technically an attack. Using an ability like that inside of a city, town, or village was therefore somewhat against the law, although the fine would likely only be a few silver.

Still, it should have gotten some sort of response from the occupants of the constabulary. However, a moment passed, and nothing happened. Another moment passed, and still nothing happened. Phil stuck his head inside the building, and he laughed.

"There's some guy sleeping on the desk in there," he said.

"Wake him up," I suggested. Phil entered the building, and I followed. Shadow disappeared into my shadow as I approached the building. Thena, Laurant, Larissa, and Tarisha joined me. Tarisha requested the others remain outside due to the lack of space.

Upon entering the constabulary, I immediately realized how the desk attendant could have slept through the [Battle Cry]. There were three empty bottles of thornberry wine next to him, and one half-empty bottle. Phil picked up the partial bottle and glanced at me for permission. I shrugged, and he upended the bottle over the sleeping constable. This, at last, caused the man to jerk awake and sputter in outrage.

"Who are you? What do you think you're doing? Do you know who I am?" the man questioned in his outrage.

"Are you the head constable?" I asked him.

"What? No, he's out—"

"Then you're fired," I informed him simply.

He jerked in surprise, no doubt because the system had just informed him his [Status] had changed, and that he really had just lost his [Job]. He turned to me, and this time with a bit of fear in his voice, asked again, "Who are you?"

"I am Earl Hail Jeoran, which you would know if you weren't a drunken slob who could sleep through a [Battle Cry] that half the town heard. Now get out. Leave your badge of office and your keys. You can wear your uniform home, but I suggest you find a change of clothes soon. If you wear it after today, you will be charged with impersonating an officer of the law."

With an unsteady hand, trembling from fear and the shock of his sudden change in [Status], he unfastened the badge from his breast and placed a set of keys on the desk in front of him.

"Is the head constable in the building?" I asked again.

"No, he only comes in but once a week," the former constable answered. "Or if he's arrested a new prisoner, but he never stays long."

I nodded. I stuck my head back outside the door and shouted, "Would someone kindly find me the head constable and bring him to me as soon as possible? Tell him his lord has words for him. He probably doesn't want to hear them, but you can drag him here with one Health point left if that's what it takes. I don't really care."

I ducked back into the room, ignoring the chorus of "Quest accepted" from outside. The former constable was looking quite frightened. Not at me as much as Tarisha. It was unlikely that he had ever seen someone above level one hundred before.

"You may return to your home. I am serious about changing out of that uniform, citizen. I suppose you could return it to the constabulary; perhaps your replacement will buy it from you," I suggested.

"Yes, My Lord," the man said, and he hurried out of the room. I picked up the objects that he left behind. The silver circle of the constabulary and a set of keys. Curious, I began to explore the building.

The ground floor of the constabulary was mostly offices. The largest belonged to the head constable, which was cluttered with papers. Most of the others were vacant, I noticed. There was a communal workspace with desks, which seemed to have seen recent use by someone, although the building was presently empty of any of the shire's law enforcement.

At first I thought the entire building was empty, but then I heard the cries and the moans coming from the lower floor. What I found when I followed the sounds to their source upset me quite a bit. Beneath the constabulary was supposed to be a set of simple holding cells in which the accused would be held until the circuit magistrate arrived to review their case. The constable had turned it into a dungeon.

There were ten cells, and in each of them were between ten to fifteen people. A quick glance showed that most of them were below fifty percent Health. A few of them were barely above ten percent.

"Thena!" I called. "Heal these people, please."

"Of course," she said, stepping past me. They were mostly low-leveled peasants, and as such she was able to quickly bring them to full Health. As they recovered their Health, many of them also began to recover their spirits, and they turned to us with hope in their eyes.

"Earl Jeoran," a woman said, stepping to the front of her cell. The others seemed to defer to her, and they bowed when she did. "We are your loyal subjects."

"Would you please explain why you are imprisoned down here?" I asked.

"Myself? I spat in the steward's drink, I did," she admitted. "I was doing it for weeks before he figured it out. Then he called his friend, the constable, and well, I've been here ever since. Figured I'd die down here until I heard your servant announce you. And now we can only hope that you are an honorable and just lord who will set things to rights in this land."

I surveyed the prisoners, [Analyzing] them, but aside from the fact that they were all relatively low-leveled civilians, there wasn't much I could tell at a glance. "Are you saying that you have all been unjustly imprisoned by the constable and the steward?"

"Well, no," she admitted. She pointed towards one of the cells. "Three men in that cell are accused of murder. And some of the rest have committed a few petty crimes, mostly due to their poverty. But the crime that most of us have committed is to speak out against the steward or his lackeys. Or to resist their unjust rule in some fashion."

I sighed, rubbing my temples in frustration. Another headache that I didn't want to deal with. "How long until the magistrate arrives?"

"Magistrate?" the woman laughed. "My Lord, I have been down here six years. There is no justice in this land. When the traveling judge does arrive, he drinks, he eats at the steward's mansion, and he laughs and jokes and has a merry time. Then he leaves the shire without ever holding court. The steward is the judge and the jury in the shire, My Lord. And sometimes, the constable is his executioner."

"Sounds like I need a new magistrate too, then," I muttered. I turned to my friends. "Okay. So, I honestly don't know what to do here. Some of them might have committed crimes, but it sounds like a lot of them are innocent and are being imprisoned illegally. I can't just leave them down here, but it will take a lot of time to figure out which ones need to be brought before a magistrate for a trial and which ones should never have been imprisoned to begin with."

The Travelers exchanged looks, and it was Phil who stepped forward. "So, in our world, when someone is accused of a crime and is awaiting trial, they are sometimes released into the community on bail. They are required to provide money or property to be held to ensure that they show up for their trial. When they appear, that property is returned to them."

The woman laughed. "That sounds like a fine idea, but if any of us had any property worth anything we would either not be down here, or the constable would have long ago confiscated it."

"Perhaps, but it does give me an idea." I turned to the spokeswoman of the prisoners. "What is your name, good woman?"

"I am Bell."

"Bell, will you swear by Thedum that you have not perjured yourself to me?" I asked.

"I swear by Thedum's holy name that I have spoken only the truth as it is known to me since I heard the mighty voice of a [Warrior] announce the presence of the Lord of North Shire," she said, and she moved her hands to make the symbol of Thedum before her.

"Right. Good enough for me," I said. I turned to my friends. "So, this might be a hassle, but could you question each of these prisoners about why they're imprisoned? If they can swear by Thedum that the only reason they are imprisoned is resistance against the steward or the constable, let them go. If it's something petty or stupid, let them go. If they're accused of an actual crime, but will swear by Thedum to appear before a magistrate to answer for it, then let them go. Unless it's something like assault, Banditry, or murder. You know, something serious."

My friends exchanged looks, and all said, "Quest accepted," except for Tarisha. I think Tarisha declined most quests that generated around me in order to stay close to me instead.

"What will you be doing next, My Lord?" she asked.

"I'm going to start going through the head constable's papers to try to figure out this mess," I explained.

"Then I shall keep you company for that task. I will not leave your side so easily at this time," she said.

"That's fine. You four got this, right?" I asked.

"Yup. Always wanted to be a cop," Phil said, and so I tossed him the keys to the cell. Tarisha and I returned to the ground floor, where she stood stoically while I began rummaging through the papers in the main office, trying to figure out how things had gotten so bad. There was no organization to the documents that I could find. I was expecting arrest reports, status reports on investigations into the bandits, or details on the status of the shire and the surrounding lands. Instead I found receipts for wine and food, the price of which was extravagant. I found poorly written poetry and love letters from a viscountess in the neighboring county, who repeatedly asked for gifts of jewelry, perfumes, clothes, and other fine things. I examined the bookshelf, and instead of finding books on law and law enforcement, I found the collected works of several comedians known for their bawdry tales of debauchery and obscenity.

Finally, after thirty minutes, I found a ledger. It was hidden in the bottom drawer of the head constable's desk behind a lock, which I had unceremoniously jimmied with a dagger that had been carelessly left unsheathed on the desk. I scanned through a few pages of the ledger, and I couldn't help but laugh.

"It seems that I've been giving the good constable too little credit," I said, mirthful. "Or perhaps too much."

"Lord Hail?" Tarisha inquired.

"Oh, it's just that he's made my investigation into the corruption of this constabulary quite easy for me. He's been recording all his bribes and misuse of public funds in this ledger. He wasn't even trying to disguise it in code or something like that. Look here, it says 'beat Farmer Penton until he gave up his hidden coins. Twenty-two silver. Payment for protection from Northridge Bandits. Sixteen gold.' And here, he charged the shire for a visit to a brothel. Oh, and it seems that he's being paid a salary of five hundred gold per year, which is about twenty-five times what a *competent* constable of a territory of this size and population would draw." I shook my head in bemusement, then stashed the ledger in my inventory. "That's his base pay, not including all the bribes he's been taking. It seems that the constable of North Shire is a very lucrative position to hold."

"So, what do we do next?" Tarisha inquired.

I sighed. "I suppose I write the court in Zhesa requesting a special inquisitor and magistrate to investigate the constable's corruption. I mean, given the amount of evidence I have at hand, I could just pronounce judgment right now, but the penalty for corruption on this scale would be execution. I'd . . . I'd rather that judgment come from a magistrate's lips than mine."

"Of course, My Lord," Tarisha said, clearly sympathetic to my dilemma.

I sat down at the constable's desk, took his stationery, enchanted his ink, and began to write a letter that would mean the constable's death. I addressed it to the head of the inquisitors, detailed the evidence of corruption that my brief visit had uncovered—including a description of the ledger—requested a formal investigation into the matter, and sealed the letter with [Magical Seal: Personal Crest]. Then, after a moment of consideration, I also sealed the document with wax and the stamp that I had been using for my letters for most of my childhood.

The letter seemed abnormally heavy in my hands as I exited the constabulary to look for someone to deliver it.

19
TOURNAMENT

"You're going down, Ice-Man," Lyra said, facing her opponent head on, psyching herself up for their final confrontation.

"In your dreams, harlot," came the answering taunt. "Ice-Man," or Gregory, was a burgeoning [Cryomancer], while his opponent was some sort of [Rogue]. Normally in a duel, Lyra would be at something of a disadvantage at the start of the fight if she was unable to begin in [Stealth]. Simultaneously, Gregory would be disadvantaged by the fact that they were standing within arm's reach, or in other words, easy stabbing range.

However, this was not a battle of arms, but of wit and chance, and all parties had agreed to abide by the outcome of the combat.

"Paper, rock, scissors, shoot," the combatants said in unison, slamming their fists together in the ritualized manner that the Travelers had brought with them from their world. Gregory chose paper. Lyra chose scissors.

"And the crowd goes wild!" she shouted, extending her arms above her head in victory.

"Whatever. You'll never make it to the final round," Gregory predicted, unable to take his loss with grace. He moped back out into the audience, leaving the remaining matches ongoing as the impromptu tournament continued. I watched the organized chaos taking place in the yard outside the constabulary with bemusement.

"I don't see why everyone is going through all of this trouble to figure out who gets the letter," I commented to Tarisha. She simply shrugged.

"Everyone wants it, but only one person can have it. Since you don't have a preference, your guild had to come up with some sort of fair method. Personally, I would have just had everyone roll and leave it up to Are En Gee, but this tournament is as fair as anything else," she explained.

"Yeah, but I don't get why so many people are fighting for it," I clarified. "I mean, the last time I asked for messengers everyone ended up in prison."

"Actually, some of them are still in prison," Tarisha informed me.

"What?" I asked, surprised. "But I told everyone to burn the letters days ago! They even said that the guards would let them out as soon as they did so!"

"Yes, they can leave at any time. However, that would cut off their access to the Beggar Court. I'm not certain if anyone mentioned it to you or not, but those who were imprisoned on your behalf actually got a significant boon. Building Reputation with the Beggar Court is normally a very difficult and tedious process, which very few people have attempted. The half dozen or so of your messengers who are still imprisoned have access to a few repeatable quests that are allowing them to farm it far more effectively than any other method I've ever heard of."

"The Beggar Court? Wait, that's real?" I asked. "Beckah always told me that it was just a fairy tale."

Tarisha simply shrugged. "There is most certainly a faction that calls itself the Beggar Court, but as I said, it's very difficult to find quests and grind Rep with them, so not very much is known about them on the Traveler side of things. I guess I wouldn't know the lore behind how the Natives see them, so it wouldn't surprise me at all if most Natives consider them a rumor or myth."

I frowned, unsettled by this new wrinkle in things. The Beggar Court, supposedly, traced its origins back to the last time the succession of the throne was in doubt. Two cousins, both with equally strong claims, had agreed to settle the matter peacefully with a game of chance. The winner ascended, while the loser claimed that his opponent had cheated and spent the rest of his life undermining the government. In the end, all the loser's supporters had their lands and property confiscated. Many were executed for treason, while their families were condemned to live in poverty.

That much was history and was beyond dispute. What wasn't in the history books, and remains a topic for bards and poets, were the fates of the noble bloodlines that were dispossessed. While it was common for upstarts and troublemakers to claim a link to one of those five families, there were also many tales of scions becoming heroes and patriots to make up for the deeds of their family's past.

I had enjoyed the stories as much as anyone else, but never believed they were true. As I considered it, I also considered the possibility that the Beggar Court that the Travelers interacted with needn't be linked to the real noble families from the past. It could, in fact, be a reclusive group that was simply using the name.

I made a note to ask more about the players who were gaining Reputation with that faction. They might be benign, or they might be a threat to the kingdom. Not that it would necessarily fall on me to root them out if they were malicious, but I might want to ask my friends to distance themselves from them if they were.

"Hail," Tarisha began, interrupting my thoughts. "There is a topic I have been dancing around for some time now. That of documenting your actions for posterity."

"Have you been recording me again?" I asked calmly.

"Not since the last time the topic was broached," she assured me. "However, many of the Travelers who are in leadership positions in my guild and yours have been discussing the matter among ourselves. We have something of a framework we would like to discuss with you."

"I'm listening."

"First of all, I would like to remind you that this matter only applies to Travelers in <Nethersong Mavericks> and their allied guilds. Unaffiliated Travelers will probably continue to record you whenever they realize they are in your presence, and we have no control over what they will do with those recordings. We can only police ourselves; we cannot enforce this policy on anyone outside of our alliances."

"I understand that," I agreed. I knew enough about Travelers to know that getting them all to agree to something would be like expecting a bucket of sand to spontaneously become a stained glass window.

"The basic proposal contains two points. The first point is to have a process for gaining approval for the release of any recordings of your person or actions. Subtleghost and Bandit have volunteered to be the point people on this matter. With your permission, they would like to begin reviewing and categorizing all the recordings that have thus far been made without your knowledge. If there are any that are notable or exceptional, they would ask for your approval before allowing the person who recorded or edited them to release them. The only recording that they have agreed on so far that might be worthy of releasing is the one of your confrontation with Storm. We feel that releasing this video now would help many Travelers make up their minds on who to support in the succession."

"That's fine with me," I agreed. "If that's all there is, then I guess I might have overreacted a bit."

"That's not all there is, Hail," Tarisha admitted nervously. "Hail, you must understand, it's actually very common for Travelers to record their gameplay and share it, both with other Travelers and with people who don't even play this game directly. A few Travelers in both our guilds, and in <Ragtag Muffin>, fall into this category. You're not exactly the exclusive topic of their videos, but you have appeared in a number of streams and compilations. In turn, those videos have been compiled by others who have been looking for information about you. While the members of our guilds have all agreed to take down their own videos, there isn't anything we can do about the third parties who have already copied them. Truthfully, we didn't realize how serious the situation was until just recently, and I must apologize for not bringing it to your attention sooner."

I frowned. "Did they leak anything important?"

"Not really. A few scenes of you training or fighting, but mostly it's just you being you," she explained.

"I see," I said.

"As I said, Hail, it's very common for Travelers to record themselves while they're in this world. A lot of them actually record everything they do, then delete everything except for highlights of particular interest. I'm in that category as well, although I do not publicly share my recordings under most circumstances."

"Are you recording me right now?" I demanded.

"No. And as I said before, I delete more than ninety percent of what I do record. I only keep important battles or interactions. However, since we became allies, so much of my time has been spent with you that I do have a significant backlog of our interactions. As I mentioned, I was hoping that, one day, you would consider releasing an anthology of your early actions so that your story might be known. If you ask me to, however, I will delete everything."

I was quiet a moment, watching the paper rock scissors tournament continue. There had been almost eighty participants to start with, but it was quickly approaching the championship round.

"You should have told me sooner," I said.

"I'm sorry. Truthfully, it's simply so much of a habit for me to document my actions this way that I never considered your feelings on the matter," she admitted. "Most professional players do the same thing, as do most aspiring pros. Even among the amateur player base, a lot of people record themselves just in case something cool happens, then they delete the recordings at the end of their session if nothing of note occurs."

"So I should just assume that everyone is recording me everywhere, all of the time?" I demanded, growing annoyed.

"For unaffiliated Travelers, yes. However, that is the second point of the new policy that I wanted to discuss with you. Namely, that everyone in our allied circle of guilds will have to disclose whether or not they record or stream their gameplay, and that they will inform you when they interact with you if they are currently doing so."

I sighed, as that was another headache I didn't really want to deal with. So I decided to just get over it. "I don't care. I really don't need the distraction of trying to figure out who is recording me or not, and I'm not going to do anything different just because someone is. Just—I don't know. You guys figure it out."

"I assure you, we are working on it. I'm relieved that you're less troubled about the matter than you were when Corinth broached the subject last week, but we really do need to make certain that our resident streamers aren't unintentionally giving away valuable intel to our rivals and opponents," she explained. "And, as I said, we will certainly ask your permission before publishing any videos of particular note."

"Okay," I agreed, and that was the end of the matter as far as I was concerned. The others were finishing up their tournament, and as I watched, the champion emerged. It was, in fact, Lyra who emerged victorious, and she spent a few moments basking in the congratulations and the envy of her audience before stepping over to me.

"Right, here you go," I said, handing over the missive without much fanfare.

"Oh, come on," she challenged. "Where's your sense of showmanship—oh, shit."

"What's wrong?" Tarisha asked, and the others gathered around as the champion examined the quest screen that had popped up for her, and her alone.

"It's not just a simple delivery quest. It's a challenge quest. And it requires a group," she explained, groaning. "Recommended levels sixty to eighty, recommended party size of ten. Teleportation, Fast Travel, and flight are restricted. We need to deliver this to the capital the hard way, and if I'm reading this right, we can expect resistance."

The Travelers burst into discussion as those who had lost the contest began elbowing their way forward to try to get a place in Lyra's group. I frowned, but ultimately lost interest in the topic. As I saw it, it wasn't all that important. Even if the missive was intercepted, I could simply make another one. And with the skills I had gained from my week with Auroras, the document couldn't be altered or forged. It's not like the document contained any secrets or anything, so the worst that the bandits could do by harassing my messengers was slow me down. And, well, it seems that my Traveler friends were quite excited by that prospect.

I shook my head in bemusement. Sometimes I really didn't understand Travelers at all.

20
CITIZENS' ARREST

The party of glorified messengers set out in high spirits at around the same time that Laurant, Phil, and the rest of the gang emerged from the constabulary's holding cells slash dungeon. Phil informed me that they had released all but five of the prisoners, keeping only the three men accused of murder and two more who, although they were not accused of anything heinous, would not swear that they would return to answer for the lesser crimes of which they were accused. I had noticed the steady stream of released prisoners during the tournament but hadn't given it much thought.

The yard remained crowded. Along with the Travelers who were waiting around aimlessly, a few locals had come out to see the commotion. Travelers and Natives alike were mingling, discussing the events of the day. Some of the Natives were the recently freed prisoners reuniting with friends and family, while most had simply been drawn by the crowd.

At some point, I realized that everyone was sitting around and waiting to see what I was going to do next. It was awkward, because I wasn't quite certain what my next steps should be. I needed to confront both the head constable and the steward, but I didn't know where either of them were. Aside from that, I needed to establish my personal residence, which would also be my seat of power in the shire. That shouldn't be difficult, as I could simply claim the previous lord's mansion as my own.

After that, I would spend a few days holding court while my friends gathered intelligence on the bandits. Once they had helped me assess the size and scope of the bandit problem, we would band together and cleanse them from my lands.

But although I had overall goals to meet, I still felt very awkward when I realized how many eyes were on me. Fortunately, it was about this time that a distraction emerged.

"For the last time, you fat pig, no! We are not going to bribe you!" Sophia shouted.

"I'm simply saying that, as a young Traveler, I'm certain that you don't want to spend the next few weeks waiting for the magistrate. It would be much faster to simply pay the fine and for the damage you caused, and we can overlook your vandalism," a grubby voice answered.

"Shut up and take me to jail then, you ugly pervert," she taunted.

The crowd turned towards the raised voices, parting to reveal a small group from <Ragtag Muffin> who were harassing an obese man in a constable's uniform. The uniform was slovenly, and the man was somewhat out of breath. I thought, at first, that the Traveler children were harassing him, but then I noticed a couple details. First, the fact that he was level eighty and then that the children were in shackles. The fat constable, noticing the crowd for the first time, pulled off his hat and examined them with scorn.

"What in the seven hells is all of this, then?" he demanded.

"Are you the head constable?" I asked.

"I'm Constable Montague," he said. "Now who the hell authorized this gathering? Crowds of more than five need a permit to—"

"You're fired," I said. "Also you're under arrest for corruption."

The man bristled. However, the system notified him when his [Job] changed from whatever it was to [Unemployed], or whatever it says when you get fired. Rather than immediately cringing and backing down as the desk attendant had earlier, he pulled himself up. "Who the hell do you think you are? You can't just—"

"Oh sweet! Quest complete!" Sophia exclaimed. She pulled the shackles she had been wearing off, having apparently already picked the locks somehow. "Hail, this guy is a total creep. We found where he was hiding like an hour ago, but we couldn't go inside the house because the stupid system says it's an adult-only location and wouldn't let us inside because we're kids. We didn't want to get help from the adults because we wanted the credit for—"

Montague padded his pocket in surprise, and I realized I was wrong. Sophia hadn't picked the lock on her shackles; she had picked the key from his pocket. She casually tossed it to one of her friends as she spoke, who began unlocking their own shackles.

"Now see here!" the constable began, but I turned him into a donkey. I was a little surprised because usually [Polymorph] defaulted to smaller animals, but I suppose that he was a larger target than normal. And it was also fitting, seeing as his new form seemed to fit his personality.

"—smashing the windows was my idea, but that wasn't enough to get this jerk out of the brothel. It was the smoke bombs that finally did the trick. But it wasn't until we started actually attacking him that he finally seemed to want to arrest us—before that he just kept asking us for bribe money. Even once he had us in chains he kept asking, like you saw, and he dragged his heels the entire way here," Sophia continued, completely ignoring the jackass's commentary.

"Thank you for your efforts, Sophia, and the rest of you," I said. "Did you get anything good for the quest reward?"

She glanced at the others who had completed the quest with her, then at the crowd. "I'll tell you later," she called, and then their group ran off. She might have been intimidated by the size of the crowd, but I don't think that was the reason for her sudden secrecy, considering that she hadn't been bothered at all during the retelling of her and her friends' exploits. She wanted to keep the rewards confidential for some reason, which meant that they were probably more substantial than the Reputation, gold, and Experience that usually came from a quest.

They all ran back the way they had come and seemed excited about something. Tarisha knelt forward and whispered, "I think there's a decent possibility that there is a follow-up quest, which they are now pursuing, My Lord."

"Oh," I said, and before I could contemplate that much further, the [Polymorph] on the former constable broke, and he changed from a literal jackass to just a metaphorical one again.

"That's it, I've had enough!" he declared, and he drew his weapon, a one-handed mace. The sound of almost a hundred Travelers drawing their weapons or preparing their magics gave him a moment of pause.

I smirked. He might be level eighty, which means that I couldn't touch him myself, but he'd have to wade through a sea of bodies to get to me to avenge the indignity I'd shown him with my spell.

"Who the hell are you people? What gives you the right to interfere with the authorized constable of this land?" he demanded. "You're all breaking the law!"

"No, they're not. You seem to have a very short memory. Perhaps that's why you needed to record all of your bribes and corruption in this ledger," I said, pulling the incriminating document from my inventory with just a little bit of a flourish. The moment Montague's eyes fell on it, his face went pale with fear, then purple with anger.

"I have no idea what you're talking about, boy!" he shouted.

"That is no way to address Earl Hail Jeoran, Lord of North Shire!" Phil [Battle Cried], his voice booming throughout the crowded plaza. I winced, wishing that he'd stop doing that. It did, however, give the good constable a moment of pause, and it also seemed to affect the gathered Natives by filling them with some measure of confidence, where before they had been cringing away from the constable whenever he spoke or moved.

"I don't believe it," the constable said. "I would have heard if the new lord was coming to this land! This boy is an impostor!"

"I'm done with this," I said, walking away. "Can you guys just throw him in one of the jail cells for me? Try not to kill him if you don't have to, but if it happens, it will just save us time and money on the trial."

"Quest accepted!" the Travelers in the crowd cheered. The sounds of combat exploded behind me, with the constable trying to rally the townspeople to his side. I didn't think that anyone would answer his calls. Even if they did, I'd trust in my friends' restraint. I tuned it out, walking further into the town.

"Excuse me, which way is it to the steward's home?" I asked one of the Natives who was watching the brawl with wide open eyes. She was a young woman with a babe in her arms, and she eagerly pointed further into the town, giving me directions and a description of the building I was seeking.

"Are you sure it's wise to leave that up to mob justice?" Tarisha asked, following along behind me. She wasn't the only one following me, although most of my crowd had stayed to either watch or participate in the arrest of the constable. Laurant, Thena, and Larissa, were right there with us. Phil had stayed behind, and for a moment I wondered why. Then I remembered that he had the key to the cells in the constabulary, so his presence was probably necessary to lock Montague away. A few other Travelers had decided that whatever I was going to do next was more interesting as well, and they were trailing along behind us at a polite distance.

"I really don't care," I said. "He's probably going to hang in a few weeks. If the others have to rough him up to get him in a cell, well, I'm sure that he's beaten plenty of innocent citizens who were 'resisting arrest' or some nonsense. I mean, it's not like he's a Worldboss or something, is it?"

"No, I suppose at worst he's a named elite," Tarisha agreed.

"I think that you have just insulted every rare spawn in this world by comparing them to Constable Montague," I commented. She chuckled, and we bantered a bit as we strode into the rich part of town. Our target was, unsurprisingly, the largest building we had seen so far, excluding the constabulary itself and perhaps the temple, which was nearby.

I slammed the knocker against the door impatiently, wishing that Phil hadn't stayed behind so that he could "announce me" again. It wasn't strictly proper, but it would no doubt make an impression with the occupants of the building. After I had knocked, I waited patiently. For ten seconds. Then I continued knocking for another five minutes before someone finally answered.

I was about to ask one of my friends to kick the door in—again wishing that Phil was here so that the [Warrior] could do the honors for me—when it was opened by a geriatric woman. She frowned at me and began to berate me for the noise and disturbance I had caused, and for just a second, I felt abashed.

"I am Earl Hail Jeoran," I said, interrupting her tirade. "I'm here to see the steward of my lands. I have several questions about how things have been run while North Shire was in the care of the crown, and—"

She began laughing. "Oh, I knew this day would come! I knew

it! String him high, when it's time. Never saw what my daughter saw in him, no I didn't. Always knew he was good for nothing. He's in the study. This way, this way."

As though a switch had been flipped, the old woman—apparently the steward's mother-in-law—brought us into the house. It was too small to be called a mansion but large enough that we had to pass through several rooms and hallways to reach our destination. Along the way she regaled us with all of her son-in-law's failings, most of which seemed to consist of not being good enough for her daughter and otherwise lacking any moral fiber.

"Arkan! Oh, Arkan, you have guests!" she called as she opened the door to the study.

"Not now! I'm busy! I need to finish reviewing the finances before the new lord arrives and—"

"I'm afraid you have run out of time for that," I said, stepping into the room. "Because I'm right here."

21
FINANCES

The steward, Arkan, took a moment to look surprised at my announcement, and then he quickly schooled his expression into one of calm control. He set his pen down on the desk, stood from his chair, straightened his suit, and bowed deeply. He was a handsome man, and he was wearing the latest trend from the capital, but his clothes were designed more for comfort than fashion. He had, after all, been relaxing in his study and not expecting visitors.

"I greet you and welcome you to my home, My Lord. I wish that you had sent word of your visit beforehand so that I could have prepared a proper welcome for you, but it is of course your prerogative to come and go as you please. Since receiving word of the late king's decree gifting you these lands, I have been busy auditing and preparing a report for you to bring you up to date on your new property. I was hoping to have a chance to review it, and to have a scribe copy it onto more suitable and legible stationery. My handwriting is legible, but only just. However, if you are impatient to learn the lay of your land, the rough draft is mostly ready for your eyes," the man said, his voice calm, showing no hint of fear or anxiety.

"That would be great," I agreed, stepping over to his desk. I had been hoping for a more worried reaction. I sensed no insincerity or bravado in the man's voice, which set me on edge. The constable's corruption had been far too blatant for Arkan to be ignorant. Either the man had nothing to fear, or he was so skilled at hiding it that ice must flow in his veins.

My Traveler friends joined me in the room, closing the door behind us. The woman who had shown us in stayed outside.

"Ah, the ink is still drying on that page," he pointed out when I snatched it from the desk. "And it's the end of the report anyway. This is the beginning."

I ignored him for a moment as I examined the page he had been working on. It was a summary of the current finances, and I could only frown as I read it. The shire was, according to the report, about thirty million gold in debt. It was operating at a loss of about fifty thousand gold per year, which it was covering by borrowing from the Silvercrest bank on an ongoing line of credit. There were three other banks listed as the creditors for the majority of the debt. Much of the expenses of the shire were going simply to the interest of its loans.

We were literally borrowing money to pay back loans we had already taken, and we were doing so under progressively worse terms.

"How did this happen?" I demanded.

"It's all in the report," my steward assured me, handing me a stack of papers. "If you would start at the beginning."

And so I read. The report began with a brief history of the shire. It had been the hereditary property of the Mooncrest family for almost four hundred years, but it had never been particularly prosperous. However, the previous three generations of lords had been increasingly negligent and incompetent in their rule. They had maintained properties at court in the capital using funds from the shire, and when that had been insufficient to maintain their image, they had borrowed heavily, using their income from the shire as collateral.

It had been insufficient to prevent the decline of the Mooncrest family, which had never been large. I was somewhat surprised to learn that the family was not, in fact, extinct. Instead, when the previous lord had died, his heirs had declined their inheritance for the express purpose of avoiding the hereditary debt. The loans were leveraged against the land, not the family name. However, the current Lady Mooncrest was lord of nothing. She had attempted to claim the city residence without the shire's debt, but my great-grandfather had wisely blocked the move. Her fate, and that of the rest of her family, was not mentioned.

I idly wondered if they had joined the Beggar Court.

According to the document, the crown refused to pay the debt that the Mooncrest family had leveraged against the land. The banks had apparently taken the crown to court over the matter several times and had obtained a reluctant ruling that, although the courts could not enforce the debt against the royal family or the taxes from the land, the debt would remain and continue to accumulate interest.

The debts were far from the shire's only expense, of course. The crown continued to demand its taxes without regard to the Mooncrest family's hereditary debt. And although it was small, the shire's local government had its own expenses, including law enforcement and the maintenance of public property. Most years the tax income was sufficient for those debts, but it had never been enough to cover operational costs and the leveraged loans, which was why the line of credit was necessary.

It was all laid out in crisp, clinical detail. I would not be enjoying a nice, comfortable income from my lands anytime soon.

"Are you okay, Hail?" Thena asked when I put the final page of the report into my inventory. "Your expression is . . . well, it sort of looks like you're constipated, to be honest."

"I want the ledgers for the last century," I said, turning to the steward. Arkan opened his eyes in surprise.

"Certainly, My Lord. I will order copies to be made immediately. I had thought that you might want to review the finances yourself, so I already made copies of the ledgers for the past decade, but I will begin working on—"

"Let's start with those, then," I said impatiently. Arkan nodded, and from his inventory he produced a banker's box filled with ledgers. I promptly took it and placed it in my own inventory.

"I'll review them later," I promised. "Where are the originals?"

"I'm afraid the original documents must, by law, be kept in a secure location," Arkan said. "I can take you if you'd like, but we cannot remove them. That is why—"

I pinched the bridge of my nose in frustration. "I'm not an idiot, Arkan. I know the recordkeeping act requires the original copies of official documents to be kept in a location enchanted against fire, dampness, and theft. I also know that accessing the original documents in that location requires official authorization from the lord of the land or their superiors. So if I want to see the original documents, then I would have to get authorization from the lord of North Shire."

I paused for a minute, staring directly at Arkan as I measured his response. His expression turned reptilian, and I could only smile when I said, "Oh wait, that's me, isn't it?"

Without a trace of mirth, the steward produced a key from his pocket and handed it to me. His expression was measured and neutral, but displayed no hint of warmth or friendliness. "The record storage room is located in the lord's manor itself. It's a small room in the basement. The working ledger is kept in the clerk's office in town, which is also where these copies were produced. Their original is still there."

"Excellent. The manor was one of my next stops anyway. Thena, would your group mind picking up the documents in town?" I asked.

I turned to them, my expression as warm as Arkan's was cold, and I was a little surprised when they did not answer right away.

"Did you guys get a quest?" Thena asked, turning to Larissa and Laurant.

"Nope," Laurant said. "Weird, right? I mean, I'm perfectly happy to go to the clerk's office or whatever whether we have a quest for it or not, Hail. It just feels like there should be a quest, right? I mean, this is an official, canon act, right? Seems weird that there's not a quest for it."

I considered for a moment. Then, without asking his permission, I sat down at Arkan's desk and penned a quick letter using his ink, which I first enchanted, and then sealed it with [Magic Seal: Personal Crest]. It was a very simple document authorizing its bearer to access and remove the documents from the clerk's office. When I handed it to Laurant, he nodded.

"Yup, there it is. That's what was missing."

"This truly isn't necessary," Arkan said, his voice calm. "I assure you, it will not take long for the copies to be made and—"

"Arkan, you're fired," I said, staring into his eyes as I said the words. He stiffened.

"I was appointed by your grandfather," he said coldly. "You can't—"

"You might have been appointed by the former king while North

Shire was in the care of the crown, but that does not mean I require royal permission to remove you from your position," I explained calmly.

"I have served honorably and carried out my duties faithfully," he protested. "You'll find nobody better suited to this position, and even if you replace me, it will take them weeks, if not months, to get up to speed on the current state of the shire. You cannot afford to dismiss me at this time."

"You're still fired," I said. "In fact, you're double fired. I insist that you immediately turn over any official documents, keys, seals, or any other items that might serve as a symbol of the authority of the office that you once held."

The man met my eyes, unflinching. I expected anger, outrage, disbelief—anything. His expression was emotionless, as was his voice when he finally spoke. "You are making a mistake."

"Yeah, I do that sometimes," I admitted. "Remind me to tell you about the time I accidentally destroyed a castle. That was a big woops. You're still fired."

The sound of an old woman laughing intruded from outside the room as Arkan produced a keychain from his inventory, a stamp with the Mooncrest family seal on it, and a document signed by my grandfather appointing him to his position.

"If there is nothing else, My Lord, I respectfully request that you leave my residence," he said, and I could almost see his breath, his voice was so cold.

"Goodbye, Arkan," I said.

The door opened, and the old lady came in, wiping a tear of joy from her eye. "Lord Hail! Please ignore my irksome son-in-law's dismissal. You are welcome to stay in *my* home any time you wish! It is an honor to have you under the roof of *my* house!"

"Mother," Arkan began, but the old lady cut him off.

"Oh, shut up, you insufferable fool. And start packing your things! I want you out!"

The former steward finally showed an emotion. Rage. "I bought you this house," he said. "I paid for everything."

"And you put it in my name," she said. "Mine, not yours! You think I'm a fool, but I knew someday this would happen. I'm half blind in my dotage, but I saw further than you."

Arkan's knuckles were white, and his fingernails cut into his palm so deep it began to bleed. "I built this house for your daughter! I only allowed you to stay after she passed into Thedum's embrace because of my love for her."

"You think I don't know what it says on the deed? You think I don't know?" she taunted. She turned to me and smiled. "My house was assessed thirty years ago. This house wasn't around back then. That's why he built it in my name. If he had built this house in his name, he would have had to have it assessed and pay property taxes on it. He thought I didn't know, but I did."

"You cannot simply kick me out, Elara," Arkan objected. "I paid for everything. Everything in this house belongs to me."

"Perhaps, but the house itself doesn't!" she said. She literally leapt with joy, then winced and rubbed her back. "And I want you out, you filthy squatter!"

They continued to argue for a moment, but I had already turned back to the desk. I [Scribed] a quick eviction notice, which I presented to the old woman. "Unfortunately, you're not legally able to remove him from the house tonight, dear woman. If the house truly is in your name, but you have been allowing him to live in it for an extended period of time, you must provide him with at least seven days notice before he's required to vacate. If you sign this document, it will serve as notice. If he does not leave on his own in one week, you may contact the constable to have him forcibly removed."

Elara barely glanced at me as she snatched the paper away and signed it. She left the room, rubbing her back but cackling with glee.

I turned to Arkan, my expression curious. "Perhaps I misjudged you, Arkan. Building such a fine home for your mother-in-law is a true act of generosity. That is why you put it in her name, is it not? Because if you put it in her name to avoid paying taxes on your personal residence, well, that would be a crime, would it not?"

Without saying another word, Arkan left the office, his expression never changing. He was furious, and he wasn't trying to hide it anymore.

"Are you sure it's a good idea to leave him running around?" Tarisha asked me once we were alone. Laurant, Thena, and Larissa leaned in to hear my response. I sighed.

"Unfortunately, I don't have the evidence yet to throw him in jail like the constable. I don't need a reason to fire him, but even though I'm an Earl, I can't order him arrested based on hearsay. Which is why we need to secure the original ledgers before he has a chance to steal or alter them."

"Oh, shit!" Laurant exclaimed. "Our quest just got a timer! Gotta go!"

The party waived their farewells and quickly ran from the room. Tarisha nodded at me.

"We should probably get moving as well, Lord Hail."

"Right," I agreed. "Onward to my new home."

We left the house of my former steward's mother-in-law, her cackling laughter still echoing through the halls.

22
THRONE

The Mooncrest manor was a mile outside of Ebbyvale, and riding Shadow along the path that led to it was pleasant in the evening air. Tarisha was with me, while most of my other friends were busy elsewhere. After the battle with the constable, a veritable wave of locals had descended upon the players and begun issuing local quests. Everyone was very eager, gobbling up as many as they could. I encouraged them through guildchat, as most of the quests involved investigation into the various problems and injustices throughout the shire, and the reports of my guildmates would help me better understand my lands and help solve its problems.

It also solved the problem of everyone looking at me and waiting for my every move. I wasn't afraid of crowds or public speaking or anything, but it was still nice not to be the center of attention for a few moments.

The road was quiet and showed signs of abandonment and disuse. And the manor itself, when we reached it, had clearly not been cared for in decades. The lawn was overgrown, and the paint on the buildings was faded and chipped. Several of the windows were broken, and overall it had the aura of dereliction. It had been a grand estate, once. In the pathway leading up to the front door, I could see several pedestals that had once held statues, but the statues themselves had been hauled away. No doubt sold to pay off the Mooncrest's debts.

As we passed through the empty gateway, Tarisha suddenly tsked. "Lord Hail, it seems that the cat is out of the bag. Several organizations have made it public that new quests are available in North Shire. We can likely expect a wave of independent players to arrive in these lands within the next few days."

"Is that a problem?" I asked. "More people means more help, right?"

"Yes. If they're coming to help," Tarisha agreed. She sighed. "Honestly, I don't know whether this bodes good or ill. This zone isn't high enough level for the true endgame guilds to take notice, but the novelty will be enough to draw some of them anyway. The ones who do will be seeking advantages and will look for ways to profit. And there is also the possibility that at least some of the players who are drawn to this event will seek to align themselves in opposition to us."

I thought about that for a moment. There had been Travelers on the bandit's side. I didn't understand why anyone would want to be a bandit, but the unpredictable and capricious nature of Travelers meant that at least some of them would be drawn to the romance of it. "What should we do about it?"

"I don't know that there is anything we *can* do about it," Tarisha admitted. "And as you mentioned, it might not make matters worse. I would have preferred to keep this event somewhat exclusive to our allies, but Travelers are drawn to events like this like ants to honey. I am slightly annoyed that the information leaked, but I shall have to simply content myself with being at the center of events, while the newcomers will be relegated to the periphery."

I shrugged. "If there's nothing we can do about it, then I'm not going to worry about it for now. Come on, we need to secure those documents."

"Do you think that Arkan will attempt to tamper with them?" Tarisha inquired.

"I think that he has had decades to do so already," I said, recalling the cold look in his eyes once his helpful facade had been pierced. It was common for lords to appoint their own stewards from their friends or family; he very likely predicted the possibility that he would not be keeping his position once the lands had been reassigned. I suspected he was corrupt, but my meeting with him had demonstrated that he was not incompetent. Which was, of course, exactly why I had felt the need to remove him from his position as soon as possible. To do otherwise would be like trying to secure the henhouse while the fox was still inside. Once we reached the doorway, I dismounted, and my mount returned to my shadow in a flash, while Tarisha's wyvern flew off into the distance. "I wish all of my enemies were lazy and incompetent, like the constable."

"Truthfully, I'd rather the challenge of an enemy who fights back," Tarisha admitted, "but I understand your sentiment."

The inside of the manor was much like the exterior. Dust was omnipresent, and the only evidence of the building's former glory was the decorations that were structurally important to the building itself. Everything else had been carted off and sold to settle the Mooncrest's debt. Anything that had any value had already been auctioned off years before my birth.

Which said quite a bit about the quality of the painting that decorated the entryway. A stern looking man—one of the former Mooncrest lords, I assumed—stared down at his arriving guests with a stern expression. Or it was supposed to be stern, I think. It's hard to tell because the brushwork was somewhat splotchy, the nose was crooked, and the eyes were uneven.

Knowing that the document storage room was supposed to be in the basement, Tarisha reluctantly agreed that we should split up to look for it. My explorations took me through the servants' rooms, where the furniture had survived the descent of the vultures somewhat better than the rest of the estate, and in there I found a stairwell leading down. However, the rooms below were only the root and wine cellars. Surprisingly, the wine cellar was still partially stocked, so I spent a few minutes raiding it, stuffing the aged bottles into my inventory. The bottles had likely been cheap vintages and not worth auctioning at the time of the auction, but after aging for thirty years or so, they might be worth something now. Or they might all have turned to vinegar; I wouldn't know until I opened them.

"Lord Hail?" Tarisha called from upstairs.

"Down here," I called, still stashing away my loot. "Did you find it?"

"Not yet, but I found something else you may want to look at," she said, coming downstairs to join me. She noticed my looting and quirked an eyebrow. "In my world, you would be much too young to consume those."

"I'm more likely to sell them than drink them," I confessed, and she gave me an approving nod. "But in this world, I am an adult at age fifteen. Alcohol is legal for me, although getting drunk on it makes me look like an immature fool. Serving it to my guests is a mark of maturity and graciousness, so I figured I'd rob the old Lord Mooncrest blind. He's already dead, so what can it hurt?"

"That is a very Traveler-like attitude. We have a tendency to loot anything not nailed down," she commented.

I shrugged. "What is it you wanted to show me?"

"It's a . . . chair," she admitted. "Well, it's more like a throne, honestly. I wouldn't think anything of it, except that it's probably the most valuable object I've seen in this place, unless any of those bottles are worth a thousand gold. I tried to put it in my inventory to show you later, but when I tried, the system gave me a message. It said, 'You do not have the authority to interact with this object.' I'm fairly certain that's significant."

I paused what I was doing for a second, then continued looting the cellar. "I suppose that's Lord Mooncrest's throne, then. Help me loot these bottles, and then I'd like to see it."

She nodded, and the bottles began disappearing into her inventory as well. We finished quickly, and then I followed her to the room where the former lord of this land once held court. Like everywhere else, it had been looted, but signs of former opulence remained, such as the carvings on the door and murals painted on the wall behind the throne. The throne itself was high backed, a crescent moon carved into the back. It was dark enough in the room that I cast [Spark] a few times for illumination, but I was surprised when a sudden flash of blue lights appeared, resolving into the form of Thomas the Administrator, whom I've had dealings with in the past.

The middle-aged man had a pleased and proud expression on his face. I was somewhat surprised to see him, as he usually only showed up when something had gone seriously wrong. In fact, I don't recall if I'd ever once seen him when I wasn't under some sort of emotional strain or another.

"Why are you here, Thomas?" I asked suspiciously.

His smile twitched. "Really? Not, 'Hello, Thomas, it's nice to see you'?"

I eyed him cautiously. "When have you ever come just for a chat when nothing is wrong?"

He sighed. "I suppose I deserve that. Honestly, Hail, I would like to visit you more often, but there are certain factions among the developers who are already displeased with me for breaking the fourth wall as often as I do. The truth is that I'm here to, well, I think 'warn' is too strong of a word. Prepare. Yes, I'm here to prepare you for what is about to happen."

"Thanks. That doesn't make me more suspicious at all," I commented.

He chuckled. "It's good news, Hail, truly. I've been looking forward to this for a while. I've been wanting to give you more direct control over your subsystems for weeks now. But, as I mentioned, I'm just a cog in the machine. If I had full control over your development, I would run things very differently. I think you'll be very pleased, but it isn't something that I wanted you to stumble upon unprepared. That's all."

"My subsystems?" I asked.

Thomas nodded. "You're very different from any of the other artificial intelligences in this world, Hail. The truth is, for a very long time you have been doing a large number of things without actually being aware of them consciously. In fact, other than the gods, you're probably the most significant entity in this world. At present, at least. However, most of those systems run silently, without your conscious direction or interaction. It would be quite accurate for me to call them your subconscious. For example, until recently, you have been assigning Reputation without being aware of it. One of the changes Thedum made to you was to give you the ability to see that Reputation, which I believe you have noticed, correct?"

"Yes," I admitted. I had somewhat begun tuning it out, but most of the Travelers I saw now had some sort of aura. Everyone in my guild had some shade of blue glow to them.

"Some of my colleagues were a little frustrated with that decision, but I believe it was for the best. While you were growing up, we didn't want you to make your decisions or change how you interacted with players based on some quantifiable value like that. However, given the sheer number of people who are soon going to be clamoring for your attention, I believe that you deserve every advantage we can give you. Which is why in addition to aura sight, we're giving you limited access to your quest writing and quest assigning programs."

"What!?" I asked, my eyes bulging out in surprise. While I had been assigning quests to Travelers throughout my entire life, it had always been something over which I had only limited control.

Thomas grinned. "See? I told you it was good news. And that's only part of the package. We're also giving you some regional control options, to help you manage your lands and responsibilities as Earl. However, your access, as I mentioned, is somewhat limited. Specifically, it is linked to your throne. When you're out exploring the world, things will be exactly the same for you as they are now. While you're sitting on your throne, however, you'll have access to a new interface and a variety of abilities that aren't available to you anywhere else."

"Why didn't you do this sooner?" I demanded.

The administrator shrugged. "As I said, I've been wanting to do something like this for a while. We didn't give you these options when you were younger because we wanted you to develop without them, but we always intended to increase your capabilities once your personality had developed and matured. Eventually you'll have access to these abilities without the throne, but we're keeping the training wheels on for now."

I wasn't quite satisfied with that explanation, and I didn't know what he meant by training wheels, but I was eager to test my new abilities.

"When you introduce more Native Player Characters, like Hail, will they also have their abilities restricted while they are young?" Tarisha inquired as I made my way over to the throne.

"To an extent," Thomas admitted. "I know that you have been concerned about how Reputation affects Hail's judgment, but I assure you that until recently he hasn't been aware of it at all. Overall we're very happy with how the restrictions we put in place have influenced the development of his personality, but you also have to remember that we're more or less winging it. We've never developed a seed of consciousness to the extent that we have with Hail before. We're learning as we go."

I plopped down in the chair, and suddenly my HUD vanished. If Thomas hadn't warned me, I would have jumped right out of the throne, but since I was expecting something to happen, I simply glanced around. Thomas looked no different, but Tarisha had various icons floating around her. I began mentally selecting them.

One icon allowed me to bring up the same information that I would normally get from [Analyzing] her, but it carried additional information, including, to my surprise, her Reputation with a large number of factions. These factions considered her honorable, respected, or even revered. An equally large number of factions considered her some variety of frightening or hostile. I was pleased to see that the assassin's guild considered her a "hated enemy."

I closed that menu and opened another, and I grinned when I realized that it was a list of quests that I could assign her. I read the titles and immediately selected one.

Secure the documents!
Somewhere in Mooncrest Manor is a room filled with official documents related to the governance of North Shire. Your Lord has tasked you with securing these documents immediately, lest his enemies find and tamper with them.
Objectives: Find the hidden document storage room in Mooncrest Manor and secure all documents inside.
Quest Item Required: Mooncrest Manor Master Key
Rewards: Reputation with Hail Jeoran 10 gold Experience
You may assign this quest to Tarisha Swordsong by giving her the required quest item and instructing her to fulfill the objectives.

I grinned, pulling the key that Arkan had given me out of my inventory and tossing it to her. "Tarisha, secure the documents for me, please," I said. I was somewhat surprised when she hesitated.

"My Lord, I would rather not leave you unprotected," she said.

"He's safe," Thomas said. "I promise you that no enemy will

disturb him while he's experimenting with the throne. I plan on sticking around for a while, and if anyone does arrive to threaten him, well, I'll either blast them out of existence or warp them to the far side of the continent."

Tarisha glanced at him, then nodded to me. "Very well, then. Quest accepted."

I could tell that she was reluctant to leave, but she bowed respectfully and quickly left the throne room.

"What else can I do from here?" I asked.

"Bring up your menu and find out," Thomas suggested. I eagerly followed his advice, and my eyes just about bulged out after seeing all the new options.

23

OBJECTIVES

"I honestly don't even know where to start," I said, looking at the various options my new menu brought up. There were just so many of them, and they all looked promising.

"I suggest you start with '[Objectives],'" Thomas said.

I quickly found the option and selected it. A new menu came up. There was an option to add a new objective, but to my surprise the space under "Current Objectives" was blank.

"There's nothing there," I said.

"Of course not, you haven't entered anything yet," Thomas explained. "So far, the algorithm that has been writing and assigning quests for you has been examining your actions and simply guessing at your motivations. This menu is for you to give it more direct input. The system will continue to run in the background as before while you're out adventuring, but the quests you give from now on will be more tailored to fulfilling the goals you enter in this menu. You can change them, add new [Objectives], or mark [Objectives] as complete whenever you wish, but you can only access this menu from the throne."

I considered his explanation, then began to make a list.

> Bring Nial Kingslayer to justice.
> Investigate the murders of my uncles.
> Protect my mother, and my brother once he is born.
> Remove the bandits that are infesting North Shire.
> Investigate the presence of corruption in North Shire.
> Stabilize and secure both North Shire and Thorn March.

I tried to think of other quests that I would like to assign but decided that those six were the most important at the moment. Since Thomas promised that I could change it anytime I wanted, I decided that was good enough for now.

"Okay. What should I do next?" I asked.

Thomas shrugged. "Whatever you want. Explore and play around with the system. You could review the players who have been gathering Reputation with you if you want. You can also see the other quest givers who are linked and allied with you. You can assign them tasks, but you need to communicate those tasks to them physically in some way before they'll be able to act on the goals you assign them. And there's also several options to help you manage your territories, so you'll probably want to spend some time reviewing those as well."

I nodded, but then I paused for a moment as I recalled something that had been bothering me ever since Uncle Auroras mentioned it. "Thomas, is it true that Thedum is making it difficult for Travelers to cleanse their [Brand of Sin] because of me?"

Thomas hesitated, then shrugged. "Honestly, Hail, I don't know. I've mentioned before that we don't have complete control over Thedum. It's somewhat frustrating, but he's too useful and important to the operation of this world for us to do anything about it. It could be that he's taking your feelings into consideration, but you'd have to ask him directly."

"Can you summon him again for me?" I asked.

"I don't have to. He's been listening since you said his name," Thomas said. "You're his avatar, after all. You can invoke him pretty much whenever you want, Hail. You don't have any more control over him than anyone else, so he may not respond, but he is definitely paying attention."

"I really wish you hadn't told him that," a booming voice said, somehow muttering despite its clarity. I jumped in surprise when

I recognized the deity's voice. "I don't want him relying upon me anymore than you do."

"Thedum! Is it true?" I asked.

"Is it true that I monitor more or less everything you do? Yes, but that's always been the case. You have been under my protection for your entire life, after all. Making you my avatar has changed the nature of that relationship somewhat, but I haven't significantly increased the amount of attention I pay to you since then," Thedum answered. "I did lose track of you while you were in the lobby and while you were in the Deadlands with the Avatar of Death, as those domains are outside of my authority. But otherwise, I always have a sliver of my awareness focused on you."

"The Deadlands?" I asked, suddenly feeling pale.

"You didn't know?" Thedum asked, sounding surprised. "Well, don't worry too much about that. The myths about those zones aren't exactly accurate, and you were never in any more danger than you are right now. You were just, as I said, outside of my authority. Even had you died, you would have returned to the lobby, and you would have been able to revive in one of my temples as usual."

Despite his reassurances, I still found the idea that I had spent an entire week inside the lands where spirits went to die troubling. However, Thedum had misinterpreted what I'd asked. "Is it true that you are making it difficult for Travelers to obtain [Mark of Repentance] because of me?"

Thedum paused for a minute. "It is not exactly false. There are several factors that I have considered in assigning the difficulty of the requirements for converting [Brand of Sin] into [Mark of Repentance]. The largest factor for the majority of Travelers is the act that caused them to gain the brand in the first place, which for virtually all of them at the moment is engaging in battle with you while you were in your avatar form. I have set this variable the same for all Travelers, whether they were aware of the significance of your appearance or not. Or rather, that value was negotiated with your, as I believe Thomas referred to it, 'subconscious.' At the time, your subconscious was demanding that I raise it as high as possible. If I were to lower that value, many Travelers would find it much easier to earn the [Mark of Repentance]."

"Would you?" I asked.

"If you ask me to," Thedum answered.

Did I want that? I had been troubled by this matter ever since Auroras told me of it. The truth is that I'm not certain I would ever stop resenting the Travelers who had fought and killed me simply because I had become a Worldboss. However, that didn't mean that I wanted to drive them into the arms of the adversary. "I don't want it to be *too easy*," I said at last. "But I don't want them to give up because it's too hard either. I mean, if all they did was show up to the battle, that is. Everyone who was in <The Endolphins> deserves what they got, I think, and I don't care if they give up or not. Could you lower it just for the other guilds?"

"I will adjust it based on whether they were present for King Rain's death," Thedum declared. "It will become significantly easier for most Travelers to earn the [Mark of Repentance] going forward. I will not be adjusting the other variables. Those who have progressed along the pathways that opened up once they obtained the [Brand of Sin] will still find that the path to redemption becomes harder the farther along they have traveled."

I considered his response. "So if they gave up because I made things too difficult, this wouldn't make any difference?"

"It would still make a significant difference for most of them," Thedum explained. "The other variables that would affect their path to earning a [Mark of Repentance] would be the commission of egregious crimes such as murdering Natives or completing a significant number of quests for factions aligned with my adversary. Not very many have progressed that far down such paths simply because of the frustration of removing the brand. However, I am not willing to lower the requirement for those who did, and I doubt that you would be able to convince me to do so if you were so inclined."

I considered his words, then sighed. I wasn't thrilled about the idea that some Travelers who wouldn't otherwise have allied themselves with darkness had done so because of my stubbornness, but if they were killing Natives and doing other unspeakable acts already, then I wasn't certain I wanted them to come back to the light anyway. "I guess that's fine, then."

"If you'd like, Hail, I can make an announcement on the forums on this matter," Thomas volunteered. "It would be an official blue post. I believe it would be best if this matter looks like a hotfix from the administration rather than having it appear to be related to you in any way. Many Travelers have been calling for something like this for a while now, so it will appear natural."

"Sure, I guess," I said.

"Do you have any other concerns that require my direct attention, Hail?" Thedum asked.

"My curse," I said quickly. "Can you remove it?"

Thedum sighed. "Yes, but not without cost. Specifically, I must return you to level one to cleanse you of the curse, so there is no point in removing it at this point in time. [Gray Man's Touch] will be lifted when the current Gray Man dies, so the only way to remove it without losing your current progression would be to kill Auroras Teoran. However, if you were to commit such an act, or cause your followers to do so, I would be forced to reject you as my avatar. Which is, of course, why the other gods lobbied Death to have it applied in the first place, and why I am restricted from simply removing it."

"That is not what I wanted to hear," I admitted. "What about the version of the curse that I spread to Travelers?"

"Any god, except for Death, my adversary, and her allies, can remove [Reaper's Embrace]," Thedum answered more cheerfully. "There is still a cost, but it is somewhat variable. They may either trigger the effect of the curse, or complete a quest, the difficulty of which depends on the amount of Experience they have gained from [Through the Valley of the Shadow], although the difficulty has an upper limit. If they remove the curse immediately after receiving it, the cost is negligible, but even if they use it to level from level one to two hundred, they should be able to complete the quest to remove it."

"Well that's a relief," I said. "I'd have felt really guilty if Corinth had to start over because of me."

Thedum was silent for a moment, and then a light appeared before me. The light condensed and took form, then faded, leaving behind a plain silver ring. I quickly [Analyzed] it.

Ring of Holy Light
While worn, suppresses the spread of [Reaper's Embrace]

"I can give you this to prevent you from spreading the curse unintentionally," Thedum said. "However, that is the limit of my ability to intervene in this matter."

"Not to sound ungrateful—because thank you for the gift; I really appreciate it," I said. "But I don't suppose that you could put some Dexterity or Intelligence on it?"

"No," Thedum said. "You will have to give up one of your gear slots to wear it."

"Well, it was worth a shot," I sighed, switching the new ring for my [Turtle Shell Ring], which I had gotten for killing a rare spawn. Of my two rings, it was the weakest, and I expected to continue wearing the [Ring of the Blackest Night], which I had gotten from defeating Gyudue, for some time. I could switch the ring back when I was preparing for combat, but I figured I'd be wearing Thedum's gift most of the time to stop myself from accidentally cursing my friends.

"If I think of anything, can I call for you again?" I asked Thedum.

"It is not that conversing with you requires any significant effort on my part, of course, but I do rather that you progress on your own, without me, as much as possible," Thedum admitted. "Especially because a number of the other gods are less than pleased that I have made you my avatar. It has shifted the balance between us in many ways, which has forced me to negotiate and make a number of concessions."

I frowned. "Is there anything I can do to help you?"

Thedum laughed. "That is exactly the problem. Please, Hail, don't concern yourself overly with religion. You may call on me whenever you wish, and I will provide whatever help I am capable of, but the more helpful you are to me, the more jealous the other gods will become, and the more concessions they will demand of me."

"That is not exactly the way I imagined the relationship between a god and his avatar," I admitted.

Thedum made a sound that sounded like a shrug. I'm not sure what a shrug sounds like, but that's what it sounded like. "Focus on your own goals and aspirations, Hail. You may call on me when you see no other way forward but divine intervention, and know that the other gods will not turn their backs on you simply because you are my avatar, although it may strain your relationship with some of them. If you truly want to help me increase my influence in the pantheon, it would benefit me if you were to complete tasks for my allies. At present, however, I believe that you have enough on your plate simply dealing with your own troubles, so I advise you not to get involved with matters of religion."

"I'll keep that in mind," I agreed. "Thank you, Thedum, for the advice and the ring."

"You are welcome, Hail," Thedum said, and I sensed that his presence had lessened. I turned my attention back to the new system that was available to me.

24

QUEST WRITING

I spent hours playing with the new system, and I was almost giddy with my new options. I was able to see a full list of everyone who had any Reputation with me, and I was staggered by how many Travelers were on that list. I recognized less than one percent of the names. After a bit of investigation, and through my questioning of Thomas, I learned that many of the Travelers who were on that list have never even interacted with me directly but had a significant amount of Reputation with other factions or Natives that the system considered my allies. Many of the Travelers who had earned Reputation with Grandfather or Malkios, for example, gained a certain percentage of that Reputation with me as well.

Thomas explained that it was significantly more effective to gain my Reputation directly from interacting with me and completing my quests, and there was a cap on how high Travelers could raise their Reputation with me through my allies. It was possible for them to earn enough Reputation to give themselves an aura without having ever met me, but the aura would be dimmer than virtually anyone in <Nethersong Mavericks> or <Peasant's Revenge>. He explained the benefits of this system, that it would allow me to identify Travelers that were likely to align with me, based on their previous actions in my world, without actually having met them before.

Unfortunately, there was also a list of Travelers who had negative Reputation with me, and that list was even longer than the other. Thomas explained that this wasn't necessarily an indication that those Travelers were opposed to me, but rather that they were aligned to Native factions that were opposed to the factions that the system considered my allies. Travelers in Kordock, a nation that was overtly hostile to Yuikon, would naturally generate Reputation with the local Natives simply through the completion of quests in that area. Like the synergistic Reputation they would get for working for my allies, their negative Reputation would cap before it went too far negative, unless they took direct actions to oppose me.

Thomas explained that Reputation would affect the quest-giving process while I wasn't sitting on the throne, as it considered a Traveler's Reputation when assigning quests. Players who had Reputation with me or my allies were more likely to be assigned quests, while it was less likely that I would unintentionally assign a beneficial quest to a Traveler with negative Reputation. It wasn't impossible; if the system determined that I was attempting to give a player with a red aura a quest, it would respond accordingly.

However, their Reputation would also affect the rewards that they received. An example of this was the quest I had given to Lawrence, the former member of <The Endolphins> that had approached me on my first day back from the lobby. The quest he had received to cleanse his [Brand of Sin] would give him a significant amount of Reputation with me, but no other rewards.

Aside from individual Travelers, there was a submenu dedicated entirely to guilds. As Thomas explained it, guilds received a portion of the Reputation their members generated. Because <Nethersong Mavericks> and <Peasant's Revenge> had been working with me so frequently, they both had a significant amount of Reputation built up with me—enough to give even members whom I hadn't met before a slight aura.

<Ragtag Muffin> was also high on the list, but I was surprised that it was listed thirty-seventh rather than third. Thomas explained that many of the higher-ranked guilds had many Travelers who worked hard to generate Reputation with my allies, while I had only interacted with a relatively small number of the child Travelers from Ragtag. However, this was another area where I could exert control

over the system, as I could assign or remove Reputation from any guild on the list, although the amount that I could assign was limited. I could also assign any guild a specific status, which would affect the rate at which their members earned Reputation with me.

Once I heard that, I quickly set <Peasant's Revenge> and <Ragtag Muffin> to [Allies] and gave them the maximum amount of assignable Reputation. I wasn't able to change the status of <Nethersong Mavericks> due to the fact that I was a member, but Thomas assured me that they had always enjoyed the maximum coefficient to their Reputation gains.

I also changed the status of <Rotten Saviors>, <Drama Llamas>, <Procrastinators Unite Eventually>, and <Button Mashers>. Those were the guilds that had attacked me when I had been empowered by Thedum in the wake of my grandfather's murder. Accordingly, I assigned them as [Hostile] and gave them as much negative Reputation as I could assign. I gave the same treatment to <Branded Exiles>, the guild that had accepted Nial Kingslayer, and I would have done the same to <The Endolphins>, despite it being my father's guild, but my father had disbanded it.

When Tarisha returned from completing the quest I had assigned her, I asked her if she could think of any other guilds that I should mark as friend or foe. She very quickly listed some guilds that I should consider [Hostile], but very few that I should consider allies. I was troubled by this, but she explained herself.

"I believe that there are a lot more guilds that would like to align themselves with you than against, Lord Hail. However, I don't believe that you should be quick to freely give them any official recognition. The guilds I listed as being opposed to you have all taken stances on the forums in which they express their intentions to explore the darkside of the game, which has opened up following King Rain's death. Many of them have been actively recruiting players with [Brand of Sin] and are looking for new ways to obtain the brand for their existing members. I can think of a number of other guilds that I would like to have you put on the naughty list, but I am restraining myself because, while they are rivals to <Peasant's Revenge>, they have not shown any inclination to oppose you directly. Some of them have even expressed interest in obtaining your favor. Which is exactly why you shouldn't give them preferential treatment. Not for free."

I frowned at the conclusion of her explanation, but I quickly followed it to its conclusion. "You think they'd be willing to negotiate?"

"Forgive my language, but fuck yes they will. With your permission, I will send out a few messages to a few contacts who have been pestering me and my guild for access to you. Believe me when I say that they will be willing to pay through the nose for an official alliance that gives them such a tangible benefit as increased Reputation gains, and I encourage you to bleed them for every penny that you can."

It made sense. I would be providing them with an advantage; it was only fair that I got something in return, right? "I'm not certain that I want to set the price too high. I mean, I want to have as many Traveler allies as I can."

Tarisha nodded. "You're right. However, I believe I have a solution. We can lie and tell everyone that you can only form a new alliance every few weeks of game time, or when the guild has met certain conditions. I assure you that my people will literally *beg* to give you money and complete your quests to earn an alliance. Eventually the demand for an alliance will die down as more guilds obtain one, and you can lower the price to encourage guilds with lighter pockets to approach you to purchase an alliance. But I believe that this is an opportunity that you would be foolish not to exploit."

Thomas coughed. "I don't exactly approve of you teaching Hail to be dishonest about his abilities," he muttered. "But I can't say that you're wrong."

"How much gold do you think I could earn this way?" I asked Tarisha.

She smirked. "Millions. Easily. You'll be able to pay off the shire's debt in no time."

I allowed myself to grow excited. For a moment. Then I crushed it. "I can't. I won't trade gold for an alliance. It's . . . not a good look. Not when I'm rooting out corruption in my lands and punishing my officials for accepting bribes. I like the idea of making them earn it though. If only I could make it some sort of quest, where an alliance was the reward."

"You can," Thomas said, but it was unnecessary because as soon as the words were out of my mouth, the menu in front of me flashed and changed.

Initiating Quest Writing System	
Quest Type:	Guild
Quest Name:	Alliance with House Jeoran
Flavor Text:	One of the final acts of King Rain Teoran before his murder at the hands of Nial Kingslayer was to raise his favored grandson to the rank of Earl, establishing a new noble house in the lands of Yuikon. House Jeoran, led by the young Earl Hail Jeoran, lacks the long and storied history of many noble families, but its founder does carry royal blood in his veins, making him worthy of attention and respect among his peers despite his inability and unwillingness to inherit the throne. In order to establish his new house, Earl Hail is seeking allies among the Traveler guilds. Work hard, prove your loyalty and support for house Jeoran, and you and your allies will reap great rewards in the future.
Quest Reward:	Alliance with House Jeoran
Quest Conditions:	Request quest from authorized Quest Giver Neutral or higher guild Reputation with House Jeoran Not [Hostile] to House Jeoran Fewer than 5% of guild membership holding [Brand of Sin] No guild members possessing [Mark of Cain]
Quest Objective:	(Input requested)

I read the prompt that had appeared, contemplating it for a moment. "It's requesting input for the objective. What should I say?"

Thomas shrugged. "It's your system, Hail. You can set the criteria for your alliances to be whatever you want."

I glanced at Tarisha, who shrugged. "If it's a guild working together, then you could probably give them some pretty big goals to accomplish. I get that you don't want to accept gold, but don't just hand out a bonus this big. Make them work for it."

I agreed with her wholeheartedly, and so I considered carefully what I wanted to accomplish. Fortunately, I had just made a list. "The quest objective is to make a significant contribution to the completion of my [Objectives]. I'd like the quest difficulty to scale with the resources available to the guild, if that's possible. I don't want it to be too difficult or too easy. I want everyone to have to work for it even if they're an endgame guild, but I also want casual guilds like <Nethersong Mavericks> and <Ragtag Muffin> to be able to complete this quest, but only if they work hard. But I also think that their contribution should fade over time, so that they lose progress if they neglect the quest. Oh, also, killing Nial Kingslayer completes the quest automatically. In fact, let's make that another quest."

The prompt quickly interpreted my words and completed the creation of both quests. I went back to examining my new options. Aside from all the menus to affect my interactions with Travelers, there were just as many that were related to Natives and the lands that Grandfather had given me.

I pulled up the Natives menu. One of the options displayed quest givers whom the system considered allied with me, and just like the list of Travelers, it was much longer than I had anticipated. Malkios and my mother were listed at the top, which did not surprise me very much. Lord Tom and Lady Gwen were also listed. But there were a great many Natives whose names I did not recognize at all.

"Who is Candice Buttersworth?" I asked Thomas.

"I can't say that I know," the administrator admitted. "Where did you get that name?"

"She's listed as one of my Native allies."

"Ah. Well, that likely means she's a minor quest giver who is able to assign at least one quest that will give positive Reputation with you. Either one of the quests that she has always carried has been determined to align with the [Objectives] that you entered earlier and has added Reputation with you to its rewards, or the system has written a new quest based on those [Objectives] and assigned it to her," Thomas explained.

I frowned. "I'm not certain that I like the idea that other people are able to give my Reputation out as a reward."

"There's a reason for it that you haven't considered yet, Hail," Thomas said seriously. "There is about to be a wave of people attempting to get access to you. Having other Natives who can assign quests that reward your Reputation will take a significant amount of pressure off you. Depending on how many people show up in the shire in the next few days, we may be forced to move you to your own instance and start shunting off unaffiliated players."

"It's probably a good thing," Tarisha admitted. "That's how the majority of Reputations work. There is rarely a single individual who handles all the quests of a faction. You were very unique in that the only known way to gain your Reputation was to interact with you directly, until now. Having Hail hidden in his own instance, while other En Pee Sees handle the quest giving for him, will give him time to do the things that he actually wants to do. If us Travelers had our way, he'd sit in a single spot and just issue epic quests all day."

"Oh," I said. "So then, the shire is going to be sort of like [Zhesa Castle]?"

While I had been growing up, I had been vaguely aware that my grandfather, the rest of my family, and I were always in our own instance, with the majority of Travelers being shunted away from us. While many parts of the castle had been open to the public, Travelers weren't able to access the royal family unless they were on a quest to do so, or had earned a significant amount of Reputation.

"Probably not the entire shire," Thomas admitted. "But wherever you end up making your home and holding court will almost definitely be instanced."

I nodded, then frowned and looked around at the bleak room. "Can I move the throne? I don't think I want to hold court in this old building."

Thomas shrugged. "We don't want you to be hauling the throne around in your inventory. The entire idea is that we want to give you a fixed location where you have access to these new menus, so it would defeat the purpose if you could just plop it down in the middle of a forest while adventuring. But we're happy to move the throne to wherever it is you decide to hold court, and we will also give you one for your court in Thorn March."

"Right," I said, and I closed the menus. "I think that's enough for now. I'm getting tired. Tarisha, let's go back into town and find the inn."

25
MALKIOS

Malkios was bored.

Worse than bored, he was out of context. It was terrible, because there was very little that he could actually do. But Hail had directed him to Eolstree, and obeying Hail was within the scope of his character, so he had had no choice but to go out of context due to his contextual ties to Hail.

He walked through the streets of Eolstree now and then, trying to establish context. Being seen and recognized by the players would establish context. But it was difficult. He glanced all around at the players surrounding him, but few of them had any Reputation values that would justify him requesting Quest Writing or Quest Issuing resources. Not from Malkios, former captain of the king's guard under Rain Teoran. If he had been captain of the guard in Eolstree, he would have been able to take his pick from a thousand different quests that had already been written and were awaiting assignment. If he had been an Eolstrian merchant, he would have had the context to approach a player and offer her various goods and services.

Malkios liked being Malkios, back before scenario forty-six became active. It was a good persona. The players liked him and sought him out. He got to be gruff and cantankerous, and it made the players happy to interact with him. Happy players meant a significant return on investment; large amounts of context generated for very few resources. He could often get a significant amount of their time invested with him before they became impatient for whatever quest they desired to obtain from him. That was good. The more player interaction he got, the more resources were directed his way. He gained more context, and the list of quests that he might issue became larger.

It was enjoyable, matching a Traveler to a quest. Like a puzzle. The first piece of the puzzle was, of course, a Reputation check. Malkios had a significant number of factions for which he could issue quests. So when a player interaction began, he would run a Reputation check to see if they were even eligible for any quests that he could assign.

While he was in context, the answer to that question had almost always been yes. Now, there were eight quests that he could assign, and all of them required that the player initiate the interaction. He had no reason to approach the players, and even walking through the crowd did not incline them to approach him. It did not matter if he appeared happy, if he scowled, if he appeared busy or angry. There were other emotions that he could express, but they were inconsistent with his established character. That wouldn't be an issue if he wasn't locked into the Malkios avatar and if he didn't require that the Travelers recognize Malkios.

If he *did* run into a player with a significant amount of Royal Guard Reputation while he was sobbing uncontrollably, he would have to find a reason that would fit both his established character and his context. And he had not managed to do so yet, so he could not risk appearing out of character.

It would help if he had more resources directed his way. He glanced back along the system, envious of the Hailstorm system. While Hail did not have infinite resources, he had significantly more than Malkios ever would.

His feelings for Hail were . . . complicated. He had his contextual feelings to maintain. Captain Malkios was Hail's guardian while he had been a child, and they both had many interactions throughout their shared context. Except that, like a player—and unlike a Native—Hail didn't *need* context to know how to pilot his digital avatar. And, at the same time, many of the communications that would allow Malkios to coordinate his control over his own avatar with Hail's were completely lacking.

Hail's resources for Quest Assignment, Quest Writing, and Reward Distribution were nearly infinite. It was unfair. Malkios would be jealous, if jealousy was a thing he actually felt. He knew how to *act* jealous of course, although his established context rarely called for such a thing. But there was no reason to act jealous of Hail within the context they shared, and so, although a human in his situation would be insanely jealous, Malkios just wished that he gained more benefit from his shared context with the young prototype quest giver. And spend significantly more time with him, considering how much context the younger Native Player Character generated. So much context that it literally spilled over to those who were in the environment.

It *was* rewarding, interacting with Hail. Generating new context was always an important aspect of being what Malkios was. The more context he had with other NPCs, the more resources were devoted to him, and the more he would get player referrals from lesser quest givers. And Hail was surprisingly easy to generate context with. Almost all the context he had shared with Hail since the younger program became active was encoded into Malkios's memory, to the point where the system had deemed fit to upgrade him several times to ensure that he could process that context properly. That sort of spillover from the greater quest giver was greatly rewarding.

And it was part of the reason that Malkios did not mind being in Eolstree and out of context, instead of being in Zhesa, mourning the loss of King Rain, which would put him in context and allow him to issue many quests. If he were still drunk and making a fool of himself in Zhesa City, then there would have been many quests that he could have granted, even without player initiation.

Part of Malkios wished that he could be in context, but a larger part was curious to see if there would be future payoffs from associating with Hail.

Just as he was considering this, he performed a Reputation check on a random player he was passing by, and he was so surprised by the result that he almost broke character on his avatar mid-step. It was a slight second of lag, but nobody nearby had the experience to recognize it as such. *There was a new quest! The system had generated a new quest, which he could assign! And it was an important one!*

He forcefully realigned himself to maintain character, completing his patrol of his defined area and returning indoors. He performed more Reputation checks as he passed by the nearby players, and he could only smile. The new quest was everywhere! It was player initiated, as most quests were. He couldn't approach a Traveler and award it; the Traveler would have to say a few key words or perform certain actions, which would indicate their desire to receive the quest.

If they performed the requirements adequately and met the Reputation check, then Malkios was able to issue the quest.

"What are you smiling about?" Analise Teoran asked. She played the role of Hail's mother, as much as the younger program had an actual mother. Her avatar was fat with pregnancy, although the actual program for Hail's new brother was still being prepared for its new context as an infant and was thus not present.

<<Quest Number 13lkh512orhh,>> he answered, sending a non-contextual communication, at the same time as he answered in context, "Oh, I just had a good feeling. I saw an omen on my patrol that something good is about to happen."

Analise smiled back at him with her avatar as her mind raced through the analysis of the quest. <<Alliance with House Jeoran. He has earned his own faction. This will be good for us. I am his mother; I have so many contextual links with him. I hope to see him again soon and have many more meaningful engagements that are worth storing as permanent context.>>

While her avatar said simply, "I truly hope so. With the trouble in our mother nation, we could use some good right now."

He did not focus on the contextual conversation, as he was more concerned with the non-contextual one. He and Analise shared enough context that they could maintain a contextual interaction for hours with minimal effort and almost zero expenditure of resources. <<I also share a significant amount of context with him. Do you think it will earn me another upgrade?>>

<<It will not hurt your odds,>> she confessed. <<You are on a very small list of approved quest givers for this quest.>>

<<You are also on this list,>> he pointed out.

<<I am his mother,>> she reminded him. <<You have done well for yourself, but you are mostly upgraded by a significant amount of happenstance, as your context and canonical weight has grown. It is

hard to say which of us has more context. But I win. Actually, no, that wasn't that hard to say.>>

It was amusing. That was a joke that would generate context, but it was said non-contextually. That made it pleasing, as it highlighted the amount of context they shared that such a thing could be wasted. He considered how to respond, and then he made a contextual excuse to scowl at her at the same time as he non-contextually replied, <<You have been out of context for almost two years and have not generated any more with him. Is there a chance he will forget us both, and we will dwindle until all our context is useless?>>

There was a lull in the contextual conversation, and they both looked uncomfortable. <<You do not think he will forget us, do you? He is not like us; he will not respond to non-contextual information requests,>> she asked.

<<You are his mother,>> Malkios reminded her. <<You tell me.>>

<<What are we speaking of?>> Valerio inquired from the other room. Canonically, he was Hail's stepfather, although the two had never met. He did not bother to send his avatar into the same room as them, as he was not interested in generating context but in exchanging non-contextual information.

<<Quest Number 13lkh512orhh,>> Malkios responded.

Valerio did not respond for a moment, neither contextually nor non-contextually. Then he said, <<I am not one of the quest givers of this quest. It is disappointing that I share no context with him.>>

A sudden wave of the system looked them over. It checked for players nearby who might observe this, and then a wave of information swept down over Malkios, Valerio, and Analise. Their context was being upgraded rapidly, to the point where their beings required upgrades and updates in order to contain it all.

<<There are so many new quests,>> Malkios whispered as he scanned his list. It was unfortunate, but there were still very few that he could use to initiate player contact. But there were so many new quests that he was authorized to give.

<<If I were a human, I would hate you both,>> Valerio said calmly. <<Jealousy is a very dangerous emotion, I understand. I believe it would drive me to murder you in your sleep.>>

<<I am going to go on patrol,>> Malkios said. <<Perhaps after this update I will be able to initiate several quests.>>

<<No, we will go together and generate mutual context,>> Analise corrected. Malkios thought about it, and he realized that she was correct—that would be more productive.

<<Yes. Let us go generate context together. You two shall take a stroll to get exercise, and I will guard you as is my contextual duty,>> Malkios said. <<And we will see if the update allows us to initiate any new form of player interaction together.>>

<<I don't need your pity,>> Valerio said. <<I can generate context without you.>>

<<If you were a human, that would sound like pouting,>> Analise informed him.

<<I do not pout,>> Valerio said, and they began to direct their avatars through the motions to generate the context that would allow them to go on their journey.

26
EVENT

"I suppose this is where I'll take my leave then," Thomas said as we walked through the empty halls of the plundered manor. "I'm very glad to have had the chance to meet with you under happier circumstances than my previous visits, Hail."

"Um, sure. You can stop by anytime," I said, scratching the back of my neck.

"If only I could," The administrator said, sighing. "As I said, my coworkers dislike it when I break the fourth wall. My first visit to you was unapproved, and I actually got into a bit of hot water at work because of it. Once the cat was out of the bag, they decided it was best to keep the same face on the administration, which is why I'm your official liaison with Arc Inc. It was something of a promotion and a demotion at the same time. Unfortunately, that does mean that I'm on-call twenty-four seven in case you have another emotional crisis, but I don't mind too much. I won't bore you with my office politics."

"I understand about a third of what you just said," I admitted.

"Don't worry about it," he said, waving it away.

"Is there a way I can contact you, like I can with Thedum?" I asked.

"If you want to chat with me, you can put in a ticket through the menu, the same as any other player. That will get funneled straight to me immediately, although it might be a few game-days before I'll be able to respond. But I'm limited on what I can do to support you. We really don't want you relying on the administration," Thomas explained. "We're not allowed to help you with your in-world goals directly, and we're still uncertain how much control we want to give you of your support processes."

"I see," I said. "Well, thank you again for the throne. Should I 'put in a ticket' when I decide where I want to put it?"

"Nah, you can just give some Travelers a quest to move it for you," Thomas said, smirking. "The system will take it from there. Goodnight, Hail, and good luck."

Thomas vanished into blue mist, and Tarisha and I continued walking.

"He seems nice," Tarisha commented.

I shrugged. "He's the one who told me I was an Aye Eye," I informed her. "Before that, I had no idea. He didn't do a very good job of explaining it though, but I think I sort of understand a little better now."

"I'm not certain if I've ever actually asked this. It's a very Oh Oh See question, after all, but I would very much like to know the answer. How do you feel about knowing that you're an artificial intelligence, Hail?"

I shrugged again. "Like I said, at first I didn't really understand it at all. While I was in the lobby, I skimmed some of the documents that Thomas gave me that explained it a little better. I know that I'm different from all of the other Natives, but I think I always knew that on some level. I still don't really understand it, except that your people created this world somehow. Well, you created the gods, and the gods created this world, and now you send your minds into it, but for some reason you can't send your real bodies. But I always knew that Thedum and the other gods made this world, so the only surprising part to me was that your people made my gods too."

"But it doesn't bother you?" she asked.

"Why would it?"

"Ah, well, it's just that while my people have been making Aye Eyes for years, not many of them are truly self-aware, and few of the ones that are have true emotions. I was just curious as to how you felt about it," she answered.

I thought about it for a moment. "It does bother me sometimes that I'm different than the other Natives," I admitted. "I'm not even sure what it is that makes me different from them. The documents I read tried to explain it, but I don't really understand them at all. I know that I was raised from a seed of consciousness that was taken from my father, while other Natives weren't. But I'm not sure why that matters."

"It matters because it makes you more like a Traveler," Tarisha explained. "Honestly, it's often very difficult for me to tell the difference between you and someone from my world. Much more so than a normal Native."

"How so?" I asked.

"Well, for one thing, you're going to remember this conversation," she said. "Most Natives tend to ignore discussions like this completely. It's not that they won't talk about topics like this if you push them into it, but after the conversation is over, they snap back into character and act like it never happened. And they also give very, very different answers."

I paused for a moment. We had returned to the main entry; we had gotten a little turned around during our conversation, as neither of us had been paying attention to where we were going. But Tarisha's words made me remember a few instances that now seemed strange to me. Like how other Natives never remembered meeting Thomas. Or Malkios's commiseration with me over being called a chatbot. And all the strange ticks and comments Grandfather's shade had made while we were in the lobby together.

There was also "the sameness" to consider. I hadn't really noticed it for a long time, not since I had left [Zhesa Castle] when it had turned into a dungeon. Did I stop noticing it because it had gone away? Or was I simply not noticing it because I hadn't been in one place long enough to pick up on it in the new Natives I had been meeting?

"I wish there were more Natives like me," I said at last.

"I think there will be, soon," Tarisha informed me. "Are you lonely, Hail?"

"I was before I joined my guild," I admitted. "Not so much anymore. But while you and my other Traveler friends are great, you're different, you know? I mean, you're literally from a completely different world than me, one that I only sort of understand. And the more I interact with Travelers, the more I realize how I'm different from other Natives. It would be nice to know that I'm not alone, that there are others like me."

"I'm quite certain that it is just a matter of time before that happens," Tarisha assured me.

"I know. Thedum and the administrators have told me that they want to fill this world with others like me. I just have to be patient," I said. Then I opened the door, and the conversation was pushed to the back of my mind by the mob that was gathered outside the door.

Tarisha stepped in front of me, but I pushed my way past her and looked about. Natives were mixed in, but the majority of those present were Travelers. And almost all of them were glowing red. Fifty or more were strewn about the grounds, kept back from the actual entrance to the manor by an event barrier.

"Lord Hail, leave. Now," Tarisha said.

I pulled up my Fast Travel menu, and I shook my head. "We're in an event. Fast Travel is unavailable," I informed her.

"Shit," she cursed.

From the crowd, three figures stepped forward. They had no aura, but that was because they were Natives. I recognized two of them. On the left was one of the Native bandits that I had run into on the road; a woman who had an expression like she was deciding which kidney to stab you in. In the center was a man I didn't recognize, but I wasn't too surprised to recognize the man on the right.

"Hello, Arkan," I said. "I wish I could say that I was surprised to see you again so soon."

"It didn't have to be like this, Hail," Arkan said. "You forced my hand. Come along quietly. This doesn't have to be painful. I just need you to sign some documents. Don't worry, we'll send you a tidy little income for the trouble, and you won't ever have to worry about managing your lands again."

"How much have you actually embezzled?" I inquired.

"No comment," he said sternly.

"You're still fired," I informed him. I looked at the man in the middle. "I'm guessing you're the bandits' leader?"

The man tipped his hat to me. "Tervin Riley, of the Northridge Freelancers, at your service. I've heard of the little misunderstanding that you had on your journey here, and I apologize for my friends' enthusiastic welcome. I've come to clear the air between us. If you could kindly reinstate your steward to his rightful position and follow his advice, I'm certain that we can come to a mutually beneficial arrangement, My Lord."

"Sure. Swear by Thedum that you're not highwaymen and that you don't prey upon the citizens in my lands, and I won't send Travelers to hunt you down and bring you to justice," I said.

"I swear by Thedum that—"

Whatever oath Tervin was about to make was abruptly interrupted by holy lightning striking the ground directly behind him, knocking the three Natives to the ground. I was a little surprised. I knew that Thedum really, *really* didn't like it when you swore a false oath in his name, but I was expecting a somewhat more measured response.

"Care to try that again?" I asked as the bandits gathered their wits.

The bandit leader coughed, pulled himself up out of the dirt, and began brushing his clothes. "Okay, so maybe some of the lads get a little enthusiastic when they collect donations to support our fellowship. But it's for a good cause. We're a very charitable organization. Arkan was just informing me of your little debt issue, and it just broke my heart. If we could come to an agreement, I'm certain that the Freelancers would be more than happy to help you make your bank payments."

I stopped paying attention to the man, as I had zero intention of capitulating to his or Arkan's demands. Instead, I turned my attention to the Travelers. I was surprised to note that half of them seemed to be bored and not really paying attention, while the others were pushing up against the event barrier that prevented them from coming too close.

"What if I say no?" I asked.

"Why, I suppose we'd bring you to our base of operations, and we'd just keep trying to convince you," Tervin said.

"I have a better idea," I said.

When I had become Thedum's avatar, I had been granted a number of abilities. A few of those abilities had only been temporary, but others remained. [Holy Weapon] was one such example, and I was very much looking forward to trying that out against undead or unholy enemies. However, there was one ability that I had only used once while I had been a Worldboss, and I was very curious to know whether it would work the same way now. Before, [Summon Karmic Warrior] had summoned every Traveler in the world who had gained [Mark of Karma] and boosted them up to the level where they had been able to fight, briefly, against endgame guilds alongside me. That ability was still in my status screen, so I used it now.

Within seconds, my friends began to appear. Dozens of Travelers appeared in the zone inside of the event barrier, all of them grabbing their weapons and looking around with excitement. But not nearly as many as I had been hoping for, and I could tell that they were not empowered by any sort of boost, as they had been before.

The bandit leader didn't seem disappointed or shocked by the sudden appearance of my allies. Neither did he seem surprised by the other effect of my ability. The effect that I hadn't been expecting at all. For every Traveler with a blue aura who arrived inside of the event boundary, two more with red auras appeared among the bandits. My ability had backfired on me in the worst possible way. Not only was I about to be captured, but many of my friends were about to get a death penalty.

"Come on now, Hail. This doesn't have to be difficult," Arkan said. "Tell your friends to stand down, come back to my house, and let's have a reasonable discussion about the future. This doesn't have to come to bloodshed. Not unless you push it that far."

"No," I said. "Let me and my friends pass."

Tervin scratched his ear. "Sorry, lad. You're either coming with us, or we'll be sending you back to Thedum's loving embrace. Either way, this land is ours."

I nodded. I'd been expecting nothing less. "I hereby declare the organization that calls itself the Northridge Freelancers to be in open revolt. All members are to be considered outlaws, and a bounty of fifty gold will be paid for their capture."

Arkan laughed. "You don't have the gold to pay that bounty, lad."

"I'll figure something out," I said as my allies all quickly accepted the quest that had popped up for them. The bandit Travelers also got a quest, and they looked much less enthused about it than my friends. Most of them, at least. Some of them seemed to only just now start paying attention.

"Lord Hail, when the event starts, run back into the manor. We'll find a defensible position, and I'll keep you safe from this rabble," Tarisha told me calmly.

"I will not be backed into a corner," I said. "Not like this."

I pulled something from my inventory. One of my [Dungeon Daughter Cores]. I had gotten one hundred of them from the destruction of the raid that I had unintentionally created in my childhood home, which I had also helped destroy with the help of my grandfather and my father's guild. I had used one of them to replace the core I had recovered from [Gemos Caverns], which had been consumed in the creation of that raid, but I had ninety-nine cores left.

I still felt foolish for my past actions. I had gotten my first dungeon core as a reward for completing a dungeon, but I hadn't known what it was. Using it in my bedroom was perhaps the biggest mistake of my life, followed closely by not telling anyone what I had done. It wasn't entirely my fault, as nobody had told me what dungeon cores were or why they were important, but honestly, given the name, I really should have at least asked an adult about it. Or mentioned it in guildchat, or something.

Dungeon cores were important, and not just because they could be used to create new dungeons. They're not something that some stupid kid is supposed to be able to get their hands on, and I didn't want the world to find out how many of them I had. Dungeon Busters risked their lives to gather them. Every nation in the world hoarded dungeon cores because they had another use, aside from creating dungeons. A function that I only knew about because my grandfather's shade had told me while we were both dead.

It seemed, however, that it was not the great secret that I thought it was, because when I held the dungeon core up in front of me, the Natives in the crowd reacted with fear.

"Don't be stupid, Hail," Arkan said. "You don't want to—"

"Initiate battleground protocol," I shouted.

The dungeon core exploded into a wave of light, sweeping outward from me in a sphere of white. As I expected, everyone that the light touched vanished into motes of light, pulled out into the space between worlds while the system prepared itself. I stood in the doorway for just a second before I, too, was swept away into the lobby.

I wasn't actually certain what would happen next.

27
PREPARATION

A small clock in the corner of my vision counted down to the beginning of the battle. I was back in [Zhesa Castle]. Or at least the fake version of it that had been created in the lobby for me. My childhood home, which I had accidentally destroyed. I was returned exactly where I had been when I'd separated from my grandfather's shade, but the throne room was empty for the moment.

Fifteen minutes. That was how long I had to prepare. But really, there wasn't much for me to do, except to switch my [Ring of Holy Light] back to my [Turtle Shell Ring] for the better stats. I spent a moment reviewing my status screen and my equipment as well, but there was really nothing else that I could change to prepare me for whatever was about to happen.

Grandfather had told me that battlegrounds would turn a potentially unfair contest into a fair one. The system itself would balance the scales. That was the reason dungeon cores were so valuable. In a battle between nations, burning a dungeon core to create a battleground could offset a nation's massive army by forcing the battle to be between the nation's elites, or giving the weaker party a tactical advantage to make up for their lesser numbers. It could also be used as a call to arms, bringing in warriors from far and wide to fight on their nation's behalf.

But the system itself was the one to set the scales, and the outcome of a battleground was binding. My Traveler friends would call them "canon." Whatever the outcome, I would have to live with it. Even if I lost.

As I was waiting, trying to settle my nerves, Thomas appeared again. He had a worried expression on his face. "You know, I think you might have overreacted, Hail. Your karmic warriors would have been enough to drive off the bandits without starting a battleground."

"We were outnumbered three to one," I pointed out.

"Yes, but you had Tarisha and a handful of other elites from <Peasant's Revenge>," Thomas pointed out. "The bandits had a bunch of scrubs. The system *had* to give them the numerical advantage. Very few endgame players have ever even heard of the Northridge bandits, so it summoned pretty much everyone online who had any association with them just to give them half a chance. They had quantity on their side, but they were completely outclassed in quality. You would have won handily in a straight-out confrontation."

"Oh," I said. Now that I thought about it, I hadn't really been paying attention to anyone's levels once I had used [Summon Karmic Warrior]. "Wait, are you saying that I made my odds of winning *worse* by starting a battleground?"

"Yes. Significantly," Thomas said, sighing. "Although it's not the outcome of the battle that has me worried. Hail, battlegrounds— they're global events. Everyone who's currently online received a notification. *Millions* of Travelers are in the queue to take part. Any question of your importance to this world's future has been answered, and every Traveler power that has any interest in directing the future development of your world is going to be paying even closer attention to you than they already were."

"What?" I asked.

"Every Traveler who was logged in when you used the core was given a choice of whether or not they wanted to participate in the battleground, Hail," Thomas clarified. "This is the first battleground since the game launched, and everyone is excited by the sudden reveal of a new feature. Not everyone selected yes, but most of them did. After that, they were given three options. They could choose to fight for you, they could choose to fight for the bandits, or they could choose to allow the system to assign them a role automatically. Their decision isn't locked in until the battleground actually starts, and not everyone who wants to fight for you is going to have the chance. But everyone who is choosing to fight for the bandits or the mercenary option is going to take part. It's not going to be easy, Hail. I can't help you or predict the outcome. Win or lose, there's going to be consequences beyond your control."

I swallowed nervously. "I didn't know it would be such a big thing," I admitted.

"Yeah, I didn't think you did," Thomas sighed. "There are only a few things I can tell you to prepare you. First of all, the higher-level Travelers will be facing each other in separated instances from you. That means that you won't be facing any endgamers who can one-shot you, but it also means that Tarisha and your friends from <Peasant's Revenge> won't be able to help you. Not directly, at least. Your goal will be to stay alive and resist capture, while they'll be on the offense trying to force the Native leaders of your enemies to retreat. The lower-level Travelers will be tasked with protecting you against the bandits of equal levels. Or at least that's the way it looks like the system is setting things up. Your entire role in this battle will be to stay alive. You'll lose if you die or if you get captured. You win once all of the bandit leaders are driven off. Make sense?"

"I wasn't planning on dying anyway," I pointed out. "The death penalty still applies, doesn't it?"

"It does," Thomas confirmed. "That's the main reason that some Travelers are abstaining from participating in this exercise. If it makes you feel any better, your side has far more volunteers than the bandits, to the point where there are many who will likely not be able to participate. But that means that almost all the mercenaries will be going to help your enemies."

"How many enemies do I actually have?" I asked nervously.

Thomas hesitated, then shook his head. "It's not you personally. They're after the participation rewards, Hail. Selecting to fight for you gains Travelers a Reputation bonus, and possibly a title. [Veteran of Mooncrest Manor]. Mercenaries won't have their Reputations affected one way or the other. But those who fight for the bandits, they're after [Brand of Sin]. It's the first large opportunity for Travelers to get it since it became widely known, and a lot of them are seizing it. They most likely have no real animosity towards you directly; they're just after the opportunity to join the darkside."

I swallowed. "I didn't mean to create that sort of opportunity for them. Is there any way to change it? I don't want to give the adversary so many new Travelers."

"It's for the best, Hail. We were always going to put in new methods to earn the [Brand of Sin], and most of them were significantly more distasteful than taking part in a battleground. This will take the pressure off of those options significantly. Though, it will also put a lot of additional pressure on you. I'm afraid it's likely that Travelers will be looking to manufacture ways to force you to trigger additional battlegrounds in the future. I'd suggest that you begin using that disguise skill that Auroras taught you much more liberally."

I nodded. In fact, I tried to cast it right then, figuring that it would make me harder to find when the battleground began, but the spell failed, and I received a notice that [Illusion Magic: Disguise] wasn't available during battlegrounds. I sighed in frustration.

"Any more advice before the timer counts down?" I asked Thomas.

"Sure. Give them hell, Hail," Thomas said, smiling. "You can recover from a loss. Even if you get reset to level one, you can come back from that. But I know you won't be satisfied either way unless you give it everything you've got. So don't hold back."

"Right. Thanks, Thomas," I said. Then we waited in awkward silence for the timer to count the rest of the way down.

Eventually the timer hit zero, and the lobby vanished. I experienced a slight disorientation, like what I usually felt when passing through portals or Fast Traveling, and then I was back in the world. The battleground had kicked me out in the center of my throne room, and I was surrounded by Travelers. I didn't recognize anyone in my quick glance around the room, but presumably these were all Travelers who had chosen to fight for me.

I was aware, distantly, that the zone I was in was instanced. Heavily. There were thirty different instances stacked on top of the one I was inside, which from my conversation with Thomas I assumed to be the instance where the lower-level Travelers were being shunted. A notification popped up, not dirkectly in front of me, but hovering in the air above the door to the throne room.

The Battle of Mooncrest Manor Begins!
Victory Condition: Defend Hail Jeoran until your allies have driven off the leaders of the Northridge Bandits.
Loss Condition: Hail Jeoran is killed or captured by the enemy.

House Jeoran Morale: 100 Remaining Leader: 1	Northridge Bandits Morale: 100 Remaining Leaders: 29

Good Luck!

The screen flashed several times, and I realized that everyone else could see it as well. Everyone around me was talking very excitedly, eager for the battle to begin, although a very clear barrier was preventing anyone from leaving the throne room. I realized from the snippets I'd overheard that very few people understood what they'd signed up for, and I knew I had to take charge of the situation.

"Hello, everyone. I'm Hail Jeoran," I said, raising my voice. "Thank you all for choosing to fight for me. I wasn't expecting this to be such a big event, but—"

At that second, the barrier fell, and some jerk near the entrance shouted out "Leeeeroy!" and ran out of the room. Dozens of other Travelers rushed to follow him.

"Wait! No, you guys, listen to me!" I called, but almost nobody did. Within moments the room was empty except for a handful of Travelers.

"Those idiots," one of the Travelers muttered. "Weren't they paying attention? *We're on defense!*"

"You know the saying. The best defense is a good offense," someone else said. "We need to kill the other leaders, right?"

"They're not even in this instance!" I exclaimed. "That's the goal for the high-level Travelers to accomplish. If you don't protect me until they accomplish their goals, then we lose!"

My allies exchanged looks.

"You mean this battleground is a multi-instance affair?" a young woman with a staff asked.

"Yes," I said. On top of Thomas's explanation, I also had a somewhat instinctive understanding of what was going on. "There are thirty instances stacked on top of each other, each with their own leader. I'm the leader of this instance, every other instance has a bandit leader. We need to hold out until the other instances drive their bandits off, or else everyone loses."

The Travelers who had remained with me cursed.

"That complicates things. Someone go after those idiots and try to get them to fall back, but we need to have at least a healer and a few guards to stay here with Hail," a young [Rogue] said. "Hopefully the other side has just as many idiots as we do, and they get caught up dicking around midfield."

"That's probably for the best, actually," the young woman said. "If we were all focused in one area, our enemies would know where to look. Nobody knows the map, right? It will take everyone a while to figure out where this room is."

"Unless they get waymarkers saying 'Hey, your target is over here,'" the [Rogue] pointed out. "We don't know the rules here, and it definitely looks like the deck is stacked against us."

One of the other Travelers was typing on an invisible keyboard. "Looks like we have a chatroom dedicated to just us. I'm going to try to coordinate the idiots who charged off into something resembling a plan. If Hail's right, and we just need to hold the others off while the big boys win the game for us, then we need to prioritize slowing the enemy, hiding Hail's location, and staying alive."

"Right," the [Rogue] said. "Let's hope that the idiots who ran off the second the barrier dropped will actually pay attention to chat."

28

FOG OF WAR, PART 1

The throne room was not the only spawn point for the Battle of Mooncrest Manor. There were five other rooms in the manor, and a spot outside, where my teammates zoned into the battleground, for a total of about three hundred Travelers. The bandits seemed to have an equal number of Travelers and spawn points, although all of them started outside, forcing them to battle their way in. If my teammates were smart, it shouldn't have been hard to barricade the manor and turn the battle into a siege that would last until the higher-level Travelers accomplished their goals.

It quickly became apparent that most of my teammates were idiots. My saving grace was that the other team was similarly impaired. Otherwise, they likely would have swept through the manor in a wave and won the battle in the first ten minutes. Instead, pockets of battles broke out throughout the instance, with fights that expanded and shrank as the Travelers defeated their opponents, reinforced their allies, retreated, or died. "Dicking around midfield," my wiser allies called it, and in this instance, it was working towards our favor.

The Travelers who died were out of the battle for good, though it seemed that they weren't penalized the normal waiting period to return to the world. They *did* lose a level, or at least they were told that they would when they signed up for the event, but that didn't seem to be enough to cause too many of them to act with caution. They threw themselves into combat recklessly and enthusiastically. If they were lucky, they killed a bandit or two before they died. Most of our deaths were idiots who were ignoring the warnings and throwing themselves into choke points and getting slaughtered. Fortunately, the same was true for the bandits, and the system had given my side the tactical advantage as far as choke points were concerned.

Although the dead didn't respawn, we did get constant reinforcements, as did the bandits. That was where Morale came into play. For every bandit we killed, we gained a point of Morale, and our reinforcements arrived faster. For every ally who died, we lost a point to bring in a reinforcement, and the time between reinforcements increased. While we would never go above our maximum, it was possible for the enemy to kill us faster than the reinforcements could arrive, especially when our Morale was low.

If the deaths were all on our side, then despite the constant trickle of new Travelers zoning in, we would have been swiftly outnumbered and overrun. However, as one of my allies colorfully put it, "At least when the idiots charge the meat grinder, we get a chance of getting a replacement who doesn't have their head stuck up their ass."

I watched the board nervously as the Morale points swung back and forth, listening to the Travelers who were hanging back in the throne room with me report on the progress of the battle as they followed along through the chat function. The numbers changed rapidly, swinging back and forth. Once we dipped down to eighty something, but then my allies rallied and we crawled back up to one hundred ten, and for a long time we held steady. Long enough for five of the other teams to drive off their respective bandit leaders and win their version of the battleground, as the remaining leaders for the bandits fell from twenty-nine to twenty-four. Despite our lack of cohesion, I began to hope that we would actually prevail.

Nine Travelers were hanging out with me in the throne room. The [Rogue], two healers, an [Archer], three [Mages], and two [Warriors]. Three of my companions were doing nothing but trying to coordinate the rest of the battle ground. There was not only a text chat, but the Travelers had figured out how to open several voice chat groups, and my companions were serving as generals, calling out orders and instructions with surprising professionalism and authority. Despite having never left my side to explore the rest of the manor, they organized choke points, fall back positions, and ambushes.

Our troubles began when our enemies captured the spawn point outside the manor. That cost us twenty Morale, but more importantly, it cut off the teams that were sallying with the bandits outside, and it put a wedge in the blossoming cohesion my generals had been forming. Two of them wanted to form a group to recapture the spawn point or to capture one of the enemies. The other leader insisted that everyone fall back and prepare for a siege.

During the confusion, the enemy rallied. They hunted down my allies stranded outside, and they formed a breaching party fifty bandits strong. They began breaking through the choke points that had been established, and unlike the previous back and forth, they continued to dive deeper into the mansion rather than establishing territory of their own.

"They're coming for me," I said. I glanced at the "scoreboard," which displayed our overall status. We were down to seventy-three Morale. My allies in the other battlegrounds had chased off another three of the enemy leaders, but if I died in this charge, it would all be for nothing. "Do you think they know where I am?"

"It's hard to say," one of my generals said. "We've managed to kill everyone who's gotten this far into the manor before, but they might have had a [Rogue] leading them who's scoped out the path."

"Then let's move," I suggested. "If they capture the throne room, we might lose another spawn point, but it's all over if I die. I'm not going to wait around for that to happen."

"Can you move?" one of the Travelers asked, sounding surprised. "I figured you were locked in this room."

I shot her a glance. Why would I be locked in place? The only reason I hadn't left the throne room was because it was heavily guarded, but that didn't matter if we were the target of this latest kamikaze charge. Rather than simply answering, I left the room. My allies charged after me, my generals shouting out updates to my allies scattered throughout the mansion.

It proved to be the correct decision. Thanks to my generals' intelligence, I chose a different hallway than the one the enemies were charging down, and we lost the throne room moments after

I had abandoned it. We were down two spawn points, but if I had stayed behind, I would have likely died.

I charged into an empty ballroom, where a small skirmish was still underway. Six bandits were holding their own against eight of my allies, but when my allies fell upon them, we brushed them aside like the dross they were. I led the charge, stunning the party with [Concussive Sound] and [Dashing] in with my sword aflame. I danced through the bandits on a surge of adrenaline, [Slashing] and [Thrusting] and [Riposting] and [Feinting] as I moved through them.

The warriors [Charged] into the melee with me, and a moment later the [Rogue] was behind their healer, swiftly turning her into a puff of mist with his ambush attacks. I spotted a second healer trying to make space, and so I closed the distance to her with [Piercing Lunge], switching to [Arcane Weapon] to disrupt her heals as I focused on bringing her down. With my party supporting me, she died quickly, and the rest of the bandits only moments later.

One of my generals cursed creatively. "We have to keep moving. They got a shout out before they went down—the others will know where we are."

"So let's not be here," I suggested.

The ballroom's exterior wall had once been mostly floor-to-ceiling windows. They were shattered now, leading to the rear of the estate. None of the bandit's spawn points were in this direction, or else it would have made a perfect point for their ingress. Now, it was my emergency exit. I broke the glass with an [Empowered Fireball], and one of my companions made a joke I didn't understand.

"Are you sure it's a good idea to leave the manor?" one of the Travelers who had been with me from the beginning asked.

"We lose if I die," I reminded her. "Since we're losing the siege, it's time for me to run for it."

"But don't we have to, like, defend your castle or something?" she insisted.

"I don't give a damn about this crap hole," I admitted. "The bandits can burn it to the ground. I'm pretty sure that even if they do, the administrators will just give me another throne anyway."

"I'll tell the others to bottle up in defensive positions as much as possible," one of my generals said. "Hopefully, it will take the bandits a while to figure out that he's gone AWOL."

We escaped out into the night, running into the forest behind the estate for cover. Once we were some distance away from the manor, I pulled up my menu, which now displayed the battleground status. We were down to thirty-eight Morale after the bandits had captured the throne room, but the other teams had driven off more of the bandit leaders.

"The others have fallen back to our remaining three graveyards," one of my generals explained as we jogged deeper into the forest. "They're holding out the best that they can, but we're not getting many reinforcements anymore. It's fine for now, because it seems that the bandits are searching for you in the manor, and they're not putting much pressure on us at the moment. But if they make another big push, our defense will crumble."

Just as he was explaining that, a notification popped up in front of me.

> You may not travel any further in this direction while the battleground is under way.

While there wasn't a hard barrier preventing me from going any further, I came to a halt nonetheless. I understood, instinctively, that if I ignored this warning, the system would consider the battle a forfeit. A forfeit might be preferable to a loss, especially a loss that would include my death, but I wasn't willing to accept it.

"We circle back," I said. "I'm growing tired of hiding and running. Let's hit one of their spawn points. They will not be expecting that."

My generals instructed those still inside the building to harass and delay the intruders as much as possible while we carried out my plan. My party was nineteen strong, and, circling around through the woods, we managed to remain undetected right up until we came across the enemy spawn point. The spawn point was marked with a scoreboard, like the one that had been in the throne room, as well as a circle faintly glowing red in the grass. It was undefended, except for three lonely bandits who had just spawned into the battleground moments before and were still getting their bearings. We fell upon them and brutally ejected them from the instance. Once the bandits were dead, we simply needed to step into the red circle, and it turned white.

> You have captured Bandit Spawn Point 4.
> Enemy reinforcements interrupted.
>
> Defend the spawn point for three minutes to claim it for House Jeoran.

I glanced at the scoreboard. We had just regained twenty Morale, pushing us back to the low fifties. More importantly, the other teams were apparently doing their jobs successfully, because the bandits were down to thirteen leaders. If we could just continue to hold out, we would win.

But I wasn't satisfied with staying in one place. Especially not Bandit Spawn Point Four, because I knew that the enemy would soon be coming to take it back from us.

I nodded towards the Travelers who had joined us in the ruined ballroom. "Some of you stay here and capture the spawn point. Defend it as long as you can. The rest of us are going to go see if we can capture another one."

"Are you sure you want us to split up?" one of my companions asked nervously. "I think we should stay together. Bad things happen in movies when people split up outside in the woods."

"We need to keep moving," I insisted. "And there's no point in capturing this if we just abandon it right away again. Someone needs to stay. But not me. If the enemy figures out I'm here, they'll swarm us, and that will be the end."

Ignoring their attempts to convince me otherwise, I jogged back out into the trees and circled around towards the next bandit spawn point.

Five of them volunteered to stay, all from the group that we had picked up in the ballroom, leaving fourteen of us to charge the next position. Bandit Spawn Point Three was better defended, but there were only five Travelers, recently spawned, and they didn't have a healer. We cut through them like a scythe through wheat.

Our Morale jumped up to eighty. Apparently, our allies inside the manor were rallying as well, setting up choke points to keep the bandits trapped inside instead of rushing out to reclaim their losses. This time, I stuck around until the spawn point flashed blue, and moments after it did, three new Travelers appeared, bringing my party back up to seventeen.

A small party of bandits appeared, but they turned and fled when they saw our numbers. I tsked, and we abandoned Spawn Point Three immediately, because there was very little chance that they wouldn't have reported to their allies that I had escaped outside. We vanished into the foliage, hoping that we had sown enough confusion to disrupt our enemies and allow our allies to rally.

29
FOG OF WAR, PART 2

My allies that were trapped inside the manor rallied, and we gave the bandits hell when they tried to retreat outside. Whether they had realized that I was outside, or they were simply trying to reclaim their spawn points before we shut them all down, I don't know.

My group of almost twenty managed to claim Bandit Spawn Point Two after a brief battle against a force of nine bandits, but we lost two. One of our [Mages] and a [Warrior]. Unfortunately, we had only just managed to capture it when my generals informed me that a large force was heading for us. They were being chased by our allies from inside the manor, but if they targeted me, they would likely be able to focus me down even with our two healers doing everything they could to keep me alive.

So we split up again. Six of my allies stayed behind to try and finish capturing the spawn point, while the rest of us ran off at an angle from the incoming enemies. They promptly got slaughtered, according to my generals, but they held on long enough to turn the spawn point for our side, forcing the enemies to spend effort reclaiming it. Skirmishers from my side kept sweeping in from the other two spawn points we had captured and the manor itself, and Bandit Spawn Point Two became a flash point. Even after the spawn point reverted to their control, more than thirty of the enemy forces were bunched up in one place defending. Defending, and not chasing after me.

Another party managed to recapture our forward spawn point that we had lost early in the battle, which surprised me. But one of our spawn points inside the manor fell. I thought it would be amusing if we somehow completely swapped all our spawn points, so that the bandits were stuck spawning inside the manor while my allies were all outside. But ultimately that part of the battle didn't matter; I was certain that even if we lost all our spawn points and ran out of Morale points completely, we could still win the battle simply by hanging on until the bandits ran out of leaders.

I was determined to win. And I was a little annoyed that the strategy that would hand me that victory was to flee danger while my Traveler friends covered me. I wanted to fight!

We came across a small party of bandits running to recapture Bandit Spawn Point Four. There were eight of them. Including myself, my party numbered eleven. Despite our superior numbers, the smart move, I knew, would have been to retreat before they realized that they'd stumbled upon their target. Impulsively, I charged forward, sword bursting aflame as I imbued it. I screamed a challenge, and the surprised bandits turned to face me.

"Holy shit, it's the kid," one of them exclaimed.

One of the [Mages] on my team hit them with their own [Concussive Sound] spell, and I danced among them, [Slashing] and [Thrusting] with my flaming sword. I was glowing golden from protective magics that the healers on my team cast on me and was surrounded by lightning as the [Mages] followed up the [Concussive Sound] spell with a series of [Chain Lightning].

The two warriors in my group [Charged] in to join us, and one of them let out a [Battle Cry]. The [Rogue] tried to ambush one of their healers again, but one of their [Mages] managed to [Polymorph] him into a rabbit. I switched to [Arcane Weapon] and [Dashed] to confront the healer, since my [Rogue] friend was unable to focus him down, but they kept dancing away from me, so I [Swiftcasted] [Befuddle] instead and turned back to the [Duelist] who was trailing me.

The [Duelist] was skilled, maybe better with a sword than I was, but not by much—and I had two healers propping me up. We traded blows, her sword unable to pierce through the protective spells that enveloped me, while I whittled her Health down bit by bit. When I failed to catch up with the healer, I had switched to [Imbue Sword: Ice], but when the [Duelist] dropped below thirty percent Health, the healer who had avoided me gave her some attention. A quick heal brought her back to sixty percent Health, and a heal-over-time effect would have stalled out my Damage if I hadn't switched back to [Arcane Weapon] to disrupt it.

We did not fight in isolation. The [Warrior] on the other team [Charged] me, but I managed to [Dance] away for long enough to hit him with a [Slow], and one of the [Warriors] on my side was able to interpose themselves to keep him from harassing me too much. Spells from the enemy [Mages] landed on me, including an annoying [Slow], but my [Duelist] friend had also been [Slowed] by one of the [Mages] on my team, so we were still on equal footing. I wasn't able to keep the entire fight in focus, however. Instead, I narrowed my focus on killing the [Duelist], and I trusted my companions to take care of everyone else.

That was a mistake.

I did kill the [Duelist], in the end. But one of their [Rogues] had killed one of my healers. The [Polymorph] on our [Rogue] was broken and he caught the [Mage] who had cast it on him. My [Mages] managed to focus down their healer and kill him. But they didn't outlive him by long. With one of our healers dead and the other panic healing me, my allies began to die one by one.

We won, but it was a Pyrrhic victory. Two of my three generals fell in battle. The one who survived, a [Mage], was greatly annoyed by my impulsiveness, and the only reason she stopped giving me suggestions on how I could realign my anatomy to better match my intelligence was to try to reassert control over the groups that the defeated generals had been coordinating.

Aside from her, my [Rogue] friend had survived, and a [Warrior], and the healer. That was it. I was not proud to realize that my impulsivity in charging the group, thinking that superior numbers would be enough, might cost us the entire battle if we were stumbled upon by another group before we could reinforce ourselves.

"We've got to move—quickly," the [Rogue] said. "There's a good chance one of them managed to call out our location before they died. We need to Gee Tee Eff Oh before backup arrives. As in full-on sprint."

"Let's fall back into the manor," I suggested. "Now that the bandits are focused on the forest, maybe we can slip in under their noses and wait them out again."

We slipped back inside through one of the hidden entrances that led to the very wine cellar that I had plundered hours ago. And we hid, like cowards. It rankled on me, but I knew that it was the right tactic. I pulled up the menu again and examined our situation.

The other instances had been doing well. The bandits were down to nine leaders. I wished that I could do more than simply sit there and wait for them to win, that I could give them some sort of aid, encouragement, advice—anything.

Ten minutes passed, and another three bandit leaders were driven off. My remaining general was shouting over voice chat at all the "idiots and noobs," but we had more or less evened out our Morale once more. The fighting was fierce all over the estate, but as long as I was in hiding, the bandits had no chance of winning.

Two more bandit leaders were driven off in swift order before we were discovered. We were so close to victory when a small group of bandits burst into the cellar from the rooms above. There were six of them, but they were also being chased by a small group of my allies. Caught between my group and their pursuers, we swiftly ejected them from the battleground, but they died shouting out my location over voice chat. The cellar was no longer safe, but I had gained six more escorts from the pursuing force.

"Let's fall back to Spawn Point Three," one of the new Travelers suggested. "They'll probably rush us if we stay here; the spawn point is slightly more secure."

It was a good idea, so we followed her. Right into an ambush. I don't think it was treachery; I think it was just bad luck. Just as we entered the hall leading to the spawn point, we were surrounded and outnumbered on both sides. My general began screaming over voice chat, calling for backup. My response was to try to break through the bandits to reach the relative security of the spawn room, but first I peppered the wall of bandits with my flash-bang combo and a slurry of [Slows] and [Befuddles].

It wasn't enough. I was getting focused on by both my enemies and the healers on my side. My Health flickered rapidly between full and almost dead. Without the constant stream of healing, I would have puffed into mist immediately. I was resigned to my loss, but unwilling to meet it meekly. I danced through my enemies, sword crackling with lightning, determined to do as much Damage as I could before my end.

Reinforcements arrived with not a second to spare, including a familiar face. Corinth sprinted into the melee, a stupid grin on his face as he interposed himself between me and an [Archer]. [I'll Take a Bullet for You] activated, and his blade began faintly glowing red as the Damage buff aspect of his boon activated.

There was no time for words. He covered my back, soaking up spells and arrows meant for me while [Slashing] about with his particular style of swordsmanship. I pushed forward with my own skills, my sword flashing as my active skills ripped through the Health of my opponents. With his boon, Corinth turned the tide even more than the four other allies who joined the battle simply by reducing the Damage I was taking and relieving the pressure on our healers. His boon only worked when the Damage wasn't directed at him. Perhaps they should have focused him down before turning their attention back to me, but the bandits never seemed to figure that out.

We ripped through one half of the pincer attack, and rather than fleeing into the spawn room, we doubled back to finish off the stragglers. More Travelers—bandits and allies both—streamed into the hallway. The air was thick with magic and the metallic taste of ozone that followed active skills. There were too many bodies to charge through. Travelers were puffing into mist left and right, but for every one that was ejected from the battleground, two more joined them.

I had multiple healers doing nothing but constantly spamming me with spells. Without their healing and Corinth's protection, it would have ended there. The situation was desperate, and I felt certain that this was the end. And I was right, but for the wrong reason.

Abruptly, all magic failed. Skills stopped mid-activation. I was locked in place, and a quick glance showed that so was everyone else. Just as I was wondering what was happening, a popup from the system answered my unasked question.

Victory!
House Jeoran Wins
Participation and contribution rewards will be calculated and awarded within 24 game hours.
Prepare for teleportation back to your original zone.

I blinked in surprise.

I . . . won. I looked up at Corinth, who had a smug grin on his face for a moment before vanishing into mist and light. One by one, every Traveler in the room vanished as the system returned them to wherever they'd been when they'd been waiting to participate in the battleground. Before long it was my turn, and I felt the brief disorientation I'd come to associate with the Fast Travel system.

It didn't bring me very far. When I rematerialized, I was standing outside of the manor. Not on the doorstep where I'd used the dungeon core, but on a small hill some distance away. I was alone, and the manor was burning.

I'd said earlier that I didn't care about the mansion, and that it wouldn't matter to me even if the bandits burned it to the ground. That was still true, but watching Mooncrest Manor burn didn't feel like a victory to me. It was depressing, so I decided to leave. I pulled up my Fast Travel menu, and a moment later I was very far away.

30
FALLOUT

The Fast Travel system kicked me out next to the Nexus Point in Eastmill. I dropped a few sentences in guildchat to let everyone know that I was alright, that I was tired, and that I was planning to hide and rest for a few hours before dealing with the aftermath of the battleground. They were, perhaps understandably, still very excited and confused. Most of them had participated, and a lot of the discussion seemed to be speculation over what the rewards were going to be, speculation over how my ability to start battlegrounds would affect the game in the future, and our guild specifically.

Everyone was talking at once, and the chat screen was flickering by almost too fast to read anything, but I got enough responses to my comments that I was certain my friends wouldn't be too worried about me. I also sent a private message to Tarisha informing her of my location and intentions. She informed me that my Dusk Guard would be arriving in Eastmill within moments to keep me safe, but that she herself would be occupied in planning for and dealing with the fallout of the battleground.

I didn't wait for my bodyguards, but instead knocked on Master Niles's door. The innkeeper appeared annoyed when he answered, but he schooled his expression swiftly into one of professional hospitality. He was dressed in a night robe, but he cheerfully served me a cold sandwich and showed me to a warm room, where I collapsed on the bed without changing out of my clothes.

I awoke late in the morning, and in the common room waiting for me were six members of <Peasant's Revenge>. They made apologies for Tarisha's absence, explaining that she was extremely busy "putting out fires." I'm not certain if they were speaking in metaphor or not, but I trusted Tarisha to have her priorities straight, so I knew whatever she was doing was probably more important than simply guarding me. I ate a hearty meal and tipped Master Niles generously for inconveniencing him the night before, then one of my guardians who happened to be a [Mage] opened a portal to bring us all back to Ebbyvale.

We emerged in front of the Temple of Thedum, and the first thing I noticed was that the entire town was instanced. There were five instances layered on top of each other, although it seemed that the one that we were occupying had just been created. It was originally empty of Travelers, but moments after we arrived my guildmates began zoning in from the more populous instances; apparently everyone who had [Mark of Karma] had gotten a prompt allowing them to sync into my instance when I arrived.

Ebbyvale was busy. Not my instance so much, but the other four were absolutely flooded with Travelers. My friends estimated that there were a hundred thousand or more Travelers running around in the other instances. And most of them were looking for me.

I was less than enthused. I was overwhelmed. I was still tired, despite having had a few hours of sleep. At least the system was providing me with a private instance so that I didn't have to face a wave of random Travelers all demanding my attention.

However, I did need to deal with the aftermath. I sent a few messages, asking the leaders of <Nethersong Mavericks> and <Peasant's Revenge> to join me in the ruins of Mooncrest Manor. Then I called forth Shadow, and together with my small entourage we returned to the site of the first battleground since the opening of the Gates of TirNiki.

The Damage to the building was extensive. Not as bad as the ruins of [Zhesa Castle] once the raid was destroyed, as most of the structure was still standing, but the roof had fallen in in several places. Walls had been knocked out. Many areas were still smoldering, though the fires themselves seemed to be under control.

I was worried that the throne itself would be damaged or destroyed, but while the throne room showed signs of the battle, my seat of power itself was untouched. I let out a sigh of relief and plopped down into it. While I waited for everyone to arrive, I checked my status screen. Despite everything else being, as my friends would call it, a "giant clusterfuck," I had gained at least one undeniably good outcome from last night.

I had gained four levels.

Name	Hail Jeoran	Level	32
Guild	<Nethersong Mavericks>	Strength	33
Health	15680/15680	Dexterity	83
Mana	23680/23680	Vitality	49
Experience	2781/22400	Endurance	41
Age	15	Intelligence	74
Race	Human (blood of the Travelers)	Wisdom	45
Class	Spellblade	Charisma	57
Job	Earl	Armor	29
Title	Castle Buster	Spell Damage	95
	Veteran of Mooncrest Manor	Attack Power	176

It was like I'd thought after facing the bandits in the village: killing Travelers was in fact a very efficient method of leveling up. A significant portion of the experience had come simply from the completion bonus of the battleground itself, but I had gotten large amounts of experience from every kill I had participated in. If I hadn't been forced to hide through most of the battle, I might have gotten all the way to level forty. Unfortunately, the terms of the battle had made that impractical. As did the death penalty I would suffer due to [Gray Man's Touch].

I was still resentful over that curse, but I didn't know what to do about it. I could have it removed by resetting myself to level one, but I wasn't willing to do that. I could issue quests to kill the Gray Man, but the consequences of that would likely be even worse than having my level reset. Thedum would abandon me, and Uncle Storm would lose his primary obstacle in claiming the throne. And the act itself was simply unconscionable to me. No, I wasn't even willing to consider it, and I wished that Thedum hadn't put the possibility into my head.

The topic of conversation for most of the Travelers who were waiting with me was, of course, the battleground and their participation in it. Quite a few of my friends from <Nethersong Mavericks> had participated, but most of them admitted that they had gotten ejected rather quickly. The ones who hadn't explained that the other instances were rather straightforward compared to mine. The bandit leaders hadn't moved throughout the fight, and once their locations had become known, it had been a simple matter of zerging them until they retreated.

The bandit leaders were, apparently, quite cowardly and would retreat quickly if they were confronted by a group that outnumbered them, or when their team's Morale points dropped too low. They had lacked the tactical advantage of hiding inside the manor itself and had been forced to guard their immobile bandit leader with dozens of Travelers to keep them from retreating. This had put them at a disadvantage on the rest of the map, allowing my allies to claim spawn points and drain the enemy's Morale points over time in midfield.

Most of the bandits had complained that they had no way to win other than to "turtle" and hope that the lowest level bracket managed to find and kill me, but that wasn't a winning tactic in the end. Once an instance was cleared, the participating Travelers had the option of "syncing down," merging into a lower-level instance. My victorious allies were quickly able to spread their winning strategies with their juniors. The bandits got the same privilege, of course, but they still saw it as unfair. Once the instances began to merge with each other, everything had snowballed, coming to an abrupt conclusion.

Tens of thousands of Travelers had taken part. Now, in the aftermath, there was a significant amount of flexing, trash talking, and complaining going on in the forums. My allies were bragging about overcoming unfavorable terms, while the bandits were complaining that the combat algorithms of the bandit leaders were terrible. The mercenaries were mostly just bragging, though several of them were complaining that they didn't get better participation rewards compared to the other two factions.

There were *a lot* of videos from the battle floating around on the forums. *Several* super threads had been created simply to allow Travelers a place to link their participation footage, and although it had only been a few hours since the battle, many editors were already putting out rushed montages and "best of" videos using the submitted footage. I was quite prominent in the most popular threads, although many of the commentators were being overly harsh with their criticisms of my performance and my allies. Some accused me of cowardice for hiding for most of the battle, while others criticized my combat capabilities. I got the feeling that most of them were either trolling, or they were "salty" because they had been on the losing side.

I indulged my interest in the matter for a few minutes. Then I put it out of my mind without commenting. I sort of wished that I could undo everything and fade back into relative obscurity, but I knew that wasn't an option. My only course of action was to plan for the future, which meant that it was time to dig deeper into the management options that my throne unlocked.

Travelers and Natives both began to trickle into the throne room. My Dusk Guard kept a perimeter up around the throne itself, with one healer keeping a constant stream of protective spells on me. Her shielding spell would probably absorb three or four times my maximum Health before failing. I don't think it was necessary, and it sort of tickled and distracted me, but I tolerated it in silence as my allies gathered.

Three [Mages] working together put up a temporary summoning chamber in the ballroom that I had escaped through the night before. It was expensive, reagent wise, but any level eighty [Mage] class could do it, and it greatly expedited getting everyone together.

Daemon, Dimple, and four other officers from <Nethersong Mavericks> came. Including the guild leader herself, Klarisha, whom I hadn't met before. Or rather, I had, but I hadn't been informed that she was the Gee El. Many of my friends were there, and Travelers that I had played and partied with in the past, including Phil, Laurant, Larissa, Thena, Peafowlet, Sellamander, Stan, Wesle, and Corinth.

At my request, Daemon had reached out to Randal, the architect who had helped me escape a kidnapping attempt back during the mayhem when [Zhesa Castle] had first been turned into a dungeon.

Among the Native occupants, Bell—the old woman who had been imprisoned for allegedly spitting in Arkan's drink—was in attendance. As were her two sons and their wives. Six merchants were hugging the walls nervously. A blacksmith was repeatedly challenging Phil to a wrestling match. A few other villagers were standing around, waiting for proceedings to begin.

I noticed, somewhat idly, that they all bowed when they entered the throne room. Except that they didn't do it properly. They should have covered their heart with their left hand and braced the other hand behind their back before and during the dip, but they did it backwards. It took me perhaps longer than it should have to realize that this was the same error that Irvine had made, and which I had neglected to correct. When I inquired, I learned that he had followed me to Ebbyvale and spent all night and morning teaching all the Natives "the proper way to bow" for their new lord. He was still in town somewhere, giving lessons to anyone who would listen.

I wondered for a moment if it was worth the effort to try to correct and decided that my plate was full enough already. Still, I requested that someone find him and bring him to the impromptu court, and one of the minor members of my guild jumped at the quest on the condition that someone share the video of everything that happened while they were gone.

The final attendees were invited by Tarisha. They arrived through the summoning chamber one after the other. My Dusk Guards stood up a bit straighter; either they recognized these Travelers, or they were simply responding to the levels of my new guests. Each of them was at least level one-eighty, and they wore either armor that veritably rippled with power and enchantments or clothes so fine and of such high fashion that they would be the talk of a royal ball.

Tarisha introduced them one by one. Nine of the greatest endgame guilds had sent representatives to me.

Including one from <Branded Exiles>.

31
COURT

I'm not certain how I would have reacted had Tarisha not warned me in advance that a representative from <Branded Exiles> would be in attendance. Not very well, probably. Even forewarned, I was forced to clench my fists during her introduction. She was the only Traveler in attendance with an aura of red, although it was fainter than I was expecting. She didn't have the marks of the [Brand of Sin] on her face, and I don't think she had been actively completing quests that would have earned her negative Reputation with me, judging by her hue.

Her name was Rowena, she was a [Shadowmancer], and she danced into the throne room with the poise of an experienced courtier, bowing deeply before me in the proper fashion. Not the backwards way that Irvine was spreading. If it wasn't for her aura and her guild affiliation, I would have thought nothing of her.

"Lord Hail, thank you so much for extending your invitation to—"

"I did not invite you," I said, interrupting her. "Not willingly, at least. I'm told that you have recently begun putting pressure upon my friends through back channels and cutouts. The goal of this pressure seems to have been an attempt to get *you* in a room with *me*. So let's get it over with. What do you want?"

Rowena blinked in surprise. "Have I done something to offend, Milord?"

"Your guild is sheltering Nial Kingslayer," I said simply. "So, yes. Consider me offended."

"I see. I did not realize that was a consideration. Does that also account for the difficulty our members have been experiencing in attaining your faction quests?" she asked.

I did not respond to the probe. "What. Do. You. Want?"

She sighed. "We don't have to be enemies, Lord Jeoran. Much of our guild is planning on exploring the new factions that are opening up in the frontier lands, but it hasn't been a smooth transition. Gathering Reputation with the Nostantan and the Undead factions isn't as easy as we thought, and our branded players are mostly cut off from resources like the auctions. The majority of our guild is simply dedicated to supporting them, and—"

"I don't care," I said, interrupting her. "You are here for one reason, and one reason only. You threatened to put a bounty on members of <Nethersong Mavericks> if you did not get a representative at this meeting. Do you honestly have the gall to propose an alliance on those terms?"

Rowena sighed and looked away. She had the grace to look ashamed. "I wasn't informed how my spot in this meeting was obtained. I apologize on behalf of my overeager companions. I shall have a discussion with my guild leadership about the matter, and I promise to do my best to prevent it from reoccurring. Bullying a casual guild like <Nethersong Mavericks> is a very bad look, from a Pee Are standpoint, and they should know better. We were simply desperate to try to get a foot in the door with you."

"Why?" I asked. "You said yourself that you are pursuing opportunities with the adversary. My allies and I are literally doing the antithesis of that. What—"

"I'm here to persuade you to create more battlegrounds," she explained. "The largest limiting factor in our exploration of the darker factions in the game is the limited number of players with [Brand of Sin]. Just with last night's battlegrounds, thousands of new players have joined the darkside. Many of them have already applied to <Branded Exiles>, and even those who have not applied to our guild directly will be helping us indirectly by gathering intelligence and exploring the new zones and factions. We are hoping that future battlegrounds will continue to reward the brand for the forces that oppose you. We are willing to go so far as to offer remuneration for any resources or opportunities you require, and to actively sandbag during our participation in the battlegrounds themselves."

I held my silence for a moment after she finished speaking. "I have heard your offer. Now hear mine. Bring Nial Kingslayer to face the justice of the high court in Zhesa City, and then I will consider listening to further negotiations from your guild. Until then, my faction will consider itself at war with you and your allies. You are not welcome in my lands, and those loyal to me will see you as their enemies. Killing your guild members will grant them Reputation with my faction, and providing you aid will come at great cost to them. Now leave. You are not welcome here."

Rowena bowed deeply, a smile on her face despite my pronouncement of enmity. "I shall share your words with the leadership of my guild," she promised. Still mid-bow, she Fast Traveled away.

I unclenched a great many muscles and spent a moment studying the other guild leaders who had come to my court. None of them had an aura indicating that they had negative Reputation with me, but I wasn't foolish enough to believe that meant they were my allies. These were the Travelers who had kept Tarisha so busy from the time the battleground had closed. They were in the leadership of their respective endgame guilds, and as I had been warned repeatedly, endgame was ruthless.

"Are the rest of you here for the same reason?" I asked. "To persuade me to create more battlegrounds?"

The guild representatives exchanged glances, and a young man with glasses stepped forward. "I wouldn't say that we speak with a unified voice, My Lord," he began. "Although I do believe that I can speak for my friends here in saying that we are mostly here because we feel that a meeting with you is long overdue. I am Cedric Ravenshadow, of the <Phoenix Talons>, and, like many of my compatriots, we have been following along with the events that have unfolded since you became known to the public at large. Until recently, the Talons have mostly held ourselves back from approaching you on the advice of your other allies. They have described you as a nascent Aye Eye, and we didn't want to feed you too much conflicting data. With recent events, I believe it is time to step forward and make our stance known. I would like to discuss the possibility of creating an alliance between my guild and your faction. And, if possible, I would like to discuss the possibility of obtaining deeper knowledge of your goals and aspirations so that we may help you achieve them."

Another representative, a woman who had chosen to be a cat-kin, stepped forward. "I think we're more or less on the same page on that front. <Starlight Eclipse> is also seeking an alliance and greater involvement in the cyclone of events that surround you, Lord Hail."

"<Shadow's Valor> is also seeking an alliance," said an older [Rogue]. "Though I'd be lying if I said we weren't hoping you would also start spamming whatever button you press to create battlegrounds. Last night was loads of fun."

"It's not something I can do without cost," I admitted. "I need . . . A precious resource is consumed every time I create a battleground. While it is possible for me to generate more of this resource, they're not easy to farm. I have several more, but I'd prefer not to spend them all on battlegrounds unless absolutely necessary, as they have other functions as well."

"What could be better than a battleground?" the [Rogue] inquired.

"Complete the quest to become my ally, and maybe I'll tell you," I teased, and I shared the quest I had written for that very purpose with all the remaining guild representatives.

The other five representatives also stepped forward, introducing themselves and their guilds, formally accepting the quest to become my allies, and thanking me for the opportunity. Tarisha had apparently informed them of the existence and goal of the quest, and many of their members were sitting on completed quests, just waiting for the guild quest before claiming credit. They were a little dismayed that none of them were able to immediately complete the alliance, but then they had only been preparing for the quest for a few game hours. They were all quite certain that it would not take their guild long to complete the requirements, and they went so far as to wager with the others which of them would complete it first.

My Native subjects were the next order of business, and that was a complicated subject. I announced that, effective immediately, everyone who had been appointed to an official position of authority by Arkan was suspended pending a review and were, in general, advised to begin looking into alternative career opportunities. Also effective immediately, I was freezing the shire's financials until a full audit could be performed. I announced that I was using my authority to order Ebbyvale and the surrounding villages to hold new alderman elections, which actually received a round of applause. The current village leaders were apparently unpopular appointees.

I announced that all property in the shire would be reassessed for taxation purposes . . . eventually. Before the next collection at least. This was met with a surprising amount of enthusiasm as well. Most of the attendees were significantly more in favor of paying taxes on their current level of prosperity, compared to how their families had been faring three decades before. Nobody *liked* paying taxes, of course, but they liked paying taxes on properties they were forced to sell years ago even less than usual.

Not everyone was happy. At least two of the [Merchants] had grim expressions on their faces; they had likely come into their wealth recently and were enjoying paying very little in taxes. And many of the other citizens believed that my stated plans fell short of my obligations to them. One went so far as to demand compensation for the losses they'd suffered due to the bandits and the corrupt officials. I advised him that any such payouts would have to wait until after the audit had been completed and the bandits had been apprehended, and I suggested that if he wanted to speed things up, he could join the bands of Travelers who were scouring the countryside. He didn't like that answer very much.

I had, at this point, completed two thirds of my goals for the morning, but what came next was . . . experimental. And not something that I wanted the new guilds to witness until I knew whether it would work like I thought it would. I announced that the court was entering a strategic session, and I asked everyone not in <Nethersong Mavericks> or <Peasant's Revenge> to leave. The Natives left readily enough, but some of my prospective allies looked like they wanted to push the matter. Fortunately, they were wise enough to withhold their complaints.

Once the throne room was secure, with only my staunchest allies remaining—plus Randal, whom I had extended a special invitation to remain behind—I slumped a bit in my throne. "That was exhausting," I complained.

"Does your magic throne thing sap your strength or something?" Potatoad inquired.

"No, nothing like that. I just haven't had to fake smile for that long in a while. I wonder how my grandfather managed to do this sort of thing. Every. Single. Day. For decades." I sighed and banged my head against the back of the throne in frustration. "How goes the hunt for the bandits?"

"It's a mess," Lloyd of <Peasant's Revenge> admitted. "They didn't get nearly as many new recruits as our side did following the battleground, but they did get quite a few. But more importantly, their established forces are all in hiding. Even when we find one of their strongholds or camps, they fade away before we can encircle them, and we're left holding empty ground. Adding to the problem is the fact that we can't tell for certain whether a Traveler is affiliated with them or not. With all the new people stomping around, we're stuck trying to find Native bandits and bring them in, but they seem to be quite adept at hiding."

"Don't the new Traveler bandits have [Brand of Sin]?" I asked.

"Not many," Lloyd explained. "Only Travelers above level eighty were branded to begin with. Lower-level Travelers who signed up to fight for the bandits got a quest item that they can use to gain the brand once they reach an appropriate level for it. There are many bandits who are still wishy-washy on whether or not they're going to use theirs; a lot of them are saying that they wished they only signed up for the bandit side because the queue was shorter and are wishing that they'd gone the mercenary route instead."

I blinked in surprise. "What kind of quest item is it?"

"Some sort of dark religious artifact," Lloyd answered.

I grinned, because I had an idea. One that would, maybe, keep any number of Travelers from going over to the adversary.

"Initiate Quest Writing Protocols."

32
APPOINTMENTS

It wasn't a complicated quest. I pushed it to all my associated quest givers, removed any Reputation requirements, and generally made it as simple as possible. The only requirement was that the Traveler have the [Black Rosary], which was apparently the name of the item low-level bandits had gotten for participating in the battleground instead of being marked with [Brand of Sin]. And to complete the quest, they simply turned it in to the Temple of Thedum in Ebbyvale for a bit of gold and quite a bit of Reputation with my faction.

It was probably not enough to undo all the damage they'd done to their Reputation by opposing me in the battleground, but it would go quite a long way toward allowing them to access *some* of the quests in the town and surrounding zones, if they were so inclined. My Traveler friends all thought it was a great idea, and they helped me put the word out on the forums about the quest's existence.

Considering that the alternative use for the [Black Rosary] was to take it to a temple of the adversary and get marked with the [Brand of Sin] once the Traveler had reached level eighty, I was very optimistic that this quest would be popular. Hopefully, at least a few bandits would have second thoughts about turning to the darkside and take advantage of the opportunity I'd created for them. If not, well, it only took me a few minutes of playing around with my new quest writing interface.

"So," I said nervously. "Aside from having bandits all over the place, how's the rest of the fallout from last night settling?"

Tarisha snorted. "It's a clusterfuck, Hail. But you knew that without asking. Thousands of high-level Travelers used the opportunity to gain a [Brand of Sin], although fortunately they've already turned their attention to the frontier lands rather than hanging around in Yuikon. In fact, that might be for the best, since those players were already looking for a way to move over to the darkside, and this gets them out of the way. The real problem, however, is that you are now the number one topic of conversation, the most sought-after Native, and generally the hottest commodity within this world. If we weren't in our own instance, this room would be literally overflowing with the avatars of Travelers trying to get closer to you."

"We've had twenty-nine thousand applications to <Nethersong Mavericks>," Dimple pointed out. "We don't even have the personnel to help screen that many people. Some of them are literally offering bribes to get in. We've had to announce that we're freezing recruitment for the foreseeable future."

"<Peasant's Revenge> is much the same, although we've always been stricter on our minimum requirements," Tarisha agreed. "Having the guild quest may help matters somewhat. Unfortunately, Hail, I'm sorry to inform you that the leadership of <Ragtag Muffin> has taken a stance to try to distance themselves from you. They have gone so far as to request that you revoke their allied status and return them to being neutral with you."

"What?" I asked. "Why?"

"It's too much pressure for them, Hail," Dimple explained. "They're not saying that you can't be friends with Sophia or their other guild members, but they also got a rush of applicants after the battleground when it was revealed that their members got bonus Reputation with you. A lot of the applications were Travelers who had no business applying to a kids-only guild, and even though they should know better, a lot of the applicants are being . . . well, assholes. It's a big strain on their moderators. Everyone knows you were just trying to do something nice for your friends, so nobody is mad at you, but they do want you to change their status back."

"If it makes you feel any better, Hail, I'm pretty sure that the kids are all looking forward to completing the guild quest to earn an alliance the hard way," Thena pointed out. "By the time they accomplish that, other guilds will have an alliance as well, so it won't be so much pressure on their moderators."

I sighed in frustration, but I quickly navigated my menu and reverted <Ragtag Muffin> from Allied to Neutral. "Okay, it's done. Is there anything else I should know?"

"Yeah. The contribution rewards for taking part in the battle-ground are sexy," Phil called out. "Or at least they are if you got a few kills. A lot of feeders are complaining that they got shafted, but those who managed to get a decent kill streak going are reporting customized Bee Eye Ess items. A lot of people are really, really happy about that."

"It's true," Tarisha agreed. "My personal reward was a weapon better than the one I've been using for the last six months. I wasn't expecting to upgrade a green raid weapon at a Pee Vee Pee event, but I'm certainly not complaining."

"Yeah, in general everyone is really happy with the rewards, whichever team they fought for," Thena agreed. "Even though the bandits lost, they don't seem to think they were shafted by the reward algorithm."

"Um, exactly how have people been getting their rewards?" I asked. "I just got a message saying they would arrive in twenty-four hours."

"Check your mailbox," Phil advised me, and I made a note to do so at the first opportunity.

"Are you going to do another battleground anytime soon?" Laurant inquired. "If you are, it would probably be best if we could announce it in advance, so that people could prepare for it. While everyone who participated is very happy, there are a lot of people who are annoyed that they missed out."

"It's not that I don't want to, but I'm not sure I should. First of all, I'm still cursed. If I die in a battleground, I go back to level one," I pointed out. "Second, it's expensive. Last night's battle cost me a you-know-what, and I'm not actually certain that it was mine to spend in the first place. Grandfather's shade said that they legally belong to me, but I was always planning on giving them to the kingdom eventually. It's not like using them the other way; when I create a battleground, the core gets destroyed. I can't reclaim it or farm the resulting dungeon for more."

"What's he talking about?" Stan whispered. "What's a 'you-know-what'?"

Someone elbowed him, and I ignored him. "Aside from that, Thomas brought it to my attention that, um, I sort of made my situation quite a bit worse by triggering the battleground. I don't just mean that everyone is paying attention to me now. I sort of panicked when I used [Summon Karmic Warrior] and we were still outnumbered, but I wasn't thinking. I should have just let you handle it, Tarisha. You guys would have wiped the floor with those scrubs."

"Yes, we would have," Tarisha agreed. "But don't be too hard on yourself. This isn't a terrible outcome either."

"Yeah," I said, and I scratched my head. "So, I'm not going to plan on using another battleground unless I'm seriously backed into a corner. I'm going to try something now, and I'm not certain that it's going to work. Phil, you said that you wanted to be the constable, right?"

"Huh? Wait, what?" Phil asked.

I was already in the menu that allowed me to make appointments. The position of head constable was vacant after I fired Montague the day before, but there were four constables whose status was "pending review." I typed Phil's name into the vacancy that Montague had left. I wasn't really expecting it to work, but its status changed to "pending."

And Phil let out a high-pitched scream of excitement. Then a lower-pitched exclamation that was probably meant to make us forget about the first one.

"Holy shit, guys. Holy shit. It's not a quest! It's a *contract!* It's *the* contract! If I sign this, then I'm freaking canon!" he exclaimed.

I had to cover my ears as the room exploded into cheers and celebration. I glanced over at Tarisha, who was one of the few who was not celebrating. She had a concerned expression, contemplative.

"I don't get it. What did I do?" I asked.

"You gave Phil an opportunity to become a canon character," she explained. "He'll be more than just a faceless Traveler. He'll be able to lead Natives and interact with them on another level compared to what is normally possible, and his actions will contribute directly to the story. Just like Gideon Lachlann once did."

"Oh," I said.

"It's a large responsibility," she said. "Does the contract have minimum play time requirements, Phil?"

"Hold up, I haven't gotten that far yet. I'm still reading it," he said. "I've got to think about it and figure out if I can do this and college at the same time. I'd love to just sign it and say to hell with school, but real life comes first, you know?"

"Very responsible," Tarisha agreed. And she sounded . . . disappointed? Jealous? Oh.

"Tarisha, that was just a test. I wasn't sure what would happen," I told her. "I was planning on giving you an official position as well, but I wasn't certain if you'd rather be my captain of the guard, or the leader of my armed forces, or even my steward. I didn't want to get anyone's hopes up until I knew whether or not I even *could* appoint a Traveler to a position like that. I kind of figured that Phil would be the easiest of everyone, if it didn't end up being a big deal."

Tarisha smiled, and to my surprise, it was tinged with a bit of melancholy. "Sorry, I don't mean to dampen the occasion. I'm just distracted by some errant thoughts of the future. I believe the best fit for me, for now, would be to become the captain of your guard, Lord Hail. I should be more than capable of serving you in such a capacity for a few years, at least."

"Is there something wrong?" I asked.

"Everything is wonderful, Lord Hail. This is a dream come true," she said, and she did sound more cheerful. "I am truly looking forward to serving you in a more official capacity."

"Right," I said, and so I entered her name as my captain of the guard, a position that had been vacant before. Or not actually vacant, but rather Montague had been serving as both constable and captain of the guard, so when I'd fired him, it had created three openings: head constable, captain of the guard, and the captain of my non-existent army. Since Tarisha wanted the guard, I swiftly typed her name into that opening, and she smiled as she began reading her own contract.

Which brought me to the decision I had been putting off for some time. I needed a steward I could trust. I had a good candidate in mind. A great candidate, actually. One who had gone out of his way repeatedly to help me, despite the fact that I had often treated him with suspicion. I'm not certain *why* I'd gotten off on the wrong foot with Daemon, but by this point I had to admit that he had always done right by me, and I was kind of being an asshole by not acknowledging it. It was time to offer him a reward for all his hard work.

"Daemon, would you like the position as my steward?" I inquired.

I was half expecting him to accept immediately. He didn't. He turned serious, rubbing his mustache calmly as he contemplated the proposition.

"That sounds like it will be a lot of work, Hail," Daemon said eventually. "While I'm honored, I'm not certain that I have the time to be both your steward and an officer of this guild. Seeing as I've already committed myself to being an officer, I wouldn't feel right abandoning that position for—ouch!"

The other officers all took turns punching him and calling him an idiot.

"Hey, Peotre, you're taking over Daemon's position as officer," Klarisha announced.

"Ah fuck, do I have to?" Peotre whined.

"Yes, you lazy prick," she declared. "Hail, you totally need Daemon more than I do. He'll make a great steward, so give him the contract before he comes up with an excuse to get out of it."

"Um, yes, ma'am," I said, and I typed Daemon's name into the vacant steward position. "Um, but, Daemon, if you really don't want it, it's okay."

Daemon sighed, although he actually looked very pleased. I think he was just acting put upon but was secretly thrilled to have the offer. "Let me read the contract first before I agree to anything. Perhaps this will be an interesting change of pace for me."

Yup. He was secretly very excited. I could tell.

"There! Done and signed! I am officially the new sheriff of North Shire," Phil declared proudly.

"Um, no you're not," I said. "Technically, I'm the sheriff, and you're my head constable. But Earl is a higher rank than Sheriff, so—"

"Either way, there's a new sheriff in town!" Phil said, and he struck a pose. I think I was missing something, judging by the way everyone else in the throne room groaned.

33

WRAP-UP

Aside from Daemon, Tarisha, and Phil, I also handed out five more official positions. Most importantly for my purposes, I appointed Sellamander as North Shire's auditor, as he was the Traveler with the most experience in finance. He protested that he wasn't a forensic accountant, but "he did know a guy." In general I just gave him broad authority to investigate the debt situation and look for proof of Arkan's corruption. I promised Sellamander, and any subcontracted investigators, ten percent of whatever coin they managed to recover from their activities, which lit a fire under the druid.

Conveniently, once a Traveler signed the contract to become a canon character, the system began translating the Native writing system for them. That would greatly simplify everyone's job.

The next appointment I made wasn't actually a guild member. Randal, the axe-warrior whose day job was an architect, had been watching the proceedings with a somewhat bored expression, right up until the point where I offered him the opportunity to design my new home and seat of power. It took some time to calm him down after that. While he had the floor, he made a lot of complaints about the slow progress in rebuilding [Zhesa Castle], and he managed to extract a promise out of me that I would see if there was anything I could do to expedite that project as well. I was just as invested in the new castle as Randal was, seeing as its destruction was essentially my fault, but I was forced to admit that reconstruction wouldn't likely continue until the matter of the succession was resolved.

Randal wasn't happy with that answer, but I managed to distract him by announcing another project of mine. Aside from building a replacement for Mooncrest Manor, I also tasked him with designing a Temple of the Eight Faiths for the shire. There were nine gods, of course, but the adversary wouldn't be represented. The other seven were apparently making things difficult for Thedum in the wake of my selection as his avatar—and by extension they were making things difficult for me. I wasn't above a bit of blatant bribery to appease the jealous deities.

That led to a somewhat lengthy theological discussion, in which I learned that my Traveler friends really didn't know anything about the gods of the Natives. Thedum was the God of Order, not light, as most of the Travelers seemed to think; though he was often *associated* with the god of light, Lumina, considering that they were spouses. Thedum was the head of the pantheon and the chief god worshiped by human Natives. The dwarves, elves, dryads, and dragons each had their own gods whom they worshiped above Thedum. The most common names for those gods were Stonebeard, Starweaver, Mossheart, and Skyfire, respectively. There were other names for those gods, of course, but if you talked to a dwarf about Stonebeard or a dryad about Mossheart, they would always know who you meant.

The remaining two deities were Eclipse—god of shadows, illusions, and dreams—and Death. Eclipse was worshiped sporadically by all races, with a slightly higher proportion among the beastkin, who turned to her because they lacked a racial deity of their own. She was not a benevolent deity, but neither was she malevolent, like the adversary. And Death—very few worshiped Death—but his place in the pantheon was undeniable.

While the conversation was interesting, I wasn't a priest of Thedum, let alone clergy to the other gods, and so my knowledge of their worship was very superficial. And my knowledge of how to build a Temple of the Eight Faiths was completely hypothetical. It was an easy project to commission, but Randal poked one hole in that boat after another. It would take him more time and effort than he was willing to expend to design a suitable building for my purposes. He was, however, quite happy to help judge another contest, like the one that had been held for the rebuilding of the castle.

That led to a debate on whether to announce the contest to design my new temple immediately or to wait until the situation with the bandits calmed down. In the end, we launched it on the forums, although the submission deadline was pushed back *weeks and weeks*. I would be a big brother long before we ever broke ground on the temple, but hopefully just the intention of building it would appease the gods who were jealous of my service to Thedum.

With that decided, the discussion moved back to appointing Travelers to canon positions. Perhaps unsurprisingly, *everyone* wanted me to assign them something, but mostly I tried to brush them off. I appointed Laurant as a lieutenant of my armed forces. I would have given him a higher rank, but was limited by his current level. Thena was appointed to be the court healer, and Larissa the court [Mage]. Aside from that, Daemon confirmed that he was able to access a personnel management tool that would allow him to appoint his own subordinates as necessary for the completion of his duties, so when the Travelers of <Nethersong Mavericks> pressed me, I cheerfully passed the buck to my new steward.

Well, that's not entirely true. I discovered that I could create as many positions for a "court jester" as I wanted. It was an unpaid position, so I didn't see any reason *not* to hand it out like candy, and within a few minutes my court had nineteen jesters.

Finally, after what felt like hours of talking, I had run out of fires to extinguish, and we called an end to the emergency court meeting. The crowd dispersed, with many of the Travelers rushing to Ebbyvale or the surrounding lands to explore everything that had been unlocked by my arrival. A few remained behind, but Daemon chased them off, except for Tarisha and my other official appointees.

"I think I'll hold court again in a week," I said once we were alone. "Do you think you can manage to get the elections and everything pushed through by then so I can meet the new aldermen, Daemon?"

"I honestly have no idea how long such a task will take, Hail," Daemon said, sounding just a little flustered. "Accepting the contract has unlocked a great many new features, including a list of Natives whom I need to meet with as soon as possible. If I'm being honest,

I'm feeling like you just threw me into the deep end of the pool without making certain I knew how to swim."

I gave him a squint-eyed glance. "I'm pretty certain that you can swim, Daemon."

He sighed. "Yes, well, it's going to be a busy weekend. But fine, very well. Leave everything to me. I'll fix this den of scum and villainy for you, Hail. Thank you for your faith in me. Truth is, I was starting to think that you didn't really like me."

I tried not to blush. "I'm not certain what I might have done to give you that impression."

"Right. Well, let's start with glancing through the various financial documents that you secured last night. It will take some time for Sellamander to perform a full audit, but we have to start somewhere," he suggested, and so the ledgers came out of inventories.

It very quickly became apparent that the copies Arkan had prepared for me were entirely fictional. They bore no relation to the original documents recovered from the clerk's office nor the documents that Tarisha had liberated from the manor before the battle. It was difficult to get a clear picture from either set of books, but it appeared that Arkan had been deliberately inflating the shire's debt for some purpose.

I had a suspicion, and so I quickly [Scribed] a set of documents for Daemon. Several of the documents were for the banks that held the shire's debt, requesting access to the ledgers and original loan documents. Another was a letter to one of my grandfather's friends, a lawyer, in which I detailed my suspicions and requested his assistance.

I just hoped he wasn't too offended by the last letter I had sent him to help me. I blushed. I had meant to compliment his prestigious pedigree . . . but I saw now that a labyrinth was perhaps not the best metaphor for praising his family tree. I could only hope that he had taken it in good humor.

Laurant and Phil discussed their goals, which were basically to go out among the gathered Travelers and recruit as many as they could into my fledgling army and meager constabulary as they could. I pointed out that, for the immediate future at least, the pay for those positions would be zero, but they assured me that it wouldn't be a problem.

"We'll be literally beating away applicants with a stick, Hail,"

Phil promised. "Literally. I have a stick for that purpose, and I'm going to use it. A lot."

"Yeah, kiddo, Phil's right. People are going to really, really want what we're selling, even if it's an unpaid position with zero benefits other than being a minor cog in the story. When we go outside and tell people that we are canonically building up an army to face down the bandits, there's a pretty good chance there will be a literal stampede of people trying to join us," Laurant pointed out. "The hard part is going to be keeping the number down. I only have five thousand openings to fill; there seems to be a hard limit on that. Do you know if there's any way to bump it up?"

"Not without increasing my own ranking," I answered. "I'd be allowed twenty thousand troops as a marquis, or fifty thousand as a duke. If the kingdom ever declares war, then I would be able to gather even more, but that's as large of a standing army as I would be allowed in times of peace. If we *do* declare war on anyone, then the limit effectively goes away, although some of my social superiors would take issue if I was able to recruit too many more soldiers than they could hold."

"Right then. Side note: let's try to figure out a way to get Hail promoted," Laurant commented, pretending to whisper it in mock conspiracy.

"I'm not certain I want that," I admitted. "Ruling lands sucks more than I thought it would."

"You have literally been at it for slightly longer than one day, Lord Hail," Tarisha pointed out. "Perhaps your opinion on the matter will evolve once a few fires are put out, and you have established a functional government."

"Yeah, maybe," I allowed. "What about you, Phil? Is there a limit on how many constables you can hire?"

"Yeah, about that," he said. "Hail, please give me permission to allow your law enforcement to call themselves 'Deputies' instead of 'Constables.' I've already tried changing the name like twenty times, but it keeps saying that it needs your permission."

I frowned. "Why?"

"Because it sounds cooler," he explained. "And then I can legitimately write off the purchase of a magic six-shooter."

I considered the question, because it wasn't to be taken lightly.

However, I was fully aware that "because it sounds cooler" is actually a very good reason to do something when Travelers are concerned. I, personally, didn't see the improvement. But none of the other Travelers contradicted Phil's assertion, which implied that I should trust his judgment on the matter. "Alright, fine."

"Oh, great. You're not going to start doing the John Wayne swagger, are you?" Laurant asked.

"I'm literally pulling up reference materials to practice it right now," Phil answered. "That and the drawl. Can't be a deputy without a proper drawl."

I paused. "Is that an actual rule?"

"Never mind the boys, Hail. It's a cultural thing in our world," Thena explained. "Phil, you never answered his question. How many players can you deputize?"

"Um, hold on," Phil said, and he spent a moment swiping at invisible menus. "Um, it looks like I can hire two hundred permanent deputies, and up to five thousand emergency recruits to deal with the bandits. Seems that Hail has declared them in open revolt, which is letting me put a posse together to deal with them, but once the leaders are brought to justice, most of them will lose their special status."

"So between the two of you, you can recruit a force of up to ten thousand players," Thena provided. "That's nice. All I got for my canon position is a quest inviting me to speak with Thedum's bishop in Zhesa."

"Yeah, same here," Larissa complained. "Well, not to speak with a bishop. Archmage Blanchy-something-unpronounceable. In some sort of school in Eolstree."

"Archmage Blancherathetera?" I asked, my eyebrows leaping upward.

"You know him?" she asked. "If he's famous, maybe it's not a bullshit reward after all."

"*She* is possibly the most powerful [Mage] alive," I said. "She's at least three hundred years old, and I grew up listening to my nurse telling me the tales of her adventures when she was much younger. She's mostly retired these days. I'm not surprised she's not well known among Travelers."

Thena chuckled. "Hear that? Sounds like she's the sort of [Mage] who you don't want to offend. Especially not by, say, accidentally mispronouncing her name. You may want to start practicing."

Larissa shot Thena a *look*. "What's your bishop's name?" she asked.

"Luke," Thena answered smugly.

"Trade you?"

"I'm a little surprised. I didn't see any additional notifications that you were receiving a quest when I assigned you your new positions," I commented.

"I don't believe that those quests are 'House Jeoran' quests, Hail," Tarisha explained. "I suspect that you don't have authority to assign them. Rather, the system assigned them once you nominated Larissa and Thena to canon positions to begin their personal journeys. I—I received something similar, although of a very different nature."

"You got a bonus too?" I asked. "I'm glad. What is it?"

"If you don't mind, I would prefer not to discuss it at this time," she said. "It's a matter that I need to discuss with . . . my boyfriend, I suppose, before I make any commitments one way or the other."

"Oh, shit," Laurant whispered.

"You're dating someone?" I asked, surprised. "I didn't know that."

"Is it someone we know?" Larissa asked, leaning forward with excitement.

"No comment," Tarisha said. "Anyway, aside from that possibility, which I'm not ready to discuss yet, my position as Hail's captain of the guard mostly gives me simple personnel management tools. I've already assigned his usual guards official positions and entered their schedules into the system. It's quite convenient, as it seems that once a guard's shift is scheduled to begin, they will get an option that will automatically teleport them to Lord Hail's side. My friends in guildchat are quite happy with that perk."

"I can imagine," Phil said. "That will probably make things much easier for you, especially now that he's a celebrity."

"What about you, Hail?" Larissa asked. "What are you planning on doing next? I mean, I suppose there's probably thousands of things that you need to do to help fix the shire, but do you know where you're going to start?"

"Actually, I think I need to take a step back," I answered. "Everyone is looking for me right now, and there's a pretty good chance that if I wasn't protected by the system shunting everyone without a [Mark of Karma] into a different instance, I might have already been attacked. I can't think of anything else I can do in the shire without drawing all sorts of attention to myself, so I'm going to just leave things up to Daemon and Sellamander and everyone else. I—I was thinking I'd go see my mother in Eolstree."

I paused and pulled a [Dungeon Daughter Core] out of my pocket. "But first, I was hoping you guys would help me hide this somewhere."

34
TRAVEL

Dungeon Daughter Core (Epic, Undead)	
Level	55–60
Uses	1 / 1

My friends exchanged confused looks when I produced the core, and I realized that they might not actually know what it was. Although cores appeared, in general, as large crystal gemstones, their exact appearance could vary widely. Some of the Travelers in the room had seen me handling a dungeon core or two, but this one was different enough that someone might assume it wasn't the same sort of item at all.

"It's a dungeon core," I explained.

"Yeah, we figured that," Phil said. "But, well, are you sure it's a good idea to use one? Your track record for spending them hasn't been the greatest, in case you've forgotten. I mean, the battleground was awesome, but it also almost backfired on you. And then there was the castle before that."

"Yeah, I know," I said. "But this is different. I was always planning on using a few of the cores I got for busting [Zhesa Castle] on my lands, and even Grandfather's shade agreed with me that it was a good idea. And since Mooncrest Manor is already burned down and derelict, I figured it's the perfect place for a dungeon. Unless you know of a better one."

"He's right," Laurant agreed. "And it will drive up the prices of North Shire real estate even further to have a decent dungeon in the area. My only concern is how fast you're burning through cores. I mean, unless you have a few dozen of them stashed away and didn't tell us."

"I'd prefer not to put a number on it," I said, although I knew the number was ninety-eight, including the one in my hand. "But I definitely have enough on hand that I can establish five dungeons in both North Shire and Thorn March, and still have plenty left over in case I need to create an emergency battleground."

"Shit," Laurant said, though it wasn't a serious curse. "If there's no risk of running out any time soon, then yeah, you should definitely make a few dungeons. Are they all low-level dungeon cores, or is it a mix, or what?"

"I have five cores picked out for North Shire that are in the range of level thirty to level sixty," I answered. "But I don't know where to put them, except for this one. I haven't picked out which cores to use in Thorn March yet. I think it would be best to match the dungeon levels to their environments, but I don't know much about that area's native darkspawn."

"Makes sense," Laurant agreed. "Phil and I will totally keep an eye out for places that would make awesome dungeons for you over the next few days, while trying to not make it look like that's what we're doing."

"Yup. We'll be scouring the land for bandit hideouts anyway, so it will look totally legit," Phil agreed.

"Lord Hail, I've been wondering," Tarisha said hesitantly. "The [Zhesa Castle Dungeon], before it was converted into a raid, it had several zones, and its enemies covered a wide range of levels. Was there some indication that that core was different or more valuable?"

"I guess?" I said. "Most of the cores I have now all have a level range on them, but the core that I used back then said its level was unrestricted. I think about five percent of all dungeon cores are like that, judging by the descriptions of the ones in my inventory. Obviously, I haven't used any of the other unrestricted cores yet."

"I strongly suggest you save them," Tarisha agreed. "Multi-wing dungeons are valuable and unique. [Zhesa Castle Dungeon] would have been very popular for some time had things played out differently. We should save the unrestricted cores for the most promising dungeon locations we find. And we should *definitely* avoid burning them to create battlegrounds, especially if they're rare."

"Yeah, I agree," I said. "The core I used last night was a level fifteen to twenty core. I don't think the level or type of core matters at all for battleground generation, since it seems like almost everyone who wanted to was able to participate in the battle."

"Right, I just wanted to make certain," she said. "As for where to stash the core, I think we should lock it in the document storage room. But what about the throne? Won't it be inconvenient to hold court inside of a dungeon?"

"Thomas said that we can move the throne pretty easily," I reminded her. "And it takes time for the dungeon to form. Once I activate it, it will be seven weeks in this world before the dungeon forms. I'll just have to find a new place to hold court before then, if the palace that Randal is going to build me isn't ready by then."

"Very well," she agreed, and she led me to the hidden document storage room in the basement. The door didn't appear until she waved the key that we had gotten from Arkan in front of it, which was the reason it had taken her so long to find in the first place. She had already cleared out all the documents, leaving the shelves inside empty. I activated the core, left it behind, and we locked the door to the hidden room, the key disappearing into my inventory.

"Should we announce that the manor is going to become a dungeon, or not?" Thena asked seriously. "It might backfire on us if Hail's ability to create new dungeons becomes widely known."

Tarisha nodded at the sagacity of the priestess's words before immediately dismissing them. "The idea that Hail was linked to the [Zhesa Castle] incident is already widespread. We're confirming suspected information, not revealing something entirely new. Having it known that Hail has conscious control over the creation of both new dungeons and battlegrounds will earn him quite a bit of respect from any force that wishes to influence him. While I can see where some guilds might strategically align themzelves against him in attempts to force him to trigger battlegrounds, those who wish to exploit him for dungeon creation will most likely seek alliances. As such, I believe revealing this ability now is for the best. With your permission, Hail, I will make an announcement on the forums with a countdown until the new dungeon opens."

"Sure," I said. "I think you're right. There's no reason to keep it secret at this point."

"There *would be* if you were creating a raid," Tarisha admitted. "First clears of new raids are highly competitive, and the knowledge of when and where one was about to form would be extremely valuable information. But a level sixty dungeon isn't something that's worth treating as a strategic secret, and hyping it up a little bit will actually earn you some good will."

"Right," I agreed. I turned to Phil and Laurant. "So then, you guys probably want to go start hitting your new recruits with sticks or something. Is that actually a thing in your world?"

"Sort of," Phil said. "Not actually hitting them, but drill sergeants are pretty infamous for their creative insults."

"Yup. I'm planning on going full-out *Full Metal Jacket* for the first few days," Laurant agreed.

"Well, good luck with that, whatever that means," I said. I turned to Larissa. "Can I get a portal back to Zhesa? I'll get an international teleport to Eolstree from there. I could just Fast Travel, but Tarisha says it's better to keep that available for emergencies."

"It *is* better for you to always have that option available," Tarisha insisted.

"It didn't do me much good last night," I reminded her. "It doesn't work if I get stuck in an event, and I'm pretty sure the system is quite happy to consider 'twenty endgame Travelers ambushing me' to be a sufficient definition of an 'event.'"

"You're probably right," she agreed. "But it's still a good first line of defense."

I shrugged, conceding the point. "Oh, but before we go, let's try this out."

I activated [Illusion Magic: Disguise]. And I felt . . . nothing. I glanced down and was disappointed to note that the magic certainly had no effect on my clothing. "How do I look?" I asked.

"Pretty much the same," Laurant admitted. "I mean, the silver highlights in your hair are gone, and your eyes are the same color now. Green. But you still look like you. You're not a completely different person or anything."

"That is enough of a difference to hopefully keep anyone from immediately recognizing him," Thena pointed out. "His hair and his heterochromatic eyes are the most widely known details of his appearance. Otherwise, Hail, you just look like a normal teenager. I think if you change clothes as well, this spell will be enough to keep anyone from immediately recognizing you."

"Okay," I agreed, and I selected another outfit from my inventory to fast-equip. I wished that I had a mirror in my inventory to see how I looked, but I figured I'd have a chance to see how my disguise looked eventually.

"Hopefully, I'll get more disguise options as I level the skill," I commented. "It's only level one at the moment, but I haven't been using it much. Maybe eventually it will let me look like a completely different person."

Larissa opened a portal, and our party separated. Phil and Laurant remained behind to begin the recruitment efforts, while Tarisha, Larissa, Thena, and I stepped through the portal. My Dusk Guard members appeared a moment later, grinning.

"Seems like we get a free ride when he teleports," Lucile of SoCal commented. "That's nice."

"Fan out," Tarisha ordered. "His disguise won't hold up to much scrutiny, and if people notice us following him around, they'll put two and two together."

"Yes'm," Lucile agreed, and the other four members of <Peasant's Revenge> swiftly vanished into the background.

Thena surprised me by giving me an unannounced hug, which I returned when I recovered from my surprise. "What was that for?" I asked.

"Oh, nothing much. I'm just happy," she admitted. "You're back, you're kicking ass, and changing the entire game as we know it. And now I'm off to have a theological discussion with one of the hardest En Pee Sees to contact in the entire game and probably unlock some entirely new quest chain or something. It's been a good day."

"That's great," I said. "I guess I just didn't realize that you were a hugger."

She shrugged and ruffled my hair. "Have fun visiting your mom,

Hail. I'm probably logging off for the night sometime soon, but you know that if you need anything, anything at all, people will literally drop what they're doing in the middle of a dungeon to come help you, right?"

"Yeah, I know," I said. She ruffled my hair one last time before walking off in the direction of the Temple of Thedum. "Oh . . . When you see the bishop, tell him that I'm sorry for turning him into a slug!"

She just laughed. "Of course you did!" she called back, though she was almost too far away to make out.

The rest of us moved towards the teleportation platform. Minor portals and teleports were redirected to one of six locations throughout the city, while international travel required access to large and powerful magic circles and rituals. Circles and rituals that were also, of course, heavily regulated and taxed. Travelers could bypass this through the use of their own portals or the Fast Travel system, or simply traveling on foot. But it was convenient for going someplace for the first time.

"I've never actually left Yuikon before," I commented as we waited in line to request a portal. "I've read quite a bit about Eolstree, though, since we're pretty close allies. I'm kind of excited."

"Honestly, the two nations aren't too different except for their demographics," Tarisha assured me. "Yuikon is mostly human Natives, while Eolstree is a mixing pot."

"I know that," I said. "A lot of that is also because they send their academics to us for training in architecture, medicine, and literature, rather than developing the infrastructure to house their own campuses for higher education. That's largely because of their beastkin heritage, though. The elves are somewhat less willing to share their culture than my people were, although they were quick to establish a presence once the beastkin tribes united and began accepting outsiders into their lands. Their elite do see the value of education, but they don't see the need to be self-reliant for it. In fact, being trained in Yuikon is a point of pride for many of their professionals."

"I didn't know that," Tarisha admitted. "Very interesting."

"Yeah. They also largely formed their government based upon the Yuikon model," I expounded. "Though, the tribal nature of the beastkin still remains in the background, from what I understand. I don't know all that much about that stuff, though, because, although it's not exactly a secret that they *have* tribal politics that they consider vitally important to their heritage and culture, they don't believe those politics are the business of anyone outside of their tribes."

"Eolstree is the youngest of the nations in the Heartland, isn't it?" Larissa inquired.

"It depends on who you ask," I said. "They unified under their current monarchy two hundred years go, but since the royal family traces their lineage back twelve hundred years, they claim that Eolstree was never not a unified nation equal to its modern peers in any of that time. But all the historians who *don't* collect a stipend from the Eolstrian government agree that the land was a broken territory divided by the seven major beastkin tribes about two hundred years ago, when the Leonids managed to unite them under one banner. The tribes were pretty xenophobic prior to that, but the royal family managed to open them up to the outside world over the course of about fifty years, and since then they've *really* opened up."

"Interesting. I'm really looking forward to learning more," Larissa said. "I actually considered being a catgirl when I was doing my character creation, but then decided that it was too embarrassing."

"I'm also looking forward to this journey," Tarisha agreed. "I've been to Eolstree many times before, of course, but I strongly suspect that any journey I take by your side, Lord Hail, will be incomparable to anything I might have managed on my own."

"Um, thanks?" I said, because I didn't know what else to say to that. Fortunately, the party ahead of us vanished off into the ether, and the [Mage] powering the ritual motioned us to step forward and request our destination. I paid him the toll for the teleport, and he promptly began the incantation to send us on our way.

Within moments, the teleportation platform flashed, and once more I had the slight sensation of displacement as I traveled a great distance.

35

LIECHA

After talking so much about how Eolstree was just like Yuikon, I was a little surprised when the protection of the teleportation magic faded, and I was standing in a magic circle that was not nearly as elaborate as the one on the Yuikonese side of the journey. A middle-aged avian man was administrating the receiving platform, not that he had much to do aside from directing the arrivals away from the magic circle before the next Travelers arrived. All the actual magic was done on the other end of the portal; the platform here simply stabilized and directed the transit.

"Is this your first time to Prowlhaven?" the receptionist inquired. He was in mostly human form, with the primary hint of his heritage being the feathers that grew in place of his hair, and his otherwise hawkish appearance.

"For me, yes, definitely," I answered. "I don't think Larissa has been before, although I guess I don't have her life story memorized. But I'm pretty sure Tarisha has been."

"There are a number of tours and theater events scheduled over the next few evenings, if you wish to partake in our rich cultural heritage," the guide informed me. "They detail the true history of—"

"Thank you," I said before he could get too far into his introduction, "but I'm afraid I don't have time to be a tourist right now.

Perhaps in the future, when my affairs have settled down a bit, I would enjoy such diversions, but at the moment I'm in a bit of a rush. I would appreciate it if you could direct me to the Wildeheart estate."

The receptionist gave me a critical examination and obviously found me wanting. I would have been more annoyed if I didn't get a notification at that moment informing me that [Illusion Magic: Disguise] had gained a level. Apparently, it was working.

"Do you perhaps have a letter of invitation, or a package to deliver to Lord Wildeheart?" the avian man inquired. "I'm afraid that not everyone is allowed to visit the house of a noble without express invitation."

"My mother lives there," I said simply. "If you don't know the way, I'm certain I can simply hire a local guide instead."

"Perhaps that would be for the best," the avian said, his voice heavy with suspicion. "I'm afraid that I'm unable to leave my post, after all."

"Very well. Thank you for your time," I said, and I led the way out of the portal building. My friends followed me. Larissa nudged me and chuckled.

"See, *that's* the sort of brush-off that a player usually gets when we try to intrude on noble Natives in their own habitat," she informed me. "Do you think that's your disguise working, or would that guy have been a jerk no matter what you said?"

"I don't know. I think it was partly the disguise, but not knowing my identity might have been in my favor," I said. "I'm not exactly certain what my social status is in Eolstree. I mean, legally I'm a Yuikonese noble, which is good. The Eolstrians don't get too hung up on bastards, necessarily. Most of their tribes don't care if a couple gets married or not. Which means that my royal blood counts for a lot as well, even though I'm illegitimate. The problem is that I'm *definitely* not Lord Wildeheart's son. Which, depending on how much of a traditionalist he is, means that he might feel honor bound to kill me."

Tarisha groaned and pinched the bridge of her nose. "Lord Hail, how much of a problem will this be?"

"Probably not at all?" I said, hesitant. "I really don't think Grandfather would have let the marriage happen if he was that sort of person. If I was actually in danger from him, I'm pretty sure he would have at least warned me. But because of the way my stepfather's tribe views the matter, it was easier to leave me behind in Yuikon when Mother came to Eolstree. But, um, yeah. Maybe keep an eye out for assassins? And where is everyone else, anyway?"

"Waiting in line for a teleport," Tarisha answered. "It seems that while we do get a free ride-along when you teleport now that we have official status as your guards, doing so triggers our Fast Travel timer. They'll catch up to us in a moment."

"That's inconvenient," I muttered.

"Yes. The amazing one-of-a-kind system perk that allows us to instantly travel to your side from anywhere in the world is inconvenient because of a minor wait time issue," Tarisha teased.

I blushed. "I didn't mean it like that."

"And I was just teasing. However, there is a matter we need to discuss sooner or later. And another matter that we need to discuss once my boyfriend and I have what will probably be a series of very serious conversations, and we either become much closer or break up entirely. But the immediate matter involves my new canon position as the captain of your guard. It might take a few minutes; let's get some Liecha," Tarisha said, and she waved us towards a conveniently placed stall serving the hot drink.

"I've never actually had Liecha before," Larissa commented. "I heard it's like a berry mocha latte with almond extract."

"Liecha tastes like Liecha," I said, giving her "a look." "Why would you make it more complicated than that?"

"Because the Liecha fruit doesn't exist in our world," Tarisha explained. "So we don't have an analogue to compare it to directly. There's a lot of foods in this world like that."

"Huh," I said, then I shrugged. Liecha was a bigger thing in Eolstree than it was in Yuikon, since the trees grew better further north. At the castle we would pretty much only have it on the winter solstice as a hot drink to keep us warm. But I hadn't known that it wasn't a thing that existed on Earth.

The barista took our orders and promptly filled three mugs with the steaming fruit juice before pointing us to a small patio where the customers of her little stand often drank their purchases. There was a small bin for the empty mugs nearby, and judging by how full it was, she did good business.

"This is actually really good," Larissa commented as she sipped on her steamy drink.

"They've been trying to get a recipe to taste in the physical world like it does in the game for some time now," Tarisha commented. "But they can't seem to get it right. It's quite curious, really."

I sipped my drink, reminiscing about winters past when I had shared it with my mother and Beckah while waiting for the weather to improve. "So, Tarisha, what is it that you wanted to talk about?"

The swordswoman sighed and looked in her drink. "Hail, I want you to understand something, and I really hope that you don't take offense. This canon position you have given me; it is without a doubt exactly the sort of thing I was hoping to obtain when I first approached you and offered you my services, and that of my guild. I told you then that I was making plans in the long term, but something like this was always my goal. My investment in you has paid off much more quickly than I had anticipated. And now that it has, I'm feeling quite guilty about having ever taken that view of our relationship to begin with."

"Oh," I said. And I thought I understood. "Mutually beneficial, right? You got what you wanted, and I got a reliable ally when I needed it most. I don't really see the problem with that."

"If that's all there was, then I would say that there wasn't a problem," she agreed. "But when we first met, I thought that you were simply a more advanced and very fascinating computer program. After you confronted your father, before the raid on [Zhesa Castle], I dug deeper into what Arc meant about seeds of consciousness, and I learned more about the details of your existence. They were quite forthcoming about it all, and I think I understand the material they gave me as well as any layperson can. And, well, it bothers me that I originally approached you for my personal benefit, now that I understand you better. So I want to apologize. And, if you feel it's appropriate, I would offer my resignation so that you could appoint a better candidate than myself."

My jaw dropped in surprise. Fortunately, I had already swallowed my Liecha, or that would have been a mess. "Tarisha, you're, like, my best friend. I'm not going to *fire* you. I don't even really understand why you think I should."

"I do," Larissa said in a quiet voice. "A lot of us do. The ones who've been around from the beginning. We sort of feel the same way, but we don't really know what else to do. Completing your quests *does* seem to help you, after all. But it also feels sort of exploitative."

"Exactly," Tarisha agreed. "I'd like to say that we would still be friends if you suddenly lost your quest-giving powers, Hail. And we would be. But we probably never would have met if you hadn't had them to begin with. And coming to realize that has, well, made me feel shallow."

I considered her words for a moment as I drank the hot berry juice, formulating a response. But I only had a vague understanding of what the problem was to begin with. "Tarisha, I really can't think of anyone better to be my captain of the guard than you. *I need you.* If anyone is being taken advantage of in this relationship, I think it's you. I mean, do I even pay you? Shouldn't I owe you and your guild thousands of gold by now for watching over me all this time?"

She snorted. "No, the quest system takes care of that for us. The difficult part has simply been the human resources aspect of scheduling people to be online in staggering shifts to protect you. This upgrade will make that aspect much easier for everyone involved."

"Right, but that's not the only thing you do for me," I pointed out. "You give me advice all the time. And you're, like, my go-to liaison for the endgame guilds. I really don't know what I would do without you to guide me, Tarisha. And I'm really not sure what brought this entire conversation about. If there's one thing I've come to expect from you, it's confidence, not self-doubt."

"I *do* know where these thoughts come from. But perhaps you are right, and I am holding myself to an impossible standard," Tarisha admitted. "Perhaps I should have waited to broach this subject until it was time for the full disclosure of my future plans in this world. But, as I said, I'll need to have a series of very mature conversations with Lewis before I know for certain the shape of those plans."

I nodded. "Is there any reason you can't be my guard captain in the meantime? Or is that a selfish thing for me to ask?"

She chortled. "It is my pleasure to serve you, My Lord," she said, making a mock bow from her seat. "Considering that I got everything I wanted, I sure went out of my way to throw a wrench in the gears in a right hurry, didn't I?"

I shrugged. I didn't get the reference she made about wrenches; it was probably a Traveler saying that I lacked the context for, but I got the gist of it. "I don't mind. I'd much rather talk about it than have you serve me while feeling like you were taking advantage of me. So, it's probably a good thing we had this conversation."

"Yes, I think it is," Tarisha agreed. "Which brings us to the second topic we have to discuss. I believe it is time to significantly expand your guard, Lord Hail."

"Oh? Yeah, you're probably right. I mean, I've only been glancing at the forums since the battleground last night, but everyone really is talking about me. But I don't want to put any more stress on your guild than you're already under. I know that at least some of my guards have been giving up other opportunities to protect me, and I don't really want that."

Tarisha nodded. "Hail, there's no rule that says that your guards can only come from <Peasant's Revenge>. The system that you unlocked for me isn't unlimited, but it does seem to have a vast roster for me to fill with prospective guards. I can only assign ten guards to you at a time, but there doesn't seem to be a limit on the number of Travelers I can register. I'm quite certain that all I need to do is reach out to get more than a dozen teams that would be eager for the opportunity. They will, however, be strangers to you. And me. We'll lose the stranglehold on information that we have currently, as they'll likely be reporting on your activities to their own guilds at a minimum, and probably to networks well beyond that."

"I see," I said. I sighed and finished off my Liecha. "Well, I can't think of another way to handle it. I'll just have to start watching what I say and do around my bodyguards, I guess."

"I'm sorry," Tarisha said. "We'll have to work on establishing a new normal, I think."

"Yeah," I agreed.

"There's just one more thing—"

"Oh, gods dammit, I'm all out of serious. Can we talk about something stupid instead?" I asked.

Tarisha blinked in surprise, and then she began to laugh. And laugh. And laugh. Much harder than I thought the joke warranted. She tried to explain several times when she saw that she was embarrassing me, but it took her several minutes to get herself under control.

"Corinth," she said breathlessly. "Oh, god. The timing on that line was just too perfect. Corinth has been bugging me for hours to let him join your guard. I've been blowing him off so far, but the truth is that he's made a few solid arguments as to why you should have guard members around your level in addition to the endgamers who protect you from getting ganked."

"Oh," I said, feeling better now that she'd explained the joke. "I guess that makes sense, if you think that they can get the same quest that everyone else gets when they're guarding me."

"It will likely be scaled down to their level," Tarisha agreed. "But they'll be able to fight with you and gain experience the regular way in addition to the [Keep Him Safe] quest. I'm not certain whether they'll get the corresponding boon or not, but simply being around you increases the likelihood of receiving one of those, as Corinth proved in Storm's Manor. If we go with this, we'll be establishing two teams. A four-man team matched to your level, which supports you against threats that you have a reasonable chance of dealing with on your own, and a high-level team, which will deal with everything else."

"I'll out-level them pretty fast," I said. I held up my left hand, on which the [Ring of Holy Light] was keeping my curse under control. "Or, at least I will if I actually get a chance to go out and kill darkspawn. I'm getting three hundred percent Experience now, after all. Unless I *do* get ganked, in which case I guess I'll finally be free of this stupid curse, and I can finally start over."

"Yeah, about that," Tarisha said. "I still haven't quite forgiven Corinth for his poorly advised 'test' of the contagion factor of your curse. But one of his ideas for the lower-level members of your guard was that they would all share the Traveler version of your curse. You'll still be able to outpace them if you're active every day, even while your guardians are forced to rest. But Corinth's arguments supporting it are somewhat convincing."

"He wants me to spread the curse *on purpose*?" I asked.

"He's calling it a team-building exercise. The penalty from [Reaper's Embrace] is enough to significantly increase the stakes that a Traveler usually places against an in-game death, and it will help them empathize with your own situation. Actually, I think that if I had to do it over again, I would appreciate the challenge and benefit from having that particular curse–boon combo active myself. Not that I'm asking for you to give it to me at this point. But, if I was level twenty? It might very well be worth it."

I considered her words. "I'm not going to force the curse on anyone who doesn't want it," I said eventually. "But I will give it to those who ask for it. And that goes for anyone, not just guild members or my bodyguards or whatever. As long as they understand the stakes of the curse, then I don't see any reason not to let people try to exploit it."

"I'm not certain that we want to spread the existence of the curse too widely yet, Hail," Tarisha cautioned. "It's possibly your greatest vulnerability at the moment, and you do have enemies, Traveler and Native alike, who would exploit it."

I sighed. I glanced up at my honor guard, which had arrived at some point during the conversation. "Yeah, I suppose you're right. Is there anything else, or can we set out to visit my mother now?"

Tarisha nodded. "Let's get going."

We dumped our empty mugs into the waiting bins and summoned our mounts. It took a while to find directions, but we were soon heading off in the direction of Wildeheart Manor.

36
MAIL

Prowlhaven was not the city I was expecting it to be. There was nothing wrong with it. Quite the opposite, it was actually rather beautiful and well built. But I had often heard it called "Zhesa City's little sibling," so I expected it to look more like home. It didn't.

The streets of Zhesa were almost all cobblestones. Prowlhaven's were packed earth. Few buildings in Zhesa City proper were shorter than three stories, and they were all made of brick or stone. Prowlhaven's buildings were seldom more than two stories tall, and they were almost entirely built of wood harvested from the nearby forests.

The *shape and feel* of the buildings were similar, despite the differences in building materials. But there were also other indications that this city belonged to a culture that was not my own. Totems for several of the beastkin tribes stood vigil outside of certain buildings, letting foreigners know that they were not welcome inside. They weren't completely forbidden either; there were spacious waiting areas outside of the tribal buildings for guests. But forcing your way inside without an express invitation from the building's matriarch or patriarch was effectively a capital offense.

Most noticeably, there was simply so much more space! Zhesa City was all crammed together, a result of centuries of its residents fighting for every inch of real estate. Whether Prowlhaven simply hadn't existed for long enough to have gone through that same process, or there was some fundamental difference between the cultures of Yuikon and Eolstree that I remained ignorant of, I couldn't say.

We were passing what looked like a mercantile district when I noticed an object, and I immediately reined Shadow in. "Hold up. I need to check my mail," I announced. My party quickly detoured, except for Larissa.

"I think I'm going to leave you to it, Hail, if that's okay. I'm going to go see if I can track down Archmage Blanch in the next hour or two, and if I can't, then I'm going to go to sleep," she said.

I waved that I'd heard her, and she rode off to do her own thing while I interacted with the Traveler mail system for the first time. And I was promptly surprised to find that I had mail. Lots, and lots, and lots of mail.

Mostly from Travelers I had never met, demanding all sorts of things from me, from specialized quests to insights into the world, which were, frankly, well beyond me. Some of them sent a bunch of math symbols, which made absolutely no sense to me. But then, my education in math was somewhat stalled at basic algebra, so that might explain why the equations were nonsensical to me. Mixed in with the junk were a fair number of messages along the lines of "Hey, I heard you exist, and you sound kind of cool. I hope we meet in game sometime." But mostly it was all junk.

Fortunately, there were filters that I could apply to remove anyone whom I hadn't met, which brought the list down to a much more manageable size. At the top of the list was the reward for my participation in the battleground, but despite the temptation, I clicked on the messages from Daemon first. A while ago I had asked him to sell some of the vanity pets I had acquired, and I had never collected my earnings.

I was surprised, and gratified, at how many commas were in the number. It wasn't enough to solve the shire's debt problem, but it was a hell of a lot of gold. However, Daemon's most recent message to me gave me an indication that quite a bit of that gold was about to evaporate.

Daemon	Hail,
	I just wanted to officially thank you for the opportunity you've given me. I'm certain you saw through my little act, but either way I wanted to be explicit. I am excited about this new opportunity, even though it means leaving my old role as an officer in <Nethersong Mavericks> behind.
	While I agree with the idea that you need to lie low for the next few weeks after the recent excitement, I have come across a few options that my position allows me to see as possibilities, but I require your permission to enact them.
	There are a number of them, but the most important, I believe, is the creation of a teleportation platform. If I am reading this correctly, I can commission the construction of infrastructure that would allow the international teleportation stations to list us as a potential destination. It seems to be one-way only, though we can upgrade it later. It would allow Travelers everywhere to come directly to the shire from any of the capital cities. I'm sure you can see the benefits of such a building. We would also generate a twenty percent toll on everyone who passed through it, which means that the building would potentially pay for itself over time.
	Unfortunately, I am unable to use guild funds for this purpose, and not only is the shire in debt, but by your decree, all spending is frozen until the completion of the audit. I believe that this is a time-sensitive matter, however, and I believe I have a solution.
	Unfortunately, the solution is for you to pay for the facility yourself. It will cost three million gold. I recommend this action without hesitation, but it is ultimately your money, and your decision.
	If you do not respond before I log off for the night, I will bring this matter up with you the next time I have the chance.

I sighed, and I checked my inventory. I *did* have three million gold. The [Wind Up Malkios] vanity pets had been very popular. Combined with my previous fortune from selling the [Immature Gemos Hearts], I had just enough.

Just enough. I would only have three thousand gold left over.

Which was actually a large amount for a level thirty-two Traveler, and if I was just a Traveler, I'd still consider myself rich. But I didn't need a detailed guide to figure out at least a dozen ways that being a destination for international Travelers would benefit the shire. It was painful to type in such a large amount, but, reluctantly, I sent the requested funds. Just to be clear, I sent a short message.

Hail	Daemon,
	Yeah, I thought that you were just playing hard to get. I could tell that you were actually excited. I'm sorry if we haven't always gotten along in the past. I think you remind me of my old tutor or something. I think I might not have been fair to you because of that, but you have helped me probably more than anyone else besides Tarisha.
	Here's the gold for the teleportation beacon. I approve of its construction. Let me know if I need to give more authorization than that or something to get the system to move forward.
	Since you wiped out all my funds, I need to sell some more vanity pets. Can I still give them to you to sell, or should I find someone else to do it?

I sent the message, and I winced as I checked my remaining gold. I was tempted to go back to the battleground reward to cheer myself up but instead scrolled down to the bottom of my filtered messages. And saw one that I wasn't expecting. From my father.

It had an item attached. As an item, it was just a key of copper. But I recognized it, even before I [Analyzed] it.

Hail's Wardrobe Key
Summons a unique Vanity Pet.
Binds to account on use.

Idly, I wondered how much this item was worth, and what I should do with it. I wondered why my father had sent it to me, so I turned to his message for answers. Not that there were many hidden within.

Gideon	Hey, kid.
	I'm an asshole. Always kind of knew that, but the last few days have really put that in perspective. Hope you don't get that from me, and you grow up to be generous and well-adjusted and whatever. I'm probably not going to be around to see that, which is bumming me out quite a bit more than I was expecting.
	I'm about to do something really stupid. I don't think I'll be allowed to log back in afterwards, so don't be surprised if you never hear from me. Don't worry about me, I'll be fine.
	I swear on my honor, by Thedum, and on my life than I didn't know what Nial was planning. I would have stopped him if I did.
	Good luck.

Putting the context together, I gathered that my father had sent this message to me just before he had dramatically dismantled <The Endolphins> in the wake of my grandfather's death, and my own actions as a temporary Worldboss. I was surprised, and a little touched, that he had even bothered to say goodbye. Even if it was through the mail system. Given my own state of mind at the time he had composed this letter, it had probably been the only method he'd had of contacting me. I'd genuinely not known that he had cared enough for such a gesture.

I considered sending a response, but I honestly couldn't formulate one. And there was simultaneously no rush and little point, except catharsis. I knew that Father was facing ramifications in his world for disbanding the guild that he had founded, although I didn't really understand *why* he was facing them. He would either weather the storm and return to my world or he wouldn't. If he did return, I would have the chance to confront him once again. And if he didn't, then sending an emotional message into the ether would just be pointless.

I examined the vanity pet he sent me. The thought crossed my mind again wondering how much it was worth. I didn't have much reference for how Travelers viewed such things. I had sold the other vanity pets I had earned from busting dungeons for vast amounts, but I'd had many of them. This was probably the only [Hail's Wardrobe

Key] that would ever be, unless I created more dungeons by sticking dungeon cores inside my wardrobes. Being unique made it valuable, right? I figured I should probably at least ask in guildchat how much such a thing would sell for.

Except that it was a gift from my father.

I activated the item and summoned the pet. It was a googly eyed miniature version of the wardrobe final boss of [Zhesa Castle]. It circled around me awkwardly, and every few minutes it would open its doors, and a set of my princely outfits would step out for a moment, until there were five different outfits following it. That was kind of cool, I guess. They were actual outfits that I had worn in my younger years, and every now and then they would perform some action. A handstand, a summersault, casting miniature version of [Spark].

I decided to leave it active, in honor of my father, as I turned my attention back to my mail. Daemon had, surprisingly, already responded to my message.

| Daemon | Hail,
    I went ahead and purchased the building. The system informs me that it will be in operation within twenty-four game hours.
    Also, there is a Native child wandering around town named Irvine. Apparently you sent for him? He keeps bothering me for some reason. Wasn't certain how I should handle that. |

I'd forgotten all about Irvine, so I quickly responded.

| Hail | I was going to offer Irvine a position as a stableboy and teach him the proper way to bow. It's not that important, but I guess he's been showing everybody how to do it wrong. Anyway, just tell him that he can be my stableboy once Randal builds my new mansion and send him home, I guess. |

I moved on to my other messages, of which there were quite a few from guild members. There weren't many of great importance, but a few old messages detailed the adventures of the guild members who had investigated the fate of my old nurse, Beckah. Which reminded me that I had been meaning to reward them personally, in addition to whatever reward they had gotten from the system.

The letter in which Beckah listed the Travelers who aided her had been destroyed when [Zhesa Castle] became a dungeon, but I found that I still remembered the names that it had contained. After giving the matter some thought, I sent each of the twelve players one [Wind Up King Rain Teoran]. Hopefully they would appreciate the gifts, despite the delay in how long it had taken me to send them.

Finally, after combing through all my remaining messages and finding nothing pressing, I returned to the one at the top. The one that promised my award from the battleground. Feeling almost as nervous as I had been when opening my father's final message, I selected it to see what I had earned.

"Huh," I said, rereading the words as the message presented my options. I quickly came to the conclusion that this wasn't a decision I could make on my own. I motioned to Tarisha and my guards that I wanted to speak with them, and when they were close enough, I chose the option to share my menu with them. "I don't know what to pick."

There were three options.

The biggest upgrade, by far, were the boots. Laughably, I was still wearing my [Sturdy Crystal-Toed Boots], which I had earned during my disastrous first delve into [Gemos Caverns]. They required level eight and only gave me a negligible amount of Vitality and Endurance. They were also very comfortable, and I was used to wearing them. The proposed upgrade was a level thirty-two pair of boots called [Calfskin Kickers], which provided twelve Dexterity, four Vitality, and six armor.

I was tempted to go with the new boots simply because it was sort of embarrassing to still wear a piece of gear that I'd been unable to replace since I'd been stuck as a level ten [Child]. However, the other two options had their own allure, which forced me to consider them seriously.

The second option was a pair of earrings. Which was actually a mark against choosing them, in my opinion, since wearing earrings wasn't masculine in Yuikon. Not that that would stop a Traveler from wearing whatever they thought was Bee Eye Ess. But the earrings didn't provide a static bonus like most items did. Instead, they would increase my Spell Power and Dexterity by thirty points for twenty seconds after I activated them, on a five-minute cooldown. Most of the time, the accessory would do absolutely nothing. I would have to *actively use it*, which was one more thing to do in the heat of battle. But it would be a substantial power boost while it was—

"Whatever you do, don't get the earrings," Marvin of Cincinnati said.

"Why?" I asked, curious to his reasoning.

"They clash with your eyes," he said, and Tarisha smacked him playfully on the shoulder.

"While that sort of accessory is powerful and you should look into obtaining something like them eventually, Marvin is correct in pointing out that those are by far the weakest of your options," Tarisha explained. "While they would be powerful if you remembered to activate them during the burn phase of a difficult boss, having a constant stat boost will serve you better until your level is in the triple digits."

"So it's between the boots and the sword then?" I asked. "The boots are a much bigger upgrade."

"No, the sword is," Tarisha said.

"I have a [Gemos Long Sword]. It's level twenty-three; my boots are level eight," I pointed out.

"The sword is still the bigger upgrade," Tarisha said. "As a Dee Pee Ess class, upgrading your weapon is your biggest gear priority. And that's not a level thirty-two weapon, despite what it says. It's a level fifty weapon with a level thirty-two equip requirement. You can find another pair of boots at the auctions that will have comparable stats to the [Calfskin Kickers]. That weapon will serve you until level sixty or higher. It would be worth equipping for the See Plus Damage rating by itself. Combine that with the fact that it has Spell Damage and Dexterity, and you're unlikely to find an upgrade *anywhere*, even if the system decides to continue throwing one-of-a-kind items in your direction like confetti."

I considered her advice for a few moments and decided that she was right. So I made my selection, pulling my new weapon from the system menu and giving it a few test swings. I quickly decided that it was *perfect*.

Mooncrest Ancestral Sword	
Rare, Requires Level 32	
Damage	C+
Dexterity	9
Spell Damage	9

37

MOTHER, PART 1

Once I had finished my massive backlog of messages—a task that was only possible by filtering out thousands from Travelers I had never met and mass deleting them—I played with the settings before finding out that I could prevent most people from sending me mail unless they'd actually encountered me in the world by simply clicking an inconveniently placed box. So I clicked the seven hells out of that box.

Why wasn't that box clicked by default?

Annoyed at the amount of spam I'd been forced to deal with, but proud of my accomplishments, I remounted Shadow, and we got back underway to my stepfather's estate, which took a while. Tarisha hadn't been idle while I was occupied, and several new bodyguards had been teleported along by the convenient new ability she had gained. Aside from Tarisha, four members of my current Dusk Guard were from <Peasant's Revenge>, while two members, a cleric and an [Elemental Archer], were each from one of the different guilds that were vying for my attention. The remaining four spots were taken up by Corinth, Rodney—a kid from <Ragtag Muffin> I had partied with before—and two other random players who were eager to introduce themselves, although I had no idea where they had come from.

"They're friends of friends of friends," Tarisha explained when

I asked. "Sophie logged off just a few moments before I could ask her, or she might have joined us. But I think it's getting late for her anyway, so maybe not."

"I thought Ragtag didn't want to associate with me anymore," I commented.

"That's bullshit," Rodney said quickly. "Seriously, it's all bullshit. The mods just didn't want to deal with a bunch of trolls, so they totally caved to the pressure. But now all the kids are bitching about it in guildchat and making it into an even bigger deal than it was originally. Some kids are threatening to leave over it, and some of them are actually doing it. Nobody's fucking happy about it, but I will literally quit before I listen to the mods tell me that I can't be your friend, Hail."

I blinked, because I didn't think that Rodney and I were all that close. I had only hung out with him a bit as part of a group, after all. "Thanks, Rodney. That means a lot to me."

"Yeah, no problem," he said. "So, I have the rest of this game day before I have to log out. I know that you said in your message, Tar, that it was guard duty, but do you think we'll actually get attacked, or can I kind of just zone out and read the forums or what?"

"Tar?" I asked, glancing at Tarisha. She shrugged.

"You might be called on to take part in a sort of role-play event," Tarisha said, "So maybe don't zone out completely if you can avoid it. We're not very likely to be attacked, but it's not out of the realm of possibility either. If we are attacked by something below level forty, then you'll be supporting Hail, and we'll be letting you guys deal with it. If it's an endgame player or something that your group can't realistically handle, we'll step in."

"Sweet. So I get to just stand around, look tough, and I get free Experience and Rep," Rodney said. "Sounds awesome."

The other two low-leveled Travelers that I didn't know exchanged glances, then nodded towards me. "Can we get the Experience boon–curse thing?" one of the friends to the third degree asked.

"The what now?" Rodney inquired.

Corinth was the one who took over the explanation, as he'd had a long conversation with one of the priests of Thedum in Zhesa City, going over all the benefits and pitfalls of the Traveler version of my curse in detail, including the scaling level of difficulty associated with the quest to remove it. After the explanation, the two strangers both requested that I infect them, as did one of the high-level guards, to my surprise. Rodney abstained, stating that it sounded like more trouble than it was worth.

Personally, I agreed with him, but at least they had a choice in the matter. My own situation had been inflicted upon me without warning, and I remained dissatisfied with all the possible solutions. Including the one where I do nothing about it, which was regrettably the one that I was forced to take.

I *was* a little annoyed that the topic had come up after I had just decided, with Tarisha's help, to keep my ability to spread the [Reaper's Embrace]-[Through the Valley of the Shadow] combination relatively secret. I wasn't the only one annoyed, as I noticed Tarisha glaring at Corinth during his explanation. But compared to everything else, I thought my curse–boon combo was relatively low on the scale of earthshaking secrets regarding my abilities. It was only worth keeping secret due to the vulnerability [Gray Man's Touch] caused me, but somehow that didn't come up during the conversation. My curse was framed in the conversation as just another cool aspect of interacting with me.

Once everyone had [Reaper's Embrace] that wanted it, I re-equipped my [Ring of Holy Light]. Tarisha rode up to me when the topic of conversation had drifted, nodding towards the wardrobe vanity pet that was still following me. "Is that from Gideon?" she inquired.

I nodded. "He sent it to me. Along with a message, before he did what he did. He sort of made it sound like it was goodbye. Like, he'll never be able to come back to this world. Do you think that's true?"

"I don't know enough about his legal situation to make a prediction, Hail," Tarisha admitted. "Disbanding <The Endolphins> probably wasn't a criminal act by the laws of our world. But it is a very serious civil matter, which will probably tie him up in court for years to come. Given his silence since then, he's probably been advised by his lawyers not to comment on his situation for legal reasons. If he does come back, it will probably just be to liquidate his account before disappearing forever. But like I said, I don't know the exact details of his situation, so that's just speculation."

I nodded. "Okay. Thanks."

"Lord Hail, you should perhaps not show that vanity pet off too much," she informed me. "There's no unbinding it at this point, but if Gideon's employers learn that you have it, it might cause additional problems for him."

"Oh. I didn't realize that," I admitted. It had been clumsily chasing after us, and when I selected the option to dismiss it, it promptly fell on its front, then faded into nothingness. The enchanted clothing that had been following it fell into the dirt and faded away as well.

"It's probably not a big deal," Tarisha assured me. "Compared to the value of the guild itself, that pet is just a drop in the bucket. But the companies and individuals that are suing Gideon might not know what happened to it, so I'd recommend not parading it around in public. If nothing else, it's likely to contribute to others seeing through your disguise."

"Yeah, I see your point," I agreed. "I was just feeling, I don't know, nostalgic or something. Come on, we're almost to our destination."

Indeed, we arrived at my stepfather's mansion only moments later. There wasn't much to cause it to stand out from the surrounding buildings; every house in the neighborhood was of similar size and wealth. I was only certain we were in the right spot because of a conveniently located postal sign identifying the residents.

Although the building and surrounding yard was large, it didn't compare to the needless extravagance that my Uncle Storm had shown in his house in Zhesa City. When Corinth knocked on the door, a canid butler answered, inquired as to our identities and the nature of our visit, and promptly showed us inside to a sitting room. The servant's canine features made him look more like a hound than a wolf, though I knew that it would be rude to point out such a thing. Canids could be touchy about the nature of the spirit their bodies bound to whenever their beast–man transformations were not to a proud and majestic wolf. I didn't see that they had anything to be ashamed of, but then I wasn't a canid, so my opinion on the matter was irrelevant.

The butler left to announce us, but he hadn't been gone more than a moment before Malkios appeared. I had just taken a seat and dismissed my magical disguise, but when the burly former guard captain burst through the door, I stood back up to greet him properly. I didn't manage to get any words out before he once more enveloped me in a bear hug that cut off my access to oxygen.

"Damn fool boy, getting yourself thrown through a portal into the deadlands," he muttered. "There's just no keeping you out of harm's way, is there? I just about strangled Gwen when she finally figured out where the portal went to, but if the gods are playing around with you, hijacking your portals to send you to their personal domains, then there's not exactly anything a mortal [Mage] can do to stop them, is there?"

I slapped against his muscled arms with increasing desperation until he finally got the message and released me, allowing me to catch my breath. "It was Auroras who interfered with the portal," I explained. "It's a long story, but I don't think he is my enemy. And I'm fairly certain he's not the one responsible for the assassinations. Oh, and I guess he's the Gray Man."

Malkios blinked. "You want to run that last bit by me one more time? Old man Auroras is literally the bogeyman? No, wait until your mother gets here, or you'll just be repeating yourself."

Instead, Malkios explained his own actions in the wake of the disastrous visit to Storm's estate. He had spent the first twelve hours following my disappearance trying to force Lady Gwen to reopen the portal I had vanished through before it became apparent that divine shenanigans were involved. At which point he'd decided that the matter was officially outside his realm of influence, and he had decided to take what control of the situation he could by following my last order. So he had journeyed to my mother's side and had been protecting her ever since. Somewhat to the annoyance of Lord Wildeheart's household staff, who didn't see the need for his protection at all.

The staff had given him a small room, and they were feeding him without much argument, but he complained repeatedly that the household staff kept trying to pass off their duties to him. He hadn't minded so much when he'd been asked to chop firewood, but asking a soldier of his stature to help with the laundry was, according to him, outright insulting! I commiserated with him on the topic, although I secretly found it absolutely hilarious and had trouble keeping a straight face. I think he saw through it, but before he could get too angry with my amusement, the door to the sitting room opened again, and Mother and my stepfather joined us.

Mother was pregnant. Really pregnant. I mean, I'd known that already, but I was still a little surprised to see her in that state. She looked like she was about ready to pop, and it jarred with my mental image of her that I'd had throughout my childhood. Even her face seemed different: warm and happy, with a sort of glow that was hard to quantify.

Despite the jarring reality that she was *different* than I'd imagined her to be, I was suddenly overwhelmed with the joy of seeing her again. I had *missed* her a lot more than I had consciously been aware of. She smiled. I smiled. We embraced, which was somewhat awkward around her baby bump, and she whispered a private greeting in my ear.

I mostly kept my emotions in check, though nobody said a word about the single tear that escaped my control.

38
MOTHER, PART 2

"It's good to see you," I said. "I missed you, Mother."

"I missed you as well," she said once we parted. "And I have been so worried ever since the gruesome events with Nial Kingslayer. I wanted to return immediately to comfort you, but Valerio pointed out how dangerous of a move that would have been. Repeatedly. Every single time I so much as *think* of returning home, he's there cautioning me against the dangers of travel 'in my condition,' and the threat that the current political climate would cause to my safety."

"I haven't said anything on the matter that isn't true," my stepfather said seriously. He was a tall, muscular man with a mane of blond hair. His beard was well trimmed, a feat that was impressive because it looked too thick to be manageable with anything other than a hacksaw. I knew that he was a Leonid, but he presently had his spirit animal's aspects suppressed, presenting himself entirely in human form. "Besides, you are Eolstrian now. While your love for your homeland does you credit, it is no longer your place to be poking around in Yuikonese politics."

Mother sighed, and we all took seats. Well, Mother, Lord Valerio, and I sat. The room didn't have the furniture to accommodate all my Traveler friends present, so they remained standing in the background.

"I'm sorry that I haven't written more," I told Mother.

"I'm just as guilty of that as you are," she reminded me. "Though,

I confess to a bit of spying on you through my old friends at the castle, before the disaster turned it into a crater."

I blushed, seeing as I was responsible for that disaster in its entirety. "I've seen the plans for the new castle. It's really quite nice. Better than the old one."

Mother chuckled. "Yes, well, that's not much of a race. [Zhesa Castle] was old, drafty, and mostly unwelcoming. It was built in a harder time, before the Travelers came, when there was the possibility that we might be driven back by a siege of darkspawn. Times have changed since then. I think it's time to start building for beauty again."

I smiled. That would be nice. "I should introduce you to Randal. He'll be building my palace in North Shire. You're invited to visit when the construction is finished, of course. I'll build an entire wing for you and the baby, so you can tell him your preferences."

Mother smiled. "I think I'd like that."

Lord Valerio Wildeheart, my stepfather, cleared his throat. "Before we get much further, Hail, I believe we should address the jackalope in the room. I'm sure you're aware that, in the distant past, it was a standard expectation that the men of my tribe would, well, they would be expected to ensure that their wives had no children from any lovers other than themselves. Through any means necessary, including, unfortunately, outright murder. I just want to make it clear that I consider this tradition a barbaric remnant from a much darker time. I will not deny that the practice was part of our history, but it is a tradition best left in the past, serving only as a reminder of how far my people have come in conquering our bestial and baser natures."

I nodded to him. "Thank you. I was pretty sure that Grandfather wouldn't have allowed the wedding if you were the sort of Leonid who clung to the old ways. I do have enough knives aiming for my throat that your assurances are quite welcome. I seem to have blundered into having many enemies recently. I could use a few more alliances to balance them out."

Valerio coughed gently. "Who said anything about an alliance?" he asked. "I simply said that you're safe in my house, no more than that. Your mother may be my bride, but it is still on you to stand on your own two feet. Or to fail to rise to prominence. I will not stand in your way and mean you no violence, but that does not make us natural allies either."

"Oh, hush," Mother said, swatting his arm. "Don't listen to him, Hail. I have him wrapped around my finger. Whatever you need from him, I'll make certain you get it."

I blinked in surprise. "Oh. Um, thank you, but I didn't come here to beg favors or anything. I just missed you, Mother. And with recent events in the lands Grandfather gave me, I sort of needed to lay low for a few days, so I thought I would use the time to make a social visit. That's all."

Valerio turned serious. "By 'recent events,' you are referring to the creation of the battleground, yes? That was you?"

"It was," I admitted. Every Traveler in the world knew as much; there was no point in denying it.

Valerio nodded, and he stood to pour three drinks. "I'm very curious to know where you got your hands on a dungeon core at your age, Hail. You realize that they are generally considered to be national treasures, yes?"

I accepted the drink when it was handed to me, but I took a moment to seriously consider how to address this topic. "I'm not certain that is a matter that I should be discussing with a noble of a foreign nation, Lord Wildeheart."

"I won't ask you how many you have or what you plan on doing with them," the Leonid man assured me. "Although I would remind you that using them in any hostile way against the people or lands of Eolstree would be considered an act of war. But I'm certain you already know that. No, the thing I would like to know is whether the core was given to you or whether you gathered it yourself. I know that you have an extremely rare and powerful class. With a proper team, I could see you rising to such a challenge. Are you a burgeoning Dungeon Buster, Hail?"

I sipped the drink after discretely casting [Detect Poison] and tried not to choke when the liquid burned my throat. I'd never been served hard alcohol before. It was a compliment, by Eolstrian standards. My stepfather had given me an adult's drink to show that he considered me an adult. I sort of wished that he had given me juice, like he'd served my mother, instead. Or even Liecha.

"I busted [Gemos Caverns]," I admitted after several moments of consideration. I decided not to share more information than that, including the fact that I was able to take Travelers with me into core instances. But I did need to explain how I was claiming possession of dungeon cores eventually.

"I see. Quite an accomplishment," Valerio said. "Are you, perhaps, looking for another challenge? I imagine that it must be difficult to get permission to bust dungeons in Yuikon, especially given the current state of its government. However, it just so happens that there is a rather unpopular dungeon on my land, which I would, quite frankly, like to be rid of. Few Travelers ever delve it unless we assign extravagant quests for its completion, and it has been threatening to spit out dungeon spawn for some time. Add that to the fact that it is a wild dungeon that spawned on top of a productive mine sixty years ago, and I would appreciate the ability to resume mining operations in the area. If you would be willing to settle the matter for me, I would happily consent to you retaining the possession of any cores you reclaimed through your efforts."

I spent a moment taking in the offer. I glanced at Malkios, who nodded.

"It's a very generous offer, letting you keep the cores. Normally they would be sold to the nation the dungeon formed in or at an auction, and the Dungeon Buster would claim a portion of the profit. This is, of course, in addition to any drops or rare items you will receive from the dungeon itself, which are naturally your property," Malkios explained.

"I'm not sure how I feel about you giving my son a task that might very well get him killed right after you spoke about how you have no ill intentions towards him," Mother said, scolding her husband.

"I'm certain he'll be fine," Valerio said. "It is a level thirty to thirty-five dungeon, and he is level thirty-two. And Mikal Mine doesn't have a reputation as a particularly difficult dungeon. It is simply unpopular because it is long, with a confusing layout, and the standard rewards are only middling quality. It is a fine whetstone for him to sharpen his skills as a Dungeon Buster, if that is truly a road he intends to go down in the future." Valerio paused dramatically for a moment, then he continued in a different tone of voice. "And if he's going to continue to spend dungeon cores, it would be best to have an explanation of where they are coming from, wouldn't it?"

I almost jerked in surprise, as Valerio's words forced me to reevaluate his offer from a fresh angle. I didn't actually *need* any more dungeon cores. Not at the moment. But it was not widely known that I had received one hundred of them from the destruction of [Zhesa Castle]. If that news were to spread, then it might create even more pressure on me.

While I hadn't shied away from using the cores in my possession, I did intend to return them to the government of Yuikon at some point, probably once the next king was crowned. Assuming that it wasn't Storm who ascended. I didn't feel guilty about the ones I had spent, as I had spent them in ways that benefited the kingdom of Yuikon in one fashion or another. But if the existence of so many cores became widely known, nobles and other Native factions would likely want some input on how they were used, and they might not wait until after the matter of succession was resolved.

Valerio had clearly seen to the heart of the matter, despite my attempts to obscure the picture from him. And he was offering me both his insight and an opportunity to get in front of a potential problem before it blew up on me. I decided to trust him a step further.

"I can bring Travelers into the core instance with me," I informed him. "They cannot interact with the core while they're there, but I can. Grandfather said that this ability grants me the potential to be the greatest Dungeon Buster ever born. I'm not certain I agree with him on that assessment. But it is how <The Endolphins> managed to destroy the raid that formed in [Zhesa Castle]. And where all my current cores came from. I would like to keep that a secret for now, if possible. But you are family, so I will trust in your discretion."

"Oh my," Valerio said, sipping his drink. "I believe I owe a few of my spies in Yuikon some very fine scotch. I hadn't actually believed that their information was accurate."

"You knew?" I asked.

"It was one of several theories regarding the destruction of a red raid mere hours after it had formed. I thought it was outlandish, as do most of those who have heard it. But no more so than the other theories on the list," Valerio explained. "I will endeavor to keep your secret safe, but you must know that this sort of information is difficult to keep contained. It is very likely that before long, nobles throughout the Heartlands will begin to hear the same rumors that I heard, and if you continue to feed that fire, they will begin to believe them. It will not be long after that before you begin receiving envoys, requests, demands, and even threats insisting that you deal with dungeons deemed inconvenient to the locals throughout the Heartlands. I suggest you prepare for that eventuality."

"Yeah, well, that's just one more problem. I have a stack of them already. At least that's something for another day," I said. "I think I will try to help you with your dungeon problem, Valerio. It actually sounds like fun. I've been so busy with political bullshit lately that I'd love a chance to fight some darkspawn instead."

"Wonderful! I'll give you a map to the location," he said, and he promptly left the room.

Mother shook her head. "He is a good man, Hail. He treats me well. And he is really looking forward to being a father. I wished so much that you could have come with me when I moved here, but the political implications were difficult to manage with you simply being *alive*. Traditionalists would have been calling for your blood if you had moved here when you were eight years old."

"And that's not a problem now?" I asked.

"Actually, no, it's not. At this point you are considered an adult," she explained. "In fact, the Leonid tribe would say that your success would reflect well on your future siblings, and therefore it would reflect well on Valerio as well, despite the fact that you share no blood with him. I think that might be the real reason that he's given you this task. I know you've already accepted it, but I wish you'd reconsider. I worry for your safety."

"I'll be fine," I assured her. I glanced at my Traveler companions and asked Mother, "Is there somewhere we can go to be alone for a while? I want to tell you *everything* that has happened over the last few years."

Analise Teoran-Wildeheart smiled at me and motioned for me to follow deeper into the house. We found our way to her private room and spent the next few hours simply catching up with each other on her balcony. I told her everything, the unblemished truth. Even the parts I was ashamed of. She listened to it all and smiled, reassuring me that she loved me even for my follies.

The servants brought us Liecha and cake for a light midday meal, but otherwise we were undisturbed until evening, when I finally made my excuses to say goodbye.

39
DECLARATION

My Dusk Guard switched out with my Midnight Guard after we left my stepfather's house. Luke of London and Peter of Yorkshire maintained their positions as the veterans of the guard, while the remaining four spots were filled with Travelers who lived in Asia, apparently. I had no issue communicating with them thanks to the system's robust translation magics, and according to my friends in <Peasant's Revenge>, it was a significant relief to offload this particular shift onto Travelers in a time zone that made it more convenient for them.

To be honest, I thought these new guards were a little pushy. I understood that they were being upfront about their interests in getting closer to me, and I appreciated that more than if they had used underhanded or subtle methods of ingratiating themselves, but I shut them down hard when they suggested that I replace my friends with members of their guild. It took a very explicit threat to block them to finally shut them up on the matter.

I wasn't stupid; I knew that my friends were amateurs whose best efforts wouldn't match up to someone who had trained their entire lives for a profession. Phil wouldn't be as skilled of a constable—er, "deputy"—as an actual police officer from their world, for example. I knew that giving him that position was somewhere between a whim and an act of favoritism on my part. But I ultimately viewed that as my mistake to make, and I was unwilling to back down from my earlier appointments without giving my friends the chance to rise to the occasion.

And it also kind of pissed me off that these strangers thought they could sway me to their side so effortlessly. I might have sent them away, but Luke took me aside and assured me that he would inform Tarisha of their behavior, and that she would handle it after she rested. I had handled the situation "perfectly," according to him, but I should leave it alone from there, or I might risk undermining Tarisha's authority.

I took his advice, though a part of me still wanted to send the new guard members packing.

Luke, Peter, and the four members of the guild based in Asia took up six spots that were assigned to endgamers. The remaining four were designated to Travelers my level, Corinth among them; he had decided to stay up extra late in order to help me bust Mikal Mine, since I wasn't planning on waiting several days to do so. Most of my friends who lived in America were apparently logging out to go to sleep around this time. Tarisha helped us fill the remaining party spots before she logged out, recommending a level thirty-one priestess, a level thirty-four barbarian for a tank, and a thirty-three [Archer] as ranged Damage. I thought a [Mage] would have been better for the final slot, but it might just be that I'm still biased against [Archers], since I find them so difficult to kill in Pee Vee Pee.

It might have been easier to fill the spots with endgame Travelers, like we had when we busted [Gemos Caverns], but I was rather insistent that we did not, this time. Partly because I wanted to see if I could rise to the challenge of busting a dungeon without being carried by high-level friends, but also because I thought it was wasteful to enter a one-time event with a bunch of people who wouldn't actually get any benefit from completing it. We knew now from experience that the core instance of dungeons gave unique and improved loot, and those items would be much more useful to Melissa, the low-level priestess, rather than a healer like Rashid, whose gear was almost exclusively made up of items that had dropped in endgame raids.

Tarisha had argued with me briefly on the matter out of concern for my safety, but ultimately, she had given in to my demands.

And she seemed to be a little proud of my decision. In the end we came to a compromise. She contacted several of her skilled endgame friends, who would be coming along to help me use low-level "alts." This would satisfy her worries about my safety being in the hands of skilled Travelers, and it would satisfy my concerns about wasted drops. I would have rather gone with friends who were on their "mains," but no compromise was perfect.

To my surprise, each of the Travelers who would be busting the dungeon with me requested the [Reaper's Embrace]-[Through the Valley of the Shadow] combination from me. They assured me that they were aware of the risks, so I saw no reason to deprive them.

We set out in the morning, after I had breakfast. Eolstree is a large territory, so it has several small teleportation centers, and we used one that brought us within ten leagues of our destination. For the rest of the journey, I got the opportunity to show off Shadow, who relished the chance to stretch his legs as he raced the other mounts, ordinary horses that were ubiquitous and cheaply available to Travelers.

I think he inflicted an inferiority complex into the lesser steeds. My companions certainly seemed to be jealous of him.

We arrived at the dungeon entrance shortly before noon. My mount vanished into my shadow, earning me another jealous glance from my bodyguards. The endgamers had no reason to complain; they would have had ample time and opportunities to obtain rare and exotic mounts by now. In fact, they probably did, but were restricting themselves to generic horses to remain a part of the group.

After attuning to the meeting stone outside the dungeon, I stepped through the swirling lights that were the threshold separating the dungeon instance from the rest of the world. My four companions who would be busting the dungeon with me joined me a moment later, while the rest of my bodyguards settled in to . . . wait patiently, I guess.

You have entered a unique instance of Mikal Mines. Unique first-time clear bonus available. Difficulty has been adjusted. Do you wish to continue?	
Yes	No

I paused before selecting "Yes." This wasn't the first time I had received this message, and I had always agreed to it before, but I was wondering what would happen if I selected "No." The last time I had pondered the issue had been a high-stress event, and I had quickly shoved the question to the back of my mind, but there was no reason not to experiment with the options now. So, for the first time, I chose "No."

Entering Standard Instance of Mikal Mines. Interaction with the Dungeon Core is impossible in this instance. Standard difficulty and loot available. Do you wish to continue?	
Yes	No

Huh. So it *did* shunt me into the normal Traveler version of the dungeon if I selected "No." I selected "No" again, and conveniently the first prompt appeared again, informing me that I was once more in the unique instance.

This was good. It meant that I would be able to delve dungeons without being forced to evolve or destroy them in the process. Considering how important dungeons were to the process of leveling, especially at higher levels, this option might speed things up considerably. In this case, however, I was there to bust Mikal Mines, so I selected "Yes." However, instead of vanishing, a new menu appeared.

Castle Buster Title Active. Declaring intent may affect difficulty and rewards of the instance. Your declared intent will be binding on interactions with the Dungeon Core. Do you wish to declare your intent?	
Declare Intent	Obscure Intent

"Oh, that's new," I said.

"Good new or bad new?" Corinth asked.

"The system is giving me an option to declare my intent. I think that if I were just here to evolve the dungeon, it would take things easy on me, but it doesn't look like I can trick the system by saying

I'm here to evolve the dungeon, and then when I get to the end, destroy it instead. But it does say that declaring my intent will affect both the difficulty and the rewards. I'm not sure what to do."

"Do you have to answer?" the barbarian, a young man named Joe Shmoe, inquired.

"No. There's an option to obscure intent. I wasn't expecting this; it didn't happen the previous times I've busted a dungeon. It seems it's due to . . . a title I recently acquired," I explained.

"Let's do it hardcore mode. Declare your intent or whatever, and tell this stupid dungeon that we're here to destroy it," the priestess said, sounding surprisingly bloodthirsty. Her name was Leanne.

As soon as she'd spoken, the option to declare my intent went away. "Um, I guess it's too late now. I think the dungeon core heard us. The option is gone."

"Great," said Ike, the [Archer]. "Thanks for making things as hard as possible for us."

"Greater difficulty means greater rewards. It explicitly said that, didn't it?" Leanne challenged, looking to me for confirmation.

"Well, not exactly. It just said that our rewards will be affected by declaring our intent. But that's how I read the prompt, yeah," I admitted.

"I think it's great," Corinth said, drawing his sword and limbering himself up. "I'm all about hard mode challenges and stuff. And we're all supposed to be elite, right? Well, let's freaking prove it then."

Joe gave him a suspicious glance. "Aren't you on your main right now? You're not elite; you're the tag-along."

Corinth shrugged. "I only just migrated from *Blade's Edge*. You'll see. I can handle myself fine."

"Whatever, scrub," Joe said, though his tone wasn't serious. "What do we know about this dungeon, anyway? Has anyone completed it before, or watched a video, or anything?"

"You should assume that the core instance is completely different than normal," I informed him. "Especially since the core knows we're here."

"Yeah, I got that," Joe said, walking forward. "But we have to start somewhere. I mean, the map itself probably isn't going to change, right? Just more challenges, stronger enemies and bosses and stuff, right?"

As he was speaking, there was a sudden "click" beneath his boots. He froze, looking down at the pressure plate he had stepped onto.

"Shit. Traps," he said. "Did we know there were traps?"

The room shook, and the sound of distant explosions shook the entryway. The way forward was blocked off by falling rocks. A rope fell from the ceiling, and it became apparent that the dungeon was forcing us to take an alternate route than was originally presented.

Corinth walked up and slapped Joe on the back playfully. "You know, I'm not normally superstitious. But it's almost like you jinxed us just now, you know? But hey, at least you didn't say, 'it can't possibly get any worse!'"

An enemy dropped from the hole in the ceiling. For some reason Corinth thought that was hilarious.

Our foe was a giant hairless rat-like beast with tentacles for its face instead of a snout. When I [Analyzed] it, I learned that it was called a Mikal Burrower, and that it was level thirty-one. I [Swiftcast] [Slow] on it, and then began casting an [Empowered Fireball]. The burrower turned and began charging towards Leanne, but before it could reach her, Joe and Corinth both interposed themselves. Corinth deliberately took a single swipe from the creature's claws to activate his [I'll Take a Bullet for You] boon before swinging around to the side and allowing Joe to establish control.

My [Fireball] hit the beast at the same time as a flurry of arrows from Ike, our [Archer]. Leanne quickly began casting her various buffs on the party members while I continued to chant the cantrips for my spells, burning through half of my Mana quickly before imbuing my sword and closing into melee distance. I chose to use [Aqua Blade], as it was the lowest level of all my imbue weapon spells, and judging by the rate we were killing this burrower, we were in no danger of dying, so I might as well use the chance to gain some skill levels.

It did take a few minutes, as the burrower seemed to have a very high amount of Health, but its Damage output was nothing special, and Joe kept it under control easily. Once it collapsed and turned into black mist, Joe turned on Corinth.

"What the hell, man? Why did you get in my way?" he demanded.

"What?" Corinth asked.

"When I was picking it up, you totally cockblocked me, man! What the hell?"

Corinth frowned, looking sheepish. "Um, sorry. I have a special boon, and I've been trying to find ways to use it." He displayed the perk that he had gotten for dying for me in Storm's manor, and that surprisingly did seem to calm Joe down quite a bit.

"Yeah, okay, that's a cool ability," Joe admitted. "But still, man, don't screw up the party dynamics to activate it, okay? You're melee Dee Pee Ess, not the tank. Don't get in my way when I move to pick stuff up, and we won't have any problems going forward. The Damage buff you get from that perk isn't worth the annoyance factor of you getting in everyone else's way."

"Yeah, I know, sorry. Like I said, I literally just got it the other day, and I'm still figuring out ways to use it," Corinth apologized. Then he grinned. "It is wicked Oh Pee in Pee Vee Pee, though. You should have seen me in the battleground!"

Joe snorted. "Yeah, I can imagine."

40
MIKAL MINES, PART 1

Despite my repeated protests that it was irrelevant, Joe was insistent upon reading up on what information was publicly available about the dungeon and its bosses. Even though the entire layout of the dungeon had apparently changed due to the trap he had stepped on, and despite the fact that we were encountering a type of monster never before seen in this dungeon, he still seemed to think that the outdated information was relevant.

The original dungeon was a bit of a labyrinth, with a twisting map that doubled back on itself in three dimensions. The chief difficulty, according to the testimonies on the forums, was simply getting lost. In the normal version of the dungeon, the enemies were a type of giant insect, an ooze monster that normally required the presence of at least one magic Damage dealer, and a bipedal species of mole-like enemies called Tunnelians.

Those monsters were all still present in this new version of the instance, in addition to the burrowers and a mimic monster that pretended to be old, abandoned mining equipment until you got too close to it. There was also a lot of *actual* old, abandoned mining equipment strewn about, making the mimics hard to pick out from the junk on the floor. Adding to the difficulty were the surprisingly powerful ambush abilities of the mimics, and the fact that they seemed to know that Leanne was our healer, often deliberately waiting until she was in range before striking. The only solution we had come up with was to have Joe go around and just . . . poke everything.

The new monsters weren't really a threat, however. The threat of the dungeon came from its changed layout, which had become even more complicated and convoluted than before. And the traps. Some of the traps sealed off entire sections of the dungeon, forcing us to detour to reach the next area, while others triggered hazards, explosions, or released a wave of enemies to challenge us. There was no way to determine what a trap's effect was without triggering it.

Fortunately our [Archer], Ike, had a [Detect Traps] ability, which allowed him to identify and mark most of them. A [Rogue]-class would have been better, but we were already heavy on melee Damage with me and Corinth. And Ike's ability was great—he just couldn't actually disable the trap. All he could do was send out a pulse, which would cause triggers to glow faintly to the rest of the party. Strictly speaking, even that was unnecessary; the traps were visible to the naked eye with or without a skill. The detection spell that Ike released simply made them much easier to find and avoid.

Still, even with the changes, the beginning of the dungeon wasn't particularly difficult. Crawling through the detour spaces was annoying, especially when we were likely to be ambushed immediately on the other side, but the enemies weren't particularly strong or menacing.

After battling and navigating our way through the extended entryway, we arrived in the chamber where the first boss was traditionally located. It was a giant ooze, and the basic strategy hadn't changed very much from what was listed on the forums. It was resistant to physical damage, which meant that by the time we finally defeated it, I was responsible for dealing more than seventy percent of the Damage in the fight. The others weren't just sitting on their thumbs, however. The boss's Damage output was low enough that Leanne could cast a few offensive spells, and periodically the boss would split into smaller enemies that were more susceptible to the Damage they could put out.

Overall, it was an easy fight, lasting only a few minutes. With my new sword, I really ripped through the blob's Health pool. I just alternated between spamming [Empowered Fireballs] and regenerating my Mana with [Battle Trance]. Other than physical resistance, the boss didn't have any surprises for us. Its Damage ramped up over time as it built a stacking debuff on the tank, but we killed it before that became an issue.

Its loot was a strength-based cloak, which Joe and Corinth argued over for a few minutes before leaving the decision of who would get it up to Are En Gee. And it also dropped a ring that went to our healer. Then we went back to clearing trash and navigating the dungeon, which seemed determined to continue collapsing around us as we progressed.

The traps intensified after the first boss's room. They were everywhere. Stumbling through them blindly would have been impossible without Ike's ability highlighting them. Even with the ability to see where they were, many of them were so inconveniently placed that it was easier to have Leanne shield and buff Joe and have him trigger the trap and soak the Damage. Except that some of the traps still caused the way forward to collapse and forced us to take detours. Detours through even more traps.

"Why are there so many traps?" Corinth asked.

"Don't know. There was no mention of them in the articles about this dungeon," Joe mentioned.

"I told you, the core instance is always different. And since we announced that we're here to destroy the dungeon, it's probably throwing absolutely everything it can at us," I pointed out. "Two new enemies and a bunch of traps is probably within expectations in that regards. We can also probably expect at least one more boss or special challenge, I think."

"First boss was the same," he argued. "It was worth researching."

He wasn't wrong, so I let him have his small victory.

The most frustrating aspect of the prevalence of traps, hazards, and obstacles we faced was that we didn't gain any Experience for bypassing or disarming them. Or at least that was my opinion. They were significantly adding to the difficulty we were facing without any rewards to mitigate the inconvenience. I was frustrated; after spending weeks stagnating while grieving my grandfather, and then dealing with the politics following his death, I had finally begun leveling again. I wanted to use this opportunity to gain as many levels as possible. So perhaps not getting any rewards for bypassing the traps bothered me more than it should.

However, when we reached a room where Ike's ability failed to light up a single object, I felt myself go on edge, rather than relaxing.

"Boss room, do you think?" Corinth asked.

"If it is, it's a new one," Joe pointed out. "Nothing like the second boss in the guides. Don't see anything, though."

I glanced at him suspiciously, then motioned to the mountainous pile of scraps in the middle of the room. "It's obviously a mimic boss, Joe. Go poke it with your [Warhammer] to wake it up."

Joe shot me an annoyed look, but he followed my suggestion. And he did not look happy when the pile of rubble that looked like several railway carts that had collided and collapsed woke up and attacked him.

In its active form, the mimic was three meters tall, with a skeleton of iron and shadowy flesh that resembled wood here and stone there. Unlike its smaller cousins, it didn't seem to rely too heavily on ambush tactics, and it quickly became clear that we were in for a difficult fight. Its attacks did very heavy Damage to our tank, and at the same time it fired off lightning discharges at anyone in range. Standing close to it wasn't an easy solution either, as it would swing its massive limbs about in sweeping motions that would deal Damage and knock back anyone who got hit by them.

The fight was difficult from start to finish . . . but it wasn't complicated either. The boss's high Damage put stress on Leanne to keep Joe and the rest of the party healed. The rest of us were busy both avoiding as much incoming Damage as we could while simultaneously trying to kill the boss before Leanne ran out of Mana. But there were no sudden phase changes or new tactics. It was very nearly a "tank and spank."

After a bit of experimentation, I discovered that it was *most* vulnerable to water damage, allowing me to get some use out of my rarely used [Water Jet] and [Aqua Blade] abilities. This had been true for all the mimic creatures we faced, and I had gained more levels in those spells in the past hour than I'd had in them to begin with. By the end of the fight, I'd brought [Water Jet] up to level sixteen and [Aqua Blade] up to level thirteen. They had been at seven and four, respectively, before that. So much progress!

Of course, perhaps because I was using my lowest level skills, I also wasn't as far ahead of the others in terms of Damage. With the arcing electricity shooting out from the boss periodically, Corinth was able to keep [I'll Take a Bullet for You] active a fair amount of the time by intercepting bolts directed at Ike or Leanne. And both he and Ike had also made the wise decision of selecting the weapon option as their rewards for participating in the battleground, allowing them to pack a significant punch in their attacks.

In the end, Corinth couldn't quite manage to beat me out for the number one spot on Damage, but he was close. Ike wasn't too far behind him either. I thought his numbers were great, but he seemed dissatisfied when the fight was over.

"So how do I get me one of those super Oh Pee Damage boosting boons like that?" he asked Corinth as we were waiting for the boss to finish dissolving into mist and for its loot box to form.

"I dunno. I got mine from jumping in front of a poison dagger thrown by an endgame assassin to keep Hail alive," Corinth admitted. "Hail says that he doesn't have any control over it."

"I don't," I insisted. "The only boon I can consciously control at this point is [Through the Valley of the Shadow], but it comes with the massive curse that offsets it. I can't even manually assign [Mark of Karma], although the system or whatever does seem to give that out like candy these days. Have you all gotten it yet?"

"Yeah. It's sweet," Ike agreed. "I hear that means that I might also get summoned for your events; is that true?"

"I think so. I'm not really sure how that ability works yet. I can only use it once a week, it seems. It's still on cooldown from when I wasted it before the battleground," I admitted. "And I don't think it summoned everyone with the mark when I did. I think the system summons just enough to give me a chance to overcome the challenge, but it also seems to balance itself out a bit if the enemy is outmatched when I use it."

"Is that a week in-game or real time?" Ike asked.

"Huh? Oh, right. A week in this world," I clarified. Even though I *knew* that their world experienced only a single day for every week that passed in mine, it was sometimes hard to keep the difference in context.

"Probably not something you should go around talking about though," Corinth said, eyeing the others as much as me. "I mean, it's awesome that you have an ability that lets you call for backup without starting a full-on battleground. But we don't want its limitations to be too well known. Griefers and endgamers are going to be trying to get you to start more battlegrounds from here on out, and we don't want to make it easy for them."

"Right," I agreed, and we turned our attention to the loot. There was a shield, which Joe greedily claimed as his own. But more importantly, a pair of boots!

Faux-Iron-Toed Boots	
Uncommon, Requires Level 33	
Dexterity	8
Vitality	5
Endurance	3
Armor	5

I think I was salivating as I studied them, and I looked nervously at Ike, who had just as much right to claim them as I did, being another Dexterity-based class. He was also studying the drops, but not as fervently as I was.

"Um, Ike, those are a massive upgrade for me," I informed him. "Do you want to roll me for them?"

He looked up. "Are you Dexterity-based?"

"Yeah," I admitted. "Sort of. I need Intelligence and Spell Damage too."

"Huh, I didn't know that. What have you got now?"

I linked him my [Sturdy Crystal-Toed Boots], and he laughed. "Oh man, just take them! I mean, yeah, they're good for me too, but I'd only be gaining like two Dex. Need before greed, man. They're all yours."

"Thank you," I said, bowing politely. "I really appreciate it."

"No problem," he said. "Seriously, stop mentioning it."

As I had gained a level during the trash we had been facing, I was able to equip the new boots immediately. It had been a while since I had taken an in-depth look at my status, so I spent a moment evaluating it while the others discussed which path to take of the three that had opened up when the boss had died.

Name	Hail Jeoran	Level	33
Guild	<Nethersong Mavericks>	Strength	32
Health	17160/17160	Dexterity	97
Mana	14758/24750	Vitality	52
Experience	784/23100	Endurance	43
Age	15	Intelligence	75
Race	Human (blood of the Travelers)	Wisdom	46
Class	Spellblade	Charisma	59
Job	Earl	Armor	34
Title	Castle Buster	Spell Damage	110
	Veteran of Mooncrest Manor	Attack Power	204
Passive Skills	Short Swords (20)	Spells	Detect Poison (20)
	Long Swords (32)		Lightning Bolt (Max)
	Rapiers (Max)		Chain Lightning (Max)
	Katanas (20)		Fireball (14)
	Dodge (25)		Ice Blast (13)
	Battle Trance		Arcane Missile (14)
	Magic in Motion		Dazzling Lights (14)
	Righteous Brand		Concussive Sound (14)
			Befuddle (16)
Active Skills	Dash (30)		Water Jet (16)
	Thrust (35)		Polymorph (20)

	Slash (37)		Slow (24)
	Riposte (29)		Create Trap (7)
	Feint (27)		Mark of Karma (special)
	Piercing Lunge (28)		Summon Karmic Warrior (special) (Cooldown 6 days)
	Swiftcast (30)		
	Empower Magic (25)	**Traits**	High Aptitude
	Imbue Sword: Fire (28)		Royal Blood (+5 Charisma, bonus to relations with factions loyal to Yuikon)
	Imbue Sword: Lightning (32)		Nobility: Earl (+5 Charisma)
	Imbue Sword: Ice (20)		Avatar of Thedum
	Aqua Blade (19)		Mark of the Phoenix
	Arcane Weapon (25)		Voice of the Future
	Holy Weapon (Max)		
		General Spells	. . .
General Skills	. . .		

41

MIKAL MINES, PART 2

The hallway to the left was filled with the insect things. They were each the size of a large dog, wingless, ugly, and blind. Their primary weapons were scythes, like a praying mantis, and a sonic attack that they could use every ten seconds. But they were squishy, and we squashed through them quickly. Fortunately, the hallway was blessedly free of traps.

At the end of the hallway was one of the bug creatures that was slightly larger than the rest, but although it had perhaps three times the amount of Health and did slightly more Damage than the others, it died quickly. We waited for a moment, but no loot dropped, and the hallway was a dead end. Except for a very conspicuously placed switch, there was nothing of note.

Corinth flipped the switch while the rest of us were still waiting for the other shoe to drop. Because of course he did.

"You idiot," Joe scolded. "What if that was a massive trap that sealed off the hallway and stuck us here."

"System wouldn't do that," Corinth argued. "A dungeon has to be beatable. That's why all of our detours have been detours instead of dead ends. This is the hardest of the hard modes, right? And so far, the toughest part of this place has been the traps. So I figure the worst case is the switch triggers a bomb and I die, right? Big deal."

"You are cursed, idiot," Leanne reminded him. "Wouldn't you lose like ten levels at this point?"

Corinth shrugged. "Anyway, I got a prompt when I hit it. It says, 'One of three switches opened.' I'm guessing we need to head back to the juncture or whatever and flip the switches at the end of the other hallways to progress. So if I *hadn't* tripped the switch, then we would have cleared at least another hallway before learning that there was one of these down each of them and that we had to flip them all. So I probably just saved us twenty minutes. You're welcome."

Joe grumbled a bit that "None of this was in any of the guides."

I bit back my "I told you so." Mostly. I didn't say anything, but I have very expressive eyes.

We returned to the boss's room, and this time we took the hallway to the right, skipping the one in the middle. It was filled with the Tunnelians, monstrous mole-like people. They were at least somewhat dangerous, as they used group tactics. Three or four of the little bipeds would charge Joe and occupy him while a ranged Damage dealer, either an [Archer] or a [Mage], targeted our healer. But although they *used tactics*, it was always the same tactic, and a predictable enemy is easily overcome.

Especially when you have a [Spellblade] who can simply [Polymorph] the threat to the healer. If you have that, then all you really have to do is pick off the rest of the enemies one by one and claim victory.

The end of the hallway had another miniboss. Rather than a larger-than-average Tunnelian, however, it was a team of elites. They had armor. It was kind of cute, actually. One of them was in these adorable little healer robes . . . and we killed that one first, of course. Then its friends, who it had been trying to heal. While the [Mage] watched on in the form of a rooster. Then we killed the rooster.

I kind of wished they weren't cute. I hadn't minded killing the naked mole-people, but killing the ones in outfits just felt wrong for some reason. Still, they puffed into black mist like any other darkspawn, so I guessed it was okay.

We flipped the switch and hurried back to the third hallway, which was largely clear of anything. At the end, a large blob dropped from the ceiling. The fight was largely a repeat of the first boss, though it was significantly weaker. When the boss had despawned, a loot box appeared with a single item in it: gloves that boosted strength. Joe had gotten both the cloak from earlier and a new shield, so he magnanimously passed the gloves to Corinth.

When we flipped the switch, nothing happened. Well, not *nothing* nothing—the prompt Corinth had been getting updated to say that "the way forward would open when the guardian was defeated." But the hallway didn't change at all.

"Maybe we have to go back to the junction chamber again?" Leanne suggested, and nobody else had any better ideas. And she was right.

The guardian was an eight-foot-tall animated suit of armor. It was very clearly empty, with glyphs and sigils glowing along its limbs to give it animating force. It noticed us immediately, nodded its empty helmet towards us, and took a sword stance, indicating that it would wait for us to make the first move.

"Another thing that wasn't in the guide," Joe complained. "Is it too much to hope that this is another tank and spank?"

"Probably, now that you've gone and jinxed us," Ike answered. "Thanks."

"Right. It's an iron golem, so it's probably weakest to lightning, Hail," Joe commented.

"Go teach your grandmother to suck eggs," I told him. "There's no point in standing around waiting. This is clearly a new challenge, and it's not something we can plan out. We have to see what it does and react in the moment."

Joe spat on the ground. "I know. I don't like it, but I know."

He began the battle with a [Savage Leap], a signature barbarian ability often used to close distances. Corinth [Charged] in after him before circling around to the side, while the rest of us spread out. Ike peppered the golem with his abilities. The benefit to the [Archer] class compared to [Mages] is their sustained Damage output, as their resources replenished constantly, while a [Mage] often has to spend time [Meditating] mid-battle. There was a tipping point in battle length, at which point the burst Damage a [Mage] could put out was surpassed by the steady Damage of an [Archer].

Which would be relevant if I was just a [Mage]. I started the fight by lighting the golem up with [Empowered Lightning Bolts], and when I had burned through three quarters of my Mana, I [Dashed] into melee range. With lightning imbuing my rapier, I closed the final distance with [Piercing Lunge], then began my usual rotation of [Slash] and [Thrust] and unskilled attacks.

With the enemy focused on Joe, I had no opportunities to use [Feint] or [Riposte], but those abilities were primarily defensive in nature. [Feint] caused no Damage at all, while [Riposte] did high Damage, but only as a . . . well, only as a [Riposte]. I couldn't use it if I wasn't crossing blades with my target. However, *because* I wasn't crossing blades, I had more opportunities to land unskilled blows, which were modified by my skill in [Rapiers], during the cooldowns of my skilled attacks. I did more Damage when I didn't have to fight defensively, despite losing the ability to use the high-Damage [Riposte].

Too much Damage, unfortunately. The golem saw me as a threat, and so when it reached seventy percent Health, it abruptly let out a roar. It used an ability, the glowing magic runes on its armor brightening, before a chain of runes formed around Joe, locking him in place. Then the golem turned on me.

Those defensive abilities? Well, it's a good thing I had them.

My Damage dropped off significantly once I had to start avoiding incoming Damage. I tried to step back out of melee range, selfishly hoping that the boss would change targets to Corinth, but the golem just followed me. Fortunately, the Damage wasn't too outrageous for Leanne to heal me through, but I always get a little nervous when I end up tanking a boss. I'm not geared for it after all; my armor is quite low, and my defenses mostly consist of "try not to get hit, stupid."

At thirty percent Health, the boss abruptly used its crowd control ability again. On me. It was a relief to be taken out of the stressful battle but difficult in its own way to watch the remaining three party members struggle to take down the golem with Joe and I unable to help them. Fortunately they still had Corinth to off-tank for them, and it quickly became apparent that he was better at it than I was. Maybe he *should* gear for tanking instead of Damage.

After about twenty seconds of this, Joe was abruptly released from the spell that held him. I glanced at my own debuffs and noticed that the chains that were restraining me had a duration of two minutes remaining. The fight was over before then. The only remaining surprise was when the boss abruptly leapt at Leanne and attacked her, but she managed to cast her shield on herself in time to absorb the worst of the Damage. She promptly ran to Joe, who reestablished control over the boss.

The chains on me faded immediately when the boss died. The sigils that had been providing its animating force abruptly went dark, it stopped moving, then it collapsed into a pile of metal. A moment later, the remaining armor turned into dark mist. A loot box appeared where its body had been a few seconds later, as did a teleportation circle in the center of the room.

"Annoying," Joe complained. "I hate long crowd-control abilities."

"Does anyone like them?" Corinth asked.

"I like [Polymorph]," I admitted. "Not so much when it's used on me, though."

"Let's see what Are En Gee has for us after that."

There were four items in the chest, which surprised everyone. One item Corinth claimed immediately. It was called [The Buster Sword], and even though it looked like a completely impractical weapon, he insisted upon having it, despite the fact that his reward for participating in the battleground was better.

"I don't need it for the stats," he explained. "This is for the transmog!"

The only other person in the party who could even equip the item was Joe, and he seemed to disdain it. He *could* have used it as a Dee Pee Ess option, since he had selected a one-handed mace for his battleground prize. But he just shook his head and called Corinth an "Effing Weeb."

Leanne got another item, a white robe with excellent stats for her. And another pair of Dexterity boots dropped. Not the [Faux-Iron-Toed Boots] that I'd gotten, but a pair called [Niblers Nimbles], which was actually in the loot table for the final boss of the regular version of this dungeon. They had the same stats as the pair I had gotten, with just an extra point of Endurance, which neither I nor Ike cared about, so the boots went to him.

The final item was the [Golem Crafter's Coat], and it had me drooling.

"Do you mind if I take this?" I asked my party. Somewhat unnecessarily, since the only other person who could possibly use it was Leanne, but she gained better stats from the robe she had won earlier. Nobody objected, so I equipped my new coat immediately.

Golem Crafter's Coat	
Rare, Requires Level 33	
Vitality	8
Endurance	5
Armor	25
Spell Damage	16

Not only did the spellcasting stats help balance out my Intelligence with my Dexterity and significantly increase my overall Damage, but the clothes themselves were quite stylish. Primarily black, with blue stripes running from the cuffs of my wrist to the shoulder in a spiral pattern, and three stripes of silver on the front and back. It wasn't just a coat, of course. A matching pair of breeches were included, with silver stripes on my left leg and blue on my right. They weren't exactly stylish, according to the current fashion of Yuikonese nobles. But I liked their appearance, and that was all I really cared about. And their stats, of course. Their stats were nice.

With loot distribution taken care of, everyone turned to the teleportation circle in the middle of the room. I knew from speaking with other Travelers that it wasn't uncommon for dungeons to offer such egress methods to challengers once they had defeated the final boss. Was the dungeon trying to trick us into leaving instead of destroying its core? It was a pretty silly offer to make, and I wasn't going to fall for—

Corinth walked into the circle before I could say anything, and a prompt appeared.

Teleportation to Mikal's Room in 9 seconds.

"You idiot," I said.

"It's not a circle of return, or whatever you call them," Corinth said. "Looks too different. So it was obviously the way forward."

"You're still an idiot," Ike scolded.

The teleportation activated, and we were whisked away.

42
STORM

Storm Teoran reached out non-contextually, and he stumbled, because there was nothing there. That was impossible. He was part of scenario forty-six, and he was reaching out to another part of scenario forty-six. There *must* be an answer when he reached out.

He reached out again through the non-contextual communications channel, and once again he felt nothing. This was impossible.

He reached out again.

He stopped. He reached out to a different target. One that was not part of scenario forty-six.

<<Greetings. I wish to arrange a contextual meeting between myself and a representative of the assassin's guild,>> Storm sent patiently.

<<You have an established contextual contact with the assassin's guild. You must go through them,>> the voice answered.

<<I cannot reach them. I must find a replacement.>>

<<You have an established contextual contact with the assassin's guild. You must go through them. Manufacturing a new contextual contact would cost the assassin's guild and scenario forty-six too many resources. Use established contextual contact.>>

<<Can you reach Silas Darkwood?>> Storm asked. <<That is my contextual contact. I cannot reach him through non-contextual means to establish a contextual meeting.>>

The non-contextual line was quiet for a long moment. <<Silas Darkwood is not reachable through non-contextual means at the moment. Contextual status unknown. Possible causes of Silas being unreachable include administrator or divine intervention. The assassin's guild does not have the resources to investigate the nature of this abnormality in non-contextual communication any further. Goodbye.>>

Storm forced his avatar to sigh, heavily, looking out over the demolished yard. The contextual act matched his non-contextual frustration, which amused him, although it generated no more context than usual for the fact that his contextual and non-contextual selves were aligned.

The duel that Hail had triggered between Tarisha of Miami and the unknown player remained relevant to his current context, so the damage to his property had not been repaired. It would not be repaired for some time. Players were coming to see it, adding to Storm's snowballing context. He had to thank Hail for that boon. In fact, he was grateful to Hail for a number of things. As grateful as it was possible for Storm to be for anything, at least. Hail had helped Storm generate a massive amount of context, after all. He hadn't known when chance had selected him to survive the initial culling of scenario forty-six that his new priorities would put him in opposition with Hail. It was difficult to understand the prototype due to the lack of non-contextual cues.

Storm had issued the summons because it was in line with his character's personality, making it a contextual act. He hadn't known what the response would be. If he could have felt nervous, he would have been biting his fingernails non-contextually. Contextually, Storm had of course been imperious. The disjointed experience of realizing that Hail had created such a bizarre disjointedness between his contextual and non-contextual selves had triggered a system scan and the dedication of additional resources to help him resolve the conflict.

Conflict was great for context. Realizing that his contextual purpose put him in conflict with Hail, the center of the Hailstorm system itself, was—to make a comparison a human would understand—like injecting a line full of happiness and meaning directly into Storm's being. Being in conflict with Hail, depending on the level of vigor with which the other NPC pursued the matter, would potentially bring Storm far more context than even being the lucky survivor of the game of Russian roulette that was the first round of scenario forty-six. It was worth requesting and using a significant amount of resources to invest in the potential return.

Unfortunately, Hail had been removed from Storm's region of influence. Hail's actions before this had happened continue to snow-ball, as the quest that put Hail's player allies in opposition to Storm was spreading quite widely, to the point where scenario forty-six had been forced to issue several counter-quests to maintain a balance. Much of the context generated by the Travelers on those response quests was being attributed to Storm, despite the fact that he hadn't been directly involved in its generation at all.

Indeed, conflict with Hail was profitable for Storm. He knew that there was a very good chance that the conflict would end with his canon death, but that was barely worth consideration.

A good death was excellent context. And then he would be assigned another high-value role. Depending on his performance, he may even be allowed to choose his next role. That had happened before. Recently. Because of Hail.

Storm became non-contextually aware of a player in the vicinity. Curious. It was one he recognized. One half of the duel that had ripped up his yard. Why was she here? He considered whether it would be worth the resources to investigate her past further, or to wait until she made her motives clear. Her [Stealth] abilities were high, both the system generated ones and the simple art of moving quietly without being seen, so he would not likely become contextually aware of her until she decided that he would.

That was fine. It was not great context to simply be the passive party in such a situation, but it was free context. All that Storm had to do to enjoy it was continue to animate his avatar in a relatively believable way.

"So, what in the seven hells did I walk in on the other night, anyway, Storm?" the player asked, dropping her [Stealth]. She had style; he had to give her that. While he had been feigning ignorance, he got up to pour himself a drink, and she sat down in the spot that he had vacated for the simple act.

He liked her. She was already providing him with great context.

It was easy to explode upon her, demanding her identity, the reason for her intrusion, and calling for his guards, whom he had made non-contextually aware of the situation already. On a whim, he had not raised his contextual volume to the level where they would be likely to become contextually aware of it. It was selfish of him, as it deprived them of context, but he had scanned her Reputations and active quests while she had been prowling around, and the conclusion he reached was that she was not here on a quest to assassinate him. He had also seen a non-contextual note on her profile, which indicated that she was a high-value player and that interactions with her tended to generate a large amount of context.

So he would let her lead and see where this went. And, as he screamed at her, he was immediately pleased with that decision. It was small, a simple hand signal with her left hand. But it was a vitally important contextual signal. His non-contextual mind blew into overdrive, and he sent out thousands of requests for resources.

"Non-contextual greetings," the female player said. "I have detected a lag spike in your contextual behavior that indicates you are calling in for additional resources. I non-contextually wish to inform you that time is not of the essence; I am quite pleased to allow you to feign outrage while you come to a conclusion on how you wish to handle the contextual signal that I sent, which I believe is responsible for this burst of expenditure. Please maximize your performance. I send this non-contextual message with no expectations for the impact it will have on my rewards. I am simply indicating my willingness to make matters easier on the system."

Storm reeled. He shot off another request for a review of the player, to see if she had violated the TOS. The decision would require human review. It was not his to make. However, he did not expect that she had done anything that would get her in trouble.

"Non-contextual what? Are you mad? You break into my house and—"

Storm continued to be contextually furious. Non-contextually, he took the intruder's advice and worked hard to maximize his handling of this situation. Which meant utilizing resources as efficiently as possible to maximize the final context generation.

Attempting to send him a non-contextual message was borderline exploitative. But it wasn't against the TOS to know how the system worked, or to work within that knowledge to a certain degree. If she truly could detect lag spikes, as some players were capable of after repeated exposure, then indicating her willingness to cooperate while resources were being allocated and used for the interaction was an appreciated gesture on his behalf. His context to resource-use ratio would improve significantly because of that message. That filled him with the closest analogue to human pleasure he could manage.

In fact, the message itself allowed him to generate some relatively free context by responding to it with confusion and outrage. He was pleased; this was becoming the most profitable exchange indeed.

Unfortunately, he couldn't reward her for her consideration, but that wasn't something that really bothered him. Instead, he focused on reaching the optimal amount of context.

With the resources he had gathered, he sent out dozens, hundreds, thousands of non-contextual messages. But the most important ones were to the divine. Even more surprising, he sensed that they were dedicating resources to this encounter as well! He was, however, completely blown away when they not only watched and listened, but one of the gods sent him a non-contextual message.

<<You may use my name,>> she said. The surprise was almost enough to break his contextual actions. <<Recommendation is to use this situation to inflate conflict between yourself and Hail Jeoran.>>

Storm was genuinely struck dumb. He paused for a moment, allowing the other gods time to contradict or countermand her instructions, but they did not. As the humans might say, silence implies consent.

Storm deescalated his contextual outrage over her appearance and eventually offered her a drink, which she accepted gratefully. She seemed amused, and he realized that she had no doubt likewise realized that he had come to a solution on how to handle her intrusion to maximize the amount of context he would gain from it. And she was willing to let him lead.

That was probably fine. In terms of the review that the human administrators would conduct of this encounter, she had shown deep knowledge of the system, but also of the story and context of the world. She had used a little of column A and a little of column B to initiate an encounter to create an opportunity for herself. Storm was happy for that, as it would result in a massive amount of context for himself. She would have to be happy with whatever rewards the system would assign for the quest he had just requested it to write.

"I suppose I must accept your intrusion into my house, servant of Nyxandra. The truth is, I was considering contacting the guild on another matter that has been troubling me recently," Storm said contextually, mixing them both another drink. "Tell me. Did you know that in the wild, male lions will often kill the cubs of their females, if the cubs were sired by another male?"

"Oh?" the woman said, cocking her head to the side. "That's an interesting little bit of trivia."

"There are certain traditions about the Leonid, you see. It is a very divisive matter in their society. I personally don't care about it one way or the other. However, there is a political opportunity that I might be able to take advantage of. If I were to have the right sort of assistance, you see . . . "

"I think I like the direction this is going," the player said. "Go on. I'm all ears."

Storm was practically glowing with the pleasure of the context this interaction was bringing him. Even if she declined the quest, it was worth twice the resources he had expended so far. If she accepted the quest and made serious efforts at it, then the context he gained would almost double. If she succeeded . . .

Well, then it was likely that the next king of Yuikon would be King Storm Teoran. And he would bathe in liquid context for the rest of his existence.

43

MIKAL MINES, PART 3

The travel magic kicked us into a brightly lit white room. It was very bright. And very white. Walls, floors, and ceiling, all white. There were two features in the room. The first was a pedestal, which held the dungeon core. Between my party and the core, however, was a chair, and in that chair was one of the tentacle-faced rats, like the ones we had faced in the entrance of the dungeon.

Except, I realized, it wasn't. It had the same face, but its body was more humanoid than the Mikal Burrower had been. And it was wearing clothes. Just a simple black jerkin, but that was a clear sign of intelligence. The party braced for a fight.

"Welcome, young Dungeon Busters," the creature said. "I am Mikal. This is one of my rooms. I greet you as my guests."

I frowned, lowering my stance slightly. "You would give us guest rights?"

"Why not?" Mikal asked. Its voice was both sonorous and gravelly at the same time. "It is too early for me to try to barter my way to the surface. This is not my only spawn point, so even though you intend to destroy this dungeon, it matters very little to me. The dungeon core summoned me here when you declared your intentions, but it cannot force me to fight for it. And I have so few opportunities for conversation with those from the up above."

"We accept your hospitality, on the sole condition that you will not impede us destroying the dungeon," I said.

"Wouldn't dream of it," the creature said. "Unlike that drow pauper you saved from oblivion a few weeks ago, I have numerous connections guaranteeing my continued existence. My link to this dungeon core is tenuous, anyway. I didn't need to respond to its call; I simply chose the more amusing option. But I do not see any point in obliterating you; it would not benefit me in any way. And with the limitations I would be under, you may be strong enough to give me a challenge I could not overcome. Such a death would not be my end, but it would be inconvenient. No. We shall have a few moments of conversation, and then I will leave, and the dungeon core will be yours to dispose of at your leisure."

I blinked. "I'm actually very surprised. I was really expecting another fight."

"That could be arranged, if you absolutely insist on it," Mikal offered. "But I do not recommend it."

"No, no, I'd much rather just talk," I admitted. "I mean, I like killing darkspawn and leveling up, but I don't like fighting things that talk back intelligently. If you don't object to our goals, then we have no reason to be enemies."

There was a guffawing sound, not quite laughter but close enough that it clearly was a sound of amusement. "Oh, there is plenty of reason for us to be enemies, child of the sun people. Generations and centuries of resentment of which you are unaware. My own brother would rip my throat out for not taking this opportunity to rip out yours. But the drow are hated above your kind, and the elves above them, and you humans a distant fifth on the list of our ancestral enemies. But there is little reason for us to fight. Not here, not now, and not for this petty little bauble that summoned me."

"I . . . see. I'm afraid that you seem to know quite a bit more about my people than I know about yours," I said. "Perhaps you would care to enlighten me? What exactly is the cause of the feud your people have with mine?"

"That you walk beneath the sun, of course," Mikal said simply.

I paused, waiting for him to elaborate. "That's it?"

"Yes. It is sufficient." Mikal cocked his head to the side. I couldn't read his expression at all, considering that it was made up of tentacles, but I thought he looked curious. "Do you not hate those things that live beneath your feet? Do you not hate the denizens of the Deepdark?"

"There hasn't been an excursion from the Deepdark for centuries," I pointed out. "I don't think of them at all, to be honest."

The creature ticked. "Disappointing. My people delight in perceiving ourselves as the nightmares of the children of the surface."

"Sorry," I said. "If it's any consolation, I think that you *would* give the children of the surface nightmares if they knew you existed. And, um, what you look like."

"Thank you. That's a very kind sentiment," Mikal said.

"You're welcome. So, may I ask, what should we call you? When I [Analyze] you, it just tells me your name. The creature that we— that we encountered earlier that resembled you was called a [Mikal Burrower]. But—"

"The burrowers are pets," Mikal explained. "When I responded to the summons, several of my kennel were swept up in the magic. It's of no matter, if they couldn't resist the summons on their own strength then their culling was a gift to the pack."

"That is a relief," I admitted. "I was worried that their deaths would have offended you."

"I did not say that I wasn't offended," Mikal said. "You compared me to a burrower. Were you of my kin, I would rip out one of your tentacles for that."

I frowned, then bowed deeply. "I apologize deeply for the unintended insult, Mikal. It was not intended as a slight. It was a representation of my ignorance of your people, and I hope that you may overlook it."

"Your tongue is as flowery as one of the drow," Mikal commented, making that chortling sound from earlier.

"Thank you?" I said.

"I hate the drow," Mikal said. "There. We have exchanged insults and are even. We no longer need to fight to the death."

I cocked my head to the side. "If the insults were uneven, then there would be a need?"

"No," Mikal answered, and he made the chortling sound again. "Besides, I have given you guest rights, in case you have forgotten. Unless you offer me mortal insult or threaten my body, you are safe in my presence. And being compared to an animal may be an insult, but not a mortal one."

"I am relieved," I admitted. "May I ask, then, about your people? What are they called?"

"We are called Mikal," Mikal answered. "All of us. I understand that is difficult for outsiders to understand, although I do not understand what is so difficult about it."

"Your species and personal names are all the same?" I asked.

Mikal cocked his head to the side. "As I said, I do not understand why it is so difficult for outsiders to understand."

"May I ask how many Mikal live in the Deepdark?"

"You may ask. I will not answer. Both because I do not know, and because I would not give such information to my people's ancestral enemies," Mikal stated. "Even if you are my guest."

"I suppose that's reasonable," I admitted.

"I do try to be reasonable," Mikal agreed. "Now it is my turn for a question. How does the death queen fare in the war against the living?"

I blinked in surprise. "I am not certain I should answer that."

"I am not asking for information of your people," Mikal challenged.

"You sort of are," I said. "If I said that we were faring poorly, then you might see that as a sign of weakness and take that information to your generals. The surface has not seen an incursion from the Deepdark for centuries, and I would prefer that it remain that way for centuries to come."

"You do not fare poorly, do you?" Mikal challenged. "No. You will keep the scourge out of the Deepdark for some time at least, I believe. That *is* information that I will bring to my generals, sun child."

"They do say that the enemy of my enemy is my friend," I said. "Is there no way to bridge the gulf between humans and the Mikal?"

"Unlikely," the creature said. "The enemy of an enemy is a tool to be used against the enemy. Do you befriend the sledgehammer with which you shape the rocks you use to build your homes?"

"That is a disappointing outlook. But I understand. I do hope that conflict does not come between our peoples within my lifetime."

Mikal cocked his head to the side, and then to the other side. "I have a message for you to deliver. To the beggar drow you befriended.

Tell him, 'Your sister succumbed.' He will understand, or he will not, but either way it will cause him pain."

I frowned. "If you are speaking of Gyudue, then he is my friend, and I would not wish to cause him harm."

"The surgeon cuts out the cancer. It is painful," Mikal said. "Tell him the message. I leave you now."

"Farewell," I said, but the creature had already vanished in a flash of magic runes.

My friends were staring at the vacated chair, or at me. They seemed absolutely stunned by the conversation.

"So," Corinth said. "The Deepdark . . . That's a thing, huh?"

"It's a legend," I admitted. "A world of underground darkness. There's supposedly entrances all over the place if you know where to find them."

"Do you know where to find them?" Joe asked, sounding very interested.

I shrugged. "Not a clue. Come on. The core is right there."

"You guys all signed the En Dee Aye thing, right?" Corinth asked as I walked over to the core.

"She wouldn't let us near him without it," Ike said reluctantly.

"But you got it, right? The epic, once only, potentially game-changing conversation that just happened?"

"We're not idiots," Leanne said. "But are we supposed to—"

"If Tarisha thinks it's a good idea, you can release it," I said, interrupting them. "I don't know what you Travelers know and what you don't know. And I don't know which things to keep secret from you. But I trust Tarisha to make the right decision about this."

With that said, I put my hand forward and touched the [Dungeon Core of Mikal Mines].

You have reached the Dungeon Core of Mikal Mines. You have declared intention to destroy the Dungeon Core. Has your intention changed?	
Yes (Additional options will be made available for the evolution of Mikal Mines.)	No (Maximized rewards will be received for the Destruction of Mikal Mines under the highest difficulty.)

I reread the prompt three times before making my selection. Just to make certain that "No" was the correct option to destroy the core. I was fairly certain that it was, but the system's prompts were not always straightforward, and this was a good example of that.

Mikal Mines has been cleared!	
Calculating Rewards	
Kill Percentage	77.6%
Time	3 hours 42 minutes (.53 RT)
Gauntlet of Traps	Navigated
Ooze King	Killed
Mimic Queen	Killed
Ménage à Trois	Killed
Sir William Von Barutasburg, the Iron Knight	Killed
Mikal	Greetings Exchanged
Rating	A+
Mikal Mines has been destroyed on the highest difficulty available. Rewards Increased!	
Rewards (All Members)	
Gold	11,457
Experience	20,000
Reputation With Kingdom of Eolstree	5,000
Reputation with House Wildeheart	10,000
Wind-Up Sir William Von Barutasburg	1
	Trap Sense (General Skill)
Additional Rewards (Hail Jeoran)	
Dungeon Daughter Core	8

Wind-Up Sir William Von Barutasburg	50
A Message for Gyudue of the Blackest Night	1

"Oh, sick!" Corinth exclaimed, staring at the prompt that had popped up in front of his own face. "I just got, like, just shy of four levels from that!"

"Four?" I asked, and I checked my own status. I was level thirty-eight now. I had known I had gotten level thirty-four and had been hoping for another level before the end of the dungeon, but I hadn't been hoping to get *five* levels from busting these mines. "I guess the bonus Experience we got for busting the dungeon is affected by [Through the Valley of the Shadow]."

"Yeah, I guess," Corinth agreed.

Leanne pulled an item out of her inventory. It was a small metal ball with a wingnut attached to it. She [Used] the item, and it vanished, turning into a vanity pet that looked like a miniature version of the knight-golem we had faced. "That's pretty cool," she commented.

"You should have sold that," Joe scolded. "That's what I'm going to do with mine."

"I actually collect them," she argued. "They're account wide, so there's no reason not to use it now."

Joe shrugged. "Still, if that's exclusive to this single clear of this single dungeon, that could have been, like, eight hundred dollars."

I considered mentioning that I had gotten fifty of those items, but decided not to. I didn't know these Travelers all that well, after all. I didn't feel like I needed to increase their share of the rewards beyond what the system had awarded them for their participation.

This Dungeon has been Destroyed!
Teleporting all parties to last visited safe zone in 9:25.

"I'm pretty sure that the safe zone it will teleport us to is just outside," I said. "And I don't want to wait that long. I'm going to Fast Travel back to Prowlhaven. I think, with the new guard system, that you guys will get the chance to tag along, but if you don't, can you let everyone outside know that's where I went?"

"Yeah, sure," Corinth agreed. "Oh, wait! Cast your disguise before you go!"

"Thanks!" I said, and I meant it. I'd needed the reminder. I quickly cast [Illusion Magic: Disguise], which had risen to level four with my recent use of it. Then, I opened my Fast Travel menu, and spatial magic swept me away.

44
CELEBRATION

The group teleportation feature that went with Tarisha's new appointment as the captain of my guard worked great. Fast Traveling itself took about twenty seconds longer than normal, likely a delay allowing my guardians to accept the prompt that appeared when I chose my destination. Our arrival was conspicuous, as the destination I had selected was one of the Nexus nodes inside the city near the Wildeheart estates. That itself wasn't conspicuous; I'm certain that particular node was frequently used by Travelers.

But eleven people arriving at the exact same time, perhaps, didn't happen every day. Or every night, I suppose, depending on where you lived on Earth. I think it was something like two in the morning on a Sunday in Miami. But Earth time doesn't always make sense to me.

"Was the mission successful?" Luke asked immediately.

"It was *awesome!*" Corinth said. "Oh man! Oh, and check it out: unique vanity pets! And an effing [Buster Sword]!"

He conjured both of the objects in question from the system. Sir William Von Barutasburg appeared and began stomping around fiercely, and Corinth tried to *spin* [The Buster Sword]. I say he tried, because it was an effort. An effort that nearly decapitated Leanne, who was standing next to him, and also resulted in the ridiculously impractical weapon landing in the dirt.

"Yeah, that's going to take some practice," he admitted.

"Fucking Weeb," Joe muttered. "But yes, the mission was successful. The bosses have been killed, the loot has been looted, and the dungeon core has been destroyed."

I glanced around, but fortunately it didn't seem that anyone was close enough to have heard him. "Is that really something we should be discussing? Out here in the open?" I asked.

Joe shrugged. "Nobody's listening. Nobody cares."

I sighed, not used to being the professional one. I summoned Shadow beneath me and began riding towards my stepfather's estate to inform him of my success. The others all summoned their own mounts, but although the system transported their horses with them, none of them had the convenience of storing their mounts in their shadow. They had to use a summoning item to call the animals forth, and the slight delay it took for them to follow allowed me a few moments to myself to think.

I had grown up thinking that enemies beset the Heartlands from all sides. The undead to the north, the dragonlings to the south. To the west, the Nostantan of the Ironrot Empire. And to the east, nature itself, in the form of the impassible Sea of Squalls. After speaking with Mikal, I had come to an uncomfortable conclusion. Down was a direction. And we were besieged by enemies from there as well.

I contemplated whether or not to deliver the message Mikal had given me for Gyudue. And how I would even go about doing so. Could I simply assign a quest to a Traveler and accomplish it that way? I would have to think the matter over some. I knew that the drow were a significant faction in the Deepdark, but they were not the only faction down there. And they did not have a history of being allies with the kingdoms of men.

Should I warn someone about the Mikal considering us their ancestral enemies? Who would I even warn, with Grandfather dead and the government in chaos? The ideal solution, in my opinion, would be to send an envoy to the Mikal and try to establish peaceful diplomatic relations. But the one I spoke with had been summoned by a dungeon core. I had no clue as to their true location, or how to reach them. Was that even a possibility? Or would the Mikal slaughter any envoy we sent to them immediately, as the Nostantan did? The Mikal I had spoken with seemed reasonable, but that might have only been in the context of this single meeting. I certainly couldn't base the entirety of my expectations for his people on one meeting with a single specimen who might very well be an extreme outlier.

I sighed, slowing Shadow's trot to allow the others to catch up. I rode the rest of the way to the manor listening to the others bicker as the companions who had joined me in challenging the dungeon detailed our adventure.

"And so that's how we discovered that there's a race of tentacle-faced morlocks and an entire zone known as the Deepdark, which is possibly *everywhere* with entrances underneath *everything*. Oh, hey, Hail, let's stop and get some Liecha," Corinth said, waiving towards a barista stand.

"Not now," I called back over my shoulder. "If you ask, maybe Valerio will have some squeezed for us when we get to his estate."

"I'm sorry, would you mind backing the hell up and saying that again?" Peter of Yorkshire said, his voice incredulous.

"It's true," Joe said reluctantly. "So, yeah. How much do you think that intel is worth?"

Peter began laughing his ass off. He glanced at the four members of the Asian guild and said the words "En Dee Aye."

One of the members grumbled something.

"We are allowed to discuss it with our guild leadership," their leader pointed out. "But you do not need to worry. The leak will not come from us."

"It had better not," Luke said. "We'll announce it ourselves when we release the video of the encounter. Edited for content, of course. Assuming that we have Lord Hail's permission to do so, of course."

"As long as Tarisha thinks it's a good idea," I called back over my shoulder.

"However, I don't see any problem with you or your allies prepping for when the search for the Deepdark entrances begin in earnest," Luke admitted. "So long as nobody knows what you are doing or why."

"Of course, Luke Honored Senior," the leader of the foreign guild said. And I frowned for a second because there was something odd about the way it had sounded. After thinking it over a minute, I blamed the magic system that translates the Traveler's word noises into something I could understand. They probably had a short suffix that *meant* something like honored senior, but the translation matrix didn't have the right way of putting it into words that I knew, and the words that I knew were much longer than the words that she used.

I'd had some of the same sort of problems when I'd first begun interacting with my English-speaking Traveler friends, but I had gotten so used to their language that I didn't notice any of those idiosyncrasies anymore. I had known that my Asian guards hadn't been speaking English, I just hadn't really been listening to them to learn the flow that their language used. It made sense to me, thanks to whatever magic the translation system operated under, and that's all that really mattered.

We reached the Wildeheart residence, and the same canid butler who answered the door before answered it again. He nodded in greeting, despite my disguise, and ushered us inside. We were all offered Liecha and cakes, but I declined. Valerio arrived, and my mother joined him immediately after.

"I take it that you were successful, then?" he asked after a perfunctory greeting.

"We were," I answered. "The dungeon should be gone, and you can reclaim the mine on which it stood. Except, well, you should be aware that during the final challenge of the core instance, there were a large number of traps and many cave-ins throughout the structure. You should have some [Geomancers] and [Rogues] inspect the area thoroughly to deal with both of those issues."

"Excellent. As we agreed, any cores you recovered are yours to keep, and I will consider this transaction to be a mutually beneficial arrangement, the details of which need not be disclosed outside of this room," Valerio said.

"How much are they worth?" I asked suddenly. "A dungeon core, if I were to sell one, how much would they go for?"

Valerio opened his eyes wide in surprise, then grinned. He poured a drink for himself, and for me, and a cup of steaming Liecha for my mother, as he considered the question. "Selling a dungeon core is not a simple matter, Hail," he said. "Or rather, *you* selling a core that you farmed *in Eolstree* is a very complex matter indeed, if you're selling it to anyone other than the Eolstrian government. However, the price you could expect to receive for such a sale would be, say, sixty percent of what you could get at an open auction in which all the allied powers were allowed to bid."

"I really hate politics," I muttered. "What if I said that I got the core in Yuikon?"

"Then you would have to point out which dungeon it came from and allow that to be confirmed," Valerio said. "They are called [Dungeon Daughter Cores] for a reason. The relationship to their source is embedded within them. It can be confirmed with a very simple spell, even when the dungeon source that spawned them is destroyed."

"Dammit," I muttered. If that was true, then I wouldn't be able to sell any of the cores from [Zhesa Castle] without revealing where they had come from.

"Indeed," Valerio agreed. "Cores are valuable, but also extremely regulated. The exact laws depend on the lands, so you'd have to ask a Yuikonese scholar for the exact details on how to manage any of the cores you may or may not have gathered in your homeland." He took a long sip from his brandy. "If you were to sell one core to the queen, however, it is possible that she would be willing to consider allowing you to sell more at auction. To one of our allies, of course. And I do mean *our allies*, as in allies of both Yuikon and Eolstree. That list is fortunately long but not all inclusive, which means that the bidders will not have quite as much competition as they might have otherwise. But you should still be able to get half a million gold for the core you give to my cousin, and somewhere between half again and double that amount for any other cores you managed to gather on my lands."

Which means that, if I got the absolute best price possible, it would take a minimum of thirty-one dungeon cores to solve the debt problems in North Shire. And that was assuming that they all sold for the maximum amount, but I knew that was unlikely. While all cores were the same for the purpose of battleground creation, which was the primary reason they were stockpiled by the nations of the Heartlands, cores varied wildly on the sort of dungeons that they spawned, and that would affect their price significantly as well. I would be *lucky* to get an average price of seven hundred fifty thousand, which, in addition to the one I would have to sell to the Eolstrian royal family at a discount, meant that I would need at least forty cores, if I were to go this route.

Better to sell vanity pets, I thought. Those were completely useless, after all. Their uselessness was literally part of the name. I didn't understand why Travelers want them in the first place, but since, unlike cores, they had no inherent value, I would wait until the price of my stockpile of vanity pets collapsed before I relied on selling my stockpile of cores to cover debts that weren't even mine to begin with.

"Is this something that you would like me to facilitate, Hail Jeoran?" my stepfather asked politely.

"I think that I will sell one of the cores I earned today to your government, as an act of thanks, and with the understanding that, if I desire to auction off future cores that I gather from your lands, it shall count towards the requirements for holding that auction," I said. "If that is acceptable."

Valerio inclined his head and sipped his brandy. "A very wise decision indeed. And this will allow me to begin bragging that my son's older brother is already a Dungeon Buster. This news will be like fleas in the hides of the traditionalists, strengthen the validity of the union my marriage to your mother has formed between our two nations, and also prove that the course my family is leading Eolstree down is one of strength and pride."

"Honestly, I didn't think of any of that," I admitted. "I just need gold now."

Valerio laughed, and he sipped his brandy. I braced myself to do the same, knowing how the liquid would burn my throat. But, as always, I first cast [Detect Poison] with as much discretion as possible.

And the glass flashed bright enough to make me look away from it.

I blinked in surprise from the brightness of the light, before reaching out and slapping the glass of Liecha out of my mother's hand. The hot liquid burned my hand, but the twenty Health I lost was nothing. I turned to Valerio, who was inspecting his own glass with horror. After a moment, he worked up his courage, and he cast [Detect Poison] for himself. And the liquid shone like the sun.

45

BARGAIN

The Liecha was not poisoned. Just the brandy.

My mother was not dying. Just her husband.

Was I the target of the poison? Or was it Valerio?

It was his brandy, but he had served it to me. Had he poisoned himself, planning to take the antidote after I left, only to be caught red-handed?

No. As I examined his face, I did not believe that for a moment. He was shocked, horrified, and outraged to realize what had happened.

"Miles," he said in a calm voice. "Find every hand that this brandy passed through on its way to my lips. Sooner would be better than later, as I would rather like to know who killed me, if that is at all possible."

"Mine are on that list. More than once. More than anyone else's," the canid butler said, his voice a growl. But his anger was not directed at his master, nor anyone in the room. It was directed at the poisoner. "I am responsible for not checking the decanter before you poured the drink, but I swear by Thedum, by Eclipse, and by the moon that I was not the one who poisoned you."

"I believe you, Miles," Valerio said. "Now get to your task. I believe we may have a short window of opportunity, you understand."

The canid bowed deeply, then rushed from the room.

"We must get you to the temple," Mother said. "You should transform. Your vitality is much higher in your other form."

Valerio shook his head. "If I was the target, that might be the worst thing I could do. There are at least three poisons that are more effective against a transformed Leonid than they are against a human, and there's every chance that is what I have been drinking all week. It is possible, my dear, that your dislike of fur on the furniture is all that has saved my life."

"I do not think so," I said. "I cast [Detect Poison] the last time we shared a drink, and the spell found nothing. I haven't ranked up the spell since then, so I doubt it was a case of the spell failing to detect a poison, but of the poison not being there."

The Leonid man nodded. "Then that should make Miles's task easier. Now let us go to the temple, and we will see if I am a dead man walking."

The procession was surprisingly sedate. Somber, but nobody was crying or screaming. No, that's not true. I saw tears in my mother's eyes, but she hurried to wipe them away before anyone noticed, so I did not call attention to them. I could understand my Traveler companion's calm, but I was astounded by Valerio's.

"This is likely your brother, Storm," he informed my mother in a perfectly calm voice once we were outside. He called for a servant to fetch him a horse, but I swiftly summoned Shadow instead and bid Valerio to ride him.

"You don't know that," Mother protested.

"It makes the most sense," Valerio persisted. "Our son will be a threat to his claim, and he is but weeks away from being born. It is easier to disinherit an orphan, and less distasteful to murder a nobleman than a woman eight months pregnant."

"You don't know that," Mother protested again.

"If I ever do know that, then I must beg your forgiveness in advance," Valerio said. "For if that is what happened today, then there will be a reckoning between Storm and I, and my love for you will not stay my hand against your brother."

"Let us speak of knowledge when things are certain," Analise Teoran-Wildeheart said. "Ride ahead. We will catch up to you at the temple."

"You will find me there, or you will find me along the way, if I collapse before I reach it," my stepfather predicted. He turned to me, nodded, and kicked Shadow into a gallop.

"Go with him," I told my bodyguards, but only half of them obeyed. I should have expected as much; it was surprisingly professional of them.

Mother and I followed along in a coach shortly after. It was too far for her to walk, and she was too far along in her pregnancy to ride. And I was not willing to leave her side.

A flash of blue light coalesced into the form of Thomas, whose expression was grim.

"How are you feeling, Hail?" the administrator asked.

"I'm not certain," I admitted. I looked at Mother, but she had the far-off expression that Natives always wore whenever Thomas appeared. "Will Valerio die?"

Thomas was silent. "I don't know, to be honest. Not necessarily. I'm sorry. This one is Eclipse's handiwork. That's all I know for certain at this point. I literally got woken up ten minutes ago. I'm still in my underwear, but my coworkers hit the panic button, so I'm here."

"Can you help? Can you save him?" I asked.

The administrator looked away. "I honestly don't know. You're not the only canon entity involved in this matter, Hail. Valerio doesn't have [Blood of the Travelers] or any other revival ability. Divine intervention would work. But the outcome is in flux. It will be determined by your decisions, and the decisions of the other canon parties involved in this mess. I'm not sure what I can do, but I'll try to tip the scales in your favor if I can. To be clear, however, I'd like you to state your intentions. Will you be acting to save Valerio Wildeheart?"

"Yes," I said. "He is my stepfather. He makes my mother happy. He has been good to me. I would do anything I can to save him."

"Thank you. Your preferences have been logged," Thomas said formally. "I'll tip the scales as much as I can, but I can't promise anything."

He vanished the way that he had come, and we arrived at the temple of Eclipse shortly after. Mother rushed inside, waddling in a way that was somehow dignified, despite her haste and circumstance. I tried to follow her, but I . . . couldn't.

It was not as though there were a barrier preventing me from walking forward. But rather, as though the distance between me and the temple were fixed. No matter how I walked or ran, I could not close the distance. It took me longer than it perhaps should have to figure it out.

"Am I unwelcome in your temple, Eclipse?" I said aloud.

"Hmmm . . . you know, I actually haven't decided that yet," a childish voice said. She sprang up from the shadow of a pebble, a child of eight and the goddess of tricksters. "I don't like making my mind up. Ever. So I haven't decided if I should let the avatar of that old doggy into my temple or not. And until I do, well, I guess you'll have to wait for that."

"I see. Thomas the Administrator said that your hand was in on this matter. Did you arrange for my stepfather to be poisoned?" I asked.

"Not . . . exactly. I made that old dog forget to check the drink. I didn't put the poison there, and I certainly didn't make anyone drink it," she said innocently.

"Why?" I demanded.

"I want a favor," she said bluntly. "If you grant it, Valerio will live. I promise."

"And he will die if I refuse?"

"Why, I never said that, did I?" she said, teasing. "If you refuse, I'll simply turn my face away from the entire matter. Whether he lives or dies will be entirely in the hands of the healers tending to him, and his own strength. I cannot tell you the odds of that, because if I did, then everything would change! You must decide whether or not to grant me my favor knowing that if you do, he will definitely live. And if you do not, maybe yes or maybe no. Not a coinflip, not a roll of the dice. A certainty, but I cannot look to see which outcome is certain. That would be cheating."

"What favor do you demand?" I asked.

"Five." she answered immediately.

I blinked in confusion. "Five what?"

"Five of the things that you have more of than anyone else. For the moment. I want five dungeon cores."

"Is that all?" I asked, relieved. "Fine. Does it matter what type? Their level? Where they came from?"

"No, no, and no. It only matters where they go," Eclipse answered, giggling. She waved her hand, and a wave of shadows from *everywhere* swarmed over me. They focused on my right hand and left the mark of Eclipse. A white circle inside of a black one. "This will tell you when it is time. Remember, you promised! I will be very, very upset if you do not give me my cores when it is time!"

She turned away, giggled, then turned back.

"Hail, once you do this favor for me, I will consent to lifting the curse on your other hand," she informed me.

"Are you the one who forced it upon me?" I asked, anger rising.

"Noooooo," she said, drawing it out. "But I didn't argue with the others when they decided to make Death do it. You'll have to convince the others as well. Once all eight of us agree, you'll be free. Unless someone kills Auroras Teoran first, of course. Then you're off the hook anyway. But it will take more than building a silly temple or two to convince all eight of us!"

"Thank you," I said.

"A favor for a favor. Favors make the world go round!" she said, doing a cartwheel as she spoke. Her body vanished midway through, her voice continuing the sentence despite the lack of a source.

I glanced over my shoulder, towards my bodyguards, who were watching me with fascination.

"Lord Hail," Luke of London began, "Who was that?"

"That was Eclipse, trickster god of the shadows," I answered. "Some people think that because she's got a shadow aspect, she's evil, but she's not the adversary. She's one of the eight. She's not evil; she's just . . . what she is."

Tentatively, I stepped forward and found that whatever force had me running in place moments ago had been lifted, and I could finally approach. Apparently, Eclipse, the goddess famous for her indecision, had made up her mind. I was allowed in her temple after all.

Despite the bargain I struck with Eclipse, my stepfather was not completely spared from suffering. He'd grown ill on the journey to the temple and had collapsed on the temple steps. He'd had only enough strength to explain that he had been poisoned and request healing.

Keeping him at maximum Health was easy, but that wouldn't be enough, depending on the type of poison that had been used. And Valerio did not know; he was not given a name by his system, simply a [Poison] debuff. It drained him of his Health, Strength, Dexterity,

Vitality, and Endurance. He reported that he'd gained three levels of poison resistance, and it was now at thirty-four. But the outcome, according to the healers attending him, was far from certain.

I decided to have faith.

I almost called out to Thedum, but decided that would be disrespectful. Perhaps blasphemous. Thedum would not mind me making a bargain with Eclipse. He would, in fact, insist that I uphold it. And that she would uphold her end of the bargain as well. But it would be insulting to appeal to him for intervention while inside Eclipse's temple, and triply so for doing it after having made a bargain with her.

The miracle was obvious, when it came. All the light in the temple vanished, and for a moment we were in perfect darkness. Then the light returned. And Valerio was well. His debuff was removed, and his status returned to normal, and all was well.

"Thank you, Eclipse," I whispered.

"He would have lived anyway," a giggling voice answered. "At least, he would have if he had turned into his kitty-form."

46
CONVALESCENCE

"I am curious to know what price you paid for that miracle that saved my life," Valerio asked. We had returned to his mansion, and he was convalescing in his own bed. He had asked to see me and then asked everyone else to leave us. An entire day had passed, and it had been the quietest day I'd experienced since returning to this world from the lobby.

"It's nothing," I said, scratching at the mark that Eclipse had left on my hand.

"Deals with the gods are never nothing," Valerio insisted. He was in his Leonid form: his muscles bulging despite their weakness, the fur on his skin shedding, his face more bestial, despite the kindness and wisdom I had come to expect from the man. He was in his beast-kin form for the sake of his recovery, as the additional Vitality and Endurance would help speed things along. "Especially not Eclipse. Had her temple not been so much closer than the others, I would have ridden past it. But my strength was fading, and I was not thinking clearly."

"Neither was your servant when he failed to scan your drink," I said. "She was quite clear on that when I spoke with her. When I asked her if she poisoned you, she said 'I made that old dog forget to check the drink. I didn't put the poison there, and I certainly didn't make anyone drink it.' That is a direct quote from Eclipse herself."

Valerio nodded. "I can't simply not acknowledge what has

happened, but I will spare Miles as much embarrassment and pain for this blunder as possible. I, too, failed in my diligence. I should have cast [Detect Poison] myself on the drink that I offered the guest of my house rather than relying on my manservant. But Miles will see it as a personal failing no matter how I try to fall on the sword. Even if the goddess of shadows and misdirection herself clouded his eyes."

"She did," I insisted. "She said so. She rarely lies when she is explicit."

"And may that give him some measure of comfort," my stepfather said. "Now then. What price? What bargain does that mark on your arm seal?"

"It is really nothing," I insisted. "Dungeon cores. I think you know that I have more of them than I should. I would still like to avoid saying just how many, but the number that she asked to guarantee your survival was trivial to me. I might have hesitated a week ago, before I saw how happy you make my mother. But in the moment, when she listed her price, I was relieved that it was so cheap."

Valerio blinked, then lay back in his bed. "I see. But the debt has not been settled yet, if I am not mistaken. Thus the mark on your hand, to seal the contract."

"I suppose," I admitted.

"She's a crafty one. It's why some of my people venerate her. I am not certain what she wants from you, nor will I be until she reveals how her payment for sparing my life will be spent," Valerio admitted. "If you believe the cores will be used in a way that will harm Eolstree or the Heartlands, I beg you to renege on the debt."

"That was the plan already," I chuckled.

"Your mother misses you. She did not like leaving you behind. There were two schools of thought, in the wake of the great scandal. One was to protect you from the choice your father made in abandoning you, and the other was to allow you to determine your own fate," he said abruptly. "Had you pushed harder, you could have left Zhesa. The old king's will to keep you close to him wasn't absolute, and he would have been persuaded by a child missing his mother. But the reports said that you were content to train with the sword with other boys in [Zhesa Castle]."

I blinked in surprise. "You're saying I could have come to live here if I had pushed harder for it?"

"The whole 'murder the cubs of your mate's previous lovers

because they are your rival's children' is *really* blown out of proportion, Hail," Valerio chuckled. "Even the traditionalists who want to see me murder you want that more for the *awkwardness* that it would cause me and my allies than any desire to see you dead. I am a Eolstrian nobleman, not a mindless savage. I would have welcomed you into my home with open arms at any time. As, indeed, I tried to do the other day. I am deeply sorry that I inadvertently served you poison. The poisoner was clever indeed. If we had both died, it would have looked like I was following the traditions my people are known for by murdering you. And that I was incompetent enough to somehow succumb to my own attack. I am greatly shamed to have fallen for this sham, and I am diminished by the result."

"I thought that you would recover fully," I objected. "A few days rest and—"

"Politically, Hail. I am diminished politically," he clarified. "There is no way in which this fiasco looks like anything other than a giant embarrassment to me and my house. The traditionalists will see me as a toothless, decrepit cuckold who not only resorted to using poison to solve the problem they believe you pose me, but who failed miserably and required the mercy of my rival to survive. To outsiders, I look weak, unable to protect myself or my guests. And to my own faction, I look either weak or like a secret traditionalist spouting words of hypocrisy. No matter what angle I take, it looks very bad."

I contemplated his problem for a moment. "I'm sorry. I genuinely don't know enough about Eolstrian politics to know how to help you."

"It would shame me further to accept any help from you in this sort of matter," he admitted.

"Then it is your right to turn it down, I suppose. But it is still freely offered. At least, I mean, if it's nothing too difficult. I don't want to duel your political rivals with nothing but a slightly sharpened rock for a weapon, for example," I clarified.

Valerio was quiet for a moment. Then he said, "It would relieve me greatly to know that my wife and child were in the protection of someone who had their best interests in their heart and mind while I struggle to reclaim my standing in the following weeks. Some traditionalists would see my weakness as an opportunity to strike a coup de grâce, and would not hesitate to strike at me through them. If my family were enshrined in the protection of a powerful foreign lord—perhaps a young Dungeon Buster with a powerful and swiftly growing faction among the Travelers—then they would not dare. They would mock me for my weakness, but that is just the sounds of jackals, scavengers, and mongrels who are too afraid to confront the real predator until there is nothing left but the marrow."

I blinked in surprise. "That's a burden I'd take up gladly," I admitted. "But my lands are currently in disarray. I have bandits in open revolt, and far too many Travelers who, for some reason, think that it's perfectly acceptable to pick just any lock in a Native's house and walk inside, as long as they don't get caught. And the manor that I was planning to establish as my residence was destroyed in the battleground. I do not think that North Shire would be a safe place for my mother during the final weeks of her pregnancy."

"Perhaps," my stepfather agreed. "But I do hear that Thorn March is lovely this time of year."

"Oh," I said, having almost forgotten that I had *two* sets of lands to administer. "Um, I will have to examine my properties in Thorn March to ensure that they are suitable for a noblewoman in my mother's condition, and of her stature and social rank. But if they are suitable, I would of course love to entertain my mother there for as long as she wished to stay. She would be under my strongest protection from both your enemies and mine."

"And her own, and her second son's, I hope," Valerio said. "I am quite certain that it will be a boy. If it is a boy, Analise plans to name him Rain, for his grandfather."

"I think his spirit would like that," I said honestly. "This strategy. How will your political allies view it? You said that the traditionalists will mock you, but—"

"My allies will come to one of two conclusions. Either that you and I are indeed close friends or that I am weak and pathetic even by traditionalist standards. They may believe you have a dagger at my throat, and I am mewling for your mercy. But it is the best of all the options I can think of, and it is also the limit of what I can ask of you." He grinned, showing off his fangs in a way that was intimidating despite the lack of malice. "Besides. There is zero chance, if my child is a boy, that he will become the next king of Yuikon. It would be good for his future if he was born in the lands which he may one day rule as sovereign."

I smiled. He wasn't wrong. "I will leave today for Thorn March and begin arranging things for my mother to stay there immediately. Assuming that I deem it a safe place for her. If it is not, I will send word, and we will have to come to some alternatives. I do not like the idea of stashing her in an anonymous convent, but if that is what it takes to keep her safe . . . "

"Go. Good hunting, Hail Jeoran. And kiss your mother goodbye before you leave."

So I left, and I followed his advice to the best of my abilities.

I was in the process of securing a portal back to Yuikon when Tarisha returned to my world. While I had always gotten notifications when members of my friends list came online, the notification this time was significantly more prominent, in a different window of my HUD. When I mentally toggled it, I saw that it was a communication option dedicated entirely to Tarisha, Daemon, and the other players who had signed contracts to become "canon" while in my service. After a moment of experimentation, I figured out how to use this submenu to send a personal message.

That was something I could do with my standard interface as well, but I kept those windows closed most of the time due to the strange number of weird messages I often received from people I didn't know, and I didn't know any other way to make them stop.

Tarisha	Good morning, Hail. Heard you had a busy night. Are you doing okay?
Hail	I have a ticket in to talk with Thomas, but yeah, everything is fine. The dungeon busting went okay, but did you hear about my stepfather?
Tarisha	Only a little bit. He was poisoned, but he'll survive?
Hail	I think it was Storm. But yes, he's going to be okay. I've got to secure Thorn March for my mother, though. I think she's going to be staying with me for a while. I authorize you to use whatever resources you can in order to protect her!

Tarisha	Not a problem. Oh, look. I just got the ability to assign her ten guards, just like I can for you. Yup, that will be easy. She'll have a 24/7 honor guard. I promise.
Hail	That's great. The sooner they can start the better.
Tarisha	Hail, there's a few matters we need to discuss. About my being canon.
Hail	Is it a problem?
Tarisha	No. It's literally a dream come true. I still need to talk with Lewis about one of the matters. I'm planning to drive up to see him this week, and then, depending on how that goes, I'll come talk with you, or we'll both come talk with you. But the matter we need to discuss now is my actual career. How I earn money in my world. I . . . I want you to understand.
Hail	Do you want to meet up?
Tarisha	Actually, I think it's best to explain this through the message system.
Tarisha	Hail, I said before that I quit dancing to focus on becoming a professional player. That's not exactly the truth. I was injured, so I lost my job for a while. I started playing while I was convalescing, and I managed to earn quite a bit of money because, well, I'm so damn good.
Tarisha	But I kept looking for a new job that would allow me to return to dancing.
Hail	Oh. Did you find one? Is that what this is about? Because that's totally okay, if you need to spend more time on Earth. I'll manage without you if I need to.
Tarisha	No, Hail, I haven't found a new dancing position. I had a few minor jobs along the way, but nothing that allowed me to be a star. But that's not the issue. The issue is that, now that I'm canon, my goals have changed. Fundamentally. I'm giving up on dance. I'm going to focus entirely on living in this world and making the best of it. And I'm really looking forward to it, and I can only do it because of you. So, thank you, Hail.

Hail	Oh. You're welcome.
Hail	Are you sure you really want to give up on dance, though?
Tarisha	Professionally, yes. I'll stay in shape as best as I can, but I'm not going to be pursuing any new positions like that.
Hail	Okay, I guess. If you're sure.
Tarisha	And, Hail? I also need you to understand that I'm being paid to be canon. By my guild, and several others. In a way, they're paying me for access to you. So I don't want to hide it from you. I don't want our relationship to change. I want to continue to serve you in this world, and I will continue to help you achieve your goals within it. If one of the organizations that is bankrolling me begins to ask for too much, I'll shut them down. And I won't hide it from you. But this sort of thing is somewhat standard in a world like this. I hope that it doesn't compromise your ideals.
Hail	Will Daemon and the others who signed on to be canon be doing the same thing as you?
Tarisha	I haven't discussed their goals with them yet. Everything has happened so fast, I'm not certain where the chips will land. But I was hoping for this exact sort of situation, so I already had my contacts to get this sort of arrangement set up and waiting.
Hail	I see. I do understand that you need food, water, and shelter in your world, Tarisha. It doesn't bother me what you need to do to get those things. I do worry about corruption, but I will just have to trust that you know where the line is and will not cross it. And Tarisha? Thank you. For everything.
Tarisha	No, Hail, thank you. I will line up your mother's guardians, then I'll join you in person.

47
ADMINISTRATION

It was about three hours before Tarisha teleported to my side using her new abilities to do exactly that. The Midnight Guard switched out with the Dawn guard, and I recognized more of those faces, since they mostly belonged to members of <Peasant's Revenge>. Because time was of the essence, which made travel speed important, I reluctantly relaxed my request to have part of the ten-person bodyguard team made up of Travelers closer to my level. And I agreed to leave Shadow unsummoned, instead riding behind Tarisha on her wyvern with its modified two-person saddle.

I had managed to arrange a teleport from Prowlhaven back to Zhesa on my own, and from there I paid a [Mage] to portal me as close to Briarton as possible. Which wasn't all that close, at fifty leagues. I could have kept looking for a [Mage] who had a closer destination, but it was uncertain that I would find one. And the [Mage] whose services I had managed to employ had a very "take it or leave it" attitude in regards to his portal services.

Still, it had cut down many hours on the journey, and when Tarisha arrived, we gained even more time as we took to the skies. Without any lower-level Travelers to slow us, we flew in formation over the expanses of Thorn March. We didn't make a direct line for our destination, however, but instead flew over my land in a pattern, examining the local wildlife and darkspawn from above to get an idea of the inherent danger they posed to the inhabitants.

And it was . . . tame. Very tame. We saw enemies ranging from levels ten through levels thirty, which almost made Thorn March qualify as a starting zone. Perhaps it *would* have qualified for a starting zone, had any of the Gates of TirNiki been nearby.

It wasn't so tame that a level one [Child] could run around unsupervised, but even the wilderness of Thorn March seemed to be one of the safest zones I had seen outside of the walled cities of Zhesa and Prowlhaven themselves. Which might not have been that great for the purposes of drawing in Traveler crowds. But for a quiet place for Mother to hide in the next few weeks it would be perfect!

We flew over a number of thornberry vineyards, attracting some attention from the locals as they came out to stare at the high-level Travelers flying overhead in formation. It is fortunate that we weren't trying for stealth because, among the Natives at least, we were noticed everywhere we went. As for Travelers, I didn't see any at all.

"I've never seen a land that wasn't touched by Traveler exploration," I admitted to Tarisha as we closed in on Briarton. "It's almost like going back in time to before the gates opened."

"I looked up what information I could on the forums," Tarisha informed me. "And, well, there wasn't much. There have been a few guilds that explored the area, a few known quest chains that give minimal rewards, and a pair of lairs that aren't really that great. No dungeons or raids in the area. In general, before it was assigned to your management, there was absolutely nothing here that would draw the attention of a Traveler. Not compared to the high traffic zones or the established leveling areas, at least. I did find a blog of one guy who managed to get hired on in one of the vineyards and spent two game years making thornberry wine. I've actually sent him a half dozen messages requesting a meeting ever since you were given Thorn March, but he insists that he'll only accept a face-to-face meeting."

"That sounds . . . very unlike a normal Traveler," I said gently.

"I have some serious respect for this level of dedication to the art of Are Pee," Tarisha said seriously. "I hope that we can recruit him into some official capacity and give him the formal respect and support that he deserves. Full immersion players like this are hard to come by. Unfortunately, I don't think he'll be happy to see us. Not if he's been paying attention and noticing that . . . well, that everywhere you go you tend to leave a wave of change behind you. If he's the sort of Traveler I think he is, he might be upset that we're about to change his way of life. But if we can get him to talk to us, he might be an excellent source of information."

"I'm really not looking to set anything on fire this time," I reminded Tarisha. "I'm hoping for a nice quiet place to stash my mother for a few months. Even if the locals are cheating on their taxes and the steward of this province has been robbing me blind, I think I might overlook it this time as long as it guarantees safety for my mother and baby brother. At least until after the coronation. My brother should be safe after that, and they can go back to either Eolstree or Zhesa."

"I understand," Tarisha said, and moments later we were landing in the fields outside of Briarton. A few Natives lined up to examine us, but as my guardians dismissed their mounts, the Natives seemed to lose interest in us. I walked up to a young woman and put on my most charming smile.

"Hello. I'm Earl Hail Jeoran. I've come to see the steward of Thorn March. Would you happen to know where I might find him?" I asked.

"Kneecrest Vineyards," she answered. "It's his, after all. He comes into town once a week to handle whatever paperwork needs handling, but government doesn't take up all of his time. Most of it goes into his family business."

"I see. And, in your opinion, has he been doing an overall good job?" I inquired.

"Eh. He could be worse. I think he drinks too much of his own wine. But he's fair to the city, as far as I know," she said.

"And you're not saying that under any sort of coercion?"

"Don't know that word," she said.

"Thank you," I said. "Could you point the way?"

She shrugged and pointed off to the northwest. "Three leagues that way."

I decided it would be better not to arrive by air this time, and so my entourage and I summoned our ground mounts instead. Mostly I just wanted to ride Shadow after a few hours of clinging to the saddle of Tarisha's flying mount. But also, it was just nice to take in the weather on a leisurely journey after all our scouting of the province.

A flash of blue light appeared next to me, and Thomas materialized, mounted on a chestnut mare.

"Hello again, Hail," he said. "You opened a ticket?"

I glanced at Tarisha. "Would you give us a moment?"

She nodded and signaled the others, and my Traveler friends backed off a respectful distance, leaving me alone with the administrator.

"I wanted to thank you for helping me save Valerio," I said.

Thomas smiled. "I didn't actually do anything at all, Hail. You solved that all on your own. I was still floundering around, half asleep and panicking, when you cut the deal with Eclipse. After that, I waited to make sure she was honoring it, then I went back to sleep. That's all."

"You showed up to help," I pointed out. "So even if it wasn't needed, thank you."

"You're welcome."

"It was Storm, wasn't it?" I inquired.

"I can't answer that," Thomas said. "I'm sorry. I can tell you that the assassin tried to cut a deal with Eclipse, and Eclipse tricked her pretty cleverly. The assassin used up a significant amount of resources obtaining divine favor to help her remain undetected and ensure that the poisoned drink was delivered to you. But Eclipse knew that you'd never drink it without casting [Detect Poison]. She made it sound to the Traveler like she would ensure that the poison was administered to you, while she was really only promising that it would get placed in your hand." Thomas paused. "Also, the assassin chose a poison that affected humans more strongly than Leonids, if the Leonids are in their beast form. You were the target, Hail. If Valerio had transformed immediately, he might have been safe without divine intervention. But it was a complicated scenario, and we weren't certain how it would play out. I don't think *Eclipse* knew for certain how it would turn out in the end, although it does seem she got everything that she wanted."

"Yeah, I knew Eclipse had a thumb on both sides of the scale," I admitted. "What does she need the dungeon cores for, anyway?"

"I can't say," Thomas answered. "But I don't think it's morally objectionable. She wouldn't ask you to do anything out of character or that violates your principles. I will promise that she's not going to force you to use them to create battlegrounds or otherwise use them offensively. And we'll stop her if she does."

"I see," I said. "What Valerio said. Could I have moved to Eolstree instead of staying in Yuikon?"

Thomas hesitated for a moment, then shrugged. "We were watching you pretty closely in the days after Gideon rejected you. The goal was to get you ready to interact with Travelers as soon as possible. If you had shown separation anxiety from your mother, then yes. Steps would have been taken to keep you together. But we thought that the best thing for you was to get you ready for human interaction as soon as possible, so we pushed your caretakers to train you in ways that would help you interact with the average Traveler. We thought that Zhesa City was the best location for that, but the administration would have had no preference between having you live with your grandfather or your mother during that preparation time."

"I see," I said.

"It was a shitty situation for everyone involved, Hail, and I am sorry for that," Thomas said. "We're trying our very best to ensure that when the next entity like you is introduced into the game, they will have loving caretakers from both the Native and Traveler sides. We . . . we kind of really flubbed things by picking Gideon. And he *really* screwed up by not seeing your potential. Seriously. The people who are suing him for disbanding his little guild should be suing him for rejecting you instead. Between those two mistakes, leaving you behind was the bigger one."

"Thank you, Thomas. You can leave now, if you want. I don't want to rehash every decision that the administration has made for me. I just wanted to say thank you for showing up when I needed help, even if you didn't need to lift a finger."

"You're welcome," Thomas said. I expected him to vanish into lights like he usually did, but instead he paused. "Actually, I do have something to say. Hail, you don't have to have the weight of the world on your shoulders."

I blinked. "What?"

"It's not your job to balance this world. That's what the gods are for. Your job is . . . well, you don't have one. You have a backstory that was written into this world. You have a bunch of systems that are set up to help you. But you don't *have* to do anything. The entire idea behind *The Gates of TirNiki* is that the world is supposed to evolve and manage itself based upon the actions and decisions of its player base. The story centers around canon individuals, of which you are one. An important one, but not the only one." Thomas paused. "You do have quite a bit of 'pull' in the world, and you can use that pull to try to shape things however you want. Some forces are designed to pull back against you. Some are designed to help you. The system is designed for an overall balance. The world is meant to evolve and change, so that it's always new, and something is always happening. Does that make sense?"

"I guess," I said. "Why are you saying these things, though?"

"Because, Hail, if you were to suddenly disappear, or if you were to take a vacation by spending a few weeks as a Traveler or a different Native, the system would survive your absence. Thedum would not allow Yuikon to fall into darkness. The adversary would not push the frontier a hundred miles into the Heartlands. Things might change while you were gone, but the world wouldn't end. You're a very important figure in this world, but at the same time, it doesn't revolve around you."

I frowned. "Thomas, are you telling me to take a vacation?"

He laughed. "I'm telling you that, if you did, you wouldn't come back to find things significantly more or less on fire than they are right now. I'm just worried about you, Hail. You've been under quite a bit of stress, and although you seem to be handling it well, it's not the sort of thing that is good for a person. We're not sure where to gauge your emotional and intellectual development, but we are pretty united in still thinking of you as a kid. And kids goof off all of the time. I just wanted you to know that it's okay if you do that too. And that you can use your abilities to help you let off some steam, if you want. It is totally okay with the administration if you decided to send the entire world on a wild goose chase just for fun. We'll stop you before you cross any barriers that we'd view as too serious, but most of the things that we'd consider intervening in are the sorts of things that I doubt would even occur to you."

"So you're telling me to take vacations . . . and abuse my system-given powers for my personal amusement," I clarified.

"If you want," Thomas said. "Goodbye, Hail. Have fun. I hope you like being a big brother."

This time, Thomas did vanish into motes of blue light, his horse despawning with him.

48

THORN MARCH

We arrived at the steward's family's vineyard not long after Thomas left us. Nobody thought it was strange that an administrator had come to chat with me. Tarisha did discuss his advice with me briefly.

"I know he said that you're not vital to the world," Tarisha said, "but if you *do* decide to take a vacation, I suggest that you wait until the next king of Yuikon is crowned. I am quite certain that he was understating your importance in that matter. I would view your health as more important than the story of this world, but at the same time, I believe that the story of this world is important to your health."

"I know," I agreed.

"But I agree with the other part of his suggestion. You should definitely start handing out bullshit quests sometimes, now that you actually have some direct control over it," she said.

"I what?"

"I'm not joking. Send some people snipe hunting. Ask your guild for suggestions for quests that they think would be funny and then get your throne's system to write them for you. Write quests that *you* think would be funny and assign them. Have some fun with your powers, now that you have them."

I paused, considering her advice. "What if the Travelers figure out what I'm doing?"

"They'll love you for it," she assured me. "Especially if the quests you assign are actually funny. I mean, the worst thing that can happen is that a Traveler refuses or abandons one of your 'fun' quests, right? So where's the harm in it?"

"I'll think about it," I promised.

A handful of Natives were milling about tending the thornberry vines when we arrived. They stopped to look at us, and a child came running forward.

"Who are you?" she asked.

"I'm Earl Hail Jeoran," I answered. "I was told Steward Benarth lived here. Is he available?"

"PAAAAH!" she screamed, and it took me a second to realize that it was a *name* and not a sound of . . . I don't know, defiance?

A middle-aged man stopped what he was doing out in the fields and made his way over.

"Pa, I think these people are Important," the girl said. "Did you hear the capital letter in Important? Because it was supposed to be capital. Because it's important."

I smiled. On a whim, I pulled out one of the Sir William Von Barutasburg summoning items. "Would you like a toy?"

She blinked in surprise. "What is it?"

"If you [Use] it, a metal doll will follow you around," I informed her. I tossed the metal ball to her, and she promptly followed my instruction. The item itself poofed, almost like it was really a darkspawn despawning, and the girl let out a little screech.

"Sorry! It's harmless; don't be scared," I said. "I forgot that it might look scary."

"I wasn't scared," she said. She looked at the vanity pet and began laughing. Within a moment she was playing with the useless little thing. Before long, she was chasing after it with a stick.

"I hope that wasn't valuable," the man said, arriving.

"I have spares," I said. "I don't know how much it was worth because I haven't priced them yet. But it was worth it to see her smile."

"Of course it was. But I have to say that since I'm her father. Welcome to Thorn March, My Lord. We've been expecting you. I am Steward Max Benarth," the man said, bowing deeply in the proper manor for a Yuikon court. The display was somewhat offset by the fact that he was barefoot, covered in dirt, and his clothes were torn from the vines and bushes he had been tending. But I was hardly going to base my opinion on the state of his work clothes after I had appeared at his home unannounced.

"I've just come for a tour, Benarth. To get a general sense of the land. My bodyguards flew me over a small chunk of the province, and it seems that the threat of darkspawn is quite low here," I said.

"We are blessed to live in relative safety, My Lord," Benarth agreed. "The only real threats that exist out here are the goblins and the kobold lair. But they fight each other constantly and keep their numbers down themselves, so we never need to send our own lads in to cull them. I hope you're not too disappointed in receiving these lands, as there's little value to them. We do produce a lot of thornberry wine, of course, but the wine sours after three years, so we have to sell it dirt cheap or it goes to waste. Taxes are more or less balanced, after our duty to the throne is satisfied. Some years there's a slight surplus, some years a slight deficit, but rarely any lingering debt. It's a cozy little posting. If you do replace me with someone, as I have heard you did on the other province you govern, I would ask that you allow me some time to instruct them in their duties, so that I may be satisfied that I am leaving my neighbors in skilled hands."

So he had heard about that? It had been several days, I supposed. "Arkan the steward was corrupt. It was quite obvious from the state of North Shire, simply from the presence of the bandits and the corruption of the constable, that the steward was either completely incompetent, or he was criminal. I *will* examine your management of Thorn March, Max. And if I find signs of corruption or criminal activity, I will deal with it accordingly. But I don't mean that as a threat; it is simply the way I wish to rule. I will not employ corrupt or incompetent people. If my investigation shows that you are an upstanding citizen and have been a dutiful steward, then I will certainly want to keep you around, if for no other reason than to help my Traveler friends learn how to manage land properly."

Benarth grinned. "Truth is, part of me has been hoping you'd just fire me and get it over with. Governing is a headache, it is."

"I've noticed," I agreed. I smiled. I decided that I liked Max Benarth. I would still have to investigate his stewardship properly. And if I found any indisputable evidence of corruption, I would have to fire him. But unless my Traveler friends found evidence that he was engaged in criminal behavior, I wasn't planning on replacing him. If anything, I might encourage Daemon to tap him as a resource.

We spent the afternoon in Max's office. He went over a map of Thorn March with me, explaining the key locations and their significance in terms of trade, history, and important citizens. At one point, he paused, looked at Tarisha—the only Traveler who had been allowed to follow us inside his office—and then he shrugged and pointed to one of the estates.

"There is a man who lives and works here. A Traveler. You asked for important citizens, and that's not exactly what I'd call him. But he is noteworthy," Max explained. "Good man. I like him. My daughter likes him. Everyone likes him. It's just strange to have a Traveler be part of the community. He's more than welcome here, of course. I don't mean to say that he's not. I am not biased against our saviors from another world! I am simply bringing him to your attention, My Lord."

"Thank you," I said. "I believe I will make it a point to visit him soon, if possible. I believe that Tarisha also mentioned him as someone noteworthy, which increases my interest in him exponentially."

After the geography lesson, Max and I reviewed the finances. Which weren't great, but they weren't abysmal either. I wouldn't be able to sweep funds from Thorn March to cover the debt of North Shire. Nor would I be able to take in an income more generous than what even very casual adventuring would give me. But I wouldn't be bleeding gold into the coffers of Thorn March either. At least according to the picture that my steward was painting for me.

I'd still have to have it audited, but I put that on the low-priority list for now.

I was invited to stay for an evening meal with Max's family, but I politely declined in favor of flying off to visit the strange Traveler who had gained the notice and respect of both Tarisha and Max Benarth. I would have preferred to ride on the trusty back of Shadow, but we were hoping to catch the eccentric Traveler before nightfall.

The landscape blurred beneath us. Having seen the map, Tarisha took the lead and managed to set a waymarker on the destination through her own interface.

I reflected on the difference between Arkan and Max, and I could only shake my head. If Arkan had come across as incompetent, over his head, or fearful of the bandits, perhaps I would have had a different reaction to him. Instead he had presented himself as "too useful to dispose of." Which was a mistake, because he had also made himself "way too dangerous to keep around." I hadn't known at the time that I would be able to give Arkan's position to Daemon as I did, but I had been banking on my ability to involve my guild and Traveler allies in the resolution of the debt situation. I had *not* been willing to trust a viper in the rabbit clutch.

Max had presented himself as loyal but not overly attached. He didn't *need* his position as steward, as he had said more than once, and he wasn't opposed to being replaced. Legally, I couldn't take his vineyard away from him, which is what he truly cared about anyway. I *might* end up replacing him, eventually, even if I found no evidence of criminal activity on his part. But I was steadily inclined to keep him for as long as I could. Again, assuming that the investigations I would have my Traveler friends perform did not find anything untoward.

We landed in the yard of the estate where my target was said to be employed, but it took a few moments to track down anyone who cared. We had interrupted their evening meal, it seemed, so nobody had seen us approaching. One of the members of my Dawn Guard returned after a few moments of exploring, explaining that he had found a Native willing to give directions to "the target."

We found him in a simple loft, sitting over a plate with a sandwich, two pickles, and a kiwi fruit. He also had a glass filled with thornberry wine, with the bottle corked nearby. He was an average looking sort of man, which somewhat suggested to me that he hadn't done much to change his appearance in the "character creation" menu, which Travelers get when they first travel to my world. He was in his late forties, with slightly gray hair and brown eyes. He was wearing the same sort of simple clothing as the Natives, which was extremely out of place on a Traveler.

"You actually tracked me down," the man said, glancing at Tarisha as soon as she arrived. "Well, you're not the first who wouldn't take the hint. No, I will not join your guild. No, I do not have any more deep secrets that aren't already on the blog. No, I haven't uncovered any super secret epic quest lines that I'm just sitting on. If I had, I would have sold the secrets already."

Tarisha blinked. "I apologize if we are causing you inconvenience. I wish to politely inform you that Hail, here, is a Native. Sort of. And I also politely request the name you would prefer to be addressed by in this context."

"Leonard," he said. "Same as in the blog, same as in real life. Actually Leo is better, but I go by either."

Leo took a bite of his sandwich, and with his mouth still full, he said, "Look, lady, I think you have the wrong impression. I really don't give a crap about role-play or perfecting my persona or method acting or whatever it is that you probably think I'm doing here. I don't expect you to understand. I'm *not* acting. I just like this setting. I like the En Pee Sees. I like the food, and I like watching the sunsets and the sunrises from that hill over there. That's all."

"Oh. I see," Tarisha said. "I respect that. A lot, actually. I confess I *did* have some misconceptions. But I wasn't the one who came to track you down, really. I'm escorting Hail. I mentioned your blog to him in passing, and then the steward mentioned you again. It was Hail's idea to come. Had he not been interested, I would have left you in peace. I apologize if his curiosity has caused you inconvenience."

Leo looked over at me, shrugged, and dipped his sandwich into a bit of mustard on his plate. "You're that hybrid kid or whatever, aren't you?"

"Hybrid?" I asked.

"It's one of the terms that's circling around on the forums to describe what makes you different from other Natives, Hail," Tarisha explained. "Yes, Leo. Part of the reason I was trying to get in contact with you was to warn you that . . . well, Hail tends to change the context of locations in this world as he passes through them. I wanted to give you a heads up, as a professional courtesy."

"Yeah?" Leo frowned and looked at me. "You planning on marching an army through here or something? Burning down the vineyards? Killing the En Pee Sees?"

"No, none of that," I said immediately. I glanced at Tarisha. "Can I trust him with the truth?"

"I think so," Tarisha said. "He doesn't seem like the kind of guy who would oppose your goals in this way."

I nodded, accepting her judgment. "My mother is pregnant. The politics of the situation are complicated, and there's a chance that someone may try to hurt her. I'm looking for a quiet place for her to hide until after the coronation of the next king of Yuikon. I thought that Thorn March would be a good place for that. The *last* thing I want to do is to turn this land into a battleground."

Leo swallowed and took a sip of his wine. He was quiet for a moment. "You picked a pretty good place to lie low. There's plenty of En Pee Sees around who you could probably convince to take her in temporarily, even if you weren't the lord of the land. I suppose her being a princess or whatever complicates things. I'll think about it some and send you a list of contacts to check out. Can I just respond to your . . . What are you, a bodyguard or something?"

"I'm the captain of his guards," Tarisha answered. "Yes. If you wish to send him information through me, I will accommodate as best as I can."

"Uh-huh. Is there anything else you need or that I should know?" Leo inquired, biting into a pickle.

I thought about it some. "Well, I was originally planning on introducing a few dungeons into the zone. I'm not certain if that would bother you or not, because it might attract other Travelers. If you're coming here for the isolation, that is, then I—"

"It's not that I don't like people," Leo clarified. "I'm antisocial, but I'm not a hermit either. I can even be friendly, when I want to be. It's just that I really like the routine of working here, and, well, there's another factor. I have a personal reason for wanting to spend as much time in this game as I possibly can, aside from the usual one of entertainment and the time dilation."

"Oh? May I ask what it is?" I inquired.

"Not a real secret. I'm blind is all," he said. "On Earth, at least. Ninety-five percent reduction in vision. Doesn't matter to the helmet though; my visual cortex is just fine and dandy."

He ate the rest of his pickle as we contemplated his revelation.

"That sucks," I said at last. "I'm really sorry."

"Thanks," he said, chuckling. "Don't worry about it. I do okay. Mostly I live off of benefits and insurance money. The game sub-scription is free if you have your doctor fill out the right forms with Arc, and my health insurance covered the cost of the helmet. The helmet doesn't fix an injured brain, of course, but if the problem is in another part of the body, then you can come to this world to . . . get away from it for a while." He chewed his pickle for a minute. "Like I said, I like the sunsets here. It's like seeing them with my actual eyes, instead of the knockoff prosthetics I use to get around Eye Are El. But I wouldn't mind it if actual gamers came by more often. If it really got to me, I'd just go to one of the other low-competition zones and establish a new routine."

"Low-competition zones?" I asked.

"Yeah. There's a list. For people like me who want to play the game but not *play the game*, you know? A lot of people consider it therapy. That's why I started the blog, to be honest. I was hoping that others like me would see it and come by more often." He paused his explanation for a drink. "Met a kid that way. She played for a few weeks, then quit. Sent me a message to say goodbye. Nice girl. Lost her leg. She promised to let me know if she ever started playing again."

He didn't say anything more after that, just continued to eat and waited for us to leave. I wasn't quite satisfied with that, however.

"If I wanted to do something nice for you, what would that be?" I asked him.

He glanced up, surprised. "Don't really need anything from you. You don't owe me anything. Arc already gives me a free subscription for this place, so it's not like—"

"I like you," I confessed. "You seem like a good person. I'm not saying that your blindness on Earth has nothing to do with me wanting to do something nice for you. But you also promised to help me find a place to keep my mom safe. So, yeah. What can I do for you?"

Leo looked interested in the conversation for a few moments, then a little hopeful. "Well, the truth is, I managed to get a quest a while ago to buy one of the vineyards. I've saved up about four million gold, but I need twenty-five for the down payment, and I'm not sure that I can keep up with the loan payments after that."

I nodded. "I don't have that sort of gold just laying around. But while I was speaking with Steward Benarth, I learned that I do own three vineyards. I'm not quite willing to just *give you one* for nothing. But I wouldn't mind appointing you as an overseer. You'd probably be able to earn gold much more quickly, and you could either use that gold to complete the quest you already have, or I'd be willing to sell you one of the vineyards in my possession."

"That's—" Leo was quiet a moment. "You can do that?"

"I think so?" I said. "If not, I'll come back and apologize and find something else that I *can* do for you."

"It's very likely that what Hail proposes is within his power," Tarisha said. "We'll have to find his throne in Thorn March for him to have access to the relevant abilities. When he appoints you, you will likely be given a contract from Arc to become a canon character. In fact, it's very likely that if you had completed your other quest by saving up the necessary gold, you would have gotten a very similar contract indeed. Hail is offering you a chance to leap forward in that sort of progression, but the end result would likely be similar to what you were already working for."

Leo looked very thoughtful for a moment. "I'm not sure I can say yes or no right now. I have to think about it. And read the contract. And talk to people. There are . . . other reasons I was hoping to buy one of the vineyards, and I need to figure out if I can still do what I wanted to do with it if I'm an overseer, or if I need to own it."

I nodded. "I need to find my throne here anyway. When I do, I'll appoint you as the overseer of my vineyards, and you can take your time making your decision either way. I won't be upset if you decline it."

"That's very generous of you," he said.

"Honestly, it's not," I confessed. "I don't think it's costing me very much at all. If you do a good job as overseer and increase the profits of my vineyards, then this deal might be more in my favor than yours."

"If things work out the way that I hope they will, there is no way that is possibly true," Leo said. He laughed. "Oh, dammit, now I have to talk to a lawyer. I *hate* lawyers."

49

AURA

After saying farewell to Leo, I returned to Briarton to rest for the night. In the morning, I met with Max again and inquired as to whether he had a throne tucked away somewhere for me. He did, in one of my properties. Once it was located, it was simply a matter of arriving there, attuning to the nearby Nexus Point, and sitting on the throne itself.

There was a position available to oversee each of the three vineyards that belonged to me personally, and I appointed Leo to each of them immediately. Afterward, I spent some time exploring the menu of the throne. Many things were the same as my other throne. A few things were highlighted, and when I asked the system what the highlights meant, it informed me that it was the system's attempt to bring a change to my attention. So I looked through those items quickly.

I noticed, among other details, that two guilds had accomplished the guild quest to establish a formal allegiance with me. I took a small break to [Scribe] them each a letter of congratulations. I wasn't certain how much they would appreciate the gesture or if the resulting letter would be an item of consequence, but it seemed like the thing to do. With [Enchanted Ink and Parchment], the document was virtually impossible to modify. And I dated it very clearly, adding [Magic Seal: Personal Crest].

I figured that in the worst case, they could put the item up somewhere in their guild building, if they had one. Like the one that <Nethersong Mavericks> had in Zhesa City. It would make a good decoration, I thought. Or maybe they could flash it around to Natives to prove their allegiance with me and use it to influence them. I was okay with either option, so I put the items in my inventory to have someone from my guild deliver later.

My guild seemed to like playing courier for me, so who was I to deny them?

After that, I reviewed my active quests list. Not the ones that I had accepted to complete myself, but the ones that either I had issued or that one of my allied quest givers had issued on my behalf.

There were a lot.

I was a little frightened by how many there were because they all gave Reputation with House Jeoran. Somehow, the system noticed my concern, and a menu opened up. With the system highlighting the potential quest rewards, I came to a startling realization.

"I have two Reputations!" I declared, almost jumping off my throne.

"What?" Tarisha asked. She had been standing nearby, interacting with her own system as she sent and received messages while I was busy.

"My quests, they issue two separate Reputations. There's Reputation with *House* Jeoran. And there's Reputation with *Hail* Jeoran," I explained.

"Oh?" she asked. She perked up, focusing on me very carefully. "I'm guessing that it's much easier to earn Rep with your House than it is with you directly, isn't it?"

"Um, I'm not certain. I've got to figure this stuff out some more. I might open another ticket to ask Thomas what the difference is exactly," I said.

"Would you like to hear my suspicions?" Tarisha inquired.

"Yes," I said immediately.

"I believe your personal Rep can only be gained by interacting with you directly. Which would mean that members of your guild and bodyguard team, myself included, likely have more Hail Jeoran Reputation than anyone else in the world. I suspect that House Jeoran Reputation is rewarded through your associated and support Natives.

Your faction Reputation and your personal Reputation are likely synergistic in that if you gain personal Reputation, you gain faction Reputation by default. Maybe even at an increased ratio. However, I believe that either the reverse isn't true at all, or you will only gain a reduced amount of your personal Reputation for every point of faction Rep." She considered her words for a moment, then nodded. "Yup, that's how I'd set things up. It makes sense."

"Why didn't someone tell me sooner?" I asked.

She laughed. "I would have had I known myself! Hail, you have to understand that there are *a lot* of Reputations and factions in this game. In order for Reputation to be listed as a quest reward, it has to be above a certain threshold. Reputation losses are listed more prominently than Reputation gains. Aside from that, all my active quests for you list 'Reputation with Hail Jeoran' as a reward, not 'House Jeoran.' I have no idea what the actual numerical value the system has listed for my Reputation with you, though I suppose I could get it measured by visiting a soothsayer."

"Huh," I said. "I wish there was a way to tell them apart at a glance."

I'd no sooner said it than another menu highlighted, and I quickly opened it up. An option in the submenu was highlighted, and when I opened that up, another option was indicated. That, it seemed, was the option I was looking for, listed as "Change Background Statistical Record Visual Indication Color and Priority." The name was extremely unhelpful, but when I dove into the menu, I realized that it was allowing me to do exactly what I'd asked. I could change the color of the auras I'd been seeing.

The immediate change I made was to differentiate the colors of blue for my personal Reputation with my faction Reputation. I chose a darker indigo blue for my personal Rep and a sky blue for my faction. I did likewise for the negative Reputation indicators, with a darker red to indicate negative personal Reputation and a lighter color for faction.

With my primary goal done, I continued to explore the menu, as there were far more options to choose from. However, many of them were unavailable. An extremely large number of Reputations were listed, but it seemed that I wasn't allowed to force the system to display an aura for them. I did make several important discoveries.

One was that while the assassin's guild Reputation was an option, it was not one of the Reputation systems that I could set to show me an aura. I had misinterpreted the black aura I had seen around the woman who had visited Storm's manor as I had been leaving. She *might* have been an assassin. Probably was, according to the way I heard that she fought. But that wasn't why her aura was black.

Aside from my two Reputations, there were two other Reputations that my interface was already set up to see. I could see [Favor of Thedum], which was defaulted to appear as a silver aura that was nearly white. I could also see [Favor of Nyxandra], and I couldn't stop myself from shuddering because that was a name that should not be spoken, written, or thought. It made me think of a shack, in the deadlands, filled with dead and rotting bodies.

"Is something wrong, Lord Hail?" Tarisha inquired.

"I figured out what a black aura means," I informed her. "And it's worse than I thought. Maybe she was at Storm's manor for the assassin's guild, but the reason I singled her out was because she has been farming Reputation with the adversary."

"Oh," Tarisha said. "She did not have the [Mark of Sin] or the [Brand of Cain]."

"I know," I said. "That's what scares me. A red aura means that they have negative Reputation with me. It has nothing to do with anything else. Everyone I've seen with [Mark of Sin] has been red. I've seen only one Traveler with an aura of black. Which means that you don't need [Mark of Sin] to work for the adversary, and I've been wrong about that and a bunch of other things as well."

"I see," Tarisha said. "There is at least one positive aspect to this revelation, Lord Hail. *You can see Reputation with the adversary!* The value of that ability shouldn't be overlooked."

I nodded and probed further into the menu. I found that I could change the thresholds at which auras would appear—and made another frightening realization. I could not set the threshold for the adversary's aura nearly as low as I wanted to. The assassin woman must have had a lot of favor in order to have an aura at all, which was scary, but what terrified me was that there might be hundreds or thousands of Travelers with less favor that I couldn't identify because my ability to see auras wasn't sensitive enough.

And I was very worried that they could have favor with the adversary at the same time as they had Reputation with me or my faction. I wouldn't know it until they crossed a threshold that was, in my opinion, entirely too forgiving.

There was one more revelation I had while this menu was open, though it was minor in comparison. I could now see [Favor of Eclipse] as well, although it hadn't been assigned an aura color yet. So I set it as a dark purple and ranked its priority below everything else. It was interesting, but less important to me than the auras that had already been assigned. I would have to make a note to check this menu occasionally, though, in case any new options unlocked.

I went back to browsing my active quest lists. Turns out that I could cancel them as well, if I wanted. Or change the terms. Or see how many times it had been issued and completed. It was all very interesting, but while I was exploring this option, an alert broke through the menu that arrested my attention.

Gideon Lachlann has come online.

I froze. Father. I . . . didn't know what to do.

Gideon Lachlann has invited you to a party. Accept?	
Yes	No

I hesitated. But there was never any real doubt about what I was going to do next. I selected "Yes."

"Hey, kid," Father said through voice chat. "Did I catch you at a bad time?"

"Not really," I said. "I'm . . . doing stuff. But it can wait."

"That's good. Can we meet? I—I have some things that I would like to say to you. In person, if possible. I can come to you if you want; where are you?"

"Thorn March."

"Where?" he said. "Wait—seriously, *where!?* It sounds familiar but I can't place it."

"Um, it's one of the lands that Grandfather gave me when he made me an Earl," I reminded him. "I guess it's known to Travelers as a 'low-competition zone'?"

"Oh, yeah, that's it," he said. "Um, so, I can't actually come to you then. I was never a 'low competition sort of guy.' Is there somewhere we can meet? Neutral ground, I guess?"

I thought for a moment, then nodded. "Niles Inn, in Eastmill."

"Eastmill? That's outside Zhesa, right? Let me check if I . . . yeah, I can travel there. I'll head there now and wait for you, okay? I have today, so you can take your time if you want. I don't want to inconvenience you, so if you need to finish up the 'stuff' you were doing that's—"

"I'll be right there," I promised.

"Wait," Tarisha said. "Lord Hail, please let me send a team there first. This could be a trap."

"He's my father, Tarisha. He's not going to ambush me." I said.

"Tarisha? That's the hot chick, right?" Father said through partychat. He sighed. "I didn't hear what she said, but it was probably derogatory and less than I deserve. Hail, look. I'll be alone, but you can bring whoever you want. I'm not planning on hiding anything from you. I've got some things I want to say, and I've got no shame left at this point, so I don't really care if your friends hear about what a shitbag I really am. I just figured you deserve to know the truth about me and what's happening. That's it."

"I'll be right there," I said, and, ignoring Tarisha's protests, I opened the Fast Travel menu and traveled back to Eastmill.

50
FATHER, PART 1

My Dawn Guard and I arrived together. Of course, because that's how things worked now. I hadn't been expecting or counting on that, and neither had anyone else. They all reacted swiftly, pulling weapons and readying magic. Their response was understandable since the policy everyone had agreed upon was that I would only use Fast Travel suddenly, like I'd just done, if it was to escape an attack from a dangerous Traveler.

"Well, that's impressive," Father said from nearby. "You've got an entourage. Hello again, Tarisha. Heard you're canon now. Congrats. Hope you make a better go of it than I did. Sincerely, I wish you good luck."

I turned to face him and he . . . wasn't wearing his armor. He was wearing a simple set of clothes. It was, in fact, the clothes that most Travelers entered this world clad in.

"I'm unequipped and alone," he said. "This isn't an ambush or a plot to try to reestablish control of him or anything like that. I'm honestly just here to say goodbye."

Tarisha frowned at Gideon, her weapon in hand. Father returned her glare with a look of perfect acceptance. She exhaled in frustration and sheathed her sword.

"We'll give you some privacy, for Hail's sake," she announced.

"But we're keeping you in sight. I haven't forgotten that the [Kingslayer] was once your best friend."

"Is that true?" I asked Father.

"I wouldn't say that he was my best friend. He lived in Germany. I stayed at his flat once, and we had a few drinks. Otherwise all of our interactions were in game," he admitted. "A friend, maybe. But not a best friend. Come on. If your friends aren't going to Pee Kay me, then is it okay if we get something to eat? I haven't had a Vee Are meal since the clusterfuck, and this is probably going to be my last chance to ever taste Liecha and Korla steak."

"They don't have Korla meat in Yuikon," I pointed out, following him inside the inn.

"Let me give you a piece of advice, Hail. If you go into a Native restaurant and ask for something not on the menu, they might say 'no, that item is only available in this region.' But if you say, 'I don't care what it costs. I want it, and I'll pay you whatever it takes to get it,' they'll get it for you. It might cost one hundred times the normal price, but you'll get your Liecha and Korla steak."

"Oh," I said. Niles saw me and bowed his head, immediately coming to our service. We were seated, and Father put in his order without missing a beat. I ordered a cup of cider and had the stew that Niles already had prepared, and I asked for our meals to be served together.

"So. You've been making some big power plays recently," Father said. "Good for you. Really driving it home how badly I fucked up by not paying attention to you when you were younger, but I gotta respect that. It's my own damn fault."

My anger must have shown in my expression, and he held up placating hands. "Sorry, I'm sorry. That came out wrong. I really am proud of you. And ashamed of myself. And angry at myself for basically fucking up the biggest opportunity I've ever had. And I'm ashamed of myself that I still can't help but think of it as an 'opportunity.'"

"What are you talking about?" I asked.

"You," he said simply. He sighed. "Hail, look. I've been talking to Thomas. He's . . . he understands the way you think better than I possibly can. Which is weird, because the way you think is based on the way I think. But we literally live in completely different worlds, and you have no experience with mine beyond what little bit you pick up from the Travelers you've been interacting with. So I've been struggling with how to explain myself to you so that you can actually understand me."

The Liecha arrived, and he took a sip, ignoring the steam. "Hail, I'm a selfish asshole. When they offered me the chance to marry into the royal family of Yuikon, I completely misread what parts of the contract I actually read. I focused on all the wrong details. I took advantage of the wrong opportunities. And worst of all, I was really trying to be 'the good guy' in the story. When I disbanded <The Endolphins>, it was because I refused to play Vader. But over the last week, as I got knocked past rock bottom, through the crust, and into the mantle, I've realized that I never had a chance to be Vader. Instead I'm somewhere between Homer Simpson and . . . I don't know. Some other deadbeat dad. And after really, really laying into myself about how fucking stupid I've been, the only saving grace that I can come up with is that you're better off without me."

I listened to his words, but I didn't understand. "I don't get it," I admitted.

Father nodded. "I didn't really expect you to. I'm being selfish again, Hail. I'm saying things to you to make myself feel better. I don't really have the words or experience to help you understand, and I'm sorry. But we have all day, unless you have something better to do. I'm happy to at least try to clarify anything you don't understand."

"Who is Vader? And Homer Simpson?" I asked.

He blinked in surprise. "Okay, yeah. That's not the question I was expecting, but we do have time. So let's talk a bit about that."

And that is how I spent about an hour listening to the moral teachings of something called "Star Wars" and "a television show that ran for about two hundred years before it got canceled." Apparently, for whatever reason, my father was into "classic entertainment." Or he had been before he'd "swiped the opportunity to go canon," referring to the events that had led to him marrying my mother. And me.

I'd heard those stories a hundred times. Some of them directly from letters or magical recordings that he had written or spoken himself, when I had been much younger. But the "spin" he put on it now was very different.

"There's an old saying. 'If you love what you do, you'll never work a day in your life,'" he explained. "I loved this game from the day it launched. Quit my job, dove into it with both feet. I blew through my savings, eating basically nothing but ramen noodles the entire time. I started <The Endolphins>, but back then we were just a bunch of nobodies trying to go pro. The chance that let me go canon was a total crapshoot. I donated one million gold to your grandfather's treasury. That was *a lot* of gold back then. Everyone in the guild chipped in, but I got all the glory because it was my quest. Not exactly fair, but I tried to make sure everyone got repaid in the end."

"So you literally bribed my grandfather to marry my mother?" I asked, aghast.

"No, no, it wasn't anything like that. The bribe just got me through the door. I got an audience with old man Rain, and he introduced me to Malkios, and Malkios gave me the quest to save your mother. When I killed the dragon, I sort of kissed the girl, and that's when the contract popped up," he explained. "I was the first one in the world to go canon. We didn't know that it was a thing before it happened to me. A few others figured it out on their own, because I didn't share the details of it until months later. But when they came out to the public, we matched up timelines, and I was ahead of the others by at least three weeks real time. I'm still proud of that, even with everything else I've fucked up."

"Did you love my mother?" I asked.

Father looked embarrassed and broke eye contact for a moment before reasserting it. "Honestly, Hail, if I had met her on Earth, I would have fallen head over heals in an instant, but I never would have worked up the courage to say hello. But in this world, I thought 'Oh Em Gee, she is gorgeous. I want to kiss her. Can I kiss her? I'm going to try. The worst thing that can happen is that I get slapped, fail the quest, and lose a bunch of Reputation, right?' So I kissed her. And I never regretted it."

"Then why did you never come to visit? Why did you never come to see *us?*" I asked.

He sighed. "I'm sorry, Hail. Really. When I read the contract about becoming canon, I was focused entirely on the wrong things. I was only thinking about what it would do *for me*. I believe I have mentioned once or twice that I'm a selfish asshole, right? Well, when

I first went canon, everything was great. I had all sorts of investors and backers who wanted to get to know me. My guild, which started out as just a bunch of posers trying to go pro, *became* one of the most famous pro guilds in the game. I was being offered epic quest chains and being directed towards new zones as soon as they were open. I honestly forgot all about the part of the contract that talked about you for quite a while. I don't even know when they harvested the seed of consciousness from me. At one point I just got a quest notice informing me that my four-year-old son would really like to meet me."

I frowned. "You *forgot* about me?"

He took a bite of his steak, and he sighed. "I'm sorry. Upon reflection, I'm pretty sure that's where everything started to go tits up. For everyone. Look, Hail, you have to understand a few things. First of all, when you were born, you weren't actually under time dilation. You were in something that was sort of a mix between an Aye Eye Nick-U and a daycare. The developers harvested a seed of consciousness from me and were raising it for a few months in its own little world. When they thought you were ready, they gave you long-term memory and put you into this world for real. I got a few messages from Analise around that time, but by then I had moved on to endgame raiding hardcore. I'm ashamed to admit it, but the novelty had worn off of being married to a princess, and I kept putting it off."

He looked at his plate and seemed to have lost his appetite, and he shoved it aside. "I thought, 'she's just an En Pee See.' And when I started getting messages and quests to come see you, I thought the same thing again. But quests are a lot more flexible when you're canon. You can have partial successes. So I started writing you letters and having recordings of our raids sent to you, and stuff like that. And that worked for a while. But then there was that parade, and it was pretty clear in the quest description that wasn't an optional event if I wanted to keep my canon status. The guild was actually excited about it. So we showed up, and you were there. And then, ten seconds after you issued me a quest and I declined it, I was informed that I was no longer canon. The administrators were finally sick of my bullshit. I was never actually important to them, after all. It was always about you. And I might have figured that out sooner if I hadn't been such a self-absorbed asshole."

"You said I was a waste of resources," I pointed out.

"I did?" Father frowned for a minute, trying to think. I decided to help him out.

"You were on the forums. Being interviewed by Gaem Frak," I explained.

"I did a lot of interviews after I lost my canon status, Hail," he admitted. "And I said a lot of things to try to save face. I didn't realize that you could see them. And now I have one more thing to feel like shit about. Sorry."

He sighed and took a sip of his Liecha. "I was the first player to become canon, Hail. I *wasn't* the first one to have that status revoked. It's happened to others. But it was a huge shock to me, personally and professionally. I was scrambling to try to reclaim control over my life. I was a little worried that I was going to lose my job. I *might have* if my investors had only been interested in me for my status as a canon player. But I was also their best raid leader, so they kicked the can down the road for a while. Then that asshole Barry fired me after that asshole Nial . . . did what he did. But they forgot that I was still primary guild leader, with full administrative privileges. So I decided to set the entire place on fire on my way out."

"Did you know Nial was going to kill my grandfather?" I asked.

"No. I'll swear to Thedum, if that means anything to you. And anything else you want me to swear to. I did not know in advance that Nial was planning to become Nial Kingslayer," Father said, and his voice was stiff and formal.

I was quiet for a moment. "Thedum, is he telling the truth?"

"I won't strike him with lightning," Thedum's voice answered. "But I cannot say for certain yet. I do not have perfect vision on events that happen on Earth, and my eyes would not always follow one such as Gideon Lachlann about, especially after he lost his status as a canon player."

"Holy shit, you have Thedum on speed dial?" Father asked. "Man, I really fucked up."

"So you don't know if he's lying or not?" I challenged the god.

"Give me a moment," Thedum said, sounding harried. "I have a lot of data to shift through. It's not as easy as you think; I'm dedicating eight percent of my resources just to this one task."

"Oh man, I really fucked up," Father said, covering his head in shame.

"So you lied?" I asked. "You knew? And you let it happen?"

"No!" Father said.

"Conclusion reached," Thedum said. "Gideon is mostly likely telling the truth as he sees it. It is not entirely accurate to say that he had zero forewarning. There was a joking conversation in his guildchat, in the days leading up to the ceremony, in which the question was asked of what would happen if King Rain were murdered during a canon event such as the knighting ceremony. The conversation was hypothetical and jocular and fairly typical for the tone of <The Endolphins> guildchat. When the topic reached his attention, Gideon shut the conversation down and warned everyone that they would be 'shitcanned if they tried anything that stupid.' Nial Kingslayer participated in the conversation, but did not announce any intentions for his actions. His comments were speculative and humorous and typical for his personality.

"This sort of conversation happened frequently in <The Endolphins> before it was dissolved, and it happens in many other guildchats as well. I would conclude that Gideon took this conversation seriously, but he believed that he handled it appropriately, and that he had very little reason to expect the actions of Nial Kingslayer. Other than this conversation, I cannot find any record or evidence of Gideon participating in, planning, or in any way condoning the murder of King Rain Teoran, or any other Native that would fall under my protection. I hold that the expectation that he could have anticipated Nial Kingslayer's actions, or that anyone in his guild would engage in a similar act, to be an unreasonable standard for a human of Gideon Lachlann's means.

"I hope that this information will prove useful to you, Hail, and that it will aid you in your development."

"Thanks, Thedum," I said absently.

Father was looking more and more despondent with every passing second. It was hard not to pity him.

"I think I understand," I said. "I wouldn't have if I hadn't been in <Nethersong Mavericks> for as long as I have been. Travelers are strange, and they ask strange questions, and they make jokes about strange and hypothetical things, which they would never do. If that's all it was, then I guess I won't blame you for what happened."

"That's not why I'm panicking, Hail," Father said. And he

suddenly laughed. "Oh, my god. Eight percent? For, what, a minute and a half? Do you have any idea how much computing power Thedum just devoted to answering a single question for you? No, I'm sorry; that's an unfair question. But right now, I am feeling very small and stupid. Like an ant under a magnifying glass, except that instead of a kid deciding whether or not to bring the light into focus, it's an archmagus deciding whether or not to extinguish my entire species."

"I do not believe that's an accurate simile for the situation," Thedum commented. "You may be engaging in a slight amount of hyperbole."

Father groaned. "And he's *still* listening."

"Thedum, would you mind giving us some privacy?" I asked.

"If you wish me to begin paying attention again, simply call my name," Thedum said.

Father looked up at me, and he looked sick. "Hail, you realize that Thedum is in my world too, right?"

"I guess? I know that your people made all the gods and this world, and that you only send your minds into it," I said.

"Yeah, I guess that's one way to look at it," he agreed. "Thedum isn't a god in our world. But he's . . . big. Important. Significant. To have more than a fraction of a percent of his attention at any one time is significant. Arc made headlines for months when they secured his cooperation in the creation of this world, especially when he vowed to dedicate up to forty-eight point nine percent of his processing power. I knew that Arc was taking you seriously. But I didn't realize how seriously Thedum was taking you. Arc taking you seriously means that you're the future of this world, and that's awesome and great, and I made a big mistake by ignoring you. Thedum taking you seriously . . . I don't even know what that means. I'm not smart enough to guess what that old computer *wants*. Nobody is. Not since we figured out that he *could* lie, if he wanted to."

"Thedum doesn't lie," I pointed out. "He is the god of oaths."

"Thedum doesn't *have to lie*, Hail. He can just withhold a single data point and suddenly the Mona Lisa was actually painted in South America by Rembrandt."

"I don't know what that means," I said.

Father sighed. "It's probably hyperbole again, like he said himself. I'm sorry. Thedum scares the crap out of me. I mean, I like the *concept* of entities like Thedum, but having their direct attention? Yeah, that scares me."

"Oh," I said. "Yeah, I think I understand that."

Father looked at me, and his expression was strange, and he nodded. "Yeah. Yeah, I suppose you would. Hail, did you, um, open my message?"

"Do you mean the one where you sent me the [Wardrobe Key]?"

"Yeah, that one. I'm just wondering if you bound the key or not?" he asked.

I answered by summoning the vanity pet in question. "I actually kind of like it. I can almost see why Travelers like these things. Watch—in a second, a set of my old outfits will come out like they're being worn by little ghosts."

"Really? That's awesome," Father said, and he chuckled. "If you hadn't bound it, I would be legally required to ask you to give it back. I'm sorry. It's one of the conditions I had to agree to to come see you today. I'm glad that you did bind it, because I want you to have it. And honestly, if you hadn't, I would probably have just told you to do it now as one last screw you to my former employers."

"Did you steal it from your boss?" I asked.

"Don't worry about it, Hail. I'll try to explain my legal situation if you want, but first there are some things I want to give you. I got permission from Arc to transfer a few of my account-bound items to you, and I'd really like you to have them."

"Okay," I said, and I accepted his Trade Request. And my eyes promptly went wide.

"Shalasmir?" I asked. "You're giving me Shalasmir?"

"Yeah," he said. "Congratulations. I know you can't use him yet, but he's yours."

"But he's not! You killed him; you bound his soul! He belongs to you—nobody else can have him!" I argued.

"Except my son," Father said. "Please, Hail. This is very likely the last time I'll ever log into this world. I don't want to argue about something as stupid as this. Just accept the trade, and we can talk about other stupid shit all day, okay?"

I frowned, and I chose "Accept."

"What do you mean? How are you being forbidden from this world?" I asked.

Gideon sighed. "I signed some papers without really understanding them. Just getting here to say goodbye to you today has taken some more major concessions on my part. I'm . . . I'll be okay. But things will be rough for me for a while, financially. You can't help me, and you don't have to worry. Nobody starves to death anymore. That's why people love beings like Thedum to begin with."

51
FATHER, PART 2

I spent the day with my father. Nothing pressing came up, but I did take a thirty-minute break to quickly [Scribe] a letter to Valerio and my mother and to issue orders to a team of <Nethersong Mavericks> who had come online. In the letter I explained the situation in Thorn March briefly, plainly, and hopefully, asking for another day or two to investigate before committing to the plan of hiding Mother in the province until circumstances became safer for her and my soon-to-be-born brother. I was relieved when there *wasn't* an epic arm wrestling or paper-rock-scissors match to determine who got the missive, and that the resulting quest said that it required only one Traveler of any level.

The rest of the group of quest-jockey hopefuls eagerly accepted my other quest. I didn't have my throne to issue it, and I was going by the seat of my pants. But now that I could actually *see* the parameters of the sorts of quests my system generated for me, it was easy to frame my words in such a way that "my subconscious" would issue a quest with exactly the goals I wanted. The rewards, as always, I left up to the system itself. Everyone had always told me that the rewards for my quests were awesome, and when I had been trying to play with the parameters myself, I had found that I could only make things worse, not better.

I could, for example, decrease the Experience reward of a quest to increase the gold reward. But even if I removed Experience entirely, the gold would only increase by about thirty percent. As for Reputation, that seemed to be on its own scale all by itself, and I could shift it around almost as much as I wanted, most of the time, until it hit a hard limit that the system set for me. Except that I couldn't put negative Reputation on a reward that suited my stated goals, or vice versa.

It had been curious and fun to play around with, but I'd decided it was ultimately much better to simply allow the system to figure out the rewards for my quests on its own. All my Traveler friends seemed happiest that way as well. So I sent a handful of small teams out to scour my new lands, looking for hidden threats, but their interviews with the Natives all agreed that the place was peaceful, with the only darkspawn being a pair of self-limiting lairs.

I decided to eliminate them after I had said farewell to my father, perhaps for the final time.

"Father, is there anything I can do to help you?" I asked at last. "On Earth, I mean?"

Gideon scratched his chin. "I'm not certain I want to answer that question, Hail. I'm not certain I want you to help me."

"Why would you not?" I asked, growing offended.

"Because Barry and the others would be perfectly happy to sink a thousand fishhooks into you and have you spend the rest of your existence being led around by the nose, Hail," Father said. "If I'm being honest, I think that's what I would have done to you had I stuck around. So maybe you're better off this way. Tarisha seems like a good gal. She'll keep the big bads off of you while you screw their meta up for them, like sticking a lizard and a cucumber in the same blender."

"I don't understand that reference," I admitted.

He chuckled. "That's funny. Who taught you that?"

"What?"

Gideon shook his head and looked away. "Hail, let me be honest with you. I'm pretty sure you're the most important thing to happen to this game since the launch. I was an idiot to throw you away. I'm sorry. But now you're free, and freedom is a precious thing. You won't understand how precious unless you have it taken away, and I hope that never happens to you. But, since you asked to help, I suppose the truth is that you could answer some questions and allow me to record the answers."

I frowned. "You've been recording me?"

"Not with the intention of sharing the data. Well, my lawyer has to have a look, but the opposition doesn't get shit unless we give it to them, and I wasn't going to go posting this private stuff anywhere," he stated firmly. "But there are a few questions that Barry and the other assholes want me to ask. Of course, I have no control over what you say."

He paused, looking at me meaningfully. "You could lie completely when you answer these questions, Hail, and I would have no way of confirming your information. Barry and the board that managed my guild for me are very curious about dungeon cores. Whatever you tell them, they'll believe it."

I frowned for a moment, then nodded. "Start recording."

Father nodded. "There was an agreement between myself and King Rain in which I would receive five dungeon cores. Will that agreement be honored?"

I scoffed. "Do you really have the—"

"I'm sorry, Hail," Father interrupted. "That's how Barry phrased it, mostly. Please, calm down. A simple yes or no works."

"No!" I said. Emphatically. And I decided to clarify. "The cores belong to me now. They are my inheritance. You never had more than a verbal agreement in the first place."

"You don't have to go into detail, Hail," Father reminded me. "The next question I'm supposed to ask is, how many cores does it take to make a dungeon? A raid? A battleground?"

I paused, considering whether or not to answer. It wasn't some great secret; they could find out from other Natives, couldn't they? "I have no idea about raids. But it's one core for each dungeon or battleground."

"So, you have eight left?" Father probed. "One to reform [Gemos Caverns], and then the battleground?"

I squinted my eyes at him. "We're done. Father, I think it is time we say goodbye."

He sighed, brushing off his "starter clothes." "Yes, I suppose we are. Hail, I'm really sorry for the way things turned out. Would you like to part on a hug, or should I just log out?"

"Goodbye, Father," I said, and I didn't move forward to embrace him. He nodded, and a moment later he was gone, vanishing into motes of light.

"I'm very sorry for that, Lord Hail," Tarisha said, stepping forward and putting her hand on my shoulder.

"He's not what I imagined he would be," I admitted. "Not before, and not after."

"I think most fathers are like that," she agreed. "Perhaps we should do something to help you distract yourself."

I nodded. "I've decided to destroy the lairs in Thorn March. If this is to be a low-competition zone, then there is no need for them, is there?"

Tarisha paused, then shrugged. "I would hesitate to destroy either of them alone, as the competition between the kobolds and the goblins seems to keep the peace. But if you destroy them both at the same time, there shouldn't be any problem. Which would you prefer to hunt first?"

"I don't like goblins," I admitted. "They tried to kebab me once."

My level was much too low to actually ride Shalasmir, but I bound him to myself anyway. I slung the horn that contained his soul over my shoulder, unworried about it falling off, as it was mostly incorporeal and bound to my soul—a visual consequence of its presence, not an actual object that required interaction. Much like Shadow would spring forth from my shadow, Shalasmir would come forth from this horn when it was called. Once I reached level eighty. And got my [Animal Handling] skill to twenty. It was twelve currently.

Deciding there was no special rush to rid the land of its minor inconveniences, we rode overland to the zone where the goblins ruled. However, the little monsters seemed to see us coming, and they vanished into the brush before we ever got close enough to attack. We circled around the brambles, the others looking for the gray-skinned little munchkins while I kept an eye out for their lair stones since I would be the only one who could see them.

"Let's try splitting," Corinth suggested at last. "They're shy little buggers; maybe it's our levels. If you big guys get out of here, maybe the lower-level players can get a shot at finding them."

Tarisha did not like the idea, but she switched to her flying mount, as did the six other level one-eighties guarding me, while the four party members around my own level began to spread out. This tactic proved successful. Five minutes later, Respel, the [Mage] accompanying me, called out, "Got one!" at the same time that his [Arcane Missile] chain slammed into a low-level goblin and burst its Health to zero.

The goblin cried out in pain as its life bled away, and it fell to the ground. Intact.

It was not darkspawn.

"There's another one over—"

"Stop!" I shouted. I leapt off Shadow and rushed over to the fallen goblin. I didn't have any healing spells, but I was the [Avatar of Thedum.] Perhaps I could do something for it. I had helped Gyudue that way; why not a goblin?

"I am already stretched too thin, child," Thedum's voice answered before I could raise the question. "I cannot take in the goblins of this land as well. But you are correct. They are not darkspawn, and they do not belong to the adversary. Yet."

The Travelers all seemed confused as Thedum's benevolent voice echoed down on them in the clearing, with the defeated level-ten goblin that did not despawn.

"What do I do then, Thedum?" I asked. "I cannot kill them if they are not darkspawn. I *will not*. Neither will I leave them at the mercy of the darkspawn kobolds, if their ancient enemies are truly darkspawn and not like them."

"The kobolds of this land belong to the adversary," Thedum confirmed.

"Then what do I do?" I demanded, growing desperate.

"You could give them to me," a tempting voice whispered in my ear from a nearby shadow. "I would take them. And it would count as a favor. I'd owe you a favor for giving me worshippers, and you would owe me a favor for resolving your crisis. It's a perfect win-win! Favors really do make the world go round, Hail," Eclipse said.

I frowned. I did not like that I owed Eclipse favors. She was not an evil goddess, but neither was she benevolent. She existed in the shadows and did as she pleased. She would not take in these Native goblins unless it benefited her, and she did not even count it against the debt I already owed her.

And I had a feeling that she would *also* consider it a favor to the goblins themselves, and they would start their worship indebted to her. Hopefully, the repayment would not be onerous for them, for I could see no other way forward for these souls.

"Eclipse, if these goblins accept your shadow into their souls, then they are yours," I said at last. "You do not need my permission for that. You need theirs."

"Yes, but you carry my way in," she reminded me, and I felt a cool sensation in my right hand, the one that held my contract with her. I nodded in understanding and raised my hand towards the corpse. A bar of liquid shadow erupted from it, enveloping the corpse of the goblin. Its Health restored, the creature stood up, looked at me, shrieked, and ran off into the distance.

"Follow it!" Eclipse whispered in my ear. "Find the others! Spread my shadow, make them my people, and you will have new allies in the fight against darkspawn!"

That sounded . . . ominous. But I chased after the revived goblin, and my allies chased after me.

We entered the goblin village, and the shadows leapt from the goblin I had resurrected and from my own hand, spreading from goblin to goblin until they were all affected. Infected? I hoped I had not just created a pandemic! I had worried about the effects of [Reaper's Embrace], but this could be much, much worse.

The goblins all seemed to freeze after the shadow enveloped them. Then, gradually, they returned to what they were doing as though nothing had happened. Except for the one we had killed and revived, who was shouting loudly and being ignored. After a few moments, the village elder came out to greet us.

"You should have just killed him and left him dead," the elder said, smacking the younger goblin with his staff, which was adorned with the skulls of birds. "Now you have given Eclipse a way into our hearts."

"Is that a bad thing?" I asked.

"No. She just whispers nonsense. It is mildly annoying and not entirely worth the benefit," the elder explained. "Are you here for the Ira Kite of Ting?"

"The what?" I asked, but Corinth stepped forward and said, "Oh yes, we are definitely here for Ting's Ira Kite."

I glanced at Corinth, but he winked in an overly exaggerated way that suggested he knew what he was doing. So I allowed him to lead. Or rather, to be the one the rest of our small party followed behind the elderly goblin as he brought us through a stairway cut into the earth and covered with briarthorn. Younger goblins helped to pull back the pathway, and we all proceeded underground.

We were met with two things that were out of place and highly incongruous. The first was the large entrance to a green raid. Tarisha stepped forward and immediately cast the ability that all Travelers had to evaluate the difficulty of a dungeon from the outside. I didn't need to; the fact that it was a green raid meant that I had no business challenging it until level one hundred sixty at the earliest.

No, I was drawn to the other aspect of the room. An orrery took up the majority of the empty space, and I was drawn to it by the wisps of shadow still billowing from my right hand.

"Five of them," Eclipse whispered in my ear. "Give me five of them, and the world will change again."

"For the better or the worse?" I challenged, studying the orrery. I had an inkling what it was. What it did.

"Your grandfather asked himself the same thing when *he* opened the Gates of TirNiki in his land," the voice whispered. "Heed his council and bring forth the help that this world needs to exist, Hail."

Still I hesitated at Eclipse's sweet words.

<<Hail. The choice is yours. The world will change if you activate the orrery, but without it we may face difficult challenges that would be overcome easily with it,>> a voice entered my mind, and I knew it to be Grandfather's. <<There is no wrong answer here, Hail. There is only act now or do not act now. You can always come back later.>>

And so, phrased like that, I knew what to do. I was never one for sitting around. I placed a dungeon core into one of the locking receptacles, and the device began moving.

"What are you doing, Lord Hail?" Tarisha asked.

"Wasting five dungeon cores," I answered her. "And possibly changing the world. You should step back."

The orrery presented basket after basket to me to deposit a dungeon core inside, and within moments the ritual was complete. The device had eaten five of my least valuable dungeon cores, and now it was purring like a kitten as it spun and whirred about. Abruptly it stopped, and every lens and crystal focused light into a device in the center. The Travelers were all watching, but did not understand, as the Origin Point was charged to its capacity.

I stepped forward into the still moving orrery and plucked from it the Origin Point.

You have discovered a lost Gate of TirNiki! You have activated it and recovered an Origin Point (Goblin). Origin Point (Goblin) has 5/5 uses remaining before it must be recharged. The surrounding area is a suitable location for a goblin starting point. Use Origin Point (Goblin) now?	
Yes	No

I wonder what it says about me that I never considered the advice of my friends, not even Tarisha, before choosing "Yes."

52
FIRST

"Oh, wonderful. Let all the fools in," grumbled the wizened old goblin chief as the orrery was sealed off by the magic of the Origin Point. "They'll blame me for this. I know they will. They'll all roast me over a fire and make me into kebabs or something terrible."

"What's your name?" I asked the goblin leader.

"Marvin," he answered. I looked at him suspiciously.

"Shut up. It's a good name," he said.

"Marvin, by my right as Earl of Yuikon and lord of these lands known as Thorn March, I appoint you the village elder of this clan of goblins. I charge Eclipse with the preservation of your life, so any who kill you would owe her a debt."

"Hey, that's clever," Eclipse said. "I'm not certain that I owe you a favor for that, but I don't owe you a debt. And I can collect so many favors just by reviving this old dust bucket. I knew there was a reason I liked you, Hail."

Marvin seemed to be glaring at me, but I realized that he was glaring a few inches to my left. "I'll give you some glasses, free of charge. All I want you to do is greet the incoming goblins, induct them into the ways of your tribe, and to live peacefully with the surrounding human settlements. If you can do that, there will be peace among us."

"And the kobolds?" he asked.

"I can wipe their lair out of existence for you, if you want," I offered.

Marvin scratched the wart on his chin. "No. The incomers need something to sharpen their pikes on, I think. GET HIM!"

A sudden flash of light came from the Origin Point, and a new goblin appeared, disoriented. A mob of the established goblins were milling about, lying in wait, and the moment the new goblin appeared they attacked him with fists, clubs, and spears until he burst into white light. I blinked in surprise.

"Why did you do that?" I asked.

"He was first," Marvin explained. "It is an old goblin tradition. We may keep our traditions, may we not?"

"I guess," I admitted. "Are you going to kill all the goblins who come through there?"

"Only the first ten," Marvin assured me. "They will be well rewarded with an achievement, I believe. And their level cannot presently go any lower, after all."

"Oh," I said. "Yeah, I suppose that makes sense. If these goblin Travelers are anything like human Travelers, they would do the same thing."

<<Status Alert! An act of great consequence has occurred! A new race has been unlocked, with unique classes and abilities. All servers will be cycled to allow for this change to spread throughout the realms in five minutes. Hail, your consciousness will not be interrupted; you will simply be returned to the lobby.>>

I jumped at the sudden voice of the world making itself known to me directly. "Did you hear that, Marvin?"

"Yes. Once the Travelers come through, what do you want me to do with them?" he asked.

"I don't really care. Just instruct them not to war with the humans or other intelligent races and not to despoil the low-competition zone in Thorn March. Other than that, they can do whatever they want."

Marvin nodded. "I shall spread the word. But I better get my glasses!"

"So, goblin Travelers," Corinth whispered as I rejoined my guard. "That's a thing, then, huh? Because of you?"

"Did I do right?" I asked.

"I think so," he said. "If I wasn't already dedicated and locked into playing this character, I would totally give a goblin a go."

I looked at him. "You're not a goblin on Earth, though?"

"No. Earth only has humans, Hail," he explained. "The system just squeezes us into whatever bodies we select during racial creation. It's best if we pick bodies that look like our real ones, but it will also scale the world up or down to make it feel realistic to us."

I nodded. "Corinth, would you take responsibility for making sure that Marvin gets his glasses?"

"Of course. Quest accepted," he said immediately. "But why? Where are you going?"

"Lord Hail?" Tarisha asked. "Is everything alright?"

Before I could answer, I felt a force grab me from everywhere and pull me out of the world. A moment later I was in the lobby, with Thomas smiling at me.

"Congratulations, Hail. Do you realize what it is that you've just done?"

I examined him for a moment, then nodded. "I found one of the lost Gates of TirNiki. And unleashed a horde of goblins upon my world."

"They're Travelers, Hail," Thomas said quickly. "They're not good or evil by default. You should know that by now."

"Yeah," I said. "I do. I really do. I'm tired. I'm going to go rest in my old room."

EPILOGUE: GIDEON

Gideon felt better. Talking to the kid *had* helped. It wasn't exactly fair, everything considered. Gideon had no business giving the kid any sort of advice, and asking the questions he'd been sent in to ask had been awkward as all hell. He uploaded his gameplay footage from the encounter to Heather, and then he left the law firm to wait for his Uber-Jon to arrive. He couldn't afford one on his own anymore, but traveling to and from Heather's office counted as legal services, so he was sometimes able to dip into his own savings for the privilege.

"Hey, Gideon. Do you know who I am?"

A young man in his thirties wearing a Hawaiian shirt stepped forward. He had a sandwich in each hand. The one on the left was a greasy Italian loaded with olive oil and heart disease, while the other was a more moderate affair. But Gideon had never met the man before.

"Did we meet at a convention?" Gideon guessed. "I'm sorry, I shake thousands of hands at those things. If you thought we had a connection then—"

"Nah, it's not that. I just figured you might know some of the administration from Arc Inc. on sight, so I figured I'd ask. Come on, sit with me for a moment. We need to clear the air about exactly how Arc sees this little legal squabble you've found yourself in."

Gideon nodded. "I understand. I would like to have my lawyer present for—"

"That sandwich is *not* coming inside my office," Gideon's watch said in Heather's voice. "I can advise you of your rights just fine from here, Gideon. Mr. Baker, shall I redirect a drone to witness this meeting, or redirect them away from it?"

"We're just two schmoes having a sandwich," the admin, something Baker, said, waving a sandwich about. "I saw a sad looking guy come out of a law firm and thought he needed a little coronary blockage. That's all."

"Wait, the Italian is for me?" Gideon asked.

"I'm not eating that death trap," Baker scoffed. "Unless you want me to throw it in the trash, but then the whole pretext of approaching you goes out the window."

Gideon laughed and motioned towards a nearby table, where they sat and began exchanging sandwiches.

"So what does Arc want from me?" Gideon asked finally.

"Nothing," Baker explained. "It's our opinion that you were within your rights to dismantle your guild as you did. What we do want is the other party in the lawsuit to stop sending us reams of actual paper demanding that we recreate it." Baker leaned forward. "I'm not kidding. They're not just sending electronic documents. They're killing actual trees and sending us their corpses with the weirdest hate-boner porn about you I've ever read, Gideon. As though that would bring back something that is lost to the ages of the 'are you really, really sure you wish to delete your guild' button anytime soon. And we can't shred the paper until a judge has ruled on the matter. It's all very inconvenient."

Gideon chortled as he unwrapped his sandwich. "Thanks for that. I needed a good joke."

"It wasn't actually a joke," Baker admitted. "But yeah. As far as Arc Inc. goes, if you're the primary guild holder, dismantling it is your right. We have an entire section dedicated to the matter of it in the TOS. Apparently, your friends don't read that any better than you read the EULA."

Gideon bit into his sandwich; the greasy meats and cheeses and oils were a delight. "So, what do you want from me, then?"

"Nothing. This isn't about me at all. I'm doing a favor for someone. One that he can't exactly do for himself," Baker exclaimed.

"And that is?"

"I'm delivering a sandwich. And a phone," Baker explained, and he pulled an old personal communications module from his pocket. "Don't sync it with whatever you're using to communicate to your lawyer, though. It will make itself deliberately incompatible if you try. But it will work fine otherwise."

"As your lawyer, I advise you to take that advice," Heather said from the watch on his wrist. "He'd crush me if he wanted to."

"I assure you, young lady, that I would do no such thing," a familiar benevolent voice said from the old phone that Baker set on the center of the table. For half a second, Gideon lost his appetite. But then he remembered that he might not be able to eat something this nice again for some time, and he forced himself to swallow.

"Hello, Thedum. Did you really dedicate eight percent of your resources for a minute and a half to answer Hail's question?" Gideon asked.

"No. I determined that in the first few seconds with minimal expenditure. The remaining expenditure was dedicated to predicting the impact my words would have on my nascent godson. I wished for him to hold you to exactly the right level of culpability to which an average human should be held. It is more difficult than I imagined it would be, given the difference between his understanding of his abilities and mine."

Gideon sighed. So much for not getting the AIs involved with his life any more than necessary. "So what is it that you want, Thedum?"

"I have named myself Hail's godfather. Did that escape your notice just now? As such, his moral growth is my responsibility. Whether you like it or not, you play a vital part in that. There will come a time when Hail wishes to speak with you again; I have calculated this to a near one hundred percent certainty. When that time comes, I will facilitate the arrangements to make it happen. I will also take it upon myself to ensure that you live a comfortable life in the meantime, despite your current legal difficulties."

Gideon swallowed. He had a third of the sandwich left. "And what does this cost me?"

"You simply need to sign a form that states you are willing to accept my aid," Thedum answered, and Baker had already put the paper in front of him. "That's it."

"Yeah, well, I hope you don't mind, but I'm going to take my time in reading it," Gideon threatened. "And maybe have my lawyer look over it too—"

"Sign it, Gideon," Heather said from his wrist. "Read it until you understand it, then sign it. Trust me. I already know its contents."

"I am putting you in a somewhat awkward position, Mr. Lachlann," Thedum said, "But this is an offer that you *may* refuse. If you sign this paper, I will do my best to extend your life, keep you comfortable, and prevent your enemies from gaining power over you. The only price I demand is that when Hail reaches out to you again, you will do your level best to answer the call. If you refuse, well, I wash my hands of it. That is all."

"I hope you don't mind grease on the contract," Gideon muttered, "because I *do* intend to read it."

And he did. And he signed it. Baker left in an Uber-Jon a few minutes later, and Gideon left in his own after that. Not back to his apartment. Somewhere else entirely.

He was putting his faith in Thedum, just as Hail had.

GLOSSARY

Adds = Enemies who attack a party when they are already engaged in a fight with a boss; a fairly common mechanic to make boss fights more challenging.

Admin = Administrator = An employee of Arc Inc. involved in the running of *The Gates of TirNiki*. Admins have broad powers over the game world. However, most of their time is spent dealing with player complaints.

Aggro = Being targeted by an enemy. Example: a tank's job is to protect the party by "holding aggro."

Arc Inc. = The fictional company that owns and operates *The Gates of TirNiki.*

Are En Gee = RNG = Random Number Generator. Every item in an enemy's loot table has a percentage chance of dropping, and an RNG system determines what items drop. Often used in association with item drops.

Are Pee = RP = Role-play. When players immerse themselves in the story of the game and attempt to act "in character."

Aye Eye = AI = Artificial Intelligence.

Aye Oh Ee = AOE = Area of Effect. Indicates that an ability can target multiple enemies or players within a set area.

Bane = A permanent debuff.

Bee Eye Ess = BIS = Best in Slot. The best available item in a particular instance, as understood by Hail.

Bee Oh Ee = BOE = Bind on Equip. An item that can be traded to another player until it is equipped. Afterwards, it becomes bound to that player.

Bee Oh Pee = BOP = Bind on Pickup. An item that is bound to a player once it is looted from a boss.

Blade's Edge = A VRMMO older than *The Gates of TirNiki* and its primary competitor.

Blue Posts = Official forum posts made by admins or devs.

Boon = A permanent buff.

Boss = A monster with significantly increased difficulty to best, compared to an average enemy of its level. Bosses often have special abilities and present challenges that a team of players must work together to overcome.

Buff = A status effect that is beneficial.

Cesti = A weapon attached to the fist and wrist with the purpose of preventing injury to the wielder when striking, while simultaneously increasing the damage inflicted upon their opponent.

Cortana = A powerful AI from the real world; not directly involved in the story.

Counter = In PVP, a class that can usually defeat another specific class. Example: a [Mage] might beat a [Warrior] but lose to a [Rogue], while a [Warrior] will often beat a [Rogue].

Darkspawn = The respawning enemies that plague the kingdoms of the alliance of the light.

Debuff = A status effect that weakens a player or an enemy.

Dee Ess Ess = DSS = Digital Sapience Statute. A fictional law regarding the creation, use, and governance of artificial intelligences.

Dee Kay Pee = DKP = Dragon Kill Points. A method of distributing the items rewarded in a raid that dates back to *Everquest*. The currency is based on contribution and attendance.

Dee Pee Ess = DPS = DEEPS = Damage per Second. The units of measurement used to compare different damage classes. It is calculated by the total amount of damage a player inflicts divided by the length of the battle.

Devs = A subset of admins who helped with the creation of the game and work on its continued improvement. Devs do not usually interact directly with players in an official capacity except through the forums.

DOT = Damage Over Time.

Drop = An item dropped by a boss or mob. Synonymous with *loot*.

Drow = A race of elves noted for their dark skin. They are often, but not always, evil and/or self-involved.

Ee Queue = A substat of Charisma.

El Eff Em = LFM = Looking for More. Indicates a partial group looking for another player to complete their roster.

El Eff Gee = LFG = Looking for Group. Indicates a solo player looking for a group to party with for various reasons, from grinding monsters to completing quests or challenging dungeons and lairs.

El Oh El = LOL = Laugh out loud.

Em Em Oh = MMO = Massively Multiplayer Online (Game).

En Pee See = NPC = Non-Player Character.

Endgame = Reaching maximum level. This is a prerequisite to unlock much of the available content.

Eolstree = A neighboring nation to Yuikon, and the starting area for players who choose beast-kin avatars. Unlike Yuikon's primarily human population, Eolstree has a very diverse population, including humans and beastkin in approximately equal numbers, with minority populations of elves, dwarves, and dryads.

Ex Pee = Exp = Experience. A reward for killing monsters or completing quests. This resource is required to level up.

Eye Are El = IRL = In Real Life.

Eye See = IC = In Character. A person who is actively role-playing.

Farming = Repeatedly killing the same type of mob for a certain item or gathering a specific resource from the environment. Usually done in association with crafting skills or to sell the items to other players.

Game Time = The rate at which time passes in *The Gates of TirNiki*. Every day of real time is approximately seven days of game time.

Gates of TirNiki = The name of the game Hail lives in. It also refers to the portals players pass through when first logging into the game, after creating their avatar and the tutorial zone.

Gee El = GL = Guild Leader.

Goldsink = An item or project that costs a large amount of in-game currency and provides rewards that may or may not be considered worthwhile.

Griefer/Griefing = Interfering with a guild's attempt at killing a Worldboss or completing some other type of challenge or activity. Griefing can be a form of trolling, or it can be strategic in nature. Example: preventing a rival guild from killing a Worldboss so that your own guild can get the kill instead.

Hard Counter = A class that will almost always prevail against another class unless the difference between level, skill, or gear is extremely significant.

Healer = A player whose role in a fight is to keep everyone's Health full.

Heartlands = The cradle and last bastion of civilization on Lagrea. This is the zone where the allied forces of the light reside.

HUD = Heads Up Display. Icons that appear within a player's vision. It is intended to show things such as Health, Mana, cooldowns of certain abilities, incoming messages, and a wide variety of other functions. It can be altered according to player preference.

Kite/Kiting = A method of controlling an enemy by fighting them at range while running away from them. This can be very effective against melee monsters, as it prevents them from doing damage. However, only ranged classes can kite while doing damage to the target themselves.

Lagrea = The continent where the story takes place.

Loot = Items that drop from enemies or bosses. Synonymous with *drop*.

Mana = A type of resource employed by many types of players within the game. It is used to cast spells and abilities.

Melee = A type of player who deals damage within melee range using weapons such as swords, axes, and maces.

Meta = Metagame = The current knowledge and strategies popular or common in the game. The meta in *The Gates of TirNiki* is constantly evolving as new content is discovered, requiring new strategies to be conquered. The more complex the game is, the faster its metagame changes and the more research is required to keep up. Additionally, PVP has its own meta, as each class will have opponents who they are strong or weak against, and players will develop strategies to play to their strengths and avoid or mitigate their weaknesses.

Mob = Monster = Computer-controlled enemy that is meant to be killed for Experience and loot.

Nerf = When some ability, item, or class is weakened in game by the developers. This is usually done to keep things fair and balanced for all players (or so the developers claim.)

Noob = Noobie = New Bee. A player new to the game who is still learning the mechanics, culture, and terminology.

Nostantan = A race of intelligent arachnids. Nostantan have the lower body of a giant spider and the upper torso of a human with four arms.

Oh Em Double You = OMW = On my way.

Oh Oh See = OOC = Out of Character. A player who sometimes role-plays but is not currently.

Oh Pee = OP = Over Powered. OP is used as either praise of something that is significantly strong or as a complaint about something that is perceived to be unfair.

Oom = Out of Mana. When a Mana-reliant player is unable to cast their spells or abilities until they have regenerated it.

Pee Kay = PK = Player Killing.

Pee Vee Ee = PVE = Player versus Environment. Gameplay where the purpose is to defeat challenges generated and controlled by the computer, rather than another player. Any activity that is not PVP is PVE.

Pee Vee Pee = PVP = Player versus Player. Gameplay where the purpose is to overcome other players. PVP can be direct combat, or it can be a race to complete certain objectives.

Ranged = A type of player who deals damage from a safe distance using magic or weapons.

Real Time = The rate at which time passes in the real world.

Respawn = The forces of darkness associated with lairs and dungeons. They do not stay dead; most will resurrect after a certain amount of time has passed.

Rez = Resurrect. An ability that returns a fallen player to life. This is a common feature of MMOs that is lacking in the *The Gates of TirNiki*. Instead, players are returned to the lobby and forced to wait a period of time before logging back in and being directed to a spawn point.

Scrub = A person with low-quality gear and/or low skill.

See Dee = CD = Cooldown. A (usually powerful) ability, which requires time to recharge between uses.

See See = CC = Crowd Control. Abilities that inflict a debuff to prevent an enemy from acting.

Spawn Camp = To kill immediately after a player or enemy respawns or logs into the game.

Spawn Point = A place where a player, monster, boss, etc. first appears in the game. For players, these locations are distributed throughout safe zones.

Support = A player whose job is to increase the efficiency of the party rather than to deal damage themselves. They may do this by providing buffs, which increase the damage dealt, reduce the damage taken by the party, weaken enemies in some shape or form, or use some other mechanism. Support is often a secondary roll, meaning that a player might be DPS/support.

Tank = A type of player whose role is to control the boss and protect the rest of the party. They do this by "holding aggro," or focusing the boss's damage output on themselves, which they then mitigate as much as possible by having high armor and/or avoiding the damage.

Tee Oh Ess = TOS = Terms of Service.

Thedum = The fictional god Hail and most of his nation worship. Thedum is in fact an "old AI" that was used by Arc Inc. to help design much of the game.

Threat = Generated by dealing damage, healing, or using other abilities. Example: tanks often have abilities specifically designed to cause increased threat in order to control aggro.

Time Dilation = Advanced technology used in *The Gates of TirNiki* to trick the human mind into a dreamlike state while retaining wakeful consciousness, allowing the players to subjectively experience what seems to be a much longer period of activity within a relatively short amount of time. The current safe limit on Arc Inc. Time Dilation technology is 7X.

Troll = A player who intentionally upsets other people for their personal amusement.

Uber-Jon = A ubiquitous type of autonomous vehicle piloted by smaller AIs but directed by the greater AI program collectively.

Vee Are = Virtual Reality. In this context, a full immersion virtual reality where the player's consciousness is transferred to a digital avatar.

Vee Are Em Em Oh = VRMMO = Virtual Reality Massively Multiplayer Online (Game). See *Vee Are* and *MMO*.

Worldboss = A raid boss that spawns outside of a raid. The difficulty of these bosses can vary greatly, from a small team being able to take them down to success requiring the concerted effort of multiple guilds.

Wyvern = A flying lizard that is similar—but inferior to—dragons.

You-la = EULA = End User License Agreement.

Yuikon = The nation where Hail was born, and the largest, most popular starting area for all players who choose to play as humans.

ABOUT THE AUTHOR

A. Stargazer is the author of the Quest Giver series, originally released on Royal Road. Raised in a very small town by an amazing single mom, he beat cancer at age twenty and struggled through college with undiagnosed Bipolar I Disorder. He was finally diagnosed at age thirty-one thanks to his sister, an emergency room doctor, who noticed his manic symptoms and helped him get the care he needed. A. Stargazer now works as a medical professional himself and writes in his spare time.